Diamonds and Mildew

To Scott
with great love.

02-06-2021

by

Marli Sieburger

ISBN: 978-1934666-24-1

Cover Design by Summer Morris

Published and distributed by:
High-Pitched Hum Publishing
321 15th Street North
Jacksonville Beach, Florida 32250

Contact High-Pitched Hum Publishing at www.highpitchedhum.net

To my son Guillermo M. Vidal
With love

I thank Nora Peña and Dr. Jessica Damián,
two dear friends who always believed in me
as a writer and never let me give up.

Dreams are the abstract reflections of a possible reality. . . and faith, the energy which keeps alive those reflections.

Book 1

One Dream, Many Tomorrows

1

MUFFLED VOICES AND THE fragrance of fresh flowers impregnated the air inside the small parlor. Silently looking at the remains of his mother's body inside the casket, Charles Merlenes remembered a time thirteen years before in the same parlor with the same people, as he stood before his father's coffin...

* * * *

Maximilien Merlenes had been a hard-working man, a good father, and an extraordinary jeweler. He was only in his early forties when Charles had found him dead, slumped over his workbench. That day remained indelibly etched in Charles' mind for he never accepted his father's death.

From an early age Charles had sat next to his father and watched him work. By the age of twelve he had begun learning about jewels. He greatly admired his father's skill in cutting and setting gemstones. Often, his father lectured him of their value. "Diamonds, as well as emeralds, are very valuable," his father used to say. "Both stones, once cut properly and set in gold, will earn three times their value." Charles paid attention to everything his father said. When his father finished a piece, he would proudly say, "People will buy the diamond, but they will also pay for my artistry." It was his father's dream to become a reputable jeweler and a very rich man.

Today, in that small parlor and surrounded by the flowers, looking at his mother, Charles realized that men were nothing—nothing but dust.

St. Denis, a small town in the northern part of France, was close to Paris. Like most small towns, all of the residents knew each other as an extended family either from attending the only church they had or by sharing drinks at the local bar on cold nights. When needed, they helped each other and acted like brothers and sisters who worshiped the same God. Life, they saw as a divine creation, each human being a creator's masterpiece. They viewed everything as good and believed the future would be as serene as the life they all shared.

At age eighteen, Charles Merlenes left St. Denis and entered the St. Francis of Assisi Seminary in Paris. He had first heard about the seminary from Father Henrique Mendonza, the parish priest in St. Denis who also was a very close friend of Charles' family. After Maximilien's death, Father Mendonza spent more time with the Merlenes family. Maximilien's untimely and sudden death left his family and the whole town in shock. While giving spiritual comfort to the family, Father Mendonza soon became strongly aware that Charles harbored a deep anger and felt concerned about him.

When Father Mendonza mentioned the seminary the first time, Charles had shrugged his shoulders showing no interest—his father was dead and nothing could change that. But Father Mendonza didn't give up and gently prodded and insisted because he felt it would be wise for Charles to leave St. Denis. Therefore, with the young man's best interest at heart, Father Mendonza approached Cardenal Filione and requested a place for him.

A year later, the seminary accepted Charles. As soon as Father Mendonza read the letter, he went looking for Charles to tell him the good news. Upon finding out that Charles was getting married and the bride-to-be was Joanna Sampaio, a single mother with a notorious reputation around town, his joy melted like ice left under a hot steamy sun.

Discouraged, Father Mendonza returned home very sad and extremely disappointed and for some unknown reason, he decided to delay Charles' response to the seminary. He decided that first he should pray, for sometimes only God knows what is right.

Wise decision. Three days later, Charles told Father Mendonza not to write to the seminary. He really wanted to leave St. Denis and had decided to seize this opportunity.

Overjoyed, Father Mendonza asked, "What about the wedding?"

"I am not getting married. I found out that the gossip about my girlfriend is true."

"I am glad you changed your mind," responded Father Mendonza.

* * * *

Charles attended the seminary for six years. During that time he learned much about the ways of the world, man, and God. He acquired an education far beyond any he could have achieved in St. Denis. Deep in his heart he knew he would never become a priest because what he really wanted to do was follow in his father's footsteps. Like his father, he had great ambitions of becoming a fine jeweler and a very wealthy man.

Although the years in the seminary seemed endless, Charles used this time wisely to learn as much as possible. He realized that the knowledge he could acquire there would be the foundation he needed to survive. The more he learned, the more he understood that his real place was out in the world. He eagerly wished to experience all life had to offer. But still, he kept hidden in his heart memories of the past, unable to forget what he knew of his Uncle Luis, his father's only brother, who filled his soul with deep hatred. Charles' intense hatred had begun on the day his father died.

* * * *

Barely twenty-four years old, Charles left the seminary in search of a new life. He strongly believed in his dreams and was determined to fight for them. He desperately wanted to achieve all that his father had been denied because of his early death.

As soon as Charles left, he went to see Ramiro Campelo, the man who used to buy the jewelry his father made. Mr. Campelo had not only bought the finished pieces, but also supplied the stones and gold at a wholesale price. He had excellent connections in the world of wholesale jewelry, owned his own retail store, and several artisans worked exclusively for Mr. Campelo.

Charles knew Mr. Campelo had respected and admired his late father. What Charles wanted most, was an apprenticeship with Mr. Campelo to broaden his knowledge and to acquire experience.

Mr. Campelo was delighted to see him. Before making his decision, Mr. Campelo calmly asked, "Why do you want to learn more about jewels?"

Looking straight into the old man's eyes, Charles responded, "Do you want to hear one reason or more than one?"

"If you have more than one, I would like to hear them all," said Mr. Campelo.

"All right," Charles said, "but first I would like to tell you something that you may not know. The death of my father hurt me profoundly. It shook my adolescent expectations heavily and because I couldn't change the events, I now must learn more about jewels. I desire to have all that was denied to my father. I wish to become rich, to make my dreams a reality."

"So, you are a dreamer?" asked Mr. Campelo.

"I believe that if dreams can meet the horizon, they dance with the sound of the waves. Perhaps I am. Yes! I'm a dreamer because I did not have the chance of becoming a sheep herder."

"Wonderful sense of humor, Charles," said Mr. Campelo. "But don't forget that dreamers always face a long journey."

"Yes sir. I will never forget your words. They will be my strength."

"I like you Charles, and I'm going to give you the opportunity you so much desire. I believe that life saves great surprises for those who skillfully use all the opportunities offered to them. You can start whenever you wish."

Charles was elated, for he had won his first important victory.

* * * *

For five years, Charles worked very hard. His dedication and the uniqueness of his designs quickly set him apart. Even Mr. Campelo often remarked, "Charles, you are like your father. You have a great talent and will go far in this business."

Ramiro Campelo's words never surprised him because Charles believed in himself. He intended to conquer the world in memory of his father. That is what he wanted and he never stopped dreaming about it. It was his intention that one day, the world would know of him—

* * * *

Charles was nearly twenty-nine with a dark complexion, dark hair, deep brown eyes and well-defined thin lips that did not smile often. He portrayed the image of a strong young man, very assertive, and ambitious.

After solemnly contemplating his mother's body, Charles went into the kitchen where he sat in a chair, silently watching the crackling fire in the wooden stove. Madame Geraldine, one of the oldest inhabitants of St. Denis, made coffee for the people who came to stay through the night to watch in silence and to pray. Instinctively, she had prepared a tray with the coffee pot and cups. Before returning to the parlor, she quietly offered Charles a cup.

"Thank you," Charles said removing it from the tray.

Madame Geraldine left the kitchen and Charles drank his coffee while gazing into the flames.

His thoughts were interrupted when his Uncle Luis entered the kitchen. "Hello, Charles. How do you feel?" his uncle said. "You have been very quiet and that worries me."

"I'm okay," answered Charles as he kept his eyes fastened on the flames.

"I would like you to know that I am here to help. You can count on me. You know that, don't you?"

"Sure!" Charles replied sarcastically, now looking directly into his uncle's eyes. "Yes, we can count on you. You have always helped us, isn't that so? What do you want? A thank you? Okay, thank you, Uncle Luis! Thank you very much!"

Luis quietly regarded his hostile nephew. He was now sorry he had tried to talk to him. Though Charles had been gone from St. Denis for eleven years, Luis realized that his hostility still remained. Ever since his brother Maximilien's death, Charles had been bitter toward him, and Luis could not understand why. Without saying another word, he turned away and went back to the parlor.

Remaining in the kitchen, Charles watched the flames in the stove as they started jumping rapidly, releasing small sparks into the air. Mesmerized, Charles stared at them, feeling the same type of heat within him.

* * * *

Just two hours after being stunned by the death of his father, Charles had started to hate his uncle. That afternoon the entire town mourned for Maximilien, the man with magical hands. The cold and melancholic night that followed would never be erased from Charles' memory.

After his father's burial, life went on. The day followed, as usual, and nothing eventful happened. Even in his house, daily life returned to normal. Charles felt that he was the only one affected by his father's death. His older brother continued to work with his uncle. His sister learned to sew and make a living from it. Even his mother continued to make the sandwiches that were sold at Mr. Almir's cafe. Charles, the youngest, still went to work at the pharmacy and also at Mr. Almir's cafe.

Uncle Luis brought milk, bread, and eggs daily, making sure

they did not lack for anything. He always said the same words to Charles, "I would like you to know that I am here to help. You can count on me." *That is true. Uncle Luis really helps my mother, brother and sister. How sad that they don't really know Luis!*

Like their mother, Charles' brother and sister never knew about their father's dreams. They didn't appreciate his talent, for they never really knew him. It was easy for them to accept his loss and be grateful for Uncle Luis' generosity.

As he watched the flames intensify, Charles realized that his bonds with St. Denis were severed. After his father's death he grew apart from his brother and sister. Furthermore, his mother, and only real link to St. Denis, now rested in a plain wooden box purchased by none other than Uncle Luis.

We all came from dust and return to dust! Charles thought for the second time. *There is nothing to lose; fear does not exist and courage has no meaning—each day... only one day less.*

While the fire quickly consumed the wood, Charles spoke aloud, "Do it tonight, Charles. This is the perfect night. Everybody is here." After hearing his own words, a shiver ran up his spine. "No. If I do it, I have to go back to Paris today. Impossible. I must attend my mother's burial."

His words kept echoing in his mind. Then he felt as if an enigmatic force was hypnotizing him, and knew he lacked the virtue to fight such a strong power. "Yes, I must do it today," he heard himself firmly state out loud. "The burial is not that important. It is the last thing which the living can do for the dead, and in such a solemn moment, the people attending only have eyes for the grave, not for the grieving family."

Suddenly, he became convinced he had found the perfect night to accomplish his task. Rising from his chair by the fire in the kitchen, Charles determinedly walked out of the kitchen. Even though at the moment courage meant nothing to him, he was filled with great determination.

Without saying a word to anyone, he left his house that night to accomplish something he never before had found the courage to do.

Outside he could barely see in the darkness. Straining to look at his watch, he realized it was 12:45 a.m. At that time of the night the streets remained empty, the silence only disturbed by the sound of the voices coming from his house. They were rhythmically praying the rosary. After Madame Geraldine had served the coffee, Father Mendonza led the mourners in prayer. The voices slowly faded as Charles walked further away from his house.

At the end of the street, he turned right and walked toward the middle of the block where he stopped in front of a big house surrounded by a concrete wall and with a large iron gate. Charles pushed the gate and it opened. As usual, it was never locked. After entering through the portal, he walked around the house to the back door. Then he pulled out his wallet and removed a well-folded piece of paper.

Wrapped in the paper were two keys, one of regular size and the other smaller. Taking the larger key, he opened the door and went inside the house. Calmly he passed through the dining room and stopped in front of the bedroom door. When he looked carefully for the safe, he found it in its usual place. Next, he took the smaller key and opened it. Charles removed three bundles of bills and put them in his pockets. Then he closed the safe and retraced the way he had come in. As he crossed the street, he uttered to himself, "It is done. Now...back to Paris."

Charles walked down the street caressing the stolen money. He got as far as Telo's house. Charles and Telo had known each other since childhood. Telo was a young man who had become very popular because he owned a horse-drawn carriage and made money by taking people to and from Paris almost daily.

Going to the side of Telo's house, Charles knocked several times on his bedroom window.

"Who's there?" Telo asked as he woke up.

"It's me, Charles. I need you to take me to Paris."

Telo jumped from his bed and opened the window. "Now? In the middle of the night?"

"Yes, Telo, now, in the middle of the night. Name your price and I will pay it."

Telo rubbed the sleep from his eyes and said, "In that case, consider yourself in Paris."

Telo had the carriage ready in less than an hour and soon after, they left St. Denis behind.

During the trip Telo asked, "What about your mother's burial?"

"I don't like burials. I will not attend it."

"Nobody likes burials, but it is your mother's," insisted Telo.

"That's an even better reason not to go. I have never forgotten my father's funeral."

"I understand," replied Telo. "You don't want to have this sad memory remain in your mind."

"Yes," Charles answered curtly.

They traveled on in silence. Telo did not know what to talk about with someone who had just lost a family member, and Charles appeared not to be interested in idle conversation.

Charles took advantage of the silence to quietly plan his next step toward accomplishing the goals that for the past two years had kept him sleepless. What he had done tonight would change his life forever. It meant leaving St. Denis, forgetting his brother and sister and saying goodbye to France. He could not look back. He wanted what should be his. And if nothing waited in store for him, then he would regain his nothingness. By committing this robbery, his soul had liberated itself from this negative feeling. It seemed as if he had ceased to live the day his father had died. But now, on the very day of his mother's death, he was reborn. To him, having no one to love meant having no one to hurt. Life became simple and the world more real.

The silence of the early hours shrouded the city of Paris. The absence of people in the streets made them seem solemn. Charles paid what Telo asked and immediately after, Telo turned the carriage around and headed back to St. Denis.

For a moment Charles stood in the middle of the street

watching the carriage disappear. *Telo is a good friend. Telo...his carriage...and Dimanche, his horse. I'll never forget Dimanche.*

After the carriage disappeared, Charles climbed the wooden stairs on the side of Mrs. Santine's house and entered the very small attic where he lived. The humble attic contained very little. Two old mattresses on the floor, two suitcases on top of low stools where clothing were kept, and between the mattresses there stood a small table with only a clock on top.

Charles entered, and as he stood with his head bent because of the low ceiling, he lit the lamp. After that, he knelt on the floor to wake Antoine, who slept peacefully.

"Antoine!" he called, firmly shaking his friend's body.

"What?" said Antoine, half asleep.

"Wake up, we have to talk."

Antoine opened his eyes, lifted himself on his elbows and very surprised exclaimed, "Charles, what are you doing here? Weren't you supposed to be at your mother's funeral?"

"I *was* at my mother's funeral, but I will not attend the burial. Get up, we have to talk."

Antoine took the clock and looked at it closely. "It's four o'clock in the morning and you wake me up to talk? Listen, Charles, I know you have lost your mother and you are upset, but we have plenty of time to talk later."

Paying no attention to his friend's words, Charles took a pair of pants and a shirt and threw them at Antoine saying, "Come on, get dressed. There is no time to lose."

"Where are we going?"

"To America, Antoine, just as we planned. To America!"

Still not very sure of what was going on, Antoine began getting dressed while suspiciously eyeing Charles.

"Here is the rest of the money we needed," said Charles, removing the money from his pockets. "But we must leave Paris now."

Antoine grabbed the money and looked at it in disbelief. It was real money. Everything seemed so unbelievable and he had to ask,

"Where did you get this, Charles?"

"I stole it."

"Stole it?" replied Antoine. "You, an ex-seminarian doing such a thing? I would believe almost any other story, but not that."

"Wrong. I stole it from my Uncle Luis and it was easy."

Charles' revelation left Antoine speechless. He looked at the money for a few seconds, caressed it and even smelled it. Then, he began to laugh uncontrollably.

"Incredible! Simply incredible! You know something, Charles, you are a son-of-a-bitch, but I enjoy your company. To hell with France, my friend. America is the future!"

2

France 1886

FRANCE FORTUNATELY RESTED UNDER the Third Republic and strenuously energized a great era. While the nation grew in prosperity, the French people had peacefully enjoyed their new Constitution. Cherbourg was the last French City Charles and Antoine visited before leaving the country.

They stopped at the train station and Charles glanced around in amazement. It all seemed like a dream. Each second of his life now had a new meaning. Growing inside him he felt an intense force that helped him face the new life that lay in his path.

Antoine's happiness was also obvious as he walked around with his suitcase in hand. Looking up at the sky he said, "Oh, Cherbourg, a piece of my country that I will never forget! Here I lived the best time of my life and experienced everything a young man dreams."

Antoine was medium height and extremely thin. He had big brown eyes, a sharp nose and a simple smile. For thirteen months he lived in Cherbourg. During that time he had worked harder than he had ever worked before in his life. Sometimes he spent countless hours in the water cleaning the hulls of the boats in the dock. But he was well paid for such hard labor and the money allowed him to enjoy life's pleasures, which he did extensively. Each night he found a willing girl who warmed him and helped him get rid of the cold of the sea. He lived a mundane life, but a happy one. The present was an adventure and the future...something that could wait.

At the age of twenty, Antoine had left his family home. He wished to become a sailor, and perhaps in the future, a sea captain. These dreams had been inspired by hearing stories from Captain Barbone, an old friend of his mother's.

Captain Barbone was a muscular Frenchman who appeared older than his actual age. His skin had been burned dark by the sun and his hair hung down to his shoulders. After several years at sea, when his ship had anchored in Port Cherbourg, he had gone to Paris to visit Antoine's mother only to learn she had died three years earlier. Shocked by the unexpected news, the captain drank all night and amused Antoine with the most fascinating stories he knew about the sea. He spoke of his own experiences and about the ancient sailors. Antoine woke up the next day spellbound by the stories and asked the captain, "What do I have to do to become a sailor?"

The captain answered, "First, Antoine, you must know the sea."

Because Captain Barbone's answer made a lot of sense, Antoine followed him to Port Cherbourg. In Cherbourg, before leaving, the captain helped him find a job as well as a place to stay. He also gave Antoine his word that he would take him sailing on his next trip.

While the captain was at sea, Antoine stayed in Port Cherbourg working and waiting. A year went by before the captain returned, and he had every intention of squeezing a year's worth of missed pleasures into two weeks and certainly had no time for Antoine. Without thinking, he explained to Antoine, that he was going on a short trip and would be back in two months. That day, Antoine silently swallowed his huge disappointment and decided not to believe in the captain's promises any longer. He then decided to return to Paris.

Upon his decision to leave Cherbourg, Antoine packed his things and went to say good-bye to the captain. Carrying his suitcase, he entered the captain's favorite bar. When the captain saw him, he tried to stand up, but was so drunk that he fell down.

"Good-bye, Captain Barbone," said Antoine. "We could have been good friends if I had not listened to your stories."

Two days later the captain died, whispering, "Antoine, my only son!"

Antoine was born in Paris and had never known the truth about Captain Barbone. His mother never really talked much about him. She had only told Antoine that his father had died a long time ago.

When Antoine met the captain, he knew only that he was a family friend. At that time, Antoine was living with his aunt, Francine, who ran a boarding house in order to support herself and her only son, Andre. Aunt Francine was loved by all her male friends—but not by her son and of course, not by her nephew—her lifestyle embarrassed them.

Without any explanation, his cousin, Andre, left home at the age of twenty. One year later, he had written to his mother from New York. The news made Antoine very happy and Andre became his hero—a cousin to be remembered. Antoine felt very proud of him.

They began writing to each other and in those letters Andre told him some very interesting things about the new country called America. He often mentioned the excitement of New York City.

After his bad experience with Captain Barbone, Antoine planned to work hard and save as much money as possible so he could go to America and share a life there with his cousin. This plan was already firmly in his mind when Charles became his roommate. They began to dream together.

That morning when Antoine and Charles arrived in Cherbourg, the city rested motionlessly in the arms of another calm and peaceful day. Summer filled the atmosphere with its bright sun as well as filling the air with the strong smell of the Atlantic Ocean.

As they left the train station, they walked side by side. Antoine recalled all the wonderful memories he had from the city. Sometimes they would stop and he would point out a favorite bar or boarding house where he had once lived. He felt so happy returning to Cherbourg that anyone would have thought he had been born there. They walked across town enjoying the soft sweet breeze that tenderly caressed their skin.

The port, located at the end of two parallel main streets, used to be referred to as Port Street. Port Cherbourg, where most of the vessels were anchored, was the busiest French port of its time. Numerous warehouses filled the port street while boarding houses, bars, and whorehouses lined the adjacent roads.

Antoine and Charles went directly to Madame Matilda's guesthouse, the last place Antoine had boarded and the one that felt most like a home. Madame Matilda resembled the mother he wished he had had. After seeing her and being assured of a hearty meal and a clean place to sleep, they both walked toward the port to find a man called Robert Dejaour.

Mr. Dejaour, a bald, short, fat man, was widely known, either personally or through word-of-mouth. There was always someone who had a friend that Dejaour had double-crossed. Mentioning Dejaour meant remembering a social outcast and sometimes a convenient helper because he appeared as the last resource after everything else had failed. When someone reached the end of his rope, it became time for Dejaour to step in, to set his price, and to save the poor devil. The man lived off the needs of others. Dejaour was very wise and clever, spoke two languages and knew all the illegal business that took place in town. Many sailors and captains, whom he knew well, did business with him.

When Antoine found him and told him about going to America, Dejaour said, "You are a lucky guy. Captain Alejandro Alvares just arrived from Spain."

"What is that supposed to mean?" asked Antoine with a questioning look.

"Oh, Captain Alejandro loves money. He is always ready to make money. And he is going to sail to America."

"Well, then tell him that my friend and I want to go to New York. You can find us at Madame Matilda's. I would like to have the answer today, if possible."

"I'll see what I can do," said Dejaour.

Antoine and Charles turned to leave, but they had only taken a few steps when Dejaour called them back.

"Antoine, you know that Captain Alejandro will have his price and I will have mine. You know that, don't you?"

"Of course, Dejaour," replied Antoine. "I am not new in town. You are like an expensive whore. I know how you operate."

As they left, Dejaour muttered to himself while chewing the cigar in his mouth. "My friend, your nasty comment is going to cost you more."

Almost broke, Antoine and Charles left France the next day at 4 p.m. The *Serenata*, Captain Alejandro Alvares' ship, sailed directly for New York. Charles had finally begun his journey toward a new life—it was a dream come true.

The *Serenata* sailed the Atlantic gracefully and smoothly as a seagull flying over the water. Charles felt extremely relaxed by the rhythmical movement of the ship. The *Serenata*'s movement traced the dividing line between the past he was leaving behind and the future he was sailing toward. He sensed that in the distant future, he would remember this day. And without knowing why, he thought about his mother and the countless times she had rocked him in her arms. His mother...what a sweet memory! *Au revoir France! St. Denis, the stage of my first unpleasantness is now behind and ahead, New York.* A strong smell of salt came from the sea and Charles took a deep breath of the exhilarating fresh air.

On the tenth day of sailing, Charles and Antoine went up on the deck and spent some time admiring the vast sea and sky. It had rained heavily the day before. Today the sea was surging and the waves rolled so strongly that it seemed difficult to see the horizon. It looked as if the Atlantic was rising from its depths in the form of a tail that pounded everything within its reach. The storm made Antoine remember Captain Barbone's stories. He told Charles, "The ancient sailors lived in fear of the horizon because they believed it marked the end of the world."

For a moment, Charles thought about those men who spent most of their lives sailing. While contemplating the empty space in front of them, Charles experienced fear. He felt insignificant before the vast sea and sky, and he thought about God and the magnitude of His power.

"Do you still want to be a sailor, Antoine?" Charles asked trying not to think of God.

"No, I want to work hard, make some money, marry a good woman, and have a son that will carry on my name."

"I wish I could think like you," said Charles.

"Yes, but you can't. You want to be very rich. You dream big dreams, Charles. I don't. My dreams are very simple compared to yours. And let me tell you something, I am not worried about that because if you become rich, *we* become rich–right?"

"Of course, Antoine," answered Charles.

"I say that because we ended up like brothers and companions on an adventure. Look at us now...on this ship, sailing to America together."

With a smile and a nod, Charles agreed with Antoine.

Shortly afterwards Antoine asked, "Don't you think it is time for you to tell me why you stole from your uncle? After all, without his money, none of this would be possible."

"He deserved it, Antoine," said Charles sharply. "He stole from my mother all that my father left us."

Charles' thoughts returned to that day long ago—

At the age of sixteen Charles entered his father's jewelry shop and found him slumped on the table and immediately called his Uncle Luis. When his uncle came running in and touched the body, Charles heard what he would never accept, that his father was dead. An hour later, his uncle and four neighbors removed his father's body from the jewelry shop to Charles' house.

Charles watched everything and followed them to his house in a rather detached haze, feeling the most unimaginable pain. His chest became heavy and he wanted to cry. He ran back to his father's jewelry shop, sat on the floor between his father's work bench and an antique chifferobe which his father had used to store his jewelry tools, put his face on his folded arms and began to cry. He stayed there for a long time crying, trying to accept the truth and wondering what their lives would be like without their father.

So submerged was he in a desolate state, that he didn't even hear the door opening. When the light went on in the shop, and he heard the scuffle of steps on the wooden floor, he realized that someone had come in. Charles instinctively moved under the table, and dried his eyes. Peeking out, he saw his Uncle Luis.

Quietly Charles observed Luis take some keys from the hanging nail near the window, selected one and opened the bottom part of the safe. His father had purchased that safe in Paris on recommendation of Mr. Ramiro Campelo so he could safely store the stones and the finished jewelry. From the bottom of the safe, Luis removed a small box that contained some papers. His uncle sifted through the papers and took out a small card that contained the combination to the safe. With it in hand, he turned the dial carefully and opened the safe. Without hesitation, he reached in and took out most of the money from inside and all the little boxes where his father had stored precious stones that were already cut and ready to be mounted. Luis put everything he had taken from the safe into a bag he found inside the chifferobe and left.

Charles remained quiet in his hiding place, wanting to move but lacking the strength to do so. He became terribly afraid after what he had witnessed, not wanting to face the truth that his uncle had stolen all that his father had accumulated through his long years of hard work. It took him more than a few minutes to recover. When he did, instantly the pain of his father's death diminished and a sense of intense hatred replaced it.

It was then that Charles swore to himself that this would not end peacefully. *I will expose my uncle! I will shout for all to hear of what I have seen! I must tell everyone in St. Denis that my uncle is a thief!*

But Charles had failed in doing so. Later, when he found his uncle surrounded by friends and neighbors giving support to his family, he realized that Uncle Luis was untouchable. His uncle had a very distinguished reputation. Everyone admired him; even the local priest would give him absolution without a confession. Luis' image was that of a respectable man with a firm gaze and a conservative smile. Overall, and without doubt, he always acted with integrity.

Oh, what a tragedy! Charles, who was still an adolescent with fragile bones who could barely sustain the weight of his immaturity, facing such an image of respectability, felt silenced forever.

The waves kept moving faster and more violently, breaking against the *Serenata*'s hull. They looked like mountains of water moving in from different directions. A sinister, methodical roar came from the sea. The Atlantic looked like a mad giant who smelled of salt and foamed with rage. Charles and Antoine, still on the deck of the ship, looked at the ocean in disbelief. The waves seemed higher than twenty feet.

"Oh, heaven!" Charles screamed into the wind. "We can't stay here, Antoine. Look at all the water that is coming our way!"

Suddenly, a giant wave pounded the *Serenata* furiously. The ship rocked uncontrollably. Charles and Antoine were thrown back and forth against the deck, dragged by the tremendous force of the water. Pure survival instinct caused them to grab some rope they found coiled on the railing.

"We have to go inside," yelled Antoine.

"Yes," answered Charles with the salt water drenching his face. "You go first, I'll follow you."

They looked at each other and Antoine yelled, "Now!"

For more than fifteen minutes the storm continued to rage. Charles could not reach the door. He was banged against the rail and knocked to the deck once again. Almost at the end of the deck, he grabbed on to some fishing nets attached to the back of the ship. He embraced the wad of nets and clung to them, motionless, inhaling the strong smell of fish while the water kept rushing past him.

When the storm subsided, Charles picked himself up and looked for Antoine. Charles knew he could not have reached the door, either. Antoine had been knocked down at the same time he had. Calling for his friend over and over, Charles walked around the deck. Then, desperately Charles approached the railing and looked cautiously out at the agitated water.

"Antoine! Antoine!" he yelled in panic and anguish, not wanting to believe what must be the awful truth. Charles never saw his friend again.

3

New York 1886

CHARLES' FIRST IMPRESSION OF New York was that of a majestic monument of power, far exceeding anything he had ever imagined. The City appeared to have a magical atmosphere, which appealed to dreamers.

The last days of September were rushing to accelerate the end of the summer. President Grover Cleveland was in office, and two months prior, he had presided at the unveiling of the Statue of Liberty, which majestically added a new splendor to the New York Harbor. The statue not only represented freedom, but also gave an attractive touch to the panoramic view of New York City.

The *Serenata* was docked in the port of New York City for three days. A few minutes after its arrival, Charles went to see Captain Alejandro Alvares. He asked the captain for permission to stay aboard the ship until Andre, Antoine's cousin, came to meet them. Before they had left France, they had telegraphed him, providing the name of the ship they would be sailing on and the date they sailed from France.

Though Charles felt extremely excited about actually being in America, he soon grew worried about the uncertainty of his future. Not as planned, he had arrived alone in New York. Antoine's death had also cast a dark shadow of doubt over his hopes for the new life he would be starting and dampened the joy that most immigrants felt when they reach America. The energy Charles had felt in Cherbourg had suddenly dissipated. Now, for the first time since his mother's death, he felt utterly alone.

Charles had no idea how his meeting with Andre would go, but he decided to wait for him no matter the consequences. He was determined to remain positive. Antoine's cousin would come.

Another reason Charles waited was that he felt the responsibility of telling Andre about what had happened to Antoine. To him, this meant it was the last decent thing he could do for the only friend he ever had.

On the second day after the *Serenata* had arrived in the port of New York City, Andre showed up. Andre was a short man with a full face, brown hair, and light brown eyes. He had a very light complexion and a nasal sounding voice.

Captain Alejandro introduced him to Charles and they all went to the captain's cabin where they sat down to talk. Immediately, the captain told Andre what had happened to his cousin, Antoine. After the captain delivered the sad news, Charles provided the details of the accident.

Andre listened attentively and calmly accepted the news. From his perspective, death was just a point of reference in a man's life—as equally as birth. His reasoning was that all must die some day. In his opinion, it would not make much difference if that day were tomorrow, or ten years from now. Death was already fixed in our minds. To suffer because of it was to lose our reasoning.

"*C'est la vie*, Captain," he said. "Nobody knows what would have been better for my cousin, but we do know that his death would have occurred eventually, don't we?" Standing up he added, "If there is nothing else I can do for my cousin, I shall leave."

Quickly, Captain Alejandro also rose. "What about your cousin's friend? You are not going to take him with you?"

"Why should I?" answered Andre. "He is neither a family member nor my friend."

Andre left and Charles remained seated, absorbing his words while experiencing the first great disappointment of his new life. That was when he realized that if he really wanted to stay in America, he had to face New York City alone. He spent the whole night thinking about it.

How can I face a strange country without any money? Why couldn't it be different? He asked himself again and again. Feeling exhausted from not finding an answer, he went up to the deck to look at the harbor and to enjoy the silence and peace of the night.

The sky lingering over the harbor offered no stars to illuminate the silent night. Only the moon light reflected on the bay and the *Serenata* was anchored almost motionless in the water. The serene and peaceful atmosphere instantly made Charles depressed. As sadness darkened his soul, he suddenly wished for the *Serenata* to be sailing, so he could jump into the waves and become part of the Atlantic, like Antoine. *Oh, poor Antoine! Man is only dust*, he thought for the third time. *No, Antoine is going to become part of the coral. He left France to grow as coral in the bottom of the Atlantic. I want to die, too. My father died. Some day I will be very rich, my father said.* He felt sorry for his father and his mother. *No one would weep for me.* He remembered the rhythmical movement of the ship in the water. He would never forget its smooth balancing.

Not even Charles' anguished thoughts disturbed the silence of the night, and it wouldn't have changed if the captain had not approached him.

"Charles, what are you doing here at this hour?"

"Oh, breathing the fresh air Captain. And just thinking."

"You're worried, aren't you? I don't know if you noticed, but it's two o'clock in the morning."

"No, I didn't know, but it looks like you couldn't sleep, either."

"I am awake because of your friend's cousin. I keep thinking about his attitude. He does not deserve to be an immigrant to this country. He has no compassion."

"Well, there is nothing we can do to change that. Don't you agree?"

"Yes," answered the captain.

"What do you plan to do, now that you can't count on him?"

"I came here just thinking about that," said Charles. "What to do with my life. You got here in time to help me with my decision."

"Oh, no. I don't like to give my opinion when it comes to someone else's life. I believe that we all have one life and each individual has his separate destiny."

"I do not believe in destiny, Captain," said Charles.

"What do you believe in?"

"Nothing."

"Uh-uh, very bad," commented the captain, moving his head from one side to the other. "You must believe in something. Man must have faith, Charles. That is what Don Nestor De Alvarenga Da Silva Alvares e Melo used to say to me."

"And who is Don Nestor De Alvarenga Da Silva Alvares e Melo?" Charles asked.

"He was a Portuguese navigator, a notable captain, and the one who taught me to have faith."

Captain Alejandro rested his arms on the railing as he looked out on the bay and began his story—

A long time ago there was a boy running in the streets of Barcelona. He was crying desperately and did not know where to go. His mother, his only family in the world, had just died, and he had no friends with whom to share his grief. So he ran, crying, without a destination, crossing streets, turning corners, and bumping into people like a thief trying to escape. Suddenly, through his tears, he saw a church. He stopped running and sought refuge in it. The boy sat in the last bench, covered his face with his hands, and continued to cry.

A gentleman praying in the front row stood to leave. He was a tall figure of a man with a cold look in his eyes. He wore shiny boots and had a hat in his hands. He saw the boy as he walked to the back of the church. Calmly, he approached and said, "Dry your tears young man. Men do not cry. Every man has a destiny and must have faith." After he said that, he just walked out.

The interesting part about this story is—the boy obeyed the command. He dried his tears and instinctively followed the stranger. The man went to the port, boarded a ship, and sailed away. Later, a sailor found the boy hiding on the ship. He grabbed the boy by the arms and brought him to the captain. The stranger from the church was the captain and he recognized the boy. With a stern look in his eyes he asked, "What are you doing here?"

The boy answered, "I don't know. I had nowhere else to go, so I followed you."

Surprised, the captain asked, "Why me?"

Then courageously the boy said, "Because you are the first person who called me a man. You said that every man has a destiny and that I must have faith. I would like to know what destiny is and what faith means."

To the boy's surprise, the captain smiled. "Fine, young man, I'll teach you that."

"This man, Charles, was Don Nestor De Alvarenga Da Silva Alvares e Melo, and he adopted the boy. I was that boy. He taught me not only to have faith, but also to speak Portuguese and French, and he made me a good sailor. You see, being a sailor was *my* destiny."

Captain Alejandro was a man in his early thirties, with a reassuring smile, and frequently showed his teeth when he laughed. He had very vivid brown eyes and dark hair, and beneath his nose he had a large mustache. He was a genuine man.

Later in the afternoon, a few minutes before sailing from New York, he once again approached Charles and asked him what he had decided—to stay in New York or to return to France.

"I will stay, Captain," Charles said. "Anyway, I have no

money left to pay for a trip back."

"Who said you would have to pay?" asked the captain.

"Nobody, but according to Mr. Dejaour, money is very important to you."

"True. Without it people only imagine. There is a big difference in dreaming about something and having something. I would like to be the owner of this ship one day. Captain Nestor was in command of it before and now I am. The *Serenata* means a lot to me. Now can you see the importance of money? Without it, I cannot fulfill *my* dreams. But, there is something that you should know about me, Charles. I am a good man. When I have to be good, I am never bad."

Charles looked at the captain thoughtfully, quite impressed by his wisdom. At that moment, the captain's words touched him deeply. Charles realized he knew him at that moment, and felt a great admiration toward him.

"I understand everything you just said and I believe you are an honest man. I will remember you forever. Thank you for trying to help me without any monetary reward. I have decided to stay in New York. I left France vowing never to return."

"I see. I guessed that would be your decision. You are a very determined young man," said the captain. Then he put his hand in his pocket and took out an envelope. "Take this, Charles, it is the money you and your friend paid for the trip. You are going to need it. Good luck and have faith. Plenty of faith."

The *Serenata* left the port and Charles stood on the dock watching it sail away. *One day I will pay you back, Captain. That's a promise.*

About the time the *Serenata* had sailed far out to sea and blended with the horizon, Charles heard a nasal sounding voice calling his name. Surprised, he turned around. "Andre?" he asked.

"Yes, in the flesh. I thought about this whole situation and decided to be benevolent."

"Thank you!" said Charles quite relieved. "I really need your help."

"Fine. Let's go, then."

Quietly, Charles grabbed his suitcase and followed Andre. He turned toward the sea to look once more time at the *Serenata* in the distance. And once again he thought of the captain's kind words to him: "Good luck, and have faith—plenty of faith."

4

THE ITALIA CAMPIBELI RESTAURANT where Andre worked as a bartender had just been expanded, and now it consisted of one gambling room, two dining rooms and a nightclub. The sign advertising the restaurant had finally been redesigned so that it now faced both sides of the corner.

Don Alfredo Campibeli, the owner of the restaurant, was a happy Italian. The many wrinkles around his eyes aggressively showed him to be in his late forties. His big mustache commanded respect and his three-piece linen suits showed good taste. "The way a man dresses makes a difference. It makes him distinguished," he always said in his broken English mixed with Italian. To the public Don Alfredo displayed an eloquent and warm smile that effortlessly attracted people's confidence, but behind it lurked another man—a very ambitious man.

In 1868, Don Alfredo Campibeli joined the Ferbonini family in a friendly agreement.

One night, as he undressed for bed he said to his wife Sofia, "Don Prieto Ferbonini had lunch with me today, and he asked me to enter the nightclub business. He likes the location of my restaurant and promised I would have no problems."

Hesitantly his wife asked, "What are you going to do, Alfredo?"

"Going to do? I already did it," answered Alfredo. "From now on, the Campibeli and Ferboninis will be one family."

Very disappointed, Sofia commented, "What a mistake, Alfredo, to join with that family after all that happened. You must be crazy. Don't you realize that Italians pay a very high price for their ambitions? Those like Don Prieto Ferbonini who come to America with nothing but money on their minds, only put their families in jeopardy and bring misery to their wives."

Calmly Alfredo said, "Sofia, Sofia, do not exaggerate. You don't know about the corruption that surrounds us. We Italians must unite if we want to keep our businesses safe from it. Don Prieto lost two sons because he prospered. Tomorrow, it may be someone else. We must band together and defend ourselves. I would like to see my son without financial problems in the future and my daughters in good marriages, and I think this is the right of every father."

Sofia did not give up. "No, Alfredo. I know the truth. He lost his sons because he is involved in dirty deals."

"That's what people say because very few know the truth," Alfredo carefully explained. "Sofia, wake up! We did not leave Italy to be poor. People are just people. They need something to talk about as much as they need something to eat every day. They will kill to eat if necessary, and they will talk about what is not true, as much as about what is. That is how they are."

From that day on, Sofia kept her thoughts to herself praying for her family while the restaurant prospered. Its name became synonymous with prestige and distinction—a respectable place and a safe haven for business transactions. There, shady characters greeted each other in a false, friendly manner. They sat and gambled all night without forgetting that they were enemies. In short, it created a neutral ground where they could safely meet, eat, gamble, and enjoy the company of younger women. In the eyes of others, Don Alfredo became a very successful businessman because he knew how to treat people and how to manage his money. He quickly became very rich.

Even though he seemed happy with the volume of his business, he still dreamed of expanding. Many times he stood across the street and looked at his restaurant, visualizing a sign facing both sides of the corner saying, "Restaurant Italia Campibeli." It took him eighteen years to see his dream become a reality. The restaurant expanded to have one extra dining room. Now, just as he had wished, the name of the restaurant unfolded around the corner, reaching both streets.

Don Alfredo felt he had finally achieved his dreams. He was proud of his business and he lived as a happy man. His agreement made years before with Don Prieto Ferbonini had made all this possible. Don Prieto had proved to be a man of his word. A man who acknowledged that there was nothing as cruel as injustice and that truth was the only way. He believed that two wrongs do not make a right and that one wrong and one right will not lead to justice either. Years ago he had told Alfredo, "You will never be sorry that you agreed to do business with me. I am an honest man and I always keep my word—no matter what or how. I assure you that nothing will happen to you or your family. You will have my protection just as if you were of my own family." And to that day nothing had changed.

Don Prieto Ferbonini arrived in New York a year after the Civil War. He brought with him his wife, two sons, and a small amount of money. In Milan, he had owned a small restaurant that, after certain hours, held illegal gambling. Once settled in New York, he started a business he always thought would provide a much greater profit, a nightclub with a small back room for gambling. He worked hard, avoided mixing with the local syndicates, maintained a good atmosphere at his nightclub, broke as few laws as possible, and kept a good relationship with the authorities.

It was obvious to all in Manhattan that he was prospering.

Among the people observing his success was Carls Shelrain, the leader and instigator of many illegal enterprises. Carls Shelrain decided, together with his four sons, that a conceited Italian like Ferbonini should be forced out of business. To begin his campaign against Ferbonini, every night he sent the lowest elements he could find on the streets to Ferbonini's club. Frequent fights erupted each night and Ferbonini had to hire four men to protect his business and customers.

Don Prieto Ferbonini's misery really began the same year he invited Alfredo Campibeli to do business with him. It was in 1868, a Sunday, when Saporo, one of his men, came to his nightclub and informed Ferbonini that his son, Felipe, had been murdered.

When Ferbonini heard the news, he cried out, "Who? Who did it? Who had the balls to kill one of my sons?"

"The Shelrains," said Saporo.

"Which one of them?" asked Ferbonini.

"Robert."

The next day, with his wife Angela and his youngest son Gambino at his side, Prieto Ferbonini buried his son Felipe. After the funeral, Ferbonini spent two days alone in the dark without eating or speaking to a soul. During those two days, he aged more than he had in the previous forty-eight years of his life. The changes he had gone through were obvious. His hair, which had only a few silver strands before, had turned almost all white. His eyes, which used to reflect a gentle person, were hardened forever.

Ferbonini was a small, slim man and a little over five feet. There was nothing remarkable about his image. No one would ever experience fear by looking at him. On the contrary, most of the time he acted friendly to all. After he came out of his intense mourning, he called Saporo in and said, "Bring me Robert Shelrain and one of his brothers, alive. Take the others to help you."

The incident, which caused the death of Ferbonini's son, had started with Robert Shelrain, Carls Shelrain's son, who dared to appear one night in the club with two of his men. He had come in talking loudly and challenged Ferbonini's older son, Felipe, to a game of poker. Felipe, who was helping at the bar, dried his hands and came over and asked, "What is the matter, Robert? Do you think I am afraid of you? You want to play poker? Okay, let's play."

From a distance, Ferbonini saw the commotion and he came over. He stood firmly between them. "No, Felipe. This is not a good idea. Robert, please leave."

Instead of listening to Ferbonini, Robert pushed him so hard that he fell among the tables and the patrons. Infuriated, Felipe jumped at Robert. Robert's two goons quickly pulled out their guns. To stop what could happen next, Saporo intervened. Backed up by three other gunmen, Tomas, Cafeno, and Fairboy, he said, "Drop your guns or we will shoot."

Under the circumstances, Robert decided to leave. He left offended, and at the door, he turned around and pointed his finger at Felipe. "This is not the end. I will kill you, Felipe. You will see."

Robert kept his word. The following week, Felipe was found dead in a dark alley.

Ferbonini's pain allowed him to make a pact with the devil. According to him, a war had begun. He wished for Carls Shelrain to have a partner, himself—*the devil*. And in a snap of a finger, things around them became very nasty. Only three days after the death of his son, Ferbonini killed Robert Shelrain in the back of the nightclub. "Good-bye, cock sucker," he said as he shot him. After killing Robert, Ferbonini gave Fairboy some money and instructed him to rent an apartment far away from their neighborhood under the name of his younger son, Gambino. And then, he wrote Shelrain a note:

> My friend Shelrain,
>
> The undersigned is your new partner, Prieto Ferbonini, an Italian who is not afraid of the Irish. I just finished killing your son,

> Robert, and I also have your son Steve. If you want things to stay as they are, come to see me at the address one of my men will deliver to you later in the afternoon.
>
> I am inviting you to a peace meeting. I give you my word that nothing will happen to your younger son if you follow my instructions. You can bring two of your men if you wish. I will have all my men and my son, Gambino, with me.
>
> Follow my instructions to the letter or you will all be dead. Warn your men. After reading this, give it back to Tomas. Evidence is something that could harm our future business association.
>
> Prieto Ferbonini
>
> Oh, one more thing! You can find the body of you son, Robert, somewhere in Brooklyn.

On that day, Prieto Ferbonini acted like an experienced mobster who had every detail planned. He finished writing the note and calmly turned and ordered Tomas to take it to Shelrain, and instructed him to bring it back. After that, he told Fairboy, "As soon as you rent the apartment in Gambino's name, report back to me." Then, he turned quickly toward Cafeno. "You, Cafeno, stay here guarding our boy, Steve. When it is dark, Fairboy and Gambino will come to help you take him to the apartment Fairboy finds."

Now everyone had a task, except Saporo. But Don Prieto Ferbonini had something special for him, too.

"Saporo, I want you to stay with me. We have other business to take care of."

"Yes, sir," answered Saporo obediently.

Saporo liked Don Prieto Ferbonini very much. He never forgot the day they met. Even though Saporo's size scared everyone else,

Don Ferbonini chose him as a bodyguard. He firmly said, "I want that black man there." Later, Don Ferbonini explained why he had chosen Saporo. "I like obedient black men and Saporo seems to be one."

Saporo had learned to be obedient after being beaten many times. He found it less painful to be humble. Many times he had seen his mother crying because of the beatings and when she was dying, she told him, "Be obedient my son, because the white man has no heart."

For a long time, Saporo believed her, but then came the war and he saw the white men fighting and dying for the blacks. After the war, he witnessed black men killing and stealing in order to survive. He didn't have a clear picture in his mind of right or wrong, good or bad. It seemed difficult to face freedom and indeed hard *not* to obey.

One day he caught a gentleman sexually abusing a very young black girl, and he innocently confronted him. "Out of here, Negro. All you have is size," said the man pushing him away. Without hesitation, Saporo killed the man with a pitchfork that he held in his hand. From that day on, he fled without a place to call home, and he became even more confused about right or wrong, and good or bad. The only thing that stuck in his mind was that by obeying and killing, he made changes. So, this massive black man with a pock-marked face, startling white teeth, and frightening eyes, turned into a fierce murderer-for-hire.

The other business Ferbonini had mentioned to Saporo was with a young girl called Anabella. About three hours after everyone had left with their instructions, Saporo entered the nightclub through the back door, bringing Anabella with him. With a glass of scotch in his hand and a gun resting next to him, Ferbonini waited for them to be seated at a table. As they entered, he studied the girl carefully. Saporo pulled out a chair for her and after she sat down, Ferbonini spoke to her.

"Anabella, no?"

"Yes," said the girl.

"Do you know why I sent for you?"

"I can imagine," she answered, not showing much interest, looking around very distracted as if Ferbonini was another piece in her game.

"I learned that my son was leaving your house when he was kidnapped and you saw it. And, I also know that you were seeing my son *and* Robert Shelrain at the same time. Isn't that true?"

"Yes, and if you don't know, I was also seeing your son, Gambino. I had them all," the girl said.

"Wait a second," said Ferbonini. "Let me see if I can get this right." He stopped for a few minutes to give it some thought and then asked, "You have a twin sister called Isabella, don't you?"

"Yes," answered the girl.

"One of my men informed me that your sister is my son Gambino's girlfriend."

"Correct," she replied.

"Good. I think I'm following you, but there is something that I want you to clarify for me. If your sister is Gambino's girlfriend and you Felipe's, how did Robert Shelrain enter this picture and why were you seeing Gambino?"

"Simple! Robert does not like Italians. He came to me and said that I did not have the guts to be Felipe's girlfriend and go out with him—and I said, yes, and I did."

"I'm beginning to understand," Don Ferbonini said patiently. "And Gambino? Why him? Did he also dare you?"

"Oh, no," Anabella said. "Gambino is a fool. He follows the others. Do you know what he told me when he found out I was also seeing Robert Shelrain?"

"No," answered Don Ferbonini. "I do not have the faintest idea."

"He said, 'If Robert can go out with my brother's girlfriend, so can I. I may not have pretty Irish eyes, but I have an Italian dick...' I found that funny. Don't you think so?"

"Yes, very funny," answered Don Ferbonini. "So you opened your legs to Gambino, my son, only because you found that remark funny?"

"I guess so, if you want to look at it that way. But I also wanted to see who was the bravest. I enjoy testing men's courage."

"Yes, I think you do," said Ferbonini grabbing the gun and shooting her. He had the courage to silence her forever.

"A pretty *bambina*, Saporo, but I hate *puttanas*."

Later that same day, Carls Shelrain stopped in front of an apartment door. This was the place Fairboy had rented in Gambino's name. Before Shelrain could knock, the door opened. He entered and as soon as Don Prieto Ferbonini saw him, he said, "Excellent, Shelrain. I appreciate punctuality." Waiting with Don Prieto Ferbonini were all his men, including his son Gambino and Steve, Shelrain's youngest son, who rested sitting on the floor with his arms and legs bound. However, Shelrain also came accompanied.

"Let's get down to business, Ferbonini," said Carls Shelrain. "What do you want from me?"

"Just a minute, Carls Shelrain. This is my party, and you are my guest so calm down! Because I am the one who is going to do the talking."

Only one chair was in the dreary room. It was an old and dilapidated chair that had been left by former tenants. Don Ferbonini grabbed it and sat down. Then he spoke calmly, yet distinctly. "Carls Shelrain, your plan to ruin my business started a war between us that caused family blood to be spilled. I did not want this, neither did you, but now nobody can stop me. You chose the wrong Italian to fuck with, the biggest son-of-a-bitch among all the Italians you know. The one who can calmly contemplate the death of his loved ones.

"From now on, take care of your own business and leave mine alone. I will unite with all decent Italian business owners in Manhattan and I will protect them from you. If you bother one of them, you will be messing with me, personally. I do not talk a lot, but I always keep my word no matter what. Today, you and your men will witness that I am not talking bullshit. I keep my word, even to a dead man.

"A few hours ago, before I killed your son, I promised him that I would get to the bottom of this and kill the person who double-crossed my son Felipe. The one who informed Robert what time Felipe would be alone.

"Since their fight in the nightclub, I warned Felipe never to be alone. But that girl, Anabella, was driving him crazy. Your son told me that I could not keep my word because Felipe was double-crossed by Gambino, his own brother. Shelrain...nobody tells me that I am a man of no word! Nobody!" Quickly, without further explanation, Ferbonini aimed his gun and shot Gambino, in front of everyone.

Ferbonini's action was so unexpected and revolting, that no one could believe what they had seen. Visibly upset, Shelrain said, "I was in the war and I did what I shouldn't have done, I saw what I shouldn't have seen, and I have never witnessed a crock of shit like this!"

"I believe you," replied Ferbonini. "But I am a man of my word, and I intend to prove it to you in my own way."

Next, showing no emotion, Ferbonini turned to Saporo and commanded, "Saporo, untie his son. You may leave now Shelrain, and do not forget what I have said. I have no more sons to lose, but you still have three."

When Ferbonini walked into his home that evening, he found his wife Angela, half asleep sitting with her legs covered by a blanket. He knelt in front of her and hugged her tight.

"Angela," he said, "I do not know how to lie and I can't lie to you, ever. Not even at a time like this. I just killed our son, Gambino."

She covered her mouth with both hands. The expression on her face was that of horror, and her eyes grew wild until she seemed to be lost forever. Don Prieto Ferbonini knew then that she would never be the same.

5

IT TOOK JUST ONE week to get Charles a job in the kitchen chopping onions, washing dishes, and boiling pasta at the Italia Campibeli Restaurant. He worked until the early hours of the morning and when finished in the kitchen, he helped clean the dining rooms and the nightclub. He left the restaurant long after Don Alfredo Campibeli closed it. Then he walked with Andre to the cheap apartment they shared.

Charles and Andre did not talk very much as they walked together toward their apartment. At that time of the morning, they were extremely tired. They had worked for more than ten hours and besides that, Andre was naturally quiet. He appeared to be embarrassed by his voice and preferred not to talk if not necessary. In addition to that, he seemed to be hiding something unpleasant—as if he was pretending to be something or someone he wasn't.

Slowly Charles adapted to his new environment, where work became the most important thing of his life. He worked himself in such a beastly way that his bones claimed rest. But each day he swore to himself, "I will do whatever I must, and New York will hear about me...one day."

During the long hours of stirring the pasta in the kitchen of the restaurant, he constantly thought to himself about his present situation. *Why is it that sometimes time passes, and nothing seems to happen? As if our ambitions did not exist. The lack of favorable circumstances makes one day after another very...tedious.*

In the mornings when he opened his eyes to the shoddy apartment where he lived, he breathed deeply and ordered himself, *get up, Charles. Get up and face the new day. You have to leave all those insignificant days behind. Remember, each one is one day less.*

Two months, three weeks, four days and some hours had passed since he had arrived in New York, and each day, his present job reminded him that it had nothing to do with rubies, emeralds or diamonds. Besides that, he was unable to save much money. Half of what he earned at the restaurant went to pay his living expenses, and he had practically nothing left. At this pace, it would take just about a million years before he could save enough money to open the small jewelry store he dreamed about.

This particular day he faced another boring day in the kitchen of the restaurant. He wore a big apron and stood in front of a wide, deep pot of boiling water. Clouds of white vapor rose rapidly from the pot. *Why do I see clouds of vapor instead of gem stones? Why?*

Then the vapor formed a diabolical face. It seemed to say, "Do you like gems stones? Many things have to occur before you reach them. Everything has a price; be ready to pay it."

At that moment, Don Alfredo entered the kitchen, saw Charles mesmerized by the steam that was rising from the pot and asked, "Are you okay, Charles?"

"Oh, yes, Don Alfredo."

"Be careful not to burn yourself."

"Yes, Don Alfredo."

Don Alfredo came in the kitchen looking for Vercine, the cook. While rubbing his hands together, he told Vercine that he had a special reservation for the night. Juan Carlos Catarel and

Don Prieto Ferbonini would be in the restaurant, and because of this occasion, some people who did not come frequently would also be present. "I want everything perfect, Vercine. Please try your best."

On his way out of the kitchen, Don Alfredo stopped and spoke again with Charles. "You know what, Charles? I have been thinking about what you said to me the other day. About being a waiter. I like the idea. You possess great qualities, speak very good English and know how to treat people with respect. You are a hard-worker and I would like to help you. We will talk about it later."

Just as Don Alfredo finished speaking, he heard a voice behind him. "No, I do not agree with you, father." It was Celino, Don Alfredo's son who happened to enter the kitchen just in time to overhear what his father had said to Charles.

"Why not?" asked Don Alfredo, surprised. "I always help hard working people. Have there been any problems between you two?"

"No, father. I just don't like Frenchmen."

"Not true," said his father. "You are the one who asked me to give Andre a job. Did you forget that?"

"No, I did not. But Andre is different. We are friends."

A long silence arose between them. Apparently, Don Alfredo expected more of an explanation, but Celino did not give one. A few seconds later he added, "You know what, father? Let's just leave it this way, because even if I explained it to you, you would never understand."

"Celino," his father called out, "I have special reservations for tonight. They are important customers and I want everything to go well. We will sit down and talk about this tomorrow. Even if you think I will not understand, I want to listen to what you have to say."

Quite angry, Don Alfredo walked toward the door. Then looking at Charles once again, he added, "Watch the pasta, Charles. It should not boil for too long."

Utterly indignant Celino left the kitchen after his father. Obviously, he had got himself in trouble and it appeared that Charles had won the first round. And the funny thing was, that Charles did not even know why this all had happened. He had never had any problems with Celino before. In fact, they had hardly ever spoken to each other.

Very disappointed, Charles looked for Vercine.

"Vercine, why do you think Celino doesn't like me? I have never even said an occasional good night to him."

"Jealousy, Charles."

"What? Why?"

"Men are jealous, too. Don't you know that? And they are worse than women."

"You are kidding!" said Charles. "All this just because his father wants to help me? Ridiculous!"

"Yes, Charles," said Vercine. "I guess it's better for you to think that way. Go! Go back to work. Today we have what we can call 'Wednesday full house.' Don Alfredo just told me that we are expecting special clients, some of them from Chicago. They play hard and when they come to New York, they like to eat Vercine's lasagna."

Bewildered, Charles began his work. He did not fully understand Vercine's comments. "To hell with Celino!" he snapped to express his frustration. But when he turned around, he found Celino behind him.

"So, to hell with me, huh?" replied Celino. "I will tell you something, French boy. You don't know me, but you will. I know how to surprise people, and I will arrange a surprise for you that will change the course of your life. Soon...very soon."

That night, as expected, the Italia Campibeli Restaurant was full. About twenty people came to eat lasagna with Don Prieto Ferbonini and Juan Carlos Catarel. They were all business people—from both sides of the law—who sometimes enjoyed each other's company peacefully.

Those gathered represented an underground world. Society did not agree with their methods, nor did it accept the laws of their world, but it needed their money. They gambled, stole, and killed. They had their own justice system, defended their own businesses with blood, and at the same time, helped to support those responsible for the laws.

Juan Carlos Catarel had become the personification of such a world in Chicago. To have his protection meant to be untouchable, and to gain his friendship was the best achievement a person could hope for. Tonight, he was in New York and because of his being there, Don Alfredo's restaurant opened its door to many special guests.

Catarel was forty-five years old, six feet tall, bald, and had solemn brown eyes, which gave him a pleasant look. He skillfully impressed people with his great personality. Catarel sought exactly what he wanted, always, and learned to use very precise methods to obtain it. He also had a very unique taste in women. He liked the ones who are sensitive and very feminine. Those who, to win them, you must love them.

His presence in the Italia Campibeli Restaurant that evening had a purpose. He was joining forces with Ferbonini in order to better protect their interests. They had plans for the future and together they would use their influences to expand their business in other cities.

In previous years when Catarel had approached Don Prieto Ferbonini to propose his plan, he explained, "Don Prieto, if we don't do this, some other bastard will. For the good of all, it is better if it is us. At least we operate with honesty. The politicians don't understand this, but between you and me, I think we should handle it."

Don Ferbonini never disagreed with Catarel, but he said he needed time to think about it. He was getting old and things were not the same anymore. By moving forward, he could risk his present stability, and he wished to assure that his age would not interfere with the plans.

As time went by, they got together and talked about it again until Catarel finally convinced him that age should be the reason for them to join forces. "My friend, when you retire, what will happen with the business you now protect? Shelrain will take your territory. After you, he is the strongest and the youngest. We all know that he lives as a coiled snake waiting for the right time to strike."

After Don Ferbonini heard Shelrain's name, he decided to agree with Catarel's plan.

Today, in the Italia Campibeli Restaurant, they wanted to officially seal their friendship with an agreement, letting all the Italian businessmen know that they were together.

At the bar, Andre prepared drinks for the guests while in the kitchen Vercine worked tirelessly putting the finishing touches on his lasagna. Meanwhile, Ferbonini and Catarel sat conversing in a little office located next to the gambling room, Don Alfredo's private office.

When the lasagna was about to be served, a loud explosion was heard in the gambling room. Apparently, someone had thrown a bomb through the glass. The bomb exploded immediately and started a fire. Everyone inside panicked and frantically tried to run out of the restaurant.

Charles and some of the restaurant waiters grabbed tablecloths and went toward the room to try to put out the fire. In the process, Charles saw a woman's body lying under a table. Quickly, he ran out of the room and grabbed another tablecloth. Using it to protect his body, he advanced toward her, picked her up and carried her out of the restaurant.

When Charles stepped outside carrying the woman in his arms, immediately Juan Carlos Catarel, Don Prieto Ferbonini, and Alfredo Campibeli approached him. They all looked at the woman and exclaimed at the same time, "Oh, no! Isabella!"

6

TONIGHT HAD BEEN THE first time, since its renovation, that Isabella Gabilano had returned to the Italia Campibeli Restaurant. Juan Carlos Catarel had escorted her; she was his current love interest. He saw her as an exceptional woman—intelligent, independent, and extremely beautiful. She was thirty-six years old, petite, and her beauty caused heads to turn everywhere she went. She owned a brothel, the Blue Salon and controlled the lovely girls who appeared every night at Don Alfredo's nightclub.

However, Isabella's story held more sadness than happiness. At the age of eighteen she had left home seeking to start a new life. She had left behind an alcoholic father and a schizophrenic mother and while looking for a place to live, she met Martha Elmeg, one of Manhattan's small-time madams. Martha shared her large apartment with the eight girls who worked for her and Isabella arrived to join the group as the ninth. Among these women Isabella found the family she never had, and Martha turned out to be the friend she had always hoped for.

Two days after she moved in with Martha, her twin sister,

Anabella was killed. Consequently, this incident affected her plans for a new life. After Anabella's death, her parents grieved and needed her support. Under the circumstances, she decided to go see Don Prieto Ferbonini to ask for help. At the time, she did not know he was the one who had killed her sister, but she possessed something very valuable, which would mean a great deal to him.

Whatever she had turned into something indeed very valuable because he really changed her whole life. He helped her open, together with Martha, what was soon called the Blue Salon.

The morning after the bomb incident, Charles returned to the restaurant. He felt terrible about what had happened and wanted to help clean up the mess. Having learned to appreciate Don Alfredo very much, he felt he must stay next to him to express it.

When he arrived, he told Don Alfredo that he had come to help in any way possible.

"Yes, Charles," Don Alfredo said gratefully. "I need your help. Lots of things were broken last night and we need to clean up this mess."

They both started to move tables from the middle of the room to a corner.

"Who could have done this to me, Charles?"

"I don't know," answered Charles.

"Unbelievable! I had just remodeled the restaurant!"

"Yes. I'm very sorry, Don Alfredo," replied Charles.

"No," said Don Alfredo. "Don't be, because Don Prieto Ferbonini is going to find out who did it. Even though one of his men, who is familiar with explosives told us that the bomb was not an expert job, though it had been a warning. He will dig it up. He promised me. His life was also in danger yesterday. When he left, he was very upset and desperate to start hunting for the devil. And the power of his words, Charles...oh! The power of his words could have tilted the earth!"

Before leaving the restaurant, after the bombing incident, Don Ferbonini had assured Don Alfredo that he would get to the bottom of it. He also asked Don Alfredo *not* to keep the restaurant closed for more than a day. He said that the best way to recover from an incident like this was to keep the business open. Also, he suggested Don Alfredo start rebuilding the gambling room as soon as possible. Money should be no problem.

Nevertheless, Don Alfredo grew indignant; he understood Don Ferbonini's words. A name like Campibeli could not disappear from Manhattan because of an incident like that. Immediately he followed Don Prieto Ferbonini's advice, and planned to be closed for one day only.

Helping Charles move the tables, Don Alfredo said, "I have a message for you, Charles. Don Ferbonini wants to see you."

"Really? Why? I don't know him. In fact, I saw him yesterday for the first time."

"I'm sure that saving Isabella's life has something to do with it. She is like a daughter to him and is the only person in Manhattan who gets whatever she wants from him—without much effort."

"I only did what any other person would have done," said Charles.

"Yes, I know. And he also knows that, Charles. But *you* are the one who did it. Now he wants to see you and you must go see him. Don Ferbonini is a powerful person."

"Do you think...?"

"Yes."

After a few moments of silence Don Alfredo added, "I like you Charles, and I am going to tell you what I don't tell many people. If you have that man's word, you can rest in peace."

"Thank you, Don Alfredo. I will follow your advice."

Charles went to see Don Prieto Ferbonini that same afternoon. Since the restaurant was closed, the timing was perfect. Their meeting lasted no more than twenty minutes. Don Prieto Ferbonini thanked him for what he had done, and presented him with a cash reward. The reward had come from both Don Prieto Ferbonini and Juan Carlos Catarel.

To Charles, this was the best thing that had happened to him since he had arrived in New York. He felt very happy. And before leaving Don Prieto Ferbonini's house, Charles asked *him* for a favor. He wanted him to keep the money in a safe place until he decided what to do with it. But he already knew he would buy his first jeweler tools with this money.

The Italian Campibeli Restaurant opened the next day. Charles worked all day, both in the kitchen and in the gambling room removing debris. In the afternoon, he had another surprise. Don Alfredo appeared in the kitchen and told him that Isabella was there and she wanted to see him. Quietly, Charles followed Don Alfredo to where she sat.

Isabella was dressed in a simple, but elegant blue dress with bouffant sleeves. She was also wearing very delicate white gloves. Her hair flowed naturally over her shoulders making her appear younger than her age. Her sparkling brown eyes had an exuberant brightness that only made them come more alive, and the sweetness of her smile spun her feminine appeal.

After being introduced she told Charles, "I wanted to meet and thank you personally for what you did on the night of the fire. I don't know what would have happened if you had not helped me."

"I simply did what any other person would have done in my place."

"Even so, you did something brave and I want to express my deep appreciation."

She looked at him for a moment then said, "Don Ferbonini told me he gave you a cash reward. I'm glad he did, but I also want to offer you my friendship in gratitude. I owe you my life. From now on, if you need anything, please count on me. You can find me at the Blue Salon."

"Thank you," said Charles.

She left and he returned to his work.

Around 10:00 p.m. Don Alfredo closed the restaurant for the night. It was empty because the bombing incident had frightened away most customers. Charles and two others stayed around until the nightclub closed. After that, they all went home.

While walking home alone, Charles thought about the latest turn-of-events. Don Ferbonini, the money and Isabella Gabilano. He admitted to himself that she was a very pretty woman.

When he got to his door, he took his key, opened it, and went in. Once inside he was shocked at what he found—Andre and Celino in bed, naked!

For an instant, Charles did not know what to do or think. Andre turned away from him, but not Celino. Celino stood up next to the bed, and said with contempt, "Do you like this, pretty French boy? If so, you are welcome to join us."

"Oh! This is disgusting!" Charles exclaimed as he turned around and left the apartment.

Charles aimlessly walked the streets, his thoughts in turmoil. *Andre, a homosexual? How blind and stupid have I been not to have noticed? That explains why he always talked little and kept his distance. Now Vercine's words have meaning. Vercine had said Celino was jealous...so Vercine must know about it. And probably all the other employees, as well as the customers, and perhaps all of Manhattan, except for Don Alfredo and myself!*

Charles was so glad that Antoine had never known about it. Antoine had had such pride in Andre that this would have devastated his entire affection toward him.

Besides dealing with unbearable disappointment, Charles was upset. He could no longer live with Andre and now needed another place. And the worst part was that he could not count on Don Alfredo's help.

After walking and thinking for hours, he returned to the apartment. He realized that he had to stay there at least one more night.

He went back, opened the door to the apartment and silently entered. Fully dressed, Charles lay down on the mattress where he usually slept. Though it was dark, the room seemed empty. Feeling relieved, he closed his eyes to sleep. But as his breathing got deeper he became aware of a strong and strange odor in the room. Worried, he got up and lit the candle.

"Oh, no!" Charles cried. Andre's nude body was on his bed with a dagger stuck in his chest.

Horrified, Charles went toward the bed and quickly pulled the dagger from Andre's chest. Andre's eyes were open and his mouth twisted, his face frozen in a death mask.

For a few seconds Charles was paralyzed after looking at Andre's naked body covered with blood. "Oh...what do I do now?"

He could not call the police because he had entered the country illegally and this surely would complicate everything. Then he began to feel sick to his stomach; his body trembled with fear that overtook him.

"I have to leave this place!" was all he could think to do.

Quickly, Charles picked up the money he had saved and left—leaving behind the horrible scene of death.

PERHAPS, AT ANOTHER TIME, he could have been the prince he felt like.

Each morning Celino looked in the mirror and superciliously played with that fantasy. He lived self-satisfied and confident that he could accomplish all he wanted. Also, he was very proud of his knowledge and social status. He loved to attract attention with his tailored elegance and because of this he preferred suits with small, discreet lines and silk shirts. Sometimes, he wore a carnation on his lapel, and a hat with a narrow brim of the same color as the suit. Tall, slim, and not very talkative, he preferred socializing only with people whom he considered his equals—like the ones who had given him the title, "The Prince of Manhattan."

Celino, the youngest in his family, grew up among four adoring sisters. When his mother very tenderly said "No," to him, his sisters conspired together to change her mind. They catered to all of Celino's whims. When he turned twelve, these doting women were still dressing and combing his hair. At sixteen, they would remove his shoes, and now at twenty, they all waited outside the bathroom with his towel, his slippers, and his clothes.

To Celino, women had special qualities that made them almost sacred. He could never imagine a relationship with a woman without thinking of his mother and sisters. Since he never felt free enough to have sex with a woman, his homosexuality unveiled.

The discovery that Celino and Andre were homosexuals had greatly shocked Charles. He had never been exposed to it before and consequently, could not understand homosexuality in others. Therefore, he felt a huge disappointment in himself for not having recognized it.

It might have been better if I had never left France.

That night Charles walked without direction, alone, except for the company of his thoughts. He crossed one street after another as he tried to cope with the speed in which all the events had happened and hoping he could think straight. Innocently, he planned to see Vercine in the morning and tell him the whole story. *Vercine*, he thought, *will guide me through this unpleasant situation.* But almost as fast as he came up with that idea, he had to stop it. He remembered he could not tell Vercine that Celino had killed Andre because, in fact, he had not seen it. No one had witnessed Celino doing such a deed. Then it dawned on Charles that Celino could be a suspect as well as himself. He had walked over the crime scene and had touched the dagger used to kill Andre.

When Charles faced that terrible reality, Celino's threat came to his mind. *You do not know me, Charles. I know how to surprise people and I'm going to surprise you—soon, very soon. In a way that will change the course of your life.*

"Oh! The bastard really did it!" he hissed aloud.

Suddenly, as Charles saw it his situation had become a horrible twisted mess. He lost his ability to focus on his dreams and expectations. While he paced the streets in tremendous distress, his mind kept back the least positive impression his good sense could ever have forged and he engaged in the most wild fear he could possibly imagine—going to jail for a crime he didn't commit.

Looking around, he imagined the streets getting narrow, the

sky ready to fall completely over his head. He didn't know what to do or where to go. All he knew was that he must flee. If he were caught, it would be the end of his dreams and the beginning of misery. Celino had been right, this would, indeed, change the course of his life. He knew for certain that he could never convince the authorities of his innocence because Celino would do everything in his power to incriminate him beyond a shadow of doubt.

Oh, this is the end of everything! Charles thought as he contemplated the huge emptiness of his life. He had never imagined that such a thing could happen—that he would need someone but would have no one to whom he could turn. Exhausted, in his mind he watched his whole life collapsing into a giant quagmire. Nothing worse, he felt, could have happened to him.

Hopelessly, he walked on, repeating everything that came to his mind. His words fell through the night like his life, sinking in misery. In his ramblings he came by the front of the Italia Campibeli Restaurant and crossed the street. His surroundings rested so quietly that he could hear his own footsteps. Charles kept walking just to see if by crossing streets, he could diminish his anguish. He kept going forward, crossed one intersection, turned, crossed another street and suddenly, from a corner, he saw a sign that made him abruptly stop. "The Blue Salon."

As he looked at it, Isabella's name quickly flashed into his mind and her saying, *I owe you my life.*

Her words began to repeat themselves, over and over again in his mind, until he decided to go in and see her. Now, he had thought of someone who might help him.

When Charles arrived at the Blue Salon, he walked to the bar and said to a young woman, "I urgently need to see Miss Gabilano!"

"She is already resting for the night," responded the young woman. "Who are you?"

"My name is Charles Merlenes."

"Merlenes? The French man who saved her life?"

"Yes."

"Please wait. I will tell her that you are here."

The enormous parlor on the first floor had four sets of brightly colored red and orange sofas. A medium-size bar impressively occupied one of the corners leaving the other one for a large and shiny black piano, which at the time, rested silently. On the opposite side, there were three small tables. At one of them four people were playing cards. Three young girls were sitting on one of the sofas talking, drinking, and smoking.

Charles sat apart from them, and while he waited, he observed the parlor. It was dim inside, but enough to see the paintings on the walls and the expensive drapes at the widows. Everything in the room gracefully contributed to make it sophisticated and elegant.

When the young woman reappeared at the top of the stairs, Charles panicked at first, thinking that maybe Isabella would refuse to see him. But then the girl said, "Please, come with me; Miss Gabilano is waiting for you."

Charles climbed the stairs to the third floor where Isabella lived. No other man, except Juan Carlos Catarel, had ever been allowed in her apartment. When Charles walked into the living room, she approached him with a puzzled look. It was 2:00 in the morning and even though night seemed endless in the Blue Salon, she was getting ready for bed.

"Good morning, Charles," she said.

"Good morning," he answered.

She had on a long satin robe with a feathered collar and wore no make-up at all. Her hair fell loosely to her shoulders. Her soft-spoken good morning had greatly diminished his tension.

"Please, sit down," she said. "How can I help you?"

Charles looked down feeling a little embarrassed. He had to tell her the reason for his visit, but he feared of the impact his story would have on her. Yet, at the same time, he knew that she was his only hope. He must tell her the truth. After taking a few seconds to put his thoughts in order, he finally spoke.

The first words uttered expressed his gratitude for her seeing him at such an hour, and explained that he desperately needed her help. Then, very nervously, he told her what had actually happened to Andre. He confided that he could not call the police because he was afraid he would be arrested and accused of Andre's brutal murder.

"Are you talking about Andre, the bartender at the Italia Campibeli Restaurant?" she asked.

"Yes," Charles answered.

"Oh, saints of heaven! And do you have any idea who might have done it?"

"Celino...I think," answered Charles without hesitation. Then he described what had occurred earlier when he had surprised them in bed together.

"I see. I knew that sooner or later he would smear his father's name."

Charles' story justified his courage for disturbing her at this hour of the night. He had to face the facts, and under the circumstances, everything pointed to him as being guilty. The complexity of his problems surfaced aggressively because he lived and worked in Celino's territory. If it came down to his word against Celino's, he knew that Celino's would prevail.

Very concerned about Charles' uneasy and distressful condition, Isabella said, "You are tense, Charles. I think you could use something to drink. What will it be, whiskey or coffee?"

"I'll have some coffee, thank you."

While getting up, Isabella added, "I know that this has turned into a nightmare for you, and I honestly don't know what to do to help, but I promise I will think of something. For the time being, I think we should wait to see what happens next. We need to make sure nobody will find you here. Sometimes using caution is better than rushing after a lousy solution. Now, go to the bathroom down the hall and wash your hands. You still have blood on them."

Charles quickly looked at his hands. She was right; he did have blood on them. "I did not kill him," he said in a desperate tone. "My hands are bloody because I removed the dagger from his body."

She hesitated before speaking. "I believe you, Charles. All I said was to go and wash your hands."

The next day about noon, the crime was discovered after Celino had grown upset because Andre and Charles had not shown up for work. He pretended to be worried about that and sent one of the waitresses to see what had happened. Later, when the police began the investigation, Celino volunteered his assistance and gave them information that would incriminate Charles without any doubt. And he didn't leave the station until he was assured that Charles was the person they suspected.

By Sunday afternoon, Manhattan finally re-started to enjoy a dull and whimsical calm. The patrons of the restaurant grew expectant, for they believed that at any moment, someone would arrive with the news that Charles had been arrested. Charles suddenly became the main topic of conversation. Some people affirmed that it was impossible for a cook who spent his days boiling pasta, to develop such courage. Others thought that Charles and Andre shared more than—just an apartment. A very small group sensed that the story was a set-up.

While Charles was the subject of most everyone's conversations, in Isabella's apartment he desperately counted the hours, and waited silently to see what she could do on his behalf. At first, she couldn't do much, but then her mind grew wise and forged some ideas. After she realized the police considered Charles the primary suspect, she knew his chance to get out of it rapidly diminished. Considering the seriousness of the accusation against him, she reached the conclusion that alone she couldn't give him the help he so desperately needed.

Shortly after she realized that, she went directly to Don Prieto Ferbonini for help, and calmly repeated to him word-for-word all that Charles had told her. Don Ferbonini listened patiently and then admitted that Celino was more of a son-of-a-bitch than he had thought. *Oh, it is a shame how things happen. Bad guys and good guys always tangled together.*

Then he remembered what Carls Shelrain had done to him, long ago. Now, someone else's goose was being cooked. *Poor young Charles! Left alone to be the sacrificial lamb.*

"You can help him, can't you?" Isabella asked.

"Yes, but for what? In this situation I must stay on Celino's side."

"Don Ferbonini, that man saved my life!"

A deep silence filled the room as Isabella looked intently at Don Ferbonini.

"This is not a common cause; it's my cause," she decided to add. "That man is innocent and needs my—"

"All right!" said Don Ferbonini. "I'll crack that egg. But this should end here."

"Thanks," she uttered. Then turned and left.

Don Prieto Ferbonini was known as an Italian son-of-a-bitch; however, sometimes he could act like an angel. This time he found two reasons for helping Charles—one, because Isabella had taken his side and the other because he had a kind of sympathy for good guys.

The next day, Fairboy, Don Ferbonini's right-hand man, went to the docks to make arrangements with a man named Steve Duke. And an hour later when Fairboy returned, he said to Don Ferbonini, "Everything will be ready the day after tomorrow. Charles should go to the port at 2:00 in the morning with only the clothes on his back. Steve Duke wants fifty greens for this." *Green* was the word Fairboy always used when he had to tell Don Ferbonini the price of a service.

"Fine," said Don Ferbonini. "Go and inform Isabella. Tell her that you will pick him up, and remind her that in our business punctuality counts."

When Fairboy turned to leave, Don Ferbonini said, "Out of

curiosity, Fairboy, what ship will Steve Duke put him on?"

"The *Coimbra*, Don Ferbonini. Charles will leave New York as—Jose Da Silva. He will go to Portugal. Poor devil...back to Europe. Sometimes life is shit, isn't it?"

8

WHILE EVENTS CONTINUED TO intensify, Charles' misfortune swiftly engaged him in his new reality—which was leaving New York. In Boston, Ana received a letter from Isabella.

Sister Luisa entered the school library with the letter in her hand. She stopped and looked around. "Oh, there you are!" she exclaimed. "Ana, I have a letter for you."

"I bet it's from Aunt Isabella," said Ana happily. "Stay, Sister Luisa, so you can read it, too."

New York, November 20, 1886

Dear Ana,

How are you and Sister Luisa doing? I hope well. We have very cold weather in New York, worse than last year.

Ana, you can't imagine how happy I feel that this year you decided to spend Christmas in New York. I am counting the days, hours, and minutes. I've redecorated your apartment, knowing you love white

> and blue. I chose those colors for the carpet and drapes. It looks lovely.
>
> This time we'll sit and talk seriously about your staying here in New York. You have finished all your studies and still haven't decided what to do with your life. I know you love Boston, but please, think about New York.
>
> Ana, Fairboy will come to Boston to pick you up. I don't want you to travel by yourself.
>
> See you soon,
> Your Aunt Isabella.

After talking with Don Prieto Ferbonini about Charles' complicated situation and asking him for help, Isabella returned home elated that she had good news to tell Charles. She now experienced an enormous sense of relief that Don Prieto had agreed to take care of it.

Even though her plan was working perfectly, she felt another concern regarding the fact that she was indeed becoming deeply involved in helping Charles. Don Ferbonini had warned her not to get mixed up in the situation because, depending on how it ended, her reputation could be jeopardized. She left his words in the air, waiting to be analyzed later on.

Later, when she remembered them, they began to bother her. Rapidly, they stirred her conscience in such a way that made her think of the consequences a scandal could bring, not only to herself and her business, but also to Juan Carlos Catarel. When she carefully analyzed Don Ferbonini's words, she concluded that he was right. Charles must leave the Blue Salon. It would be better to keep him away from her business. As soon as she understood that, she decided to hide him in the apartment she had prepared for Ana's arrival.

At night, with an air of confidence, she appeared in the living room of her apartment carrying a large coat, a scarf, and a hat.

Then without any explanation, she ordered Charles to put the coat on.

Silently Charles obeyed.

After he put the coat on, she said, "Excellent! You look like any man protecting himself from the cold. Put on this scarf, too, and cover part of your face with it."

While Charles was doing what she asked, she quietly stood looking at him.

"Now, put on the hat. That's perfect! You won't be recognized at all."

At 12:30 a.m. night turned darker and colder. Charles stood quietly in front of her not knowing where she had planned to take him.

"You must move to another place, Charles," she finally explained. "I have an apartment not far from here where you can stay." Then she slipped her hand inside her dress pocket and said, "Here is the key. Saporo will be here soon to take you there."

Ana's apartment, located on the fourth floor of the building, had a nice living room, kitchen and two bedrooms. There was a big mirror on the dining room wall just opposite the door to one of the bedrooms. Charles arrived there, sat in the living room and spent the rest of the night thinking about his trip back to Europe. *Why Portugal?* He then admitted Celino had indeed accomplished what he had promised—had changed the course of his future.

The next day, boredom filled his hours. He spent every minute trying to accept his bad luck and when he felt tired of his own thoughts, realized that now, not even Captain Alejandro's words made any sense.

At the end of the day, he got up from the sofa and looked around the apartment. In the kitchen he remembered that he was hungry, and there was nothing to eat. He kept looking around the apartment observing the furniture and decor. The combination of them both made it very elegant and cozy. Stopping in front of the bathroom, which smelled so clean, he immediately felt the urge to take a bath. *A warm bath would break the monotony and ease my* *mind for a while. It will be a whole day before I get to the port to hide in the Coimbra and sail to Portugal. A bath would certainly help me feel better...*but Charles hesitated. *Maybe it wouldn't be a good idea using the spotless bathroom that looks as if it has never been used. Isabella might not like that.*

For a few moments he just stood in the bathroom doorway and thoughtfully looked at it. *This might be my last opportunity to take a warm bath and use clean towels for a long time.* That last thought erased his modesty and he promptly decided to follow his urge. *If I break a rule of etiquette, I'll never know. Portugal will make me forget about it.*

Charles took a long bath and then entered the bedroom where he had left his clothes. He stood naked in the center of the room, drying his hair carelessly with a small towel, feeling extremely relaxed, thinking of absolutely nothing, when the front door opened and Isabella entered.

She had a big package in her hands that she placed on the dining room table.

While removing her coat, she saw Charles' reflection in the dining room wall-mirror. She stood quietly without moving and looked at him. She found him very attractive and not only did she observe him, but also spent some time enjoying the view. Then without making a sound, she tiptoed to the bedroom door.

"Charles," she whispered softly—not to alarm him. Charles heard her whisper and turned around extremely confused about what to do. He did not know whether to cover himself, get dressed, or what. He stood frozen in place and speechless.

To save the moment and diminish the tremendous embarrassment her presence caused, Isabella approached and masterfully took the towel from his hand. "What a rough way to dry your hair, Charles. It is going to get all tangled making it impossible to comb."

The smoothness of her voice induced him to stand still while she dried his hair. With both arms up, she moved the small towel gently, back and forth over his head. They stood so close that he could feel the softness of her skin. Their faces almost touching made it possible for him to inhale her breath. As their passionate looks intensified, Isabella's hands slowly stopped moving, and Charles bent his head and kissed her.

Magic moments create complicated situations; however, if nothing erases such a divine moment, let everything happen. After that, nothing could have stopped them from having each other.

An hour later, still glowing from their lovemaking, Isabella put on her dress and went to get the bag she had left on the dining room table. With the bag in her hands, she walked to the kitchen. Charles, who had not stopped watching her, also put on his clothes and silently followed her. "Do you like Isabella's spaghetti?" she asked.

"As hungry as I am, I could even eat boiled tomatoes," he answered. "Spaghetti is one of my favorite dishes. How did you know?"

"Telepathy," she said, happily. "Sometimes it works. The same way I knew I was going to find you naked in the middle of the room drying your hair."

"I am sorry for taking a bath without asking first."

"Don't worry. Sometimes magical things happen this way. And because of that they are magical."

She began to remove the contents of the bag. First, she took out some onions, garlic, and tomatoes. "Mmm!" she exclaimed. "These are the essential ingredients for preparing a delicious spaghetti sauce. Garlic is very important. If you forget the garlic, please...forget the pasta. Do you understand?"

He looked at her thoughtfully, "Yes, I understand."

"Oh, tomatoes! Do you know about tomatoes, Charles? They should be red and firm. My mother always asked my father what was his special touch that made his spaghetti sauce better than hers. And he always had the same answer, 'I'm Italian, and I sing when I choose my tomatoes.' Actually, my mother never discovered his secret. Being an Italian helped, but singing? What do you think?"

"That was not his secret."

"Of course not, but no one could make spaghetti like he did!"

Isabella talked endlessly and Charles never tired of listening to her. He grew more and more fascinated by her and acted like a schoolboy listening to his girlfriend babble. Everything she said sounded fabulous and all of her stories were brand new to him. Her energetic spirit suited her differences and she suddenly became the woman beyond his dreams.

That evening, Isabella revealed several things about her life. Charles found out from her that Prieto Ferbonini had killed her twin and only sister, Anabella. He also learned about Ana, her niece who lived in Boston. Also, she had said she loved Prieto Ferbonini more than she had loved her father.

When she finished her story, she asked, "What about you, Charles? Tell me something about yourself. Why did you leave France?"

Oh, why did she ask that? All that he had not wanted to remember had come back, like oil paintings hanging out of sequence on a wall.

"I want to be a rich man," he said unpretentiously. Afterwards, he talked about the rest—his father, St. Denis and his mother's burial that he had not attended. He also spoke about his uncle—whom he still hated, his brother and sister, the robbery, his friend Antoine, and finally, about what he knew best, jewelry.

Without a doubt Isabella found his story quite inspiring. He, who was seven years younger than she, had a past that made him very interesting. She saw in him an adventurous young man living an unhappy life, falling on rough times and dreaming a big dream. Suddenly, all of this made him—very desirable. Different from any of the other men she had known.

"So you left France because you wanted to be rich?"

"Yes."

"What makes you think that money is everything?"

"I didn't say that."

"No, but it sounds close to it."

"Okay. Let me explain why money is an issue in my life. My uncle stole from my father everything my father had saved in his entire life. And he did so when my father lay dead, unable to speak for himself. My father was my uncle's only brother. From his actions don't you think money is more important than feelings?"

Instead of answering she said, "Keep talking, and tell me more about *you*."

Charles talked for some time. He let her know about the seminary, which was the best decision he had made at eighteen, and that indeed, it had helped comfort his soul that had been in need of overcoming its conflicts.

"It was inside those huge and cold walls that I had the opportunity to learn about the ways of the world, man, and God. Today, I see it as something life offered me when I most needed it, and I feel grateful by accepting it."

"Things like that only happen to a few people, Charles," she said. "Life sometimes plugs in only its sour intentions. For example, to me, things did not work as great as they worked for you. In fact, when I gained freedom to shop for happy days, I discovered that I had to fight more to survive, than to fight for what I was looking for. Soon, protection became the issue because fear began to bounce back and forth inside me. Without many inquiries, I started to share happiness in order to understand feelings, and carefully, I shared passions to grasp what was missing in my life."

"Do you believe in God?"

"God and fear confused my heart when I was still a little girl. After that I gave those two words the same meaning. But the answer is yes! I grew up in the Catholic faith; however, I understood little, not really the whole idea."

"I understand. We went through different ways."

"Yes. We traveled on separate roads. You probably learned to cross the river with faith, the land with knowledge, and the days of your life with powerful dreams. Your father may have given you his wisdom. It seems that you have been given the opportunity to listen to good advice as well as to study valuable lessons."

"Precisely, Isabella, precisely."

They faced each other while the silence bounced off the walls.

"With me, Charles..." she began. "Oh! What can I say? The incidents rolled very quickly and in a confused way. The best thoughts I intended to have died with the night and the best valuable words I heard shrunk before their meanings could possibly reach out. What I had left were just crazy ideas. We all know that crazy ideas lead to crazy results—they increase our shame and rob us of our prudence—but there is a time in life when our desires for craziness never reverses. I followed these desires once, and I believe I will live them again if I have a great battle to win."

Charles looked at her thoughtfully. From whatever she had drifted, now it didn't matter. She learned something throughout her struggles.

"You mentioned my father," he commented. "He was a wonderful man. Everybody loved him. To this day I still remember things he said. As I age, I improve my way of thinking because of him. Since I left my hometown, I have changed a great deal. We all have problems understanding life and what shapes our minds might not be what lives in our heart—at least not with the same priorities. The mind holds the thoughts and the heart—only feelings. Feelings are not constant. They come and go like the rain and the wind. Sometimes it is the rain that makes the heart fertile, and sometimes it is the wind that blows away the best of it."

"I have never heard anything so truthful. You seem very romantic."

"Do not count on that because you could be wrong. I don't have much experience with women. I spent most of my life studying and working."

"Oh, I also didn't have time for romance. I still need what I missed."

She paused to see if he would have any interest in knowing

about what was missing in her life, but no. Charles only silently observed her.

"When I was a young woman trying to find a decent man for a husband, I couldn't find any. Men like you, Charles, dwelt somewhere else learning about thoughts and feelings while I was fighting for survival. New York City showed me that fishing in the river was different than fishing in the ocean. The river has a steady course, and the ocean...a fickle motion. Salt water tastes nothing but salty. Now surrounding my memories lived the laughs, cries, and noises that belong to my most painful moments. Days now pass by in simple commotion. I only wait for the bright and clear mornings because they forge my hopes, and I enjoy the quiet afternoons for they bring wonderful nights. That's all."

"Life, Isabella...it can forge very unpleasant moments. Look at me for an example of it. If it were not because of your generosity, who knows where I would be right now."

"Generosity no, Charles. You saved my life."

"I may have done that, but I'd still like to thank your generosity."

Later, while enjoying dinner, she looked at him thoughtfully, trying to determine the qualities and flaws which lead an inexperienced young man to change into such an interesting one. *Not attending his mother's funeral—was insolent; stealing from his uncle—quite insane; and disregarding his siblings—something unusual. Then, there were the other experiences he has survived. He lost his best friend in the middle of the Atlantic, saved the life of a prostitute in New York City, and even became involved in the death of a homosexual. Definitely, Charles Merlenes appears to have an unfortunate destiny. His profession—unique! His dreams—exciting!*

Isabella had him sit across from her as he ate the delicious spaghetti she had cooked. Silently, she observed his hands as he cleaned the corner of his mouth—firm, skillful, and capable of unforgettable caresses. She realized how much she liked him, and how much his checkered past and his dreams for the future appealed to her.

They spent the night together and made love again and again. Caressing her naked body, he talked about diamonds, rubies, and emeralds and he revealed the sad experience he had with Joanna Sampaio.

Joanna had been the only woman that had meant something in Charles' life, but she existed only for a brief time. She became his first sexual partner, a young and beautiful single mother he intended to marry. After accepting his proposal they planned to be married a year later. But then something unexpected happened. Charles had found her in bed with his Uncle Luis, the one he hated so much. From that day on, she had ceased to exist for him and he then decided to go to the seminary. St. Denis seemed to be too small for both him and his uncle.

At about 3:00 a.m., Isabella realized she had to go back to the Blue Salon. She quickly rose from the bed and got dressed. Charles remained sound asleep, as an innocent child sleeps after so many mischievous deeds. Before leaving she sat on the bed and contemplated him. *Oh, I do not want to lose you!*

In her mind, Charles' image replaced the imaginary prince on a white stallion she had hoped to find one day, and now she realized the man she had idolized as a lover had come too late—when the innocent girl no longer existed. *Oh, saints of heaven, why? Just tell me why?* she begged for an answer.

The saints of heaven in their serene and loving way reinforced her lack of faith by causing her, in that moment, to remember the day she received her First Communion. That wasn't a pleasant memory for her—

Her mother first helped her get dressed and then went to help her sister. Isabella was supposed to sit still while waiting, but she did not obey her mother. She got up and went to the front porch to enjoy the beautiful morning. It had stopped raining and the morning air seemed so clean and vibrant that even the green of the trees looked brighter. Isabella took a deep breath and smelled the rich wet soil. The enticing smell seduced her down the steps. Holding up her long, First Communion tunic, she started to jump over the wet ground as if she were playing hopscotch. As fate would have it, she fell. When she found herself on the ground, she grabbed a fistful of soil and squeezed it. The soil, the smell, and the evidence of a clean morning made her very unclean for her First Communion.

When her mother saw her, she screamed furiously and Isabella began to cry. The anger on her mother's face terrified her to death. She honestly thought her mother would kill her! "Mamma, please forgive me!" Isabella pleaded, very afraid and genuinely sorry. But her mother gave her a hard spanking.

She never forgot that day. Every time she listened to the rain and smelled the wet soil, she remembered her mother's fury and the first time she had experienced fear. This had happened on the same day as she had received God in her heart. Since then, God symbolized fear, and fear...was something she had learned to avoid.

She stood up firmly only for what she wanted, and resolution introduced peace.

While sitting next to Charles, she again experienced fear and knew that time for resolution had arrived. He slept innocently as her fear of losing him increased. She found that she simply adored him and her soul rejoiced by these feelings. If she could keep at least the breeze of it inside her heart, her passions would be playing cheerfully over a lovely fantasy.

Indeed, she made the resolution to keep him forever.

Fully dressed to leave, she looked at him once again. She then leaned down to smell his skin and gently kissed his lips as she whispered, "I can't let you go."

Determinably she added, "Forget about Portugal, Charles, you are going to marry Ana."

9

"WE PUT THE BOMB in the restaurant because of Celino."

"Will you be so kind to explain to Don Ferbonini what is your business with Celino," said Saporo without getting up from his chair.

There, in the presence of Don Prieto Ferbonini and Saporo, stood two very young men, one of them so afraid that he stuttered, "Celino won a poker game against us and we had to give him our asses. The cock had a gun to our heads."

"So that is what is going on," said Don Prieto Ferbonini. "Thank heaven that you are a pair of talking birds, otherwise, who knows how many people would have died."

After that Don Ferbonini ordered Saporo to cut off a finger from each one. Then he stood up saying, "This will remind you that talking birds should have concerts in their own nests. Next time I will cut off your balls."

Before Don Ferbonini left the room, Isabella, who had arrived and stayed at the door listening to the conversation said, "Very interesting meeting. Are those the bastards that almost killed me?"

"Yes," said Don Ferbonini looking at her, surprised to see her there so early. "Celino's friends," he explained.

"I heard. Apparently our little prince is involved in many businesses, no?" Then with her head held up high, she walked over and stood near the young men. "Bastards, you could have killed me!" But when following Ferbonini out of the room, she thought differently. *I am happy for what happened.*

Prieto Ferbonini walked to his study and Isabella followed silently. After he sat comfortably in his chair he said, "Let's see what brings you here so early, Isabella."

"I came to talk about Charles," she said in a very confident manner.

"What is it now? Everything is arranged for tomorrow. Fairboy will take him to the port and will give him the money that he left with me for safekeeping. Everything should go exactly as we planned."

"Those plans must change, Don Ferbonini. He is not leaving for Portugal."

"Oh, no?"

"No. He will stay here and marry Ana."

"I beg your pardon!"

"Charles will stay here and marry Ana," she repeated adamantly.

"Isabella! I have always been patient with you and—"

"This is what I have decided, so let it be. We have a peace pact. Don't forget it."

"Isabella, when I lose my patience, I can even forget what I promised."

"It has never happened and it won't happen now that Ana is about to come. You always keep your word and that is why people do business with you. Same reason I also do business with you."

"Forget the old stories," said Ferbonini. "I am an old man. Don't take advantage of it. Ana is my beloved granddaughter and I want a world of roses for her. That's what grandfathers wish for their granddaughters. So, why not allow things to follow their course? Why this sudden talk of marriage?"

"Charles is a jeweler, a good man—mature and intelligent."

"You slept with him, didn't you?" asked Don Ferbonini firmly.

"What? Is that what you think?" she asked defiantly.

"No. If you are planning on a wedding between him and Ana, I guess you didn't."

"Correct, I did *not*!"

Prieto Ferbonini kept quiet for an instant, considering her answer, measuring the amount of sincerity that existed in it.

"Oh, Don Prieto," she started to say with a sweet voice. "You have to understand that Charles is the perfect husband. What is Ana? Think about it. An innocent angel raised in a religious school. She received the best education a girl could dream of, even learned three languages, but she ignores real life. She knows the meaning of a thousand words, and probably does not know what masturbation means. This innocent and pure young girl, who can communicate in three languages, will be completely lost as soon as she gets out in the real world. The first rogue that touches her forbidden fruit will marry her. I do not want that to happen. Neither do you. Charles happens to be a good man in a desperate situation. Whatever we decide for him, he will accept."

She paused briefly and added, "Ana can solve his immigration situation, and he can solve her problem for us. I do not want her in the hands of an ordinary or perverted man with nothing to offer and no ambition in life. She is Ana, not an ordinary girl, the one we educated to be a decent woman."

Feeling an enormous sense of relief, she finished talking and sat on the sofa. Isabella thought that she had proven her point and that Prieto Ferbonini once again would do as she wished.

Don Ferbonini remained silent. He stayed in his chair with his head down, moving his fingers in a distressed manner. To throw Ana—all that he had—into Charles' arms, seemed absurd. He thought people got married because they loved each other. However, he could not completely disregard what Isabella had said, men were full of filthy thoughts and deeds.

"Don Prieto," said Isabella, while getting up from the sofa and walking toward him, "I know what disturbs your mind—love. Love is wonderful, but not relevant. If *love* exists before marriage, it will not last. Sometimes it comes too late in our lives, and sometimes never at all. Frankly, the flesh only identifies pleasure. With or without love pleasure will exist. I know what I am talking about. While your business is to cut off a body part and leave it behind as dead meat, mine is to make it erect for pleasure."

"Oh! Enough, Isabella! Enough! Please, close your mouth!" yelled Don Ferbonini. "You have said more than I wanted to hear."

"All right, you don't need to yell. People are like that; they hate to listen to the truth. Anyway, I can leave. If you don't want to help I will ask..."

"Juan Carlos Catarel." Ferbonini repeated with her. "I know about that. You keep him happy at night and he does whatever you ask in the morning. It never fails. It is not too difficult to figure out."

"Leave my relationship with Juan Carlos out of this. I insist that you stay out of it."

"I will. I am just reminding you that I may be old but not stupid. Now let's finish this conversation. In my opinion, what you have in mind is totally nonsensical, but you win. I will agree with you only because of the future of my granddaughter. I know that whether I agree or not, you are going to do what you want anyway, and in the process, you might even succeed in making Catarel my worst enemy. I cannot afford it. As I told you, I am old and tired. You will be my nemesis; I feel it. Ana is the only reason that prevents me from forever erasing your beautiful smile. Go in peace. Again you will get your way."

"Excellent!" she exclaimed clapping her hands and kissing him on his cheek. "You know what, Don Prieto? You could never kill me. I am the daughter you never had and you are the father I always wished for." Grabbing her purse she turned to leave. From the door she added, "Solving the immigration problem and keeping Charles out of jail will be your responsibility. I will take care of the rest."

As she calmly walked away, Ferbonini thought, *I don't know why I didn't kill her instead of her sister.*

For an instant he was lost in time, remembering Anabella—

She was barely eighteen when he killed her. *I like to try the courage of men*–her words. *A pretty bambina, Saporo, but I hate puttanas*–his words. With a great sadness, he said aloud, "I think I gained my just reward. I got rid of one but I will have the other, forever. And my only granddaughter happens to be the child of one of them."

Isabella left Ferbonini's house and went to see Charles. Immediately, after she stood in front of him, he understood that whatever had happened between them had died at dawn. She seemed too serious for the occasion and strange for a lover. Her impetuous look forced him back to his original position–a poor devil in trouble, and to whom she owed a favor.

As soon as she walked into the living room she said, "I just came from talking to Don Prieto Ferbonini and I have a proposition to make."

Charles remained taciturn. Her voice held a new pitch to remind him that she was dealing new cards. Instantly, he sensed her impulsive intentions draining directly from her imagination. Her desires tenderly seduced the good instincts of her soul and no virtue stood against her bizarre intention.

"If you agree to marry Ana, my niece, you will not have to go to Portugal. Ferbonini will arrange a place for you in Manhattan under his protection."

At first, Charles could not perceive her audacity. Only when she authoritatively stated, "You have one minute to decide and you should think about this seriously. Remember, you do not know a soul in Portugal and here you almost have a family." *Did he realize that she was not joking?* She wondered. And to dare him she added, "Let's see if you are a man who knows what is best for you."

The lack of modesty he saw in her forced him to participate in that dirty game she began to play. The quickness of her mind could indeed frighten even the strongest man who ever set foot on earth. Intentionally, he kept his thoughts swinging within the silence in order to combat the vibration of her last words.

"I do know what is good for me," he finally said. "Even though this is a big decision to be made in a minute, I will take the easy way. I trust it. Still water runs deep, doesn't it? If it is a matter of choice between Portugal and New York, I will choose New York." Then cynically he added, "You can go and tell my future wife that I love her."

In spite of seeing everything falling into place, as she had planned, Isabella thought Charles' answer sounded despicable. "I have no desire to start a war between us, Charles. Honestly, I only want to help you. What happened last night should be forgotten. You have a dream to accomplish and I'd like to see my niece married. According to my life's experiences, marriage is the best thing that can happen to you at this time."

"Funny, that's what my life experience tells me also."

"Ana is a charming girl," Isabella continued. "She received the best education a northern woman can afford. She speaks three languages, among them French. By marrying her, you'll open a door to the future you so desire. You will not only put an end to your present problems, but you will also have the money to start your dream business. I can't see any better way to help you. If you have any other suggestions, please let me know."

He tried to find one, but couldn't. What he wished he could do was hold her in his arms as he had the previous night, to smell the sweet smell of her soft skin and kiss her again.

"I want the best for you," she explained. "I will not forget what happened between us. I can never forget it."

While her words musically floated between them, Charles realized there was no other way. Life had to go on.

"I'm sorry, Isabella. I have no intention of making any trouble. But too much has happened too fast and I wasn't prepared. You have a point. I fully understand everything now. Let today's desires die and tomorrow's dreams live. Thank you for everything you have done. I promise to do my best to please your niece."

She looked at him quite satisfied. "Much better," she murmured, and then left.

As the door closed behind her, Charles said, "To be honest, my dear, I'm really doing this only for America!"

10

THE CHRISTMAS SPIRIT FILLED the city of Manhattan and little by little people set aside their sadness to involve themselves in the festive atmosphere. Magically, they ignored everything that had nothing to do with the season. Resting in eternal peace, Andre, was now forgotten; it was as if he had never existed. As for Charles, he had simply vanished into thin air. The urge to find him was replaced by the joyful enthusiasm that came with the last days of the year.

At this time, Celino was the only unhappy person—with the way things had turned out. He had killed Andre even though Andre had meant so much to him. His reasoning had been that Charles must pay for destroying their relationship, for becoming a wedge between them. Since Charles' arrival in New York, Andre had changed a great deal, and his new behavior created suspicions that disturbed Celino's peace of mind. Based on this, everything started and the rest fell into place.

Perhaps if the birds of New York could speak, Celino would have known what was happening. But no, birds only sing and fly. Not even in his wildest dreams could he have imagined that between him and Charles Isabella Gabilano now existed.

Ingeniously, Charles had stopped being the simple French immigrant in search of fortune. Suddenly he had attained the privilege of resting peacefully under the protection of a very powerful woman. Celino would never know that Charles had made Isabella experience emotions that she had never experienced before, and because of that, Charles became all that she did not want to lose. And even knowing that Charles arrived late in her life, she had decided he came to stay.

From then on, Charles, a handsome young jeweler who wanted to open his own shop in America, would be known as the son of Maximilien Merlenes, an old friend of her father. Charles would spend a few days in Manhattan, and then go to Chicago where he planned to carefully look for ways to invest the small fortune he had inherited from his father. Charles, born in St. Denis, France, was an only child. This was his new biography and the Charles whom Ana would meet.

Isabella started the end of the year preparations in a very happy mood. All of a sudden, she found herself very busy. It was Christmas and this meant Ana's arrival in New York. She was determined that everything must fall correctly into place. She needed to keep the ball rolling by taking care of every little detail to make the events happen naturally, since Ana was not to suspect anything. Charles would enter her life, unexpectedly, and as an experienced lover he would overcome her innocence and wake within her emotions which had been dormant. She seemed very confident about her plans—Ana would fall in love with Charles and ultimately, decide to stay in New York because of him.

The perfect realization of her dreams made her plans flow smoothly. Now, unselfishly, she dreamed the best dreams for Ana. Then, through the transparency of her own reality, she saw Charles as the man she would never stop loving, and together with Ana, her most precious treasure ever. *Could any woman ask for more? Indeed, I used to conquer my wishes, not love. Romance is still not for me.*

Three days before Ana's arrival, Charles stood by the guest room door watching Adela, the lady who came to cook and clean, carefully hanging his new clothes. *How incredibly well Isabella controls everything around her. She skillfully handles any situation, whether simple or difficult. She changes things with the velocity of a twister that flattens the land and whatever remains, is more powerful than she.*

He remembered that she failed to have any pretensions when they were in bed making love. How she performed in bed was the way he wanted to remember her.

Life really strikes in different ways. It takes with one hand and gives with the other. Scientifically, it is only a transformation. So in spite of what he thought would be the best for him, he had accepted his situation with resignation. He quietly watched how fast things shifted from one stage to another, and how quickly he lost control of his own life! And underneath all the flamboyant expectations, unquestionably he became used to the idea of being a married man.

Why do women always get everything they want?

Isabella mastered quite well the territory in which she operated. She could control the peace in New York and Chicago or create a war between the two cities because she possessed the manipulative force to do so. Smart, she knew the minds of men as well as the palms of her hands—they were all alike once they left their clothes on the chair, and that is when they became most vulnerable. She could play any game from a major position. When she asked for something—she obtained it. Whatever she demanded—someone provided for her, for she was extremely successful at making things happen. At the snap of a finger, she found Adela to help with the housekeeping. She sent Fairboy to Boston to escort Ana, and had Charles' wardrobe changed to fit her taste. Also, in the middle of all the preparations, she found time to receive Juan Carlos Catarel, who arrived from Chicago, just to see her.

* * * *

Evidently the end of the year activities prevented the people in Manhattan from knowing what was cooking in the Mafia's big pot. They simply couldn't smell the spices in the air. As a result, the Mafia moved smoothly to fixing the mistakes according to its needs—like always buying favors and proclaiming lies under everybody's noses. Not even the authorities wasted their time to spoil the savory dish.

Charles turned out to be the center of one event after another, the reason for all the back and forth movements that Fairboy had to do. Because he stayed in New York, Fairboy needed to change his arrangements with Steve Duke, and once again, he was brilliant. He created a silly story to tell the police and he paid Steve Duke to act for him. As Fairboy expected, the story appeared on the front page of *The New York Times*, which in turn, made Celino Campibeli very angry—

> The Manhattan Police Chief, Donald Kelves, announced this morning that he had received new information regarding the murder of Andre Palusque. Robert Smith, New York Port Authority manager, reported that a man identified as Jose Da Silva mugged one of his assistants, Steve Duke, early this morning. Mr. Duke declared that Da Silva wanted desperately to leave New York. He did so by leaving for Portugal.
>
> According to Mr. Duke, Da Silva confronted him brandishing a gun and saying, "Co-operate, because sending people to hell is my line of business!" Then he confessed to Mr. Duke that he had killed the 'gay French' and had thrown the bomb into the Italia Campibeli Restaurant. He said that 'big' people had paid him well for both jobs.
>
> Da Silva also confessed that he had been involved in an incident in Queens. In order to have a gambling debt erased, he had to do a job outside of his usual style and had to cut the fingers off of two young men. This incident caused both sides to go after him—the big people and the small fish—and that was why he decided to leave the city.
>
> Steve Duke admitted that this was a frightening

> experience, but luckily, all Mr. Da Silva wanted was to leave New York.

"Liar, liar, liar!" Celino screamed as he pounded the table. "I'd like to know who the hell had that fucking idea! Who invented such bullshit?"

That same day, Don Prieto Ferbonini read the account. To be precise, he read it twice and then called Fairboy. "How much did you pay for it, Fairboy?"

"Oh, Don Prieto, Steve Duke is a little bit expensive, but he did his job very well."

"And why talk about cutting fingers?"

"Necessity," said Fairboy. "Da Silva needed a reason to leave New York City quickly."

"And do you expect the police to swallow this?"

"No," answered Fairboy. "They are not idiots, but they do not have time to investigate all the cases they have. Meanwhile, my character, Da Silva, will disappear in Portugal as fast as he appeared in New York. Excellent, isn't it? And we did not have to bother the police chief or the *New York Times* editor."

"Go away, Fairboy. Go away," ordered Don Ferbonini. "I think I am letting you go too far. I must really be getting old."

In another part of the city, the two young men who had their fingers cut off heard about Fairboy's story. With the newspaper in their hands, they looked at each other and together said, "Who the hell is this Da Silva?" But as they contemplated their mutilated fingers, they accepted what the newspaper said.

Like everyone else, sometime later, Isabella read of the account. She laughed out loud. "How I adore you, Ferbonini! And Fairboy, you are the best. I can't compare you with anyone else. Cleverly you throw the whole case into one little cradle and let the newspaper sing a sweet lullaby for you. Beautiful! Unpredictably beautiful!"

At the end of the day she took the newspaper to Charles. She wished to cover with intense happiness the paths on which she walked. Any space between the ground and the sky could have been great for their love; however, their individual aspirations went farther than the planet earth. Satisfaction arrived as a result of many accomplishments—she relished it. And at that moment, she had it. She wanted to share her happiness with him because she had won—rather they had won.

Charles read the article and handed it back to her. "Poor Mr. Da Silva! From being a nobody—he became a somebody."

Wickedly, his comment reached out only to diminish her confidence. It sounded too harsh, and tasted too sour. But, Charles only said that because he did not have anything more interesting to say. The woman in front of him had cleverly turned his life into a nightmare. Now he decided to avoid any sweet conversation she could possibly think she deserved. Ambitions like the ones she pursued moved oceans and heavens, just to fabricate a new outcome, and he happened to discover that in a very quick fashion. That is why today he only wanted to sit quietly with his thoughts and savor the glorious future that lay ahead—if he could only succeed in making it glorious.

"It seems that all I do to help you is wrong," she abruptly said. "But it's okay. One day you will be grateful to me!"

"I am aware of that," replied Charles. "But I can't decide if it will be for showing me how to dry my hair, or because you are going to be a superb aunt?"

Indignant, she threw the newspaper down. "No, for putting Mr. Da Silva in your place."

11

ANA GABILANO HAD GROWN up in a very predictable environment, where she had listened to what it meant to be *good,* learned only about the *good*, and for her own *good*—only sought the *good*.

As an innocent child, she had been taken unwillingly to Boston for the precise purpose—to be utterly separated from the *bad*. That day she had such a fit that she lost her shoes, the ribbon in her hair, and spoiled and wrinkled her beautiful white dress. It took two people to lift and remove her from the waiting room at school. And when Ana was taken away, Isabella went down the school stairs with her head held high. She knew she had done what was best for Ana.

Ana had cried for an hour. The small parlor, which was the waiting room, had only one window and a few black chairs. As Ana sat there, next to her aunt, she noticed that all the women in the surrounding area were dressed exactly alike—in dark blue robes with white scarves on their heads. Instantly, their presence traumatized her.

When Ana had to face the reality that her aunt would leave and that she would have to stay, she rolled on the floor, crying and screaming with all her six year old strength. She fought against anyone who approached her. Later on, after the useless fit drained her of her energy, she fell asleep. Sister Luisa, who never left her alone, remained by her side. Ana was a beautiful child and Sister Luisa knew they would soon become good friends.

Sometime later, Ana opened her eyes and saw Sister Luisa sitting on the bed. Gradually, everything came back to her—the small parlor, the black chairs, the women with the unusual attire, and once again she started to cry. Sister Luisa patiently picked her up, talked to her, and took her to meet the other girls. They were all gathering in a beautiful room with paintings on the walls. It did not take long before Ana began playing with them and forgot about her initial shock.

In that room she learned to pray, to color, and to listen to stories. Every time she started to feel homesick, thinking about the beautiful woman who used to care for her, Sister Luisa appeared with a friendly smile, took her by the hand and told her a new story.

Ana was nine years old when her Aunt Isabella came to visit her for the first time at the school. They talked for half an hour in the small parlor that she hated. Then her aunt disappeared from her life once again. But this time Ana did not suffer from her absence, for she had become acquainted with and accepted her new life at the school.

The years that followed were excellent for Ana. She loved to read and she spent countless hours in the school library. She achieved the best grades in her class and was friendly with all the girls that shared her life. Through the years, she won everyone's love. Her classmates, teachers, and nuns all loved her. Once in a while she wrote to her Aunt Isabella and always received short, but loving responses from her. When she completed her twelfth year, she left the school to spend the afternoon with her Aunt Isabella and they went shopping together. It was an unforgettable afternoon for both of them. Ana found her aunt so beautiful that she wished one day to be like her.

When Ana was fifteen, she had gone on her first visit to New York City, which lasted one week. She stayed in the same apartment that Isabella had remodeled for her. The apartment had been purchased specifically for that purpose—for her to stay in whenever she decided to spend some time in New York. On that trip, Ana met her grandfather, Prieto Ferbonini, her grandmother, Angela, and Juan Carlos Catarel. When Ana returned to Boston, she told Sister Luisa, "Did you know that I have two living grandparents? My grandfather's name is Prieto Ferbonini and my grandmother's name is Angela. She suffers from mental problems."

Sister Luisa then confessed, "I do not know much about your family. Your Aunt Isabella has been the only person in contact with the school."

"Sister Luisa, what is wrong with my Aunt Isabella?" Ana asked. "I feel that she is not like us. Is she?"

"She is an excellent person," responded Sister Luisa. "And she loves you very much. She wants the best for you. That is why she brought you here."

"I know," Ana replied. Still without understanding.

After that day, there were no more questions.

* * * *

In spite of the distance between Boston and New York, something out of the ordinary filled the space between the two cities. In Boston, little by little, Ana grew excited about her trip to New York—and, in New York, Charles humbly spent the time lessening his expectations.

Ana had always expected to receive the best that life could ever offer her, and she hoped to receive it with the wisdom that God had already given to her. She lived ready to push aside anything that immediately would destroy her interests. She never worried too much about her future because she only had the best to give—and never experienced any deep distress. On a clear afternoon she liked to sit outside to enjoy the birds singing. No dark feelings ever disturbed her heart.

The day Charles was to meet her came like any other day. That afternoon, while dressing in the new clothes that Isabella had purchased for him, he looked in the mirror and remarked, "At last the Merlenes are moving up in the world." He looked very elegant, like a refined gentleman. *If I were Ana, I would fall in love with myself.*

Ana was supposed to arrive at 3:00 p.m. Approximately half an hour before, Isabella appeared at the apartment. She hardly spoke to Charles, and spent all her time in the kitchen giving Adela last minute orders.

Fairboy and Ana arrived on time. When they entered the apartment, Charles had just finished pouring some cognac. He was ready to perform for Ana his new role of businessman who had inherited a small fortune. Finally, the time had arrived for him to perform as the epitome of his own masculinity, and he thought that a well-dressed man with a glass of cognac in his hand would be perfect. If the truth were known, *he* really needed the drink.

Shaking with fear as most inexperienced actors feel the first time they walk onto the stage, Charles walked toward her thinking that this was probably the most important day of his life. He had the intention of giving his best performance to his audience. It was time to lie, to scheme and most of all, to love. He envisioned himself playing Napoleon Bonaparte and sarcastically he thought, *Isabella, my dear Josephine. But the French crown needs a virgin!*

"*Bonjour, Ana! Je suis Charles.* It is a pleasure to meet you," he said, holding the glass of cognac with his left hand and extending his right to meet hers.

"*Enchante*, Charles!" said Ana. "It is wonderful to find someone in New York with whom I can speak French. This is a delightful surprise!"

To make sure that everything would go as well as planned, Isabella intervined. "Ana, this is Charles Merlenes, the son of a very old family friend. He just arrived from France and will spend a few days in New York with us."

In reality, that first contact with Ana had left Charles fully surprised. He had expected a schoolgirl with braids and school shoes; a girl who was simple and devoid of sophistication. *Enchante, Charles! It is wonderful to find someone in New York with whom I can speak French. This is a delightful surprise!*

After she said that, Charles wondered, for a moment, if he were not the only actor on stage.

When Charles had complimented her, she still had on her hat and traveling cloak. He quickly put down his cognac and carefully helped her take off the cloak and hat, handing them to Adela. Ana wore a beautiful light green dress with bouffant sleeves.

From a few steps behind, Isabella silently observed Charles. He looked different. He had an unusual cold stare, a discreet smile, and appeared calm and confident.

Cleverly, Charles turned Ana's attention to him all that afternoon. He took the lead and asked her what she wanted to drink and made the decision to invite Fairboy to stay for dinner. He intentionally ignored Isabella, as if she were a part of a world that no longer existed. She did not even have the opportunity to ask Ana about the trip. In a subtle way, he established that there was no room for her in his new life, and that from now on, his word would be the last one. He pretended to think straight before she could influence his decisions with her powerful actions.

On Ana's second day in New York, she went shopping with Isabella. They returned with several boxes and a young man of about sixteen accompanied them carrying a pine tree. This was Ana's first Christmas in New York and Isabella thought she might enjoy decorating her own Christmas tree. As soon as the young man brought the pine tree inside, Isabella gave him a tip and he left.

Following the young man's departure, Charles appeared in the living room and his presence surprised Ana.

"Charles, are you already back? I thought you would spend the whole day out."

Calmly, Charles replied, "I thought so too. I just arrived. I couldn't do much. All the people I wanted to see were either busy with Christmas shopping or out of town—wrong time for business, I'm afraid."

While speaking, he avoided looking directly at Ana. He just glanced maliciously at Isabella. He was not telling the truth. He had not even gone out, and Isabella knew it.

"This is my first Christmas in New York, Charles," said Ana. "And to celebrate the occasion, Aunt Isabella thought I should decorate my own tree. What do you think of the idea?"

"Wonderful! And if you don't mind, I would love to help you. We can get started right after dinner."

"Great! I like the idea," she replied smiling at him.

Then politely he said, "You look lovely today!" Next, he took her hand and added, "Come and have a glass of wine with me."

They left the living room happily omitting Isabella completely. Charles felt responsible to keep the show going. He definitely decided–in his search for happiness–to use his common sense to accomplish his goal. In fact, his *happiness* would be for his own good no matter what happened. While walking out of the living room, holding Ana's hand, Charles observed Isabella. It was a shame seeing how fast she lost control of her own position.

Charles and Ana had dinner alone that night, and during dinner, Charles spoke little about himself and about his father. Instead, he talked about jewelry designing and about the business he wanted to start either in New York or Chicago–the reason he had come to America.

In spite of everything going well, Charles was aware that he had very little time to gain Ana's confidence and convince her to marry him. According to his businessman's story, he would be in New York for only two more days before leaving for Chicago. As he sipped the wine, he resembled a tiger stalking his prey. He was nothing more than an opportunist who felt increasingly confident as well as secure in what he wanted. Suddenly, the word '*wanted*' made him remember some of his father's sayings. *Whenever you go out Charles, always shop for the best red apples, for all good ones happen to be out of season when they are most wanted.*

This is my moment, Charles thought. *For the sake of my dreams, Ana is what I want.*

Unknowingly, Ana suddenly became the attractive eighteen year old girl and bride to be. To fulfill his wishes inside of this intricate triangle–it would be her wish, and Isabella's.

During the Christmas season, tender feelings visit our hearts, but only the strong ones furnish heat to them and hearts on fire not only burn our souls, but also leave us without fear for the future. In spite of all that she learned in a religious school, Ana would experience these feelings when Charles exuded the precise confidence. But now–sitting across from him, her innocence freely played with his weak decency–she appeared so naive that it seemed easy to convince her to make the trip to the altar. Observing her, he realized that she could be compared with the virgins painted from the Bible–fair skinned with a round face, clear eyes, and a small mouth. Her serene expression effortlessly separated her from any impure thoughts.

After dinner, Charles placed the tree in its base as Ana stood next to him, helping. She never had to struggle for accomplishments because she knew that what starts well, ends marvelously. Ana was that young girl who spent her entire life dreaming in the morning for what would become the splendor of the afternoon–she only lived for the moment and belonged to a clean world where honesty was never for sale and she never dared to test the cliché. It was not in her to think suspiciously.

Charles became her best companion in New York, making her visit enjoyable. She talked about her life in Boston and her indecision about where to live as an adult. Also, she talked about her friends and the special place in her heart for Sister Luisa. At the end, she confided how sad she felt for never knowing her mother.

"You, Charles, for example, can talk about your mother, but not me. I never knew her."

"I do not like to talk about my mother, Ana," said Charles.

"Why not?"

"I don't know. I loved her, but when I think about her, I feel guilty. I did not attend her burial when she died. I failed her."

"And why didn't you attend her burial?"

"Because I hate burials, that is why."

After a short silence she asked, "Do you have any brothers or sisters?"

"No."

"Did you ever wish you had some?"

"Honestly, I never gave it much thought."

"So what were your thoughts when you were young? Usually we wish to have a brother or sister, if we don't already have one."

"I only thought about rubies, emeralds, and diamonds."

"Oh, I see. To you they are more important than family. Is that the case?"

"No, of course not. Never!"

Ana was standing between him and the Christmas tree and Charles had the feeling what he had said gave her the wrong impression about him, so he decided to reword it.

Politely he said, "Ana, please understand me, I want to have a family. I hate being alone, but I am waiting for a special girl. The one that will be with me forever."

She studied carefully the expression on his face. Then with a shy smile, she uttered, "I understand."

Charles believed opportunity is when a bright sunny day brings to us what no other day has ever brought. Looking straight into her eyes, he defined 'that instant' as the brightest moment of their impending relationship, and romantically added, "Maybe... someone like you."

Instantly, Ana turned not only red, but also speechless. His look grew so intense, and tender, that she, who learned to stand up only for the good—stood still for the best. She couldn't move.

Charles delicately held her face between his hands and softly kissed her.

She found this so unexpected, and indeed, wonderful that she couldn't help feeling passionate and submissively available.

They extended their solemn contemplation of each other until her sweet voice uttered, "Charles, I have never been kissed before."

He sweetly placed a finger over her lips to make them silent and tenderly kissed her again.

Christmas Eve arrived and Charles did not go to Chicago. He really hadn't been going anyway. Ana Gabilano, after being kissed for the first time, only needed one night alone in her room to realize that she would like to be kissed again and again for an infinite amount of time. She was pure, but not stupid. That night she went to bed thinking about Charles' last words: *Sometimes Ana, we do things unintentionally for the simple reason that what pleases us most is suddenly, so available. I kissed you because I strongly desired your lips.* She heard what men had never told her before. Charles uttered what she longed to hear.

Words are powerful weapons. They come and go like seasons; sometimes they are hard and harm the land, and sometimes they cause remarkable changes. Unquestionably, Charles won her heart. From one day to another, she fell in love with him, and she thought that love should arrive like this, without warning. Happier than ever, she accepted their relationship and with the sweetest look in her eyes, she asked him to postpone his trip to Chicago so he could spend Christmas with her in New York. And he did as she wished.

Christmas dinner was simple—turkey and pasta to please the guests. The party consisted of Isabella, Ferbonini, Saporo, Fairboy and Juan Carlos Catarel with two of his men. After dinner, Ana announced her plans to marry Charles.

Hearing the news, Prieto Ferbonini asked, "Is this what you want, Ana?"

"I am in love, grandfather," she responded as her face radiated with happiness.

Quietly Ferbonini contemplated her sweet innocence. She was all he had left in the world.

"If you are sure, congratulations! All I want is your happiness, so you have my blessing."

Ana thanked him for his kind words and addressed Isabella. "Aunt Isabella, what do you think about it? I want your opinion, too."

Lost in thought as she was remembering the night she had spent with Charles, she was startled to hear her name. She felt a little bit embarrassed and asked Ana to repeat the question.

"What do you think about this wedding idea?"

"I don't know what to say, Ana," she answered. "This is a big surprise. I think I need time to recover. Maybe it would be better not to go so fast, don't you think?"

"Yes," said Ana. "In a way I agree with you, but Charles insists that we get married soon."

"Oh!"

Patience reduces stress, raises confidence and prepares the mind for changes. Charles waited for this moment as he would be waiting for many others.

"I love her," he said firmly, with every intention of hurting Isabella because, from now on, this would be the most fun part of it all. "I want to make her my wife. We don't have any reason to wait and I don't have time to waste. I am a businessman."

As Charles spoke, his well-defined lips moved easily and the sound of his voice raised the weight of his highly attractive presence in the room. He represented an intelligent strong young man defending his interest. By observing Charles everyone noticed in his slender figure a person who held not only a fine education but also a sharp character.

At that moment, looking at Isabella with his brown eyes, he thought, *I see myself in a big field. My life is an empty space and my mind—a river full of fish. Water is running and fish are swimming. I must get somewhere. I must set my direction. The water never stops.*

The fish always swim, and the empty space will still be mine.

"Tomorrow will be rushing unmercifully into the past," he explained. "And I want to erase all that has contributed to my wasting time. I'm a man capable of excelling my abilities. I have a great talent and I dedicate myself to my work. I do believe that my desires control the forces I need to fight any kind of resilience. I feel ready to start a stable course toward my future, and right now my time is as precious as yours."

"Charles is right, Isabella," said Juan Carlos Catarel, very concerned. "Under the circumstances, getting married is a wise decision. I understand him. A man in love can never wait. Anytime is the right time."

A long silence filled the room after Catarel's words. And when Isabella recovered from her speechless state, she politely said, "Ana, I love the idea of you and Charles getting married. Forget everything I said. We have never celebrated a wedding in our family. It is about time. Congratulations to you both!"

From his seat Charles looked directly at her. He did not miss a word she uttered. She spoke softly with her eyes fixed on his. But she saw hatred and scorn reflected in them. There was no trouble reading his thoughts at that moment, *Hypocrite, bitch, congratulations for acting so cleverly!*

Before leaving that night, Don Ferbonini approached Charles and said, "You make my granddaughter happy or I will kill you. *Capite?*"

"Yes, sir." Charles answered.

* * * *

During the last days of the year, Fairboy worked hard and did what had to be done in order to keep Charles from being found guilty of Andre Palusque's death. Charles needed to reappear in Manhattan to be proven innocent. Fairboy not only held the position but also the ability to handle it. He was a genius at finding solutions to all problems relating to Ferbonini. He became a strong diplomatic piece between the Mafia and the authorities.

Fairboy spent an extremely busy week meeting people, among them immigration agents, police, and lawyers. With Juan Carlos Catarel's assistance, he succeeded in destroying all evidence that Charles was at the crime scene, and Judge Lorenzo Stelon concluded he could safely drop the charges against Charles. Once again, Fairboy had brilliantly accomplished what he set out to do.

* * * *

Ana and Charles were married the second week of January. The wedding took place in Boston where she grew up at the school's chapel. Fairboy proudly escorted Ana to the altar. He was chosen to represent her grandfather. Everyone knew that Don Ferbonini never attended social events.

The chapel was full of students all dressed in uniforms. As Ana took her place next to Charles, one could see the envy in the students' eyes. They imagined Charles and Ana together alone in their own world of wedded bliss.

Isabella did not attend the wedding, either. She excused herself by saying that she always cried at weddings and that she hated to cry in public. But on the day Ana left New York, she told her, "Dear Ana, I am so happy for you. I know that Charles is going to make you very happy. Enjoy your wedding. I want you to do this for me because I never had the opportunity to experience the emotions of such a beautiful day."

12

CELINO COULD NEITHER UNDERSTAND nor accept what had happened. So to find some peace of mind, he went to Queens with the intention of finding out about the man named Jose Da Silva.

In Queens he searched for the two young men who had lost a card game with him and found out that it *was* true that someone had cut off their little fingers. Celino asked questions about this Jose Da Silva, but they hadn't much to say. They explained that Mr. Da Silva really injured them, and that they had never seen him before all that happened. Fearful, they didn't say who really had done it to them. It seemed unsafe to let Celino know they were the ones who had thrown the bomb into his father's restaurant.

After talking to the men for a while, Celino realized they really didn't know anything and decided not to ask any more questions. While turning to leave, the thought came to him that perhaps they could be useful in some other way. Smiling, he put his hand in his pocket, brought out a thick roll of bills and said, "I have a little proposition to make. Here is the money. Come with me to the port so we can catch this Steve Duke and convince him to tell us what we don't know." The two men were so broke that when they saw the money, they agreed to do what Celino proposed.

Together they went to the port. One of them used to work at the port and knew Steve Duke very well. They looked around carefully as they walked. The port was quiet so they waited until Steve Duke, holding a ring of keys, left his desk. When he reached the darkest part of the port, the two young men jumped in front of him and held him back. Celino opened a switchblade in a threatening way and held it against Steve's stomach.

"We want to know why you invented that story for the newspaper," he demanded.

"I can't tell you that!" said Steve Duke.

"Why not?" asked Celino pressing the blade a little harder. "Do not play with me Mr. Duke because I never learned patience. I want to know everything about this Mr. Da Silva."

"That man never existed," Steve Duke said. "The story I told to the newspaper was a lie. I received money to tell it."

"Who paid you?"

"That man...Fairboy."

After Steve Duke's confession, Celino shoved the blade in without an ounce of compassion then continued to stab him several times. The men who were with Celino became so scared they dropped the body and ran away. They had never expected that Celino would go that far.

Steve lay on the ground bleeding as Celino calmly cleaned the blade, closed it and put it in his pocket. Then he looked around, adjusted his hat, and walked away. Very angry and puzzled, he left the port. He could not understand why Ferbonini's man was protecting Charles.

Angrily, Celino walked back to his father's nightclub, trying to solve what he considered a perplexing puzzle. He wanted to know what Charles had to do with Don Prieto Ferbonini. Charles and Ferbonini had just met briefly on the day of the bombing in his father's restaurant. Cautiously, Celino started to recall details about that night and—as the events of that evening went through his mind, he saw Isabella Gabilano in Charles' arms. Then he remembered that it was Charles who had saved her from the fire.

"Of course!" he exclaimed. "Why didn't I think of that before? *She* must be the person helping Charles. That is the only thing that explains Ferbonini's role in my private war. Bitch!" he spat angrily. He turned and headed to the Blue Salon.

When Celino entered the salon, he saw Isabella next to the bar talking to two of her girls.

Seeing him coming straight toward her, instantly, Isabella knew that something had gone wrong because Celino's presence in the salon was highly unusual. She sent the two girls away and waited silently.

When he stood close to her, with great satisfaction on his face, he said, "I know everything, Isabella. Where is the French boy?"

"Calm down, Celino. Charles is not here in New York, and I guarantee you that you do *not* know everything."

"Really?" he answered, showing no surprise. "In that case, why don't you tell me what I don't know?"

"It would be my pleasure," she said. "Charles left for Boston, and he is now a married man."

"Oh? I guess I was wrong after all!" he exclaimed. "This is a big surprise. And who did he marry?"

"My niece, Ana."

Looking at Isabella, Celino laughed in a strange way like someone who had suddenly become frustrated and could only laugh. However, when he stopped laughing, he added, "I think you should look for another husband for your niece because that French boy will not live very long, my dear. I'm going to kill him. You wait and see." Then he turned around and left the Blue Salon.

As he parted, Isabella thought about and measured the weight of his words. She knew that anyone who approached him would only suffer misery. He meant nothing but bad news to anyone who did. She hated the idea of seeing everything she had planned go wrong because of someone as sick and insignificant as him. In order to avoid further complications, she decided that she must take action. *I'll go to see Ferbonini tomorrow,* she told herself. *You aren't going to get away with this, Celino. I will not let it happen. You wait and see who is going to get his way.*

Early the next day, Isabella went to see Ferbonini to tell him about Celino's visit. However, her timing could not have been worse. Ferbonini had just received the news of Steve Duke's murder and he was furious. When she stepped in, he was screaming at Fairboy.

"Who did it? Who Fairboy?"

"Apparently nobody," Fairboy answered ironically.

In spite of being sorry about her coming in at such a bad time, Isabella stood at the door and assuredly said, "Good morning, everyone! What is going on to make Don Ferbonini scream so early in the morning?"

"What are you doing here at this time of day, Isabella?" asked Ferbonini instead of answering her questions.

"I came to inform you that Celino Campibeli paid me an unexpected visit last night. He knows that we are helping Charles. He told me he is going to kill him."

"I do not want to hear about Celino's threats. I have more important things on my mind right now. Steve Duke is dead and I feel responsible for it, do you understand? Please go home and do not come back until I say so."

"Okay, I'll leave, but we should discuss this again as soon as possible. I think Celino is capable of making good on his threats."

"Wrong," said Ferbonini. "I know Celino. He would never play with me."

Unhappily, Isabella left the room terribly worried about Celino's crazy threats. She feared in her heart that he might be more dangerous than anyone expected. Ferbonini was really getting old and she feared he had stopped using his common sense.

As she walked through the dining room, she saw Saporo playing solitaire. Looking at him she remembered something he had said to her many years ago. She experienced a great sense of hope. Right then she decided *not* to rely completely on Don Prieto Ferbonini concerning Celino's crazy threats. Confidently, she approached Saporo.

"I need to talk with you in private. It is very important, please come to see me as soon as you have a chance."

A few hours later, Saporo showed up at the Blue Salon looking for her. Isabella came downstairs, served him a drink, and they sat together at a small table in the corner of the salon. Immediately after they sat down, she spoke. "Saporo, do you remember my cat Bambino and the day he broke his paw?"

"Yes, Miss Isabella. I will never forget that day."

That day had been sixteen years ago when Isabella was only twenty years old. She had a cat named Bambino that meant very much to her. A fight had broken out at the Blue Salon and one of the chairs flew across the salon, hit the cat, and injured one of its paws. Saporo had arrived at the salon, stopped the fight and afterwards took care of the cat's paw by improvising a splint with two pieces of wood. Isabella was so grateful that she told him to choose one of the girls and that it would be on the house. But without looking at her, Saporo had answered, "No, thank you."

Quite surprised, Isabella had said, "No? Why? Don't you like girls?"

"No, it is not that, Miss Isabella. It's just that I have never been with a woman before."

"What?"

His words had left Isabella speechless because that had seemed very strange to her. *Saporo is a man who can go out with a gun and kill people, but he has never fucked a woman?*

To satisfy her curiosity she asked, "Why, Saporo?"

"Oh, I am too big and very ugly. That's why."

"I can't believe you," she replied moving her head from one side to the other. She spent a few minutes looking at Saporo, thinking about his problem—and suddenly, she felt so sorry for him that she couldn't let it go. At that precise moment she decided to do something to help. Without a word, she stood up, walked to the bar and picked up a bottle of liquor. When she came back, she took his hand saying, "Come with me. You can't be a virgin forever! I am going to make love to you and—like I said—it will be on the house."

They went to one of the rooms, and did what she said. Saporo had his first orgasm with a woman that night. Thanks to her, he was freed of his fears. Before leaving the Blue Salon he said to her, "I owe you a favor, Miss Isabella. Please let me repay you one day."

"Fine, Saporo. I will keep it in mind."

She couldn't have remembered his words at a better time. What Saporo said remained in the back of her mind much like a leaf inside a book with great words written on it. The purpose of having a leaf with beautiful words inside a book is not to read them every day, but rather to open the book on the right page—one day.

Isabella had an old book with such a leaf inside and she opened it as expected—on the right day. *I owe you a favor.*

"Can you grant me that favor you once promised me?" she asked.

"Yes, Miss Isabella. You can count on it."

"I want Celino dead."

13

SAPORO CARRIED OUT ISABELLA'S wish immediately. Exactly two days after she had spoken with him, Celino's body was found on the street. Someone had attacked him from behind and had shot him twice. He died without seeing the face of his killer.

In the morning, Don Alfredo Campibeli received the news of his son's death, and the doors of the Italia Campibeli Restaurant were closed for the second time. Also, that same morning, still at the table having breakfast, Don Ferbonini learned about it. He became so angry that he stood up and yelled at Fairboy. "What is happening in Manhattan that every day I understand less and less? Fairboy, please explain. We are supposed to prevent these things and they are happening under our noses. Are we becoming careless?"

"No, Don Prieto," answered Fairboy. "But we couldn't give Celino protection. He was involved in too many things. Maybe what happened was for the best."

"For the best? Oh, Fairboy, you do not understand Italians, do you? And this is between Italians. His father has been fair with me. I gave him my word that nothing like this would happen. Ferbonini's words must not fail. Not while Ferbonini is still alive! I want to know who did this because I must avenge Celino's death."

"Yes, sir," said Fairboy leaving the room.

Fairboy walked out with the intention of following Don Prieto Ferbonini's order. However, as he thought about this act of revenge, he knew it could end badly. According to his way of thinking, Celino deserved what he had got and they should not waste their time on the matter. But, after all, Don Prieto Ferbonini was the boss. Obediently, he went to give the others the first orders of the day and when they left, he spoke with Saporo.

"I want you to stay with me all day. Don Prieto wants to avenge Celino's death. I don't like it, but that's what he wants. He is very angry."

When Saporo heard that, he said, "Wait for me here, Fairboy. I want to talk to Don Prieto alone."

Fairboy stayed in the dining room and Saporo went in to speak with Don Prieto. He entered Don Prieto's study, stopped in front of his desk, and humbly said, "Don Prieto, I have something to confess."

"What is it Saporo?"

"I am the one who killed Celino."

"What?" exclaimed Don Prieto.

"I killed Celino," Saporo repeated.

"Why, Saporo? Why?"

"Miss Isabella asked me and I couldn't say no."

Of his four bodyguards, Saporo was Don Prieto Ferbonini's favorite man. Through the years, he had come to appreciate this particular bodyguard and his loyalty. Listening to Saporo unexpectedly confessing his deed surprised Ferbonini. He would have given his own life not to experience this betrayal by his most trusted man. The whole thing seemed like a stupid game. Celino might be a homosexual, as well as a killer, but he belonged to a family that lived under Ferbonini's protection, and Saporo knew that. This never should have happened.

Feeling like part of an organized plot, Ferbonini silently opened his desk drawer and took out his gun. Saporo, like his son Gambino, had to die. He had turned out to be a traitor and traitors do not deserve to live. But at the same time Ferbonini pointed the gun, Saporo fired his.

Ferbonini's body fell from the chair. Saporo hopelessly ran toward him and knelt next to him. Already sorrowfully crying, he lifted Ferbonini's head from the floor.

"Don Prieto..." he began, but with his last words, Ferbonini interrupted him.

"No, let me talk. I love you, Saporo. You served me fairly. Isabella succeeded in destroying me. She is stronger than both of us put together. Take care of Angela for me."

Fairboy rushed into the room when he had heard the gunshot. He could only stand there speechless as he watched the scene.

"He is gone, Fairboy."

"Saporo, what happened? Why is his gun out?"

"He took the gun out to kill me because I confessed that I murdered Celino."

"What?"

"It's true, Fairboy. I killed Celino. I should have let Don Prieto kill me. I did not want this to happen. My instincts took over—to shoot first when somebody aims at me. I can't believe I did this. After my own father, Don Prieto was the man I most admired and I killed him! Tell me, Fairboy, why did I do it? Why?"

"If we knew all the answers, things like this would probably never happen," said Fairboy.

Fairboy could see how much Saporo was suffering. In all their years together, he had never seen him cry. As soon as Fairboy regained control of the situation, he said, "Saporo, you cannot stay here. I have to take you somewhere. If the police find you, you will never be free again! You will be forced to confess all your crimes as well as some others that you did not commit."

"I don't care, Fairboy. I'm despicable. I killed Don Prieto. Let them find me."

"No. This can't happen. You don't know how the police operate. They are cruel, Saporo. If they arrest you, they will torture you and make you admit to terrible things. You will be found guilty for all the crimes they have not been able to solve for the past two decades. No, I can't let that happen."

Convinced that he had to save Saporo, Fairboy closed the curtains of Ferbonini's study, and as he did it, he asked, "Why did you kill Celino?"

"Because Miss Isabella asked me to do it. She wanted Celino dead and I could not say no to her. I owed her a favor. You know why. I told you that story."

"Damn you, Saporo! Damn you!"

With determination, Fairboy separated Saporo from the body and ordered him to stop crying. Then in an attempt to clear his mind and find out what to do next, he paced the room.

Suddenly, he came up with an idea. He decided that Saporo had to disappear from New York and that Isabella would be the right person to help him. After all, she was responsible for what had happened. Swiftly, he locked the door of the study and also locked the door leading to the rest of the house. Followed by Saporo, he left to see Isabella.

On their way to the Blue Salon, Saporo asked, "Why are you helping me, Fairboy?"

"What kind of question is that Saporo? Once you beat up six guys to save my ass, and you ask me why?"

"I did it because you were alone and they were taking advantage of you."

"Okay, then pretend I am doing exactly what you did for Isabella. I'm just returning a favor."

"Thank you, Fairboy."

"All right, Saporo. Now stop talking and walk fast. I need to get my thoughts in order and plan how to get you out of New

York. You don't know it, but you have a bigger problem than you realize. Juan Carlos will search for Ferbonini's killer since they were close friends."

"I'm sorry. I'll keep quiet."

In the Blue Salon, Fairboy asked for Isabella and in a few minutes she appeared downstairs.

Before she uttered a word, Fairboy took her by the arm then whispered in her ear, "Celino and Don Prieto Ferbonini are both dead. Let's go upstairs to talk. I need your help."

They walked up to her apartment and Fairboy explained everything that had happened. He told her that they must help Saporo get away before the news spread.

"Whatever you say needs to be done, will be done. I'm ready to help," she promised.

"I need money. Do you have any here?"

"Yes, I do."

"Then get it."

Isabella went to her room and opened her closet. She took out a little wooden box where she kept the money that Juan Carlos Catarel gave her. It was what she had been saving for a rainy day and had never spent a penny of the money, but she was going to today. Quickly she walked back to the living room and gave Fairboy the money. Wide eyed, Fairboy opened his eyes, surprised at the amount of money she handed him. But besides being surprised, he was very happy.

"Excellent!" he said taking the money. "Let's go, Saporo. I will see you later, Isabella."

When Fairboy turned to leave, Saporo stepped closer to her and said, "Thank you, Miss Isabella. You have been good to me. I need to tell you something very important. The last thing Don Prieto Ferbonini asked before he died was for me to take care of Angela."

"Go in peace, Saporo. She will be well taken care of."

* * * *

Fairboy took Saporo to the port, the most logical place to begin. He went directly to see Robert Smith, the port manager who had been doing favors for him lately. There was one more favor he needed from him and Fairboy planned to use his same old tactics—he was going to use what talked the most–money.

When they arrived, Robert was just beginning his routine work, unaware of the problems he would have to face later that day. If anyone needed his full attention, he could get it without any difficulty in the early hours of the morning. Fairboy was among the people of New York City who knew this.

"Good morning, Mr. Smith!" said Fairboy.

But he was greeted with an unwelcome look as Mr. Smith said, "Oh, no! I'd rather not listen to you. And I will not."

"I need a favor in a hurry. Name your price."

"No," answered Robert Smith. "This is getting very dangerous. Look at what happened to Steve Duke. I do not want any more risky business."

Fairboy took out part of the money he had with him and was about to say something when Robert Smith interrupted him. "No, Mr. Gaspier!" he addressed Fairboy formally. "I said no more."

"Okay," replied Fairboy. "Call me a loser. I must respect your wishes. You do not want to help this time–fine, don't. However, let me make my offer. It makes no sense at all to come here and leave without even mentioning the amount of money you could easily make. We have done business before and the profits have been greater than the danger. If you say this is the last time that you will listen to me, then so be it. But let me show you what I have for you."

Putting his hand back in his pocket, Fairboy took out a large amount of money as he said, "What if I give you two months pay, and my word that I will never bother you again?"

The firm look Robert Smith had on his face disappeared instantly and his next words were, "Fine, Mr. Gaspier. You got me. What do you want?"

"I want this man to leave New York as soon as possible."

"I have the ship *Noche De Plata* leaving in half an hour for South America—Colombia. It's all I have right now."

"*Noche De Plata* is perfect," answered Fairboy giving him the money.

The last words between Fairboy and Saporo were an exchange of instructions. Fairboy gave him the rest of the money and said, "Saporo, please spend this money wisely because it is all you have. Now, listen to me. *Noche De Plata* will be going to Colombia. But I don't want you to stay in Colombia. Look for a way to go to another country because Robert Smith and the ship's captain know that you are there, and it will not be safe for you. When the news about Ferbonini's death spreads all over Manhattan, I will no longer be able to control the situation. I will have to tell the truth for my own sake, and when Juan Carlos hears that it was you who killed Ferbonini, he will ask for your ass. He admired Ferbonini greatly so I know he will do the impossible to see you dead. And the police will be around enjoying the whole situation. So make sure you disappear, forever! No matter what happens to you in South America, don't ever set foot here again. Good-bye and good luck."

Fairboy left the port and returned to see Isabella. When he saw her, he said, "I did what had to be done. He is leaving for South America. Don't forget that we both had a hand in this. Besides that, I know you asked him to kill Celino Campibeli."

"I agree with whatever you have done, Fairboy. I would never let Saporo go to prison either."

"Good! Now, come with me because I am going to give Angela the bad news about Ferbonini's death."

As they walked side by side to Don Prieto Ferbonini's house Fairboy asked, "What do you plan to do, regarding Ana and Charles?"

"I will tell them the news," said Isabella.

"Do you have the courage to ruin their honeymoon?"

"Fairboy, the man is Ana's grandfather. She must know what happened."

"All right. If you think they should know, don't worry. I will take care of it."

An hour later, Fairboy sent two telegrams. One went to Juan Carlos in Chicago and the other to Mr. and Mrs. Merlenes in Boston. They both delivered the same news:

DON PRIETO FERBONINI IS DEAD.

14

THE DEATHS OF DON PRIETO Ferbonini and Celino marked a new beginning for Charles. The time to fulfill his dreams had arrived. While looking for a place to open his business, several things happened. Instead of opening a modest business as he had planned, he opened a luxurious one in the corner where the Italia Campibeli Restaurant had been. Once again, it all had happened because of Isabella. She had the idea first and then Fairboyvon Gaspier worked on the rest.

Fairboyvon, better known as Fairboy, was a man with an incredible imagination and a unique nose for business. He always came up with outstanding ideas even though reality showed there really was nothing more to be done. On top of that, he had a lot of experience dealing with the authorities and probably knew the law as well as any lawyer because he was an expert when dealing with them.

Though Fairboy had a natural capacity to run a big industry, due to circumstances, he had ended up as Don Prieto Ferbonini's right-hand man. He enjoyed working for Ferbonini mainly because the money was always available to put his ideas into action. It was mainly thanks to Fairboy's abilities and intelligence that Ferbonini had become as powerful as he had.

After Ferbonini's funeral, Juan Carlos Catarel and Fairboy visited Don Alfredo Campibeli to reveal that Saporo had killed both Celino and Don Prieto Ferbonini.

When Don Alfredo heard that, he looked straight at Juan Carlos Catarel, and said, "I want that Negro dead. Do you understand, Juan Carlos?"

"Yes. I understand and I promise that I will take care of it."

Next, Don Alfredo asked, "Why would Saporo kill my son?"

"We don't know, Don Alfredo," answered Fairboy. "To be honest with you, the only thing we can figure out is that Celino was not what you think he was."

"What do you mean by that?" asked Don Alfredo with his eyes wide open.

Quietly, Fairboy looked at Juan Carlos Catarel. He did not know whether to tell the truth or not. Not intending to keep it a secret, Juan Carlos nodded his head, urging Fairboy to continue.

"Okay, Don Alfredo," said Fairboy. "I am going to tell you everything. Prepare yourself, because what I'm about to tell you will not be pleasant."

"Nothing is harder than losing a son the way I did, so go on and say whatever you have to."

"Celino was a homosexual and was involved with Andre, the bartender. Celino was the last person with Andre before he died. All I know is that Don Prieto Ferbonini wanted to avenge Celino's death and when I delivered the news to Saporo, he asked me to wait because he wanted to speak with Don Prieto alone. A few minutes later, I heard a shot and ran to the study where I found Don Prieto on the floor, dying, with his gun next to him. I asked Saporo what had happened. He told me that Don Prieto was going to kill him because he had confessed to murdering Celino. Honestly, Don Alfredo, I don't know the reason why Saporo killed your son. He never said why."

"*Oh, Dio mio!*" said Don Alfredo. "*Mi figlio, un omosessuale!*"

For an Italian man like Don Alfredo, that was devastating news, harder than Celino's death. It was as if his family and his dignity had also died. For the first time Don Alfredo understood why things had seemed out of place. He also had to accept the truth that everyone around him had known it all along. For a while he remained silent. Having used all his strength to face his shame, Don Alfredo no longer desired to walk through Manhattan again.

The Italia Campibeli Restaurant remained closed for an entire week. No one, except Juan Carlos Catarel and Fairboy, had been able to talk with Don Alfredo after what had happened. And everyone waited quietly for Don Alfredo's final decision regarding his business. Many entrepreneurs were interested in that corner and went to see Juan Carlos Catarel. Under the circumstances, by the end of the week, Juan Carlos felt obligated to send Fairboy to talk with Don Alfredo about the matter.

When Fairboy went to Don Alfredo's house again, he did not waste any time. As soon as he entered and sat down, he informed Don Alfredo that he had come on behalf of Juan Carlos Catarel and that Juan Carlos wanted to know of his plans regarding the restaurant.

"I want to sell everything," said Don Alfredo firmly. "I am going back to Italy with my wife and daughters. I don't want them to ever find out about Celino."

"Have you thought about this carefully, Don Alfredo? That might be a big mistake."

"No. My mistake was leaving Italy."

Then, Don Alfredo told Fairboy to inform Juan Carlos that he could have the first bid and to name his price. As Fairboy stood to leave, he asked, "Fairboy, what about Saporo? Any news?"

"No, nothing yet."

"I see..." said Don Alfredo. "But I think you know where he is."

"Really! What makes you think that, Don Alfredo?"

"You were Don Prieto's right-hand man. No one knows New

York like you do. Saporo worked with you, and he was not a bad person. Killing him would not change anything and you knew that. So you helped him get away."

"Don Alfredo," said Fairboy, calmly looking directly into his eyes like a wolf in control of his territory, "If you found yourself between a dying man and his murderer, what would you have done first? Would you have taken care of the dying man or would you have grabbed the murderer?"

After a long moment of thinking, Don Alfredo said, "I would take care of the dying man."

"That was exactly what I did," said Fairboy.

The news that the Italia Campibeli Restaurant was closed for good and that the entire corner now would belong to Juan Carlos Catarel, made Isabella extremely happy. She had learned of this while making love with Juan Carlos. He had told her of his plans to buy the corner and rent it to another restaurant owner because the location was appealing and any kind of restaurant could prosper there.

It had taken many years for Alfredo Campibeli to acquire the whole corner. Poor man. For years that had been his only ambition and if the truth were known, the corner had only brought him bad luck! But things like that only have meaning to superstitious people and apparently Isabella was not one of them. When Juan Carlos finished telling her of his business venture she asked, "Why another restaurant?"

"I don't know," answered Juan Carlos. "Perhaps it could be something else. I said restaurant because it was the first thing that came to my mind."

Isabella and Juan Carlos were lying in each other's arms talking peacefully. "Don't you think you should change the way in which you invest your money? Why always the same things—restaurants, nightclubs, and hotels. Why don't you try something new?"

"Like what, for example?" Juan Carlos asked curiously.

"A jewelry store," she said.

"A jewelry store?"

"Yes."

"But my love, the only thing I know about jewels is that they are expensive. I am a conservative man who likes to see my money in the same old basket, rather than in the one that I never weave."

"You don't know anything about jewelry, but Charles does," she explained. Then in order to have his full attention, she sat straddled over his naked body and enthusiastically began to explain further.

"Juan Carlos, my dear, it is a fantastic business. Tell me, what is the first thing a man thinks of giving a woman when he falls in love?"

"A jewel," he answered.

"You see, if the woman is his future wife, she gets a jewel. The same applies for a daughter or a lover. A jewel symbolizes affection. It is also a delicate way of expressing a feeling. Progress is leading us to a promising future; people are getting rich from one day to the next. In short, we will all be products of an extravagant society in which we want 'that' which we see, and we will do 'what' we are taught. How about a phrase like this, for example: 'When love is what matters, one jewel will say it all.' It would have a great effect on people's minds. I could be wrong Juan Carlos, but I see a gold mine in this."

She stopped talking. Juan Carlos kept looking at her, silently absorbing all she had said. *I see a gold mine. When love is what matters, one jewel will say it all. You don't know anything about jewels but Charles does.* He gently took her hands and delicately opened her fingers. With an inexhaustible silence he contemplated the diamond and ruby ring she wore. It had been his gift to her and it had cost a fortune.

"Are you serious about this, Isabella?" he asked, just to test her response.

"Have you ever heard me joke around when your clothes are over the chair? Of course, I'm serious. You and Charles can be partners. Think about it."

Juan Carlos smiled joyfully. He adored her answer. While caressing her naked body, he admired her beauty. She was the finest jewel he possessed.

"Whatever you want, my dear! So, you want a jewelry store on that corner? Then you shall have it."

* * * *

On the afternoon of September 9, 1887 at 4:00 p.m., Charles stood across the street watching two men on ladders as they painted a sign that read, "Merlenes Jewelry." His name, in bold blue letters, could be seen from both sides of the street. *Incredible!* Charles said to himself. *I never thought my beginning would be like this!*

Charles had never experienced a sensation of happiness like that before. The small store that he had originally envisioned remained buried in the past. Seeing his name for the first time in big letters, precisely in the heart of Manhattan, overwhelmed him. Finally he was beginning to feel the warmth of the sun on his glorious future.

The jewelry store had four doors and two U-shaped balconies. In the back was Charles' workshop where most of the pieces would be made. It had a large table in the center and another table, twenty-four inches wide and forty-eight inches long that was close to one of the windows. On top of the tables rested templates, grinding wheels, a sharp-pointed chisel, and light hammers. Equipment such as a grinding arbor with mounted grinding wheels, a cabochon unit, mud and wire saws, and also a safe, were also in the room.

Though Charles seemed enthusiastic, something was bothering him—the partnership with Juan Carlos Catarel. Charles had wanted to start his business small and simple, with only the essentials, and then later to expand into something more sophisticated. But, suddenly, that had become almost impossible. He had to join in a partnership or he would lose it all. When he had left France it was not to be a failure. It was just like walking in heavy rain—he couldn't avoid getting drenched.

When he had been in the process of finding a location for his store, Charles received an unexpected visitor. Fairboy approached him on behalf of Juan Carlos—then everything began happening. He learned that Juan Carlos was the new owner of the premises where the restaurant had been, and that he intended to open a jewelry store in its place with him as a partner.

From Charles' point of view, the news was an upsetting surprise and he immediately refused it saying, "No way! That will never happen!" He repeated it in different ways, "No, no, and no! Never, Fairboy."

But Fairboy's experiences had always guided him to handle things smoothly. He let Charles talk and while Charles was saying, "No, no, never," he quietly observed him with inexhaustible patience. Like a spectator, he just listened and watched until Charles' anger dissipated.

When silence fell between them, Fairboy finally, said, "Man is sometimes irrational, Charles. No one says 'no' to Catarel, and much less at a time when he is the one who protects the people's businesses here in Manhattan."

"I don't care what you think," said Charles. "I plan to open my business alone and I would like to do as I wish. From now on, I hope this remains clear between us."

"What if I say no? You don't have that right. Only the ones with power have the right to make a statement like that. Learn that as your first lesson. I want to help you, but I will only do so if you listen to my advice."

"Isabella is behind all of this, isn't she?" Charles asked.

"Who cares about that, Charles? Whether she is or not is irrelevant, Catarel has the power. You need to pay attention. I'm nine years older than you and those nine years can be multiplied by two because I aged twice as fast in this city drinking coffee in the Mafia caves and having tea with respectable politicians. And I can tell you the whole truth. There are no bad coffees or special teas, for what counts is the deal behind them. We have a great variety of people in this city and only a few can be trusted. Understand that to avoid mistakes. Drink coffee or tea with all of them, and do business with those who offer you the better deals.

"In this game it is very important to know who to discard and when. You look intelligent so you should be able to deal with it very well. But, first, you have a lot to learn about how to survive in New York City as a businessman. If you let me, I will teach you. Now, back to our jewelry affair. If you ignore the opportunity Catarel is giving you, there will never be another one like it. This I can surely guarantee."

Fairboyvon Gaspier had been born in Brest, France, and raised in New Orleans. His father worked as an apothecary and his mother a seamstress. Even though Charles was French, Fairboy never had an interest to become better acquainted with him. It was only after the trip they had made together to Boston before Charles' wedding, that Fairboy became interested in him.

Charles had remained speechless after Fairboy told him everything. He probably had never had an opportunity to hear so much sense put together in one single speech like that. With his head down, he sat for some time, thinking about Juan Carlos Catarel. About how much he hated him because Juan Carlos possessed what he most desired—Isabella!

"No, Fairboy. I will never have him as a partner. I can't accept it."

"Why not?" asked Fairboy. "Having him as a partner wouldn't be that bad. If you know how to deal with him, you can acquire everything he owns—even her. Catarel now has his cards on the table but that doesn't mean he holds the ace. She only sleeps with him; she is not his property."

"What are you trying to suggest?" Charles asked.

"Don't tell me that you don't know what I'm talking about!" said Fairboy. "Charles, my experience allows me to see 'that' which is not done in public. It is not her style to be generous with men like she has been with you. She gave you Ana, the most precious thing she had. Why did you suddenly become the perfect husband? Oh, she does not fool me. She never could."

Charles hadn't known Fairboy was aware of his feelings. He also realized he could not deny it. Like Isabella, he could not fool him either. To his surprise, he experienced a sense of relief. Now he had someone in whom he could confide.

"I love her like I never loved anyone before," explained Charles. "Even when making love to my wife I think of her. You see why I cannot be in business with that man. I hate him!"

"Love and ambition walk side by side," stated Fairboy. "To have both, we must be clever, quick, straight, and sure of ourselves. Like I said, you have a lot to learn. If I were you, I would use her as a reason to defeat him. My first step in accomplishing that task would be to keep him very close to me. In that case, a partnership. What a splendid deal!"

"You don't give up, do you?" Charles said.

"No, I don't. I cannot stand a person who doesn't try hard. Think about what I said last. You *can* have her. At least give yourself a chance."

For a moment, Charles sank into the depths of his mind where Fairboy's last words unraveled his annoyance and he saw himself experience the joy of winning—Isabella was the prize.

"You said that you would teach me how..."

"Yes, Charles."

"That means you will be at my side?"

"Just like you said."

"How do I know I can trust you?"

"It is impossible to know that. After you choose your right-hand man, you must trust him. This is lesson number two."

"So, if my right-hand man did not deserve my appreciation, it would be my problem?"

"That is the way the game is played."

Thoughtfully, Charles moved a little closer. Then in solemn silence he studied Fairboy's proposition. He clearly saw that Fairboy had a point—this was indeed his best chance to have a jewelry store in Manhattan.

"All right! You bring up an interesting point. I don't know why, but my conscience has started to tell me that I must take what comes instead of fighting for silly wishes. Perhaps I deserve the life I'm living because I know what future I would like to have. For this reason only I should learn to accept and not complain. Definitely, the greatness of any glorious future must have its sources in some...unfair present. It's a deal. Tell Mr. Catarel that I accept the partnership and *you* are going to be my right-hand man and I want you to do as I say. I will always have the last word."

"Of course. You would be the boss."

"I want to see how right you are about everything you said, Fairboy. How you can help me win my battle with Mr. Catarel."

"You will see more than that, Charles. I will help you become a powerful businessman and teach you the proper way to drink coffee and tea as well. In exchange, I want the recognition that I am capable of doing what I promise. All I want is a friendship. Someone who will bury my body when I die."

"I presume that will be the easiest part for me to do," commented Charles.

"Then, welcome to Manhattan, Charles Merlenes!" exclaimed, Fairboy, Charles' new friend.

* * * *

A few months later, the biggest jewelry store in Manhattan was ready to open, and even though Catarel owned the greater part of the partnership, only Charles' name appeared on the sign.

Fairboy was the genius behind all the preparations. He investigated all that Charles needed to know including the black market and in little time, found out who controlled the sale of gold and gemstones in the country. In order to know the jewelry industry better, he dedicated himself to researching the market and learned how things worked, advising Charles on many aspects. According to Fairboy, growing fast was important. Not many people were in the jewelry business, so Charles had the chance to become powerful in this field. Clearly seeing this possibility, he was pleased that Charles had also seen it.

On the day Charles had read the sign “Merlenes Jewelry” from across the street, he had felt like the happiest man in the world. *Why dream with so little when we can dream with so much?* And for a moment, he forgot that Juan Carlos Catarel was the man who slept with the woman he most desired in his own bed.

15

JUAN CARLOS CATAREL WAS only seven years old when the first train had entered the city of Chicago. He and the other children would never forget that day, for it was the first time they had seen a train up close.

At the young age of fourteen Juan Carlos left Chicago, returning five years later after being released from a penitentiary. He had killed his stepfather inside Dona Josepha's salon in front of fifteen people. The reason he killed him was to end the violent abuse and suffering his mother had been tolerating for years.

Juan Carlos' father had died at an early age and soon his mother brought home a lover addicted to gambling, drinking, and womanizing. The young boy grew up watching his mother prostitute herself in order to bring money into the house. When the money and food were not enough, she simply suffered the consequences.

One afternoon around 6:00 p.m., Juan Carlos entered his house to find his mother on the floor next to the stove. Her dress was torn into shreds, blood dripped from her mouth and her eyes were bloodshot. His instant reaction went further than the simple instinct of helping her. Blinded by his rage, he grabbed his stepfather's rifle from underneath the bed and rapidly left for Dona Josepha's salon.

As Juan Carlos entered the salon carrying the rifle, everyone inside turned to look at him. He saw his stepfather playing cards at a table with a pretty young lady who was wearing an extravagant red dress. Without fear or hesitation, Juan Carlos approached the table and shot his stepfather.

No one had dared try to stop Juan Carlos, and for a very long time the image of the fury in that young man's eyes had haunted the minds of those who witnessed the tragedy.

During the five years Juan Carlos spent in the penitentiary, his mother resided at Dona Josepha's salon, working as a prostitute. She had performed favors in bed to married politicians in order to lessen her son's sentence. None of them fulfilled their promises, until one day one felt genuinely sorry and helped her with her ordeal.

After his release from the penitentiary, Juan Carlos returned to Chicago. He knew life would not be easy, but he wasn't afraid because he knew he would somehow survive. His desire to rescue his mother from a life of prostitution was greater than his whole life.

Soon after arriving in town, he had begun working for Romero Garcia. Mr. Garcia owned a general store that sold everything from beans and clothes to horse saddles and carriages. He was a small man in his late forties with a narrow face, crossed eyes, and poor taste in clothes. Also, he was a swindler with a bad temper, and addicted to women and gambling. Though Mr. Garcia lacked the drive to go after new horizons, his ability to persuade people to buy his products made up for the absence of it.

The two years that Juan Carlos worked with Mr. Garcia were the hardest years of his life. He had done everything: cleaned the store, carried sacks of grain, shoed horses and changed the wheels of carriages. All that time he worked without a raise and became Mr. Garcia's right hand in the store.

Tired of the situation, Juan Carlos innocently decided to speak with Mr. Garcia about a raise.

Then, in a very unconcerned manner, Garcia answered, "Listen son, you don't deserve to be paid more than I already pay you. An ex-convict doesn't deserve to be treated like others. You have this job because your mother opens her legs for me and does whatever I want without my having to pay her a cent. That's why you have this job."

The effect that Garcia's words had on him were so strong that it erased his desire to help his mother to get rid of the life she had. With every ounce of strength in his mere twenty-one year old body, Juan Carlos threw Garcia to the floor and wrapped his hands around Garcia's throat. While choking him, Juan Carlos sensed a strong satisfaction taking over, quickly increasing his rage. "I'll kill you, you miserable son-of-a-bitch!" he shouted.

However, when he realized that he was actually killing Garcia, he suddenly and just as violently, released him. Juan Carlos remembered that the last time he had experienced that kind of fury he had committed a crime that had cost him five years of his life. *No*, he told himself, *it won't happen again. I vow to destroy Garcia in another way!*

After this experience, for the second time, Juan Carlos left the city. He hoped that somewhere, other than Chicago, life would be better. New York would be it—

* * * *

Juan Carlos could not have picked a worse time to arrive in New York. There was a tremendous uproar caused by the army's draft in the city. He saw a multitude of disoriented people engaged in every act of violence imaginable with no consideration of the consequences their actions had on them. Witnessing all of this from a remote street corner, he learned that man should never lose control of his actions. He determined never to lose his again.

New York had become a complicated city, probably too complex for a young, inexperienced man with little money in his pockets. Juan Carlos knew he had to find a way to survive and do it quickly. Going into the army was the best solution he could find.

In 1864 he departed for Virginia and for a long time did not think about his mother and Romero Garcia. All he could see, when closing his eyes to sleep, were lifeless corpses of young men like him strewn over the ground. Men stretched out along the gutter, drenched in their own blood and misery. They all killed in order to live or died because they did not have time to fight back. For the first time Juan Carlos understood that man would never stop committing crimes because their desire for crime grew instinctively, and sometimes it seemed the easiest way to fix things.

Near the end of the Civil War, something interesting happened to Juan Carlos. One night he witnessed Sofia Verdeja sneaking out of Lieutenant Gaspon's tent. Upon seeing Juan Carlos, Sofia was surprised and immediately asked, "Do you know who I am?"

"Yes. You're the future wife of Captain Balarde."

"Soldier, you saw something you weren't supposed to see."

"Yes, miss, I did," answered Juan Carlos.

"What's your name?"

"Juan Carlos."

"Just Juan Carlos?"

"Juan Carlos Catarel."

"Ah!"

Looking at each other, she asked, "What do you plan to do about this?"

"Nothing," he answered.

"Will you be able to keep quiet without asking for anything in return?"

"Yes," replied Juan Carlos. "The one thing I wish to have most after the war is money, and I don't think that a woman can provide it for me. So go in peace because I didn't see a thing."

Anxious and extremely concerned, Sofia disappeared into the night. She wondered what significance a soldier like Juan Carlos could have in endangering her project.

Sofia was not a very rich woman, but had resources of her own to finance any expenses she may have, and at the moment, she decided to follow one of her whims. That was to murder Colonel Frederick Lachimir, whom she had loved with an intense passion. After making a million promises to her, Lachimir had left her to marry another woman. Unable to face his upcoming marriage, Sofia attempted suicide but was unsuccessful. That experience made her become obsessed with the idea of killing him. She determined that he must die. Since then, all she thought about was how she could destroy that enigmatic man behind an impeccable uniform, who had deceived her.

Sofia's first step in fulfilling her vengeance was to make Captain Carls Balarde fall in love with her. He happened to be much older than she, but this meant nothing to Sofia. She needed his lieutenants and soldiers in order to see Colonel Lachimir dead.

With meticulous dedication, Sofia planned everything. The thought that Lieutenant Gaspon might commit the crime for her continued to grow in Sofia's mind. He seemed to be an opportunist who defied danger was intensely proud of the uniform he wore, and found great satisfaction in sleeping with the future wife of his captain. To him, she was a forbidden woman, and of course that made her most interesting. Out of nowhere she got the impression that being naked in front of Gaspon would give her more power than General Grant in front of his regiment. With this in mind, she became overly confident about her wishes and never gave a second thought to her crazy idea of killing Colonel Lachimir.

She envisioned Lieutenant Gaspon walking with the weapon in his hand and firing the bullet that would kill the love of her life. In her mind she watched Frederick Lachimir falling and the blood, drop by drop, staining his impeccable uniform. In slow motion she ran toward him with tears running down her face as she said, "Oh, Frederick, my love!" Then resting her head on his chest she would hear his last words, "Sofia, my sweet love!" For more than a month her mind systematically played with this insane fantasy.

Unfortunately, the incident with Juan Carlos stirred up an undesirable sensation—fear. Suddenly, she was hesitant and thought he might spoil everything. It puzzled her and she couldn't understand why a soldier, who had nothing to do with her plan, had surprised her leaving Lieutenant Gaspon's tent, just at the moment when everything seemed right for her to accomplish her deed. Being superstitious, she saw this as a bad omen and started thinking about what to do with Juan Carlos.

Not only was Sofia worried, she became extremely confused. One night, in the middle of a dream, she heard Juan Carlos uttering something to her. T*he only thing I wish to have most after the war is money.* Quickly she awoke and sat on the edge of the bed saying aloud, "He needs money!"

Leaving her bed, she paced continuously around her room, her mind lost in trying to analyze the whole situation. On one side she had Gaspon who loved sex and who might do the job for her and then on the other, she had a soldier who needed money. *What would men choose if their options were sex or money? What would they want the most?* For a long while she thought about it then concluded they would grab whichever came first. Instantly, she connected her thoughts with this new philosophy and decided to put Juan Carlos in Lieutenant Gaspon's place in her scheme. For some strange reason, she strongly believed that Juan Carlos would murder Colonel Frederick Lachimir for money.

Lieutenant Gaspon should not be a problem, she figured, because he had never heard about her plan. He could easily disappear from this whole picture, probably to spend the rest of his life trying to figure out what he had done wrong. *But what the hell! That is life!* She told herself.

Soon after she decided to alter her plans, she went to see Juan Carlos.

In a straightforward manner, she asked him, "How much money do you think you need to start a new life after the war?"

"You mean if I make it out alive?" Juan Carlos asked.

"Of course."

"I don't need change, miss. I need a great amount of money. Enough to buy a store in Chicago. Forget about it. I don't think you have that kind of money. I told you, there is no need for you to worry, I already forgot what I saw the other day."

"It is not about what you saw," she said. "It's about a job that needs to be done." Then she offered him one-third the amount of money he had in mind.

Sofia's offer was tempting. Juan Carlos looked at her as he considered what kind of job it might be. Then his common sense eagerly engaged him in this opportunity to make some money. He thought that whatever she wanted—it should be a piece of cake.

"All right, miss. If you show up with the money, I'll do anything you wish."

The very next day, Sofia brought the money and gave him half of it. They agreed that the other half would be given after the job was done. Then she explained what she wanted done. "And I want you to bring me something as proof," she explained at the end.

She departed leaving Juan Carlos surprised by the sort of job he had to do. Then he realized that it would not be as easy as he expected. Nevertheless, he wanted the money and decided to take advantage of the opportunity.

He spent two days planning the task and when he felt ready, he met with Sofia again. They set up the time and place to meet to finish the deal. She insisted he must bring some kind of proof that the job had been done and she would then deliver the rest of the money.

At approximately 9:00 p.m. a few nights later, Sofia stood waiting for Juan Carlos at the side of a deserted road holding the reigns of her horse. Anxiously she waited about five minutes before Juan Carlos arrived. He approached her calmly and got off his horse.

"The job is done. Where is the money?"

"Here," said Sofia. "But where is the proof?"

Juan Carlos immediately took a bloody handkerchief from his pocket. "Here. A piece of his finger along with his wedding band."

Without releasing the reigns of the horse, she moved closer to Juan Carlos to take the handkerchief from him. Juan Carlos quickly grabbed her arm and turned her around, opened the bloody handkerchief, which was empty, and choked her with it.

Sofia struggled in vain until her body went limp in his arms. Then he took the money out of her purse, placed her body on top of the horse, and lightly slapped it.

The horse rode off through the night.

"Killing a colonel is too risky, miss," he said softly. "Only a crazy person like you would dream about it. I think that Colonel Frederick Lachimir and I have something in common. We are both lucky."

16

A FEW MONTHS AFTER JUAN Carlos had murdered Sophia Verdeja, General Lee and his forces surrendered to General Grant, marking the end of the war. Among the soldiers returning home was Juan Carlos Catarel. Even though he did not have enough money to buy Garcia's store, he headed back to Chicago.

Juan Carlos now faced the world alone as his mother had died while he was away fighting the war. Now, he no longer needed to worry about her. As much as he had loved her, he accepted her loss peacefully knowing he couldn't have done much for her. His life wasn't an easy one either. When he returned home he still had to deal with the hatred he felt for Garcia. Juan Carlos had never put aside his desire for vengeance.

After much deliberation, Juan Carlos chose the prostitute Carmela as his helper. She had been the woman dressed in red sitting next to his stepfather that day when he had killed him. Subtly and in a devious manner Juan Carlos developed a close relationship with her. Fortunately, she easily fell for him in a way she had never fallen for any other man. And being rather naive, as women sometimes can be, she called it love and made him her favorite man.

For his own safety, he never mentioned to anyone his hatred toward Romero Garcia. In fact, he made it a point to always speak well of him. It was his intention to play his game conservatively and win fast. Garcia would pay in a proper way for what he had done to his mother.

Once again Juan Carlos returned to work for Garcia who intentionally took advantage of the situation and decided to pay him even less. But Juan Carlos did not mind since he needed to be close to him in order to plan his future misfortune and disgrace.

For the first time ever, Juan Carlos felt in full control of their relationship as well as confident that no one could stop him. No one would be in the position to save Garcia. It would be the same as when he killed his stepfather. Not a soul dared to stand between the young man with his rifle and the man at the poker table.

About a year after his return to Chicago, Juan Carlos decided that the right time had come. He was ready to put his plans into action. Carefully he prepared Carmela.

"Carmela, we must talk about our future," he said. "I want to take you away from this kind of life. I have a fabulous plan in mind, but I need to know if I can count on you."

"Of course, dear," she replied.

Intuitively, he knew what her answer would be. He had made her believe that he loved her and thus won her loyalty. Carmela was his.

"We will take advantage of Romero Garcia," he said. "I want to run him out of Chicago."

"But how?" Carmela promptly asked.

"I have a perfect plan. You wait and see"

Juan Carlos was very careful to keep his plan to himself, only explaining to her what she needed to know so she would help. Carmela's role was to seduce Garcia. When she heard that, she said, "Are you asking me to please him like I please you?"

"That and much more, dear. Much more! You will have to eat

him up," said Juan Carlos.

"Oh, that's..."

"I know," he said cutting her off. "But I need you to do it. It's for us."

"Yes," she lovingly agreed.

Juan Carlos had developed a fantastic plan—perfect for a man like Garcia.

During Juan Carlos's five year stay in the penitentiary, he had met a man named Santiago Esmerilo who had lost his mind. Santiago Esmerilo spent his days contemplating an old map that led to a treasure. He was a merchant marine who had sailed many years under the American flag. One day when the ship was out at sea and the majority of the crew was asleep, he attacked and killed two sailors and the captain because he wanted to take over the ship and sail to South America in search of the lost treasure. His foolish action caused him to have the worst experience of his life. When the ship arrived in New York, he was arrested and went straight to jail.

On the map Esmerilo had was the date 1713, and apparently it had belonged to a Buccaneer captain. The map carried the C.E.T. mark, which stood for Captain Edward Teach, known as Blackbeard. Upon Juan Carlos' arrival in the penitentiary, he became acquainted with Santiago, and often saw him gazing at the map for hours. Crazy Santiago looked at it for long hours, folding and unfolding it without ever tiring. Sometimes he hid it in his pants, and other times under the bed. "It's mine," he constantly said with madness in his eyes. "I'm rich."

During those five years Santiago had died, dreaming of his fortune and the old map ended up in Juan Carlos' hands. What had originally been a white piece of paper now had faded into an ugly yellow-color one with torn corners. In the center of the old map, some faint lines and a poor sketch of seven mountains could be clearly seen, and right next to these appeared the words Atlantic Ocean, South America, Brazil and Claros. Despite the poor condition of the map, the initials *C.E.T.* could still be read without any problems.

Juan Carlos saved the map but with no ulterior motive. After he had left the penitentiary, he just could not part with it. Each time he tried to, he felt an uneasy sensation and quickly changed his mind. *Not everyone has a treasure map for a souvenir from a penitentiary. At least I have one. Who knows, maybe it will bring me luck.* He kept it not knowing why and it proved to be beneficial because that old, faded map from the 1700s was what helped him run Garcia out of Chicago.

Along with everything else that Juan Carlos learned about Garcia, he also found out that Garcia was extremely superstitious. At times Garcia would say, "Juan Carlos, do not tell anyone about how successful my business is because people are ambitious and have the evil eye."

All these traits of Garcia's personality remained in Juan Carlos' mind for a long time. Later, these traits made Juan Carlos realize that Garcia would be unable to resist the temptation of possessing an old map of a hidden treasure. As greedy as he was, Garcia would live wondering, questioning, as well as believing in the map. Besides that, Juan Carlos remembered that many years ago a fortune-teller had predicted that Garcia would sail to South America one day.

According to Juan Carlos' plan, old Garcia would continue to live, but not in Chicago.

Garcia's misadventure started on a calm night with Carmela caressing his unusualy shaped mustache.

"Garcia, I need to confess something to you. Can I trust you?"

"Of course," he responded. "What is wrong?"

"Nothing," she said. "But I have a secret, which I have kept with me for many years."

"Whatever you want to tell me, do so. It will remain a secret. Go ahead. What is bothering you?"

"I have never told anyone about this, Garcia. You must keep it a secret."

"Carmela, you know me. You are my girl."

She looked at him closely, as if she really wanted to study the sincerity attached to his words, "All right. I hope I won't regret this."

Then, with great persuasion she began her pitch. "I have a treasure map that I took from Juan Carlos' stepfather the afternoon he died. He had wished for us to search for the treasure, but what happened, of course, was his death. I have waited all these years for someone to help me find the treasure. Now, I believe that you might be the right person. Can you help me? We could be very rich."

"A treasure?" he said full of curiosity. "Where is this map?"

Carmela removed the map from one of her drawers and opened it upon the bed. She saw Garcia's eyes light up. His expression shone with intense greediness. She let him contemplate the old map for a while until he had seen enough. Then in a sweet and coquettish manner, she picked up the map, folded it, and held it in her hand.

"Think of how we can accomplish this journey, Garcia. Meanwhile, I'll keep the map."

After that day, the desire to own that treasure took the place of everything that was once important in Garcia's life. It appeared that Juan Carlos had accurately predicted Garcia's reaction. Garcia could no longer sleep peacefully. He spent his nights thinking of the treasure that would be his and only his. He pictured that moment in his miserable stingy mind. After finding the treasure, he would throw Carmela into that same hole. It seemed so simple that he did not have to plan ahead. It would work out when the time came. And if the treasure were inside a grotto, he then would leave her there forever.

Now, Garcia had another reason to wake up everyday, and he became more distrustful than normal, spoke little, and barely greeted his customers. He even suspected his own shadow and often talked to himself. Everyone noticed the change, but everyone also knew that he had taken on Carmela as his new pastime and that she was twenty-three years younger than he. So to the others, they figured she was the reason for Garcia's unusual behavior.

One night as Garcia was closing the store with Juan Carlos, he asked, "Juan Carlos, did you and your stepfather ever talk much?"

"Very little," replied Juan Carlos happily, for he knew that his plan was set into motion.

"He never spoke to you about his travels?"

"Sometimes," answered Juan Carlos. "He was a son-of-a-bitch, Garcia," Juan Carlos said cutting him off.

"You're right," Garcia replied.

"If he were any different," added Juan Carlos, "my life would have been less painful. That miserable man had a treasure map which I saw one time. If I could find it, perhaps my life would change."

As Garcia heard this, he felt a sudden shiver. His expression changed and he looked back at Juan Carlos with a blank stare. He wanted to appear as if he wasn't giving much thought to their conversation.

"Do you know something, Garcia?" cleverly Juan Carlos continued. "Your woman, Carmela, was once my stepfather's woman. Sometimes I wonder if this map might be in her possession. I even had a relationship with her to see if I could find out what had happened to the map, but I was unsuccessful. Anyway, I still have hopes that I can find it one day. I have often heard stories of people who went after treasures and became very rich."

"Oh, stop dreaming," said Garcia. "Get your feet back on the ground. You are too old to be dreaming of treasures. Don't mention this to anyone who does not know you and run the risk of being laughed at."

Garcia had started this conversation with Juan Carlos to find out whether he knew about his stepfather's old map, and to his surprise, Juan Carlos had seen the map once. This worried him and caused him to think that he had little time. He decided he must act quickly before Carmela tired of him and before Juan

Carlos found out that she possessed the map and ruin everything.

That night, Garcia decided to sell all his possessions and leave Chicago with Carmela and the map. He told Carmela that Juan Carlos knew of the map's existence and because of that, they should not wait any longer. He informed her, "Be ready because we will leave Chicago sooner than I had planned."

A few hours later Carmela informed Juan Carlos what Garcia had in mind, and he carefully began his preparations for the final phase of his plan.

Juan Carlos waited a week before climbing the balcony and entering Carmela's room. He did it soon after Garcia had left her, and she was still lying on the bed naked, and full of disgust toward him. Juan Carlos came in, sat on the bed and said, "We must make our final move today. You don't have to sleep with him anymore."

"Oh, thanks to the angels!" she exclaimed, kissing Juan Carlos everywhere.

"Where is the map?" he asked.

Carmela left his arms, walked to its hiding place, came back and handed it to him. He opened the map to verify its authenticity, then calmly folded it, and put it in his pocket. Smiling maliciously and experiencing the taste of victory, he pushed Carmela down on the bed, grabbed a pillow and pressed it to her face until her struggles ceased.

"This is for my mother, bitch!" he spat.

He left Carmela's room just as he had entered it. No one saw him. Everything ran perfectly. While Carmela lay dead in her bed, Juan Carlos returned to Garcia's store to speak with him but Garcia wasn't there yet. After leaving Carmela's room, Garcia had gone back downstairs to Dona Josepha's Salon for a few drinks.

With Garcia away, Juan Carlos forced open the back door of the store, went in and sat down at a small table where Garcia served cognac to his best customers. There was always a tray with bottles and glasses on this table. Juan Carlos took a glass and poured himself some cognac. He attentively had kept track of

Garcia's routine and knew the man would arrive soon. And it happened just as he expected. At 11:40 p.m. Garcia entered and was startled to see Juan Carlos sitting at the table drinking his cognac.

"Juan Carlos! What are you doing here?"

"Waiting for you. Sit down and have a drink with me. We need to talk."

Garcia hesitated. He had a feeling that this was not at all good, but he pulled up a chair, and sat down to hear what Juan Carlos had to say.

"I heard a rumor that you were going to sell the store and leave Chicago."

"True," answered Garcia.

"I want to buy your store. I know how to run it and it would also be a good investment for my future."

"How? You don't have money to buy my store."

"I have my savings, and I made good money during the war."

Carefully, Juan Carlos passed an envelope across the table. "This is what I have to offer."

Quite surprised Garcia opened the envelope and counted the money inside. "You are crazy if you think I'm going to accept this," he exclaimed. "This store is worth three times more than what you are offering!"

"I know," said Juan Carlos. "Here is the rest of my payment." Silently, he unfolded the old map and placed it on the table.

When Garcia saw the map, the expression of astonishment on his face was indescribable. He felt as if his heart would fail him. *How could he have the map if no less than half an hour ago I held it in my own hands?* With a trembling voice he asked, "When did you get this map?"

"Fifteen minutes ago."

"But how?"

"In a simple way," said Juan Carlos. "Listen, Garcia, the bitch is dead. I killed her and when her body is discovered, you will have a big problem on your hands. Everyone knows that you were the last one to see her, but I'm your friend and I will help you get away. Behind the store is a carriage, take the money I'm offering you, the map, the rest of your savings, and disappear before it is too late."

"And if I refuse to do as you say?"

"I'll kill you, too."

Slowly, Juan Carlos took a dagger and placed it on the table. Then he removed a folded piece of paper from his pocket. He unfolded it and said, "Before you go, sign this document. It states that I have bought the store from you."

Garcia understood that he had lost. He looked at everything that lay on the table between him and Juan Carlos. The map, the envelope, the document he was to sign, and the dagger. Juan Carlos had his right hand resting on the dagger. Garcia considered the map once again. It was old and dirty but it could make him very rich. He signed the document against his will.

Then bearing the weight of a defeated man, he gathered some of his belongings and went to the back of the store to find the carriage. However, before leaving he asked, "Now that there is nothing left to negotiate, Juan Carlos, tell me why you didn't want the map for yourself?"

"I decided to follow your advice. I put my feet on the ground and forgot about treasures."

"You knew all along that Carmela had the map, didn't you?"

"Of course. You haven't noticed it but lately you've been thinking out loud, and I always listened."

"Poor Carmela!"

"Why?" asked Juan Carlos. "You thought of killing her, too."

"I thought about this out loud?"

"No. But I happen to know the color of your soul."

With a broken heart Garcia left Chicago with one last hope—finding the treasure.

For a while Juan Carlos watched Garcia as he disappeared down the road. *You shouldn't have fucked my mother nor have told me what that Spanish gypsy said about your future journey to South*

America. That is what gave me the idea of using my old map to ruin you.

While in Spain a gypsy read Garcia's future with the cards and told him he would travel to South America one day. About a year and a half later, Garcia left Spain bound for North America. During the trip, he remembered the gypsy's words and believed that she was quite right—only she had seen the wrong continent. Now of course, the map caused him to remember once again the gypsy's words. He headed out of town thinking about her. *It took a long time. After all she was right. There is a treasure in South America waiting for me!*

* * * *

After Garcia's departure, Juan Carlos quickly became well known and regarded as a highly respected figure in Chicago. He won the esteem of most people with his smile and out-going personality. First, he took over Romero Garcia's store, later Mrs. Josepha's brothel, and then, as Chicago grew, the hotels, nightclubs, and restaurants. The name Catarel became synonymous with Chicago.

In 1870, he met Prieto Ferbonini and they soon became good friends. One year later, he met Isabella Gabilano. He saw her for the first time in the Italia Campibeli Restaurant on the day she was celebrating her twenty-first birthday. For the occasion, Isabella had dressed in white with her hair in soft curls on her shoulders and looked as pretty as an angel. When Prieto Ferbonini introduced them, her delicate beauty fascinated Catarel. Immediately he felt attracted to her lovely smile and had an overwhelming desire for her. For the entire evening she became the center of his affection. Whenever she spoke, he listened attentively and when she smiled, he wanted to own her.

In keeping with his style, Juan Carlos promised himself that he would make her his. After that he began to visit New York and Isabella with greater frequency investing an enormous amount of time accomplishing his goal of winning her love and affection. His outstanding dedication made it possible. When they made love for the first time, he left her a beautiful ruby ring with a note that read:

> *Darling, it was divine. I chose a ruby. I hope I'm right.*
> *Love, Juan Carlos.*

Happily she placed the ring on her finger. As she said aloud to herself, "You chose correctly. A ruby is just fine!"

Every year Catarel asked her to marry him. He loved her and longed for her to be his wife. She did not belong to his past and therefore, must be always a part of his future. But Isabella kept refusing his proposals. She felt that for her, marriage was something that had lost its purpose. Too many eventful moments had happened during her life and because of them she believed she no longer had the right to think about it.

"Why marry when we are fine just the way we are?" she responded every time he asked her. After many fruitless attempts he abandoned the idea for a while, for he couldn't risk losing her. Juan Carlos loved her more than any of his possessions. In her arms his pleasure went on—limitless. He saw the beginning and end of his existence fusing into an overflowing enchantment.

In addition to acquiring just about everything he wanted from life, Juan Carlos also worked hard to fit into society. Despite his crimes, he managed to present an acceptable image of integrity and morality. He worked hard to build a sound reputation for himself based on this new portrayal. With great respect for each individual he dealt with, both good and bad, he learned how to negotiate successfully. Those who attempted to destroy him simply died with decency, because this characterized the nature of the game. It was the same as when he was in the war. If he did not kill, he would be killed and Chicago represented his personal battlefield.

As he became exceedingly rich, the residents of Chicago felt very proud of him. Juan Carlos established himself as a well-known benevolent figure by always standing next to any cause in order to offer help. He never turned his back when he could do something for the people of Chicago. If he had desired to dignify himself with any political position, he could have had the support of almost everyone. But Juan Carlos did not seek that. Politicians were supposed to uphold the law, and in his world it seemed enough only to know it. To follow the many rules by the book would be a difficult task.

According to legend, in 1871 Mrs. O'Leary's cow knocked over a kerosene lamp and started "The Great Fire," which lasted more than twenty hours and destroyed half of Chicago. Juan Carlos stayed side by side with the people of Chicago. His money helped build shelters for the homeless and assisted in the restoration of Chicago. He did everything he could for the people during that difficult time. But most of all, his good deeds made him unforgettable to the people.

His involvement in the community during the aftermath of the fire caused him to experience strong humanitarian feelings, and he ardently wished to retain that same image—of lending a helping hand—whenever necessary. While watching the new city rise from the ashes, he thought about something that had never occurred to him before—to invest outside of Chicago. New York came to mind. From Chicago's tragedy he learned he could also lose all that he owned at any time, and only the illusion of such reality created a huge wave of unpleasant feelings. Instantly he decided to take action to prevent that from ever happening to him.

Soon after that, he started to make business arrangements with Don Prieto Ferbonini, and with Don Prieto's connections he acquired some properties in New York, as well as gained the position he needed to masterfully consolidate his business transactions between the two cities.

Today, while in New York, the young jeweler from St. Denis, France spent hours upon hours cutting gemstones and melting gold. In Chicago Juan Carlos entertained himself drinking and gambling with his friends. And from time to time, someone asked him to tell the story of the Spaniard with whom he used to work—Romero Garcia. With great satisfaction, Juan Carlos would say, "Oh, he believed in too many gypsies and pirate stories. He sold me everything for almost nothing and an old dirty map of a treasure."

After Catarel's words, everyone would laugh. But in these gatherings there was always a wise-ass that asked, "And where was the treasure hidden?" To avoid their curiosity and also because he didn't want them to know what had happened with Garcia and his treasure, Juan Carlos answered, "It was in India. Can you believe it? I sent him to India."

* * * *

Destiny is a sequence of events precisely arranged in a very creative way. Whoever is in charge of the artistic job will always be a mystery. Juan Carlos' lifestyle had never been threatened until Charles Merlenes' arrival in New York. One might wonder what kind of threat Charles could be to a man like Catarel. After all, he was just a young jeweler. However, Charles not only ended up in Isabella Gabilano's bed, married Prieto Ferbonini's granddaughter, but also became Catarel's business partner.

Would Manhattan be big enough for both of them?

17

New York, October 1887

CHARLES ARRIVED AT THE HOSPITAL. He rushed in looking for Isabella and found her crying, holding Ana's newborn baby—Anthony Charles Merlenes.

"How is Ana?" he asked worriedly as he hurried toward her.

"Oh, Charles, she's dead."

"No! It can't be," he said filled with anguish.

"The doctor said her heart could not take the strain."

"I have to see her."

The doctor escorted him to where Ana's body lay and left him alone with her. Charles approached the bed, took her hands, and contemplated her silent face. He could not believe she was dead. An enormous pain swept his soul as he stood by her side. Looking down at her as he stroked her hair, he was unable to cry. His sorrow intensified and washed over him as he remembered the day when she had told him she was expecting their child. How he had hugged her tightly and blissfully told her that if it were a boy, he wanted to name him Anthony, after his friend.

How sweetly she had replied, "Anthony Charles would be perfect."

Charles also thought about their happiest time together. How he desired—above all—to love her. That night he had been drinking in the company of Fairboy when he found out that Isabella had once slept with Saporo. The news upset and disappointed him tremendously, and when he left, he said to Fairboy, "I will go home and make love to my dear wife like never before. Tonight will be our best ever. After, I hope I discover that I love her."

Unfortunately hopes are just that—hopes—his heart held a totally different feeling. Nothing happened or changed. But now while holding Ana's dead body, he knew she was the best wife he could have ever had.

Ana's love brought tranquility and peace to his life. He would have done the impossible in order to love her. Her pure heart made her perfect for mothering his children. Oh, how he would miss her terribly!

But missing Ana did not hinder his love and desire for Isabella, because that love was the poison that circulated in his blood. Each day without her deepened his misery especially since she belonged to his partner, Juan Carlos Catarel.

* * * *

After Ana's death, Charles immersed himself in his work. It ultimately became the focus of his life. Meanwhile, Adela cared for his son Anthony Charles.

Charles and Isabella's pathways rarely crossed. She visited the child often but intentionally did so when Charles was away. Strong barriers kept them apart. There was Ana's absence, the partnership with Juan Carlos and little Anthony. Isabella chose to respect the order of events that now surfaced in her life. Eagerly she pretended to play the rules decently, for she did not want to lose her rights as an aunt. She knew men very well. They were inflexible when they decided to be cruel. Above all, she wanted to enjoy little Anthony's love and be part of his life.

* * * *

Three years passed before Anthony Charles' birthday was celebrated. Isabella organized it. She planned a simple party that really surprised everyone, even Charles. He learned of the event the moment he returned home. In order not to ruin his child's celebration, he moderated his feelings to behave like a civilized person. Happily he accepted the idea and enjoyed the festive moment in honor of his son. In fact, he even managed to approach Isabella and thank her for the great idea.

They lived separate lives, but when Isabella and Charles came in contact, an unusual tension circulated between them. After he had thanked her and enjoying little Anthony's happiness, Isabella commented innocently, "Look at your child, Charles. He is exactly like you and has his mother's smile. It is a shame that Ana can't be here to see him."

"She *is* here, Isabella," Charles answered coldly. "Her memory lives here with us. Why do you always have to make things so difficult?"

"I'm sorry," she replied instantly. "I didn't mean to annoy you. This is difficult for me, too. She was my...niece, so don't forget that I loved her as well."

He glanced at her steadily ending their conversation with his meaningful silence. Then drinking his whiskey he walked away leaving her alone with her anger. His attitude greatly ruined her good mood, so she kept her distance. After they sang "Happy Birthday" to Anthony, she immediately left.

That evening Charles found he was unable to fall asleep. He sat in the dining room with a drink in his hand regretting his actions. Every time they saw each other, things like that happened. He couldn't avoid being bitter because he felt as if he were trapped in hell whenever he was around her.

After drinking almost a whole bottle of whiskey, Charles decided to go to the jewelry store, thinking to work for a while, perhaps until midnight or one in the morning. In fact, time did not matter to him as he wished to work until he could erase the whole evening from his mind.

Once there, he carefully examined the sketches of some new bracelets he was designing and tried to work on them. Soon he found himself fighting with the images inside his mind and couldn't concentrate. He lost his patience and abruptly put things down and said, "Damn it!"

Then trying to cope with his frustration, he poured himself another drink.

Charles missed the woman who owned his heart so much that he spent the next hour drinking—expecting the alcohol to help bury his frustration. Later on when he stepped outside the jewelry store, his mind failed to guide his steps. Instead of going home he went to the Blue Salon.

Immediately after entering it, he heard the sound of music mixed with laughter. He took a moment to look around. The past three years he had been celibate and only just now he realized it. His desire to become rich and to defeat Juan Carlos Catarel had made him forget the pleasures of being a man. *Damn it! I have forgotten I have a dick between my legs!*

The people in the Blue Salon paid no attention to his presence. Everyone seemed busy enjoying whatever entertainment their money had bought for the night. Silently, Charles crossed the room and went up to where Isabella lived. Instinctively he knocked on the door.

Isabella, half asleep, opened the door, wondering what might have happened downstairs to make someone come up and get her out of her bed. When she opened the door, she was extremely surprised to see him.

"You?" she stammered.

Before she could utter another word, he pushed her inside and closed the door behind them.

"You are drunk," she said. "You need strong coffee."

"No. I need a blow job."

Quickly she slapped his face with all her might. "Oh you—"

Charles advanced, held her by her arms and forced her against the wall and kissed her.

Oh, Charles... was all she could utter in her mind.

They kissed each other roughly with tempestuous passion, trying to diminish the amount of kisses they had missed since the first time. Without a word he lifted her in his arms and took her into the bedroom. Charles lost the strength to fight against his desires. Humbly, he lost all his pride because he could no longer go on without having her. At that moment he needed her as much as he needed the air he was breathing.

Wildly engaged by an endless appetite for love, they tumbled onto the bed. His lips persistently touched her warm skin seeking its delightful, sensual pleasure. His hands traveled fast over and into the most provocative places of her body that she yielded, and his eyes continuously closed and opened to intensify his pleasure and to contemplate her body's sexuality. They only abandoned their mischievous fight when magically everything mixed inside of them—

Then enjoying the peace that now cooled his heart and soul, Charles calmly dressed to leave. Without looking at her, he reached into his wallet, took out some money, and placed it on the night table.

"Oh, no!" she yelled angrily, abruptly rising from the bed. "I don't want your money!"

"You can't refuse it," he said. "This is not my first time. I'm not Saporo."

"Oh, I hate you! I really do!" she screamed bitterly, throwing the money at him in the most violent manner she could. "Take your lousy money with you and next time, go fuck yourself. I can't believe that once I thought I was in love with you."

"I did too," Charles said. Then he turned around and walked away.

Lamenting, Isabella knelt over the money that was spread on

the floor. *Why is it that men cannot forgive? I hate you, Charles. I hate you.* She cried for a long time over her unrelenting misery.

* * * *

Anthony was five years old when Charles took him to the cemetery for the first time to visit his mother's grave—on Ana's birthday. Isabella was already there dressed in black, standing motionless among the tombstones, the flowers, and the smell of the moist sacred ground. It was a dull, rainy day and the raindrops seemed so soft that they failed to make any noise.

Isabella stood under the umbrella while her eyes contemplated the flowers she had placed on the grave. Charles, too, stood looking at Ana's grave. Some thoughts ran through his mind. *Ana was not like us, Isabella. This is why she is no longer here. I lived with her. I can say she was different. Even making love with her was different.*

In Ana's arms Charles had been able to identify himself with the happiness that comforted both the flesh and spirit—not passion. Feelings such as those he felt for Isabella, easily mixed with hatred, only confused the soul and made the body wild. With Ana he had always enjoyed a pure fragrance. Through the years he understood that life had allowed him to have the best part of her. "I like you," was all that he could say to Ana in their most intimate moments, and she never complained.

Charles and Anthony remained next to the grave and together placed their flowers on top of it. Isabella stepped back quietly, just watching. Anthony had a special place in her heart, and Charles...she knew she could not hate him.

While little Anthony fixed the flowers on his mother's grave, his father and his aunt simultaneously looked into each other's eyes as if they could communicate with their own silence.

I love you.

I can't hate you, Charles.

The rain stopped and she slowly closed her umbrella. She inhaled the smell of the wet ground. Memories instantly disturbed her peace of mind—the day of her First Communion—*Mommy, forgive me...* She felt a chill run through her body. Hating the idea of staying any longer in the cemetery, she quickly decided to leave.

Delicately she lifted her skirt above her ankles to avoid getting it soiled and made her way through the graves. She passed by Celino's grave and felt her body shudder. She couldn't pass it without remembering that she had sent someone to kill him. Suddenly, many memories ran through her mind. *Ana loved Charles... I love Charles... Ana was my daughter... Why didn't I? She died without knowing the truth... Oh, cemeteries...I hate cemeteries.*

She hurried on until she had reached the outside then breathlessly stopped and leaned against the cemetery gates. She stayed there catching her breath, waiting for all of her thoughts to disappear.

Charles and Anthony came out. "Aunt Isabella, you look beautiful dressed in black," her nephew said, finally hugging her as she wanted.

"Thank you, dear. You are the first person to tell me that."

Charles kept quiet viewing the scene from behind and wondering why the gods had made her so beautiful.

"Charles," she said. "We need to have a talk. I'm thinking of moving to Chicago. I'm going to sell my business and I want to buy a house in Anthony's name. I would like to discuss this with you."

"When?" he asked.

"As soon as possible."

"Then we can talk today. I have no intention of returning to the jewelry store."

"Today is fine," she answered. "Would you have dinner with me if I cook something?"

"I don't see any reason why not."

"Would 8:00 p.m. be a good time?"

"Eight o'clock is fine."

Slowly she lowered herself and kissed her nephew on the forehead. Then as she turned to say good-bye to Charles he said, "May I ask you something?"

"Yes, you may."

"Don't wear black tonight."

"I'll try not to."

Charles arrived at her apartment promptly at 8:00 p.m. wearing black pants and a white, linen shirt. Lately, he had been dressing with incredible elegance, portraying a well-to-do successful man who understood much about things few others did—precious stones. In Manhattan he had become "that man" thirty-four years old, widowed, and with a young son who was a reflection of his own image. In most women's opinion, an excellent catch.

When Isabella opened the door and invited him in, Charles looked at her in disbelief. She was wearing black. She had on a taffeta dress with few details, tight sleeves, wide collar, and pleated skirt. For an instant he stood staring at her. He had never seen her so beautiful.

"Dinner is ready, Charles," she said. "I can serve it now if you like."

"Please, if you don't mind."

"It's okay with me. Why don't you open the wine while I serve the food."

Quietly he did as she said and ten minutes later both of them were sitting and eating the only dish she knew how to cook—spaghetti.

They talked but avoided looking at each other. It had been two years since Charles had come to see her in the middle of the night, very drunk and lost his senses. For that he could never forgive himself. Today, he wanted to be very careful and behave decently. After all they were meeting to talk about family business and he planned to leave after giving his opinion.

"Charles, I'm going to marry Juan Carlos and move to Chicago," she announced.

Surprised by the news he responded, "If that is what you want, then I don't see anything wrong with it."

"Whether I want it or not is irrelevant. We do not have to explain things like this, do we?"

"No," said Charles. "When is the wedding?"

"I don't know, yet. Perhaps at the beginning of the year, I imagine. Juan Carlos still doesn't know I have accepted his proposal."

"Oh, I understand," Charles uttered, wondering why she chose to tell him first. "Congratulations! This is indeed something significant for you."

"It is," she said curtly.

Following this exchange, there was a long silence in the dining room and when one of them spoke again, it was she. "Like I told you, I plan to sell my business and I think that Juan Carlos himself will buy it. We have already talked about this before and he liked the idea. His biggest wish is to take me to Chicago, so I believe that he may go through with the deal."

"Of course," said Charles.

"I want to buy a house and I would like for you, Adela, and Anthony to live in it. Anthony is already five and needs more space in which to play. What do you think of this idea?"

"You want to know my answer?"

"Yes."

"It is no."

"Charles, please...think of Anthony," she said softly.

"You heard my answer. No!" he said emphatically.

They finished the meal arguing over Anthony's future and happiness and at the end Charles said, "Isabella, I don't want to be rude, but I will be the one who makes decisions about what is or isn't appropriate for my son. I will ask you kindly to stay out of this."

"Fine. I'm sorry."

Into the silence, Charles poured himself one last glass of wine after dinner. Apparently they had run out of subject matters for the moment, and their individual thoughts became more important than the child's welfare.

Instinctively she started to clear the table and for some time she went in and out of the dining room, silently deep in thought that only increased the tension between them.

"Why do you hate me so much?" she finally dared to ask.

"Damn you, Isabella! Damn...you!" He said standing up abruptly. "Why didn't you ever tell me that Ana was your daughter? Why did you make me marry her? Why did you force this partnership between Juan Carlos and me? Why did you have to cook this stupid spaghetti again, and why are you wearing black when I asked you not to? Can you answer all of these '*why's*' for me? Don't you have something better to ask?"

Tears started to fall from her eyes and slowly roll down her cheeks tracing her features, making her so feminine and weak.

"I...don't...know, Charles. I don't know how to answer all of those '*why's.*' But I do have a better question. Why didn't you appear in my life when I was still pure and innocent?"

Genuinely sad, he took her in his arms. "I'm sorry..." he said closing his eyes and embracing her tightly. He held her against him as if she had always belonged in his arms and slowly breathed in the aroma of her clean and soft skin. Gently he kissed her lips and tasted the salt of her tears. Her soft lips and warm tears, his needs and their passions once again swept away his pride. While his desire for having her increased, the smooth sound of her taffeta dress roughly filled the air.

"Please, be mine tonight...I need you," he implored gently.

They made love with their souls full of distress, for they sensed they were losing each other forever. And while rushing their caresses to fill their needs, Charles experienced the fear of ending this moment too fast. He stopped her urging and slowly undressed her and himself. Tirelessly he brought his lips to every inch of her body dreaming to never forget the softness of her skin. His finger gently touched the inside of her mouth and became lost in between her legs, infinitely searching for her joy, infinitely leading the sensations of his heart and soul. The strength of his love and desires held her in his arms endlessly and under the magic contact of her fingers and lips, he loved and pleaded, until his entire existence died within her.

They slept in each other arms all night long. In the morning before leaving, Charles kissed her lips with love. "*Je t'aime*," he whispered, presuming that she was sleeping.

Soon after he left, she opened her eyes and said to the room, "He finally said it! *Je t'aime* my darling, and thank you."

18

IT SEEMED THAT GOD watched over and protected Charles. He had safely reached the most prosperous stage of his life.

Easily his path opened to lead him in the direction of his dreams. During the past five years everything that Fairboyvon Gaspier had done to enable the Merlenes' name to gain prestige in the jewelry market was a success. Charles' name grew with distinction, and he enjoyed this with great satisfaction. He felt proud of what his hands could create and knew that with them he could conquer the rest of the world. The most difficult stage had passed and more than ever, he was ready for the new outcome.

Charles and Fairboyvon were preparing themselves for a step toward the future. Gaspier wanted to attain a patent on Charles' designs. According to him, the timing was right to take action towards this matter. By protecting the Merlenes' own designs, they could secure their uniqueness and exclusivity as jewelry-makers. With those new credentials they could smoothly step ahead, and when buyers started to sift for names in order to acquire a great piece of jewelry, the name Merlenes would be the first to handle any competition. After that, they would be creating business agreements with the mine owners in South Africa to buy the stones directly from the mines, and then probably from South America.

Gaspier, as everybody now called him, became the right hand for both Charles and Juan Carlos Catarel. Lately, he had been very busy working with Mr. William Ugani, preparing the application papers for the patents.

Mr. Ugani, who had an excellent reputation as a lawyer, knew a great deal about International Laws. Every businessperson in New York City knew about his éclat and respected him highly. When Gaspier thought they could afford to pay for his services, Charles simply hired him.

A few days after hearing the news of Isabella and Juan Carlos' engagement, Gaspier met with Charles in the jewelry store. He wanted to inform Charles that everything was ready for the patent.

He said enthusiastically, "Charles, after that, nobody will stop us. I will go to South Africa myself. Five years, Charles. Give me another five years, and I promise that when the world awakes to diamonds, rubies and emeralds, the Merlenes will be in the right place to control everything. The Merlenes' jewels will be *TOP OF THE LINE.*"

Charles looked at him and smiled.

"You are a genius, Gaspier, simply marvelous. What do you think about having dinner together?"

"Excellent idea."

That night, they dined in Manhattan in a French restaurant. They had soup, and savored the rich *crepes*, and salmon *quiche*. They were very happy. Life seemed perfect.

"Do you know something, Gaspier? I would never have been this successful without you."

"No, Charles, that is not so. On the contrary, I could not have done much without such a distinguished and talented jeweler as you."

Charles raised his glass.

"Maybe... To our success. Cheers!"

"Cheers!"

They drank the wine as they laughed while enjoying that small, and yet, significant celebration. But suddenly, Charles became serious. His face changed completely.

Something wrong, Charles?"

"Yes."

"What?"

"Juan Carlos Catarel."

"There will be no problems with him," explained Gaspier. "He will agree with everything we have planned. I have to inform him that this will cost a fortune, but I will do it at the appropriate time. He will understand that in the future the profits will be threefold."

"No. It's not about that."

"It isn't?" Gaspier asked quite surprised. And after studying Charles carefully for a few seconds, he added, "Oh, I think I know what it is. It's about his marrying Isabella, isn't it?"

"I want him out, Gaspier. Out of my life and out of her life as well."

"May I ask how?"

"I don't know. You should be able to figure out how. Now, I see things from a logical point of view and I accept them with an honest understanding. Five years ago you told me that he had all the cards in his hands, but that didn't mean he would be the winner. If he marries her, Gaspier, he will be the winner, not I. You are on my side, aren't you? Once you made *me* change my mind. Why don't you make *him* change his now?"

"Juan Carlos is not like any other man who can be easily gotten rid of."

"I know. You also told me that five years ago."

"Wow...you have a good memory."

"No, I keep track of my interests."

They were silent for a moment. Charles savored the wine just waiting to see what Gaspier would say next, and Gaspier remained quiet thinking.

"Charles, tell me the best part. Tell me what you have in mind that you have not told me yet."

"Me? Nothing. That is your job."

After dinner they went their separate ways. Charles walked home expecting that Gaspier would find a solution for this problem. He loved difficult tasks and thrived on the challenge.

* * * *

Gaspier was now forty-four years old, average height, and had a large forehead typical of an intelligent person. He had salient features, a sad look, and a modest smile. Also, he possessed a pleasant voice and knew how to express himself well. Surprisingly he had never married, never loved anyone, and had never ceased being a thinker. Another side of him was that he was creative, alert, and skillful when doing his job. Ferbonini had become untouchable because he had done the right things and prevented the wrong ones from surfacing. He was the knock-knock down on the street, knocking daily without tiring and without making mistakes.

The five years he had spent working with Charles were the happiest years of his life. It became much more interesting to idealize and build one man's empire than to be merely resolving the day-to-day problems of a man like Ferbonini. With Charles, everything was exciting. This knock-knock on the street not only placed Charles in the right position but also built the foundation for a remarkable future.

Before he went to bed that evening, he thought about what Charles wanted—*If I could find a discreet way to get rid of Juan Carlos, it would be like turning over a new leaf—*

"Indeed, a difficult task; however, not impossible."

* * * *

February was soon approaching as well as Isabella's wedding.

Juan Carlos had become the happiest man in the world when she said she would marry him.

"Darling, this is wonderful! What kind of wedding ring would you like?" Juan Carlos asked quickly, thinking that this was important to keep her from changing her mind.

"Oh, all diamonds. Can you ask Charles to make a special one for me?"

Innocently, Juan Carlos responded, "Of course. Who better than he?"

Isabella loved Charles so much that she was willing to marry Juan Carlos just for the sake of having a piece of jewelry made by Charles' hands. She knew that Charles would never marry her, for he couldn't forget her past. He would probably love her until his dying day, without ever forgiving her. And perhaps he would never say "*Je t'aime*" again. But in the ring that she would wear on her finger, in the carats and cuts of those small diamonds, there would be the echoes of the "*Je t'aime*" he had once said.

As the month of December advanced, Juan Carlos became more and more involved in the wedding preparations. Marrying Isabella meant more to him than anyone could imagine. He had never desired any woman before with the same intensity he felt for her. The mere thought of losing her would have driven him insane. He once had admitted, "I would have the courage to kill her if this were to happen and then I would also kill myself, because without her at my side, I would be a miserable empty shell of a man." In his mind she belonged to him and no one else.

New York to Chicago then from Chicago back to New York. This became Juan Carlos' constant itinerary. Now, for example, he was in New York. He had just arrived and Gaspier made sure that they would meet as they had many matters to discuss and papers to sign in reference to the patent of the jewelry designs. Catarel had to be informed that his name would appear on all the documentation regarding the patent; however, Merlenes once again, would be the name exposed to the market. Juan Carlos never heard about the amount they had to spend for this transaction as well as Gaspier's idea to negotiate with South Africa.

They met in the afternoon in a cafe not far from the jewelry store and in less than twenty minutes, Gaspier had brought him up-to-date regarding the plans. They made an appointment to meet the following day with Charles and their attorney. Gaspier assured him that after this step, when it came to the jewelry business, they would be TOP OF THE LINE.

Satisfied with everything, Juan Carlos said, "I believe you. You and Charles are doing very well. I don't have any complaints and am happy with the partnership. It turned out to be an excellent investment. Isabella was right about this business."

"Yes, she has a good nose for business, doesn't she?" Gaspier agreed.

"Clever in every way," added Juan Carlos.

"Speaking of her, how are the wedding preparations coming along?" Gaspier asked.

"Oh, very well. I hope to see both you and Charles in Chicago. Isabella is very special to me. You know that. This will be the most memorable day for me and I would like you both to be there."

"No problem. You can count on it."

They sat in silence enjoying the coffee and cake that had been served. Juan Carlos loved chocolate cake. He never came to New York without visiting this cafe and having its famous delicious specialty. He poured more coffee for himself and Gaspier. And as he was serving the coffee, Gaspier laughed about something that had suddenly come to his mind.

"What?" Juan Carlos asked.

"Oh, nothing. Just remembering some of my father's customers... How old are you, Juan Carlos?"

"Fifty-one."

"You are still young and you look healthy. But you know something? You drink and smoke too much. Maybe you should stop before it is too late."

"You think so?"

"Yes, I do."

Calmly, Gaspier returned his attention to his coffee. He did not explain about his father's customers and it appeared that he had no intention of doing so. But Juan Carlos became somewhat curious.

"So tell me. What happened with your father's customers?"

"Nothing really important."

"Please, you piqued my curiosity."

"All right. They are the stupid things that men do to themselves. Many of my father's customers were like you. They drank and smoked too much. In their later years, they grew afraid of becoming impotent. My father was an apothecary and spent his entire life curing people of their ailments. People would come to my father for anything that scared them. He used to prepare some special applications for those who were suddenly stricken with impotence. What he did was extract blood from their vein and mixed it with a few drops of milk from the skin of a green papaya. Then he injected the mixture back into the vein once again. He would repeat the applications three times. Can you believe that?"

"Yes," Juan Carlos said, "Men truly do strange things, don't they? I like your story." And jokingly he added, "If I need these *applications* some day, shall I call you?"

Giving him a confident smile Gaspier answered, "Any time, Juan Carlos, any time."

In good spirits Juan Carlos said good-bye to Gaspier. When he left he was pleased with Gaspier's plans, trusting him completely. Gaspier had given him good reason to be trusted through the years and he sensed that this would never change. He walked to Isabella's apartment without a care in the world. He never imagined that those *applications* would become his wedding gift.

By the time the last week of January arrived, Isabella began to feel nervous because of all the things that she still had to resolve before leaving for Chicago. She had lived in New York since she was nine and after spending thirty-four years of her existence in that city, it seemed almost impossible to just leave. It seemed complicated and painful to say good-bye to her beloved city. Not only did she have to pack up the material things, but her memories as well—she would not leave without her memories. They couldn't stay behind as if they never belonged to her life.

Leaving New York to start a new life as Mrs. Juan Carlos Catarel represented ending one long chapter of her life and then starting a new one. She found it difficult to turn the last page. Before she could do that, however, she would have to have a good cry for the moments that would never be forgotten, for what had been sad, and for what she had loved. Also, she must cry for everything that she had never accomplished, and for what was to come. Behind those last pages lay all that she didn't know about her new life.

Suddenly, these ideas and all the activities related to her moving to another city drove her into a chilling agony, and a strange fear took over her spirit.

She accepted that Charles would never be a part of her life and that Anthony Charles had become the tie to him and Ana. The house that she wanted to buy for Charles and his son to live in was still for sale, but Charles insisted on staying at the apartment. He refused to understand that Anthony needed more space and avoided talking about the matter again.

The pain of leaving New York mixed with the doubts she had about her last minute decisions, sank her into a deep depression. She knew she had to leave New York and she wouldn't be able to see her nephew as often. She had forgotten why she decided to get married.

Unexpectedly, she felt so insecure about everything and grew so nervous about what to do to stop her crazy idea of getting married that she collapsed and began to cry.

As she was facing this difficult moment, Juan Carlos arrived from Chicago finding her in the midst of this crisis. Worried, he ran to her. "What is wrong? What happened?"

"Oh, I don't know," she replied. "Sometimes I think that we should not get married. It will ruin everything. I feel so much nostalgia for New York."

"Oh, no, Isabella! You cannot do this to me. I have already sent the invitations. You are very nervous. Let's talk about this later."

But later she refused to talk about it, and said, "I will think it over. I'll let you know my final decision."

That night was a terrible one for Juan Carlos as he could not relax and rest as he wished. Finding Isabella crying had worried him very much as he really wanted to see her happy—to be the happiest woman in Chicago. But now he was not sure if she would ever be happy. He just did not know what to do anymore. For some reason, he felt he worried about her more than he ought. This time it seemed just too much.

For many years he had dreamed about marrying her and thought that if this would happen one day, "that day" would be the greatest day of his life. Suddenly he became engaged in the enjoyment of that–great day and put his attention completely into the wedding preparations and felt so excited about his new life as a married man that he also ended up anxious.

Now seeing her suffering because of her own decisions scared him to death. He panicked, thinking that she would call everything off. Poor Juan Carlos! Life was quite strange. What had never happened–without warning–happened.

As a result of his excessive worrying, he failed to have an erection and could not make love to her that night.

Obviously, Isabella overcame her bad moment, deciding she must just be nervous. So she decided to continue with the plans. The good news calmed Juan Carlos down and consequently, all the activities fell into their normal course. Juan Carlos recovered quickly and felt confident once again, but grew quite concerned about himself. One night of impotence seemed too much to handle, and he experienced such fear after that night, that before leaving New York he called Gaspier for a private conversation.

He told Gaspier that he wanted to have the *applications* of which he had spoken.

"Can you do this for me, Gaspier?" he asked with such a serious expression on his face.

"Of course, Juan Carlos. It will be my pleasure."

"Tell me, what more do you know about it."

"Not much. Only what I already told you. That it prevents impotence."

"I mean how does this work, will it make me stronger?"

"Absolutely."

"And about this fruit? Do you think we can find it here in New York?"

"Don't worry about that Juan Carlos; I know where to get one."

"Can I count on it?"

"You certainly can."

"Thank you."

"You are welcome."

Standing up to leave Juan Carlos added, "Oh, one more thing, can you keep this confidential? I would be embarrassed if someone else knew of it."

"Not a word will escape my mouth."

Two days before the wedding celebration, Gaspier went to Chicago. On his way to the train station, he stopped to see Charles.

"I'm leaving for Chicago, Charles. Juan Carlos needs me there. I'll see you at the wedding."

"I can't believe that this is really happening."

"Never doubt your best man, Charles. Lesson number three."

With a sad smile on his lips, Charles commented, "I will keep that in mind."

* * * *

The wedding day of John Carlos Catarel and Isabella was also a special day for the people of Chicago. Those invited to the ceremony waited eagerly to meet this creature that had conquered Mr. Catarel. Some of them had heard that New York hadn't seen a woman more beautiful than her, and they knew that if she were to be Mrs. Catarel, she would be something more than just beautiful.

The ceremony and the reception were held at the same locale. It took place in the reception room of the best hotel he owned. As Isabella had wished, only two hundred people attended the wedding, all were her future husband's friends. She entered the room on the arm of Juan Carlos, dressed in soft pink—he wore a white tuxedo. All the guests instantly found them very charming.

After they were pronounced husband and wife, from the back of the room Charles said to himself, *now I really have lost her.*

Immediately the champagne was brought out for a toast. The headwaiter approached the couple to open the first bottle and when the sound of the cork hit the air, Juan Carlos clutched his chest in pain and fell to the floor. Everyone held his or her mouths open without understanding what was wrong, until Isabella screamed for help.

Two doctors among the guests immediately came forward. One of them checked for Juan Carlos' pulse while the other put his ear against his chest. Then they looked at each other in shock and pronounced, "He is dead!"

The guests panicked and a great murmur filled the room. Charles stepped closer to get a better look. Isabella was kneeling and crying over the lifeless body of Juan Carlos Catarel. No one seemed to know what to do.

Suspiciously, Charles looked around the room for Gaspier and saw that he was like everybody else standing among the guests. At first, he appeared to be as shocked as the others, but then Charles caught a knowing look in his eyes.

It was as if Gaspier was telling him, "Did you see? No gun. No blood."

19

THE VERY NEXT DAY, THE same wedding guests attended the burial of Juan Carlos Catarel. For the occasion Isabella wore black, and Charles thought she looked even more beautiful than she had in her wedding gown. Like him, no one could take his or her eyes off her.

In the cemetery standing next to Gaspier, Isabella watched the casket being lowered into the ground. In the midst of so much silence, she picked up some dirt and threw it into the hole just as she thought, *I hate cemeteries. Oh, I think I am going to faint....*

Her body slumped silently to the ground leaving everyone with their eyes wide open in surprise. Dr. Angelo Varela came immediately and took her from the cemetery. He treated her and made sure that she would stay in bed resting.

Though she shortly regained consciousness, she was ill for three weeks with a high fever. When she finally felt better and Dr. Varela allowed her to get out of bed to receive guests, Gaspier appeared in the company of a stranger.

"Good morning, Mrs. Catarel," said the stranger. "I'm Gabriel Solano, your late husband's attorney. I have come to request that you remain in Chicago for at least a few weeks. You see, you are

Mr. Catarel's sole heir, and we must discuss the details of his estate."

"Oh, saints of heaven!" she exclaimed. "We did get married, didn't we? Now, I'm Mrs. Catarel and a widow. Gaspier...please help me!" she said weakly.

Isabella let herself fall into a chair that was next to her. The new reality frightened her to death. She was now a widow and also a very rich woman. Juan Carlos owned hotels, nightclubs, and many other properties, including a bank. It was obvious she would not return to New York as soon as she had wanted.

She looked so sad as well as frustrated that Gaspier said in a comforting manner, "Hey, this is not the end of the world. The only thing Mr. Solano wants to know is what you wish to do with Juan Carlos' estate. That is all."

"Oh! I want to sell everything and return home. I miss New York."

Mr. Solano left a few minutes later, agreeing to return the next day to hear her final decision.

Soon after his departure, she looked at Gaspier and asked for his opinion. "Gaspier, what should I do?"

"Do what you said before. Sell everything and then invest the money in things that won't cause you headaches."

"And what do you think would *not* be a headache?"

With an intriguing smile, Gaspier responded, "Diamonds, my dear. Perhaps some mines in South Africa."

Quickly, the image of a daring man living an ordinary life, experiencing hardship, and with big dreams to accomplish came to her mind—Charles. *Yes, now I'm his partner.*

"Gaspier, I think that Africa is the best word I have heard since I left New York."

Even though she responded quickly to Mr. Solano, she and Gaspier had to remain in Chicago another month sorting out the details and signing the necessary documents in order to go ahead with the plans. They worked together tirelessly to accelerate this process. Finally, at the beginning of April, they were ready to return to New York.

She left behind in Chicago the image of herself created in the aftermath of Juan Carlos Catarel's death. He had died after marrying the only woman he truly loved. Everyone believed that his happiness was so great, that his heart could not bear it. Could an excess of joy really kill a man like Juan Carlos Catarel? Those who had attended the ceremony could certainly believe so. Even Charles, before looking at Gaspier had believed it. The real truth would remain forever between the dead and Gaspier—

That night when Juan Carlos had arrived at Isabella's apartment, he was worried about her and so afraid that she would call off the wedding that he couldn't make love to her. For the rest of the night he lay awake, restless and worried. Such a thing had never occurred before. And while he grew confused and scared, Gaspier's previous conversation about men and impotence came to his mind and quickly mixed with his thoughts.

The next day, he kept re-living the horrible experience of his impotence of the night before, and like a curse, he could not forget Gaspier's story about the "applications" his father used to give. Fearing that the problem would persist and seeking peace of mind, he had decided to ask for Gaspier's help. *Why not? Those apothecaries used to have many useful, interesting techniques. Papaya milk mixed with blood. People have always mixed things for good reasons, and no man in the world would get married simply to rest and sleep on a bed.*

Before returning to Chicago, he had made up his mind and feeling very enthusiastic about his decision, had a confidential talk with Gaspier and it was arranged. Two days before the wedding, Gaspier left for Chicago to do what had been requested.

Gaspier did it all in his own way. When he was young, he had seen his father extract blood from the veins of people and then inject it into their muscles to prevent acne, and he also had seen him rub papaya milk on meat to make it tender. By observation he learned that papaya milk was sticky and it formed thick little drops on the surface of the meat. From that he got the idea how to get rid of Juan Carlos. Papaya milk once in the veins would probably thicken the blood and stop the heart. He did not know for sure if it would work or if he would even have a chance to try his theory by performing the applications. However, he had decided that it couldn't hurt to throw the bait. *The fish bites when his day comes*. And ...it had happened.

No one was to know about it. Juan Carlos had wanted to keep it confidential and it would remain as he wished—

In April, when Isabella and Gaspier arrived in New York, Charles and Anthony came to the station to greet them. From there, they took the carriage which Charles had waiting for them.

During the ride, Isabella, occupied with Anthony, didn't notice the direction they traveled. When the carriage stopped and they stepped out, she was greatly surprised by what she saw. They were standing in front of the beautiful house she had wanted to buy.

"Why are we here?" she asked.

"This is now my home," said Charles. "And I would like for you to come and live in it with us."

"You bought this house?"

"Gaspier did it for me. You know how he is. He likes to take care of everything."

She stood quietly, wondering when Gaspier could have done it. Most of the time he had been with her in Chicago. *Had he known that Juan Carlos would die? No, of course not.*

Silently, Isabella climbed the steps to the front door, opened it, and went inside. Once there, she breathed in deeply. *Finally, Anthony will have a nice place to live.*

She stood in the living room for a while enjoying it. Already familiar with the layout, she knew that next to it was the dining room, then a study, the kitchen and a few guest rooms. The rest of the rooms were upstairs. The house had already been furnished and decorated quite tastefully.

"Isabella," said Charles. "This is François, our butler."

"Butler?"

"Yes. It was also Gaspier's idea."

"Pleased to meet you, *Madame*," François said in greeting.

"François? Is he French?"

"No," said Charles, "he is American, but of French descent."

Charles had decided that her room would be the one across from his.

"Aunt Isabella, would you like to know which one is your room?" Anthony asked excitedly as he held her hand.

"Of course, darling."

Led by Anthony, she went upstairs with him leaving Charles and Gaspier alone.

"Gaspier, I have decided to invite you to live here with us also," said Charles.

"Thank you," replied Gaspier. "If you are saying this just to be nice to me, then you're in trouble, because my answer is yes."

"No, Gaspier. I'm not in trouble. You are very welcome here. And before I forget, I have to ask you something. I've wanted to do so since the day of the wedding in Chicago and I have not had a chance. Were you responsible for what happened to Juan Carlos?"

"What you saw was what happened," said Gaspier. "I don't have to explain to you the technique I used when doing my job. And Juan Carlos wanted it to remain confidential."

"He knew that he would die?"

"Of course not. Not even I knew that."

"Then I don't understand."

"It is not for you to understand. You wanted him out and he is out."

"I didn't mean to kill him."

"I know. I didn't exactly plan this either. I was just doing an experiment with a fruit. Rule number four, Charles: When the job is done, there should be no more questions."

"All right, no more questions. Let's have a drink."

They went to the bar and Charles prepared them.

"To Africa, Charles!"

"To Africa!"

At dinner, they were all together again. They started to eat, when Isabella said, "Charles, I have not decided yet whether or not I will stay and live here. I like the idea, but I need to think it over calmly. Anyway, I certainly appreciate your offer."

"Why don't you think this over tomorrow?" he said. "Take all the time you need."

"Yes, I'll do that. I promise."

Looking deeply into her eyes, he spoke to the butler, "François, later when you prepare my bath, please place a small towel with my robe. I like to dry my hair with the small one."

While François responded, "Yes sir," Isabella smiled discreetly.

Fine, my darling, I will be there for you.

Book 2

The Earth is Shining

20

Brazil 1913

MINAS GERAIS WAS A LAND of honest and determined men, strong women and vast mineral resources. Its gold reached Portugal making the cities of Minas Gerais part of the country's history.

Belo Horizonte was a city where population had grown with unchecked speed, along with its rapid development of homes and stores. The sweat and tears of those who had worked on the construction of this city remained unforgotten. Their hardy resilience became a defiance of the human condition, and their strong characters displayed the determination and devotion needed to accomplish the tremendous task. Along with that, they steadfastly demonstrated to the rest of the country that their words weighed far more than their gold. Belo Horizonte soon rose as the capital of Minas Gerais. It grew with a distinguished and indestructible image of fortitude—a city with immutable style.

Mr. Felipe Castanheda, one of the most reputable attorneys in Belo Horizonte, had his office located on Afonso Pena Avenue. In his conference room was a large redwood table with ten chairs around it, eight of which were occupied.

Felipe Castanheda sat in the chair on the right side of the table, and next to him Antonio Faria, his assistant. Sergio Estrada, serving as an interpreter, occupied the seat next to a German merchant. On the other side of the table, four more merchants were seated as well: a Frenchman, an Englishman, a German-Jew, and an American. The meeting had been scheduled to begin at ten o'clock. It was now five minutes before ten, and the most important person had not yet arrived.

The anxiety of those present, under the circumstances, was normal, as they all had made the trip specifically for this meeting. The German man seemed to be the most impatient of them all. *Why hasn't she arrived, yet? Will she even come?*

The Englishman remarked, "Women! Always late!"

Worried, Mr. Castanheda glanced at his watch, feeling uncomfortable by her absence, as she was a very unpredictable young woman.

She did not believe in the good will of others and had ingrained in her mind a series of negative ideas about men. The first wound to scar her heart was caused by a man whom she should have loved, her father. As irony would have it, she had to spend most of her life dealing with men. The business that she inherited from her father did not give her any other choice. Making men wait on her could be either a premeditated incident or a deliberate accident. Entering a room full of men and feeling as if she towered over them all was an easy task for her. She did it so cleverly.

When the clock on the wall struck ten o'clock, all those in the conference room unconsciously glanced toward it. And while the German complained to himself that she was late for her appointment, the French man thought she was still on time.

Mr. Castanheda had spoken with her about this meeting the previous day. He had spent quite an enormous amount of time arranging it. In fact, she was the one who had come and asked him to find buyers for the diamond mine she planned to sell.

Logically, she would come to this meeting. But because Mr. Castanheda knew her better than the others, he also felt uneasy about her delay and thought to himself, *I hope she comes.*

When the clock struck fifteen minutes past ten, the English man sighed deeply and shook his head, silently disapproving her delay. At the same time, showing his frustration, Mr. Castanheda looked at Antonio Faria, his assistant, and felt he could guess his thoughts—*If she wishes, she can change her mind. She is the one who has the diamonds that everyone wants.*

That rich, strong-willed and liberated, beautiful young woman for whom these gentlemen eagerly waited, owned many acres of land in Minas Gerais; a vast city could be built over her property. Claros stood between Rio de Janeiro and Belo Horizonte. Four miles from her house lay a valley named Vale do Pical, where the Pical River began. Tons of cassiterite were extracted regularly from one of the banks of the river.

The operation she ran successfully, as a family tradition, was a horse-breeding business. Her family had made the horses from Claros famous around Minas Gerais. Going to Claros to buy a well-bred animal had been the wish and desire of many for more than a decade.

She was a direct descendant of a distinguished Portuguese lineage from which the men were of strong character and the women learned to stand up bravely. To the humble people who relied on her, she appeared as a goddess. To the men who negotiated with her, she became the princess of Claros. None of the great gentlemen who knew and negotiated with her had any idea of her wealth. Only a few people in Minas Gerais knew that she owned a diamond mine.

When the clock struck half past ten, the door opened and in she walked.

Mr. Castanheda and the others breathed a sigh of relief, and simultaneously stood up.

"*Bom dia,*" she said while walking toward the head of the table.

"Gentlemen, this is Miss Maria Catarina Casimiro," announced

Mr. Castanheda in English and right afterwards, the interpreter repeated his words in French and German. Those in the room bowed their heads politely and proceeded to sit down.

Antonio Faria approached her and helped her with her long coat. As soon as she sat down at the head of the table, Mr. Castanheda said, "Catarina, these men want to buy the diamond mine you are planning to sell. Each one has already made an initial bid. You can choose the best one, or consider *all* of them if you wish. They all agreed to make a better offer once they see the mine."

"*Muito bem*," she said. "Let's see them."

Antonio Faria passed five sealed envelopes to her, and calmly she opened the first one. It carried the name of Mr. Peter Marconi, the Frenchman. Catarina looked at his bid and found it very interesting. Before going on to the next envelope, she asked who Mr. Marconi was and he politely made a small signal with his finger to indicate his presence. Silently she studied him. She saw a man in his forties with a pleasant expression who appeared to be very cavalier.

The next envelope belonged to Mr. Johan Mayerhofer, the German. He was very tall, had large blue eyes and appeared to be in his late thirties. He also had made an excellent offer, which surpassed Mr. Marconi's.

Following Mr. Mayerhofer's envelope, Catarina opened the next one, which introduced Mr. James Fister's bid. Mr. Fister represented the Worshipful Company of Goldsmiths of London. He was in his late fifties with effortlessly scattered gray hair over his head and two light-colored eyes that still held a tireless look. He seemed to be very intelligent. His offer was the highest offer yet.

The envelope of Ivan Rosenblum, the German-Jewish man, did not contain any figures. He simply wrote that his offer would be whatever price she asked. He appeared to be the oldest man in the room, almost seventy years old. Catarina took an instant to observe him. *He surely wrote down something appealing,* she thought. Her price, without a doubt, would be the best offer.

Lastly, she moved on to the final envelope, which belonged to the American. She opened it calmly as she had done with the others. Suddenly her eyes opened wider in surprise. His bid was the least attractive of those she had received. Quietly, she glanced at him and saw the figure of a young man around twenty-six and quite handsome. His vivid eyes held a deliberate and piercing look that held her entranced for a few seconds. For some reason she felt perturbed, and instantly, against her will, all that was unknown about him intensely disturbed her. Quite confused, she moved her head and her eyes viewed the envelope once again, looking for his name. Anthony Charles Merlenes, representing the Merlenes Jewelry Industry of New York.

As she read his name, the others looked at her expectantly. The most important moment had arrived for them—the moment of her decision. They sat tense, like frightened rabbits staring at her, afraid of what they might hear. Individually they waited for the words that would indicate whether they would stay or leave.

Catarina wittingly spent three minutes pondering their offers with her eyes fixed firmly on an obscure spot in the room. If they had known her thoughts, they would have been surprised—*Merlenes... Anthony Charles Merlenes. He must be Charles' son.*

Despite everyone waiting impatiently to hear her decision, no one said a word. At this point, saying anything could be a terrible mistake. They all preferred to wait quietly for her announcement on who had made the best offer.

She came to the conclusion that Anthony was Charles' son, and silently closed his envelope. Self-assured, she looked at the men around the table once more, knowing they would all hate her for her decision. Setting aside the envelopes and rising from her chair, she said, "I have changed my mind. The mine is no longer for sale."

As the impact of her words sank in, Felipe Castanheda stared, with his eyes open wide in disbelief. *No, this can't be true. After all the work I have done? After all these men have traveled so far to be here?* Then, fighting to hide his disappointment, he instructed the interpreter to deliver the news to the others.

After her announcement, Catarina had no desire to stay and see their reactions.

Guiltlessly, she leaned towards Mr. Castanheda and carefully whispered something into his ear. She extended an invitation for the young American to visit Claros. Then holding her head high, she strolled to the corner of the room, grabbed her coat, and walked out.

In the aftermath of her departure, Peter Marconi, now relaxed, sarcastically commented in French, "She is like one of the Seven Wonders of the World, the Colossus of Rhodes. Very impressive."

John Mayerhofer spoke indignantly, "What does she think she has that allows her to do this to us?"

"Diamonds, my friend. She has diamonds," answered Sergio Estrada, in German.

21

JETULIO CASIMIRO'S PARENTS disembarked in Minas Gerais near the end of 1852. At that time the family consisted of three members—a husband, wife, and their four year old son, Pedro. They settled in a town named Claros. The people who lived in Minas Gerais said that the name Claros had been bestowed upon it in the 1700s by a Portuguese explorer, João Vasco. He had led an expedition of eleven Portuguese men and lived in the region for several years. The humble townspeople knew that Senhor Vasco had discovered a little light-colored stone in the Valley of the Seven Mountains, and because of this stone, Senhor Vasco named the region Claros. The Portuguese had, in fact, discovered diamonds, but in order to keep the treasures to themselves, they had told the townspeople they were merely a clear stone.

Claros was a sad place; a cold, harsh region, and its small houses were situated sporadically throughout the valley. In Cipreste Square, near the carriage route, sat a house that sold supplies such as candles, kerosene lamps, dry meat, eggs, and *aguardente*—a drink made from sugar cane. The house also kept a few rooms just for travelers to rent when they needed a decent place to sleep, and the Casimiro family chanced to stay in one of them while they looked for a home. Then, Senhor Benedito Mata, the owner of the store, sold Jetulio's father a small house he owned, located two miles from Cipreste Square.

The house Jetulio's father bought lay in the heart of Claros. Close by, there was a train station with a high platform and a ramp on each side. Alongside the station, visible above the columns, rested two large water tanks for when the trains stopped. Central do Brasil built and operated it. Eleven small houses rested along the dirt road that ran behind the train station, and beyond the tracks six more very run-down houses could be seen. They served to shelter the poorest of families who struggled to survive by farming the harsh land.

The Casimiro's three-room house was located on that side of the tracks. In the kitchen the family gathered to eat, drink, and bathe. The water was carried to the house in buckets, and the lights were small hand-held kerosene lamps. When the trains passed by, the house shook, and the air lingered with the echo made by the noise from the wheels and the steaming, hissing engines of the locomotives.

Jetulio was born in that house and when he had reached the age of seven, he loved to sit by the kitchen window watching the trains go by. This became his favorite entertainment. He liked to see the massive engines that billowed great clouds of smoke and pulled the rest of the cars. Sometimes he counted as many as one hundred. Carried in the cars were horses, cows, and sheep. Also, some cars were completely closed and gave no clues of their contents.

Jetulio and his brother knew how to write and count well because their parents had taught them. His mother had brought workbooks from Portugal and taught them their lessons. Upon his arrival in Claros, Jetulio's father hired a group of men to travel with him to buy cattle and trap wild horses. After traveling for months, his father and the band of men returned home, bringing with them many heads of cattle and beautiful wild horses to be broken and tamed. Meanwhile, every afternoon, Jetulio's mother gathered the neighboring children, sat them down at the small kitchen table, and taught them how to read and do math.

Mr. Casimiro, Jetulio's father, never lost any of his money in Claros. On the contrary, he successfully built a great life there. He had found the men of Claros to be humble, courageous, and above all, hard working. They also had wonderful abilities in dealing with animals and that helped them tremendously because they desperately needed reliable resources to support their families.

He employed all who sought work from him. In fact, he helped many of them raise their children with the milk and meat that came from his cattle. In return, he received respect, admiration, and loyalty from the people of Claros. Because of the character and honesty of the people, Jetulio's father established, in this small part of Minas Gerais, an enterprise that brought Claros to life.

Years later, across from the station where the three-room house once stood, the Casimiros built a large house. An extravagant and enormous kitchen with a three-meter wooden table and two heavy wooden benches on each side soon became everyone's favorite place. Family members, employees and friends met each other across this table on a daily basis.

Besides the kitchen, fourteen bedrooms and three living rooms, one next to the other, very well arranged, completed the vast extension of the residence. The employees who did not have families also lived there with the Casimiros and usually occupied the rooms in the back of the house.

Close to the house on the peak of a small mountain, the Casimiros built a chapel, and on Sunday afternoons, when the nearby priest did not come, the residents of Claros met there to pray the rosary together.

As the years passed, the Casimiro family became very well known. They acquired additional parcels of land and eventually much of the roads, mountains, and valleys belonged to them. Their name became known throughout Minas Gerais. Outsiders and young families came to Claros seeking employment because of what they heard about the Casimiro family.

At the age of fourteen, Jetulio started to travel with his father and the company of his men. On one of these trips something tragic occurred. His brother, Pedro became ill and died. He was buried next to the road on their way back to Claros. This unforgettable incident remained in Jetulio's memory. Pedro—his only brother. Suddenly, Pedro was gone.

Although difficult, Jetulio took his brother's place. He worked side by side with his father and learned as much as he could about their business. In fact, this turned out to be very valuable because he lost his parents at a very early age, before turning seventeen. They contracted the swamp fever, known also as Malaria, and the worse happened. Suddenly, Jetulio found himself alone and having difficulty dealing with the successive deaths of his loved ones. In three year's time, he had lost all of them. His father's death symbolized the last cars on a passing train. After that, nothing was left.

His loved ones had departed from his side, but a great fortune still remained. Jetulio inherited the vast lands of Claros. In spite of his young age, the people of the community respected him as they had respected his father, for he had a good heart. What the people could not understand was why he lived such a solitary life. The attractive and rich young man that he was, he could have had any of the many beautiful girls to choose from for his wife. However, he never gave it any thought.

Jetulio had two habits he loved more than anything—breeding horses and smoking cigars. He liked to sit alone on the veranda of his house, light a cigar, and sit for hours, gazing upon the emptiness, until a train passed by. The noise of the trains approaching the small train station cushioned the monotony of that place, so distant from other civilizations. If one day the noise of wheels and iron ceased, as well as the majestic whistles of the oncoming trains, Claros would have become a dreary place with the silence, fog, and cold consuming the warmth of the people who lived there, and they would soon perish of sadness inside their homes.

Sometimes, while sitting and smoking his cigars, Jetulio thought about Portugal, a place his mother had so often described to him. Remembering his mother's words, he imagined the happiness that existed on the streets of Lisbon. But Portugal held no special meaning for him. In Lisbon, he would just be another citizen, while in Claros he stood for more than that. Jetulio Casimiro knew he was a man without dreams but still a man of great importance throughout Minas Gerais. He intended to sit on the veranda every afternoon for many more years, watching the trains go by until the very last car of his life happened to pass.

Claros was all that was left.

A few days after his father's death, while sitting on his veranda, he saw a homeless black family, dressed in rags, with tangled hair and dirty faces, begging for food. The woman carried a child, while the man held the hand of a five year old girl, and following them was their sixteen year old boy.

Since Jetulio hated to see people go hungry, he got up and ordered Fulgencio, his servant, to fill the cans they carried with food, and to wrap some bread and dry meat for them to take for later.

As the food was being prepared, the family sat on the steps and waited. The older boy remained standing, looking at everything with interest. Sota, Jetulio's favorite dog, went to him. The boy bent down to pet her and Sota seemed to like him. When Fulgencio returned with the food and gave it to them, the husband and wife said, "May the Virgin Mary repay you double for your daily bread."

Jetulio, who had been observing the young man with the dog, approached them because the dog's behavior had aroused Jetulio's interest in the young man. Sota normally disliked blacks.

"Where are you going?" Jetulio asked the man who appeared to be the boys' father.

"To Serra Milagrosa," he replied.

"And where is that?"

"People say it is close to Ouro Preto. We don't know for sure. We ask for directions as we go."

"And what are you looking for over there?"

"People say that the Serra is miraculous, that we can lie down on the peak of the mountain and awaken in heaven."

Jetulio looked at them in disbelief. *This is absurd. Such a thing is untrue. Was this their way of putting an end to their miserable lives?*

Again he looked at the boy who continued petting the dog. *Could it be that he also believes the story of Serra Milagrosa?*

Without any further thought, Jetulio decided to offer the young man a chance. He spoke sincerely, "Why don't you leave the boy here with me? I'll give him a job, food, a home, and he can also learn a trade."

When the boy heard Jetulio, he left the dog and came closer to them. He nodded his head, showing his father that he wanted to stay. The black man silently looked at his wife. They nodded at each other. They seemed so unassuming that they did not need words to communicate. They agreed on letting the boy stay.

That day, Claros gained a new resident by the name Bihato. As soon as his family had turned and walked away, Fulgencio took him into the kitchen. Maria, the housemaid, prepared a bath for him and then brought him new clothes and a plate full of food.

After that, Bihato learned and helped with everything. He brushed the horses, cleaned the stables, applied oil to the saddles, helped Maria in the kitchen, carried water to the house, chopped wood, swept the floors, and in the afternoons, lit the kerosene lamps to light the house.

In exchange for his services, he slept on a clean bed, and in the mornings, drank hot coffee with corn bread. He also had lunch, an abundant dinner, clean clothes to wear, and a heavy winter coat. Surely he had found Serra Milagrosa. Claros became a paradise and Jetulio its saint. Bihato was overjoyed with his life.

22

SHORTLY AFTER BIHATO HAD arrived in Claros, Jetulio decided to stop traveling and dedicate more time to horse breeding. He had heard of a very good horse tamer that lived in a small village in a remote area of the valley called Rio Alto. According to others, this man could easily rope a wild horse, and in little time have it broken and tamed so completely that it seemed as if the horse had been under his care since birth.

Jetulio decided he needed someone as good as this man working for him. So, without thinking twice, he decided to go to Rio Alto to find him.

On a Sunday morning, Jetulio left for Rio Alto with Fulgencio. He rode ahead on a horse while Fulgencio followed driving a carriage, accompanied by Sota, the dog. They traveled on an overgrown and narrow path but recognized it as such because the growth had been flattened to the ground and some branches had been cut away by other travelers. Knowing there were wild monkeys in the forest that sometimes attacked and ate humans, Jetulio carried a rifle.

After two hours, they heard branches rustling among the trees.

The two men stopped and Jetulio held his rifle up attentively. Sota ran in the direction of the noise, barking furiously. When she returned, she carried a porcupine in her snout. She let it fall to the ground and lay down, crying in pain. Her snout was full of spines.

Jetulio and Fulgencio looked at her, and they both knew that she had to be put down, as it would be impossible to remove all the spines from her snout. There were too many and the wounds would become infected. Valiantly, Jetulio aimed the rifle and fired. Then with Fulgencio's help, dragged her body from the road and covered it with dry leaves and branches.

As soon as they finished, they continued their journey but suddenly Fulgencio said, "Senhor Jetulio, why don't we return home? Something bad already happened; we lost the dog. I see this as a sign that we shouldn't go on looking for this man."

"Fulgencio, I am not superstitious," said Jetulio. "The dog did not recognize the animal or the danger. These things happen."

"No. A porcupine is a bad omen. It means disgrace, pain, and blood. You may not believe in these omens, but they are true."

"Fulgencio, we must concentrate on our direction. Rio Alto is still far away."

"Yes, sir," answered Fulgencio quite frustrated.

They continued their journey in silence. Jetulio rode ahead, and Fulgencio followed in the carriage. Three hours later, they arrived in Rio Alto.

Rio Alto happened to sit in the middle of a jungle. It consisted of five *pau-a-pique* homes covered with palm fronds and a small river, nothing more. Jetulio looked around, shocked to see such dullness displayed before his eyes. The men, women, and children stood outside their little huts staring at them quietly. Jetulio and Fulgencio's arrival seemed to be a national event in that place, even the chickens came to see the spectacle.

Geraldo De Souza was the name of the man Jetulio was looking for. After Fulgencio climbed down the carriage, he asked out loud if Geraldo De Souza was there. Upon hearing his name,

Geraldo approached them.

"Are you Geraldo?" Jetulio asked.

"Yes, sir."

"I am Jetulio Casimiro of Claros," said Jetulio, "and I have been told you are a great horse tamer. I have come to meet you and offer you a job."

"Yes, sir."

Because Geraldo's hut looked so small and it appeared Jetulio would not be able to stand inside of it, they talked outside instead.

"I have decided to spend more time at home with my breeders," said Jetulio. "I need a man as knowledgeable as you to travel and oversee my men. You may name the pay for your work and bring your family with you. I guarantee they will have food and shelter."

Geraldo had never received a proposition like this. He experienced great happiness and gratitude that it came from Jetulio Casimiro, as he had heard only good things about him. Though he knew the answer, Geraldo excused himself and went into the house. He needed to be alone for a moment to organize his thoughts and get used to the idea that Jetulio Casimiro had offered him this position.

Once inside his house, Geraldo went directly to the kitchen. Mariana, his wife, was preparing fresh coffee from beans that grew around their hut, roasted in a round clay oven, and ground by hand. The mugs she served the coffee in were made from dried squash. She gave one to Geraldo and then picked up two for the visitors.

Mariana was a tall woman; in fact, taller than her husband. She had light brown eyes and long black hair that she wore in a thick braid. Quietly she approached the visitors and offered them coffee. After they accepted it, she returned to the hut.

She found Geraldo in the kitchen, standing in front of the stove with a pensive look on his face. She dared not to speak to him and stopped, waiting. Mariana understood that he wanted to remain alone. However, when he noticed her presence, he quickly drank the rest of the coffee and said, "Gather the children and a bundle of clothes because we leave now for Claros with the gentlemen waiting outside."

Mariana was the mother of two small boys, Tiago and Jose; the oldest was just two years old. That afternoon, they all climbed into the carriage with Fulgencio and left. Silently they disappeared into the forest leaving behind the men, women, and children of Rio Alto with bewildered looks.

In Claros, Geraldo along with his wife and children lived in the same house as Jetulio. In the kitchen were four doors. One of them led to the backyard, another to the pantry, and the third situated next to the pantry, led to a big and empty room which became Geraldo and Mariana's. The last door opened to a hallway and the entrance to the rest of the house. Off the hallway and next to the kitchen were two more bedrooms. Bihato already occupied one and the other became the children's room.

Upon Geraldo's arrival in Claros, he took over Jetulio's men. He began to travel with fifteen of them and sometimes they were gone from Claros for a month at a time. When he returned, he always brought new horses with him and at times bulls, raised in Bahia.

The horses that Geraldo selected for breeding stayed in the Pical Valley, a better site for them. Jetulio had chosen it as the breeding place for the horses because there were no trains passing by.

When the Portuguese man called João Vasco came with his expedition to the Pical Valley, they built a house. According to the local people, Senhor Vasco went back to Portugal leaving the other members of his expedition behind, but he never returned. The Portuguese who remained fell ill and died. A peasant from the surrounding area, merely as an act of charity, buried the remains of the last one. For some reason, he dropped dead on the veranda of the house. After that, no one ever entered that house again. The peasants always believed the owner of that land would one day return. But no, he never did.

After employing Geraldo and using his power and influence, Jetulio acquired this abandoned land with the intention of moving his horses there. As soon as he obtained it, he quickly fixed the old house by repairing the roof and extending the veranda.

When Geraldo was in Claros, he spent most of his days in the valley tending the newborn foals and taming the others. Usually he and Jetulio descended to the valley in the mornings and returned in the evening. At dinner they sat together at the enormous table in the kitchen and talked like old friends.

As usual Mariana cooked for them. Since her arrival in Claros, she had taken over the kitchen duties. She was a hard-working woman who loved to spend her days in front of the stove. As the daughter of an excellent homemaker and cook, she had learned how to make many of the pastries typical of her region. In the village where she grew up, her mother's pastries had been famous.

Geraldo met Mariana by chance. After traveling and tending a herd of cattle, he and his men had stopped in her village in search of a place to eat. Many travelers stopped at Mariana's house for a meal.

When Mariana emerged in front of Geraldo for the first time, he looked at her carefully, as he usually did when selecting the cows he purchased. He had never imagined he could be attracted to anyone as much as he was to her. After dinner, he drank his coffee, lit a cigarette and asked to speak with her father. Geraldo told him that he liked Mariana very much—enough to marry her.

Mariana was the fifth daughter in a family of nine girls. When Geraldo ended the conversation, her father told Geraldo that if he wished to marry her, it could be arranged for the very next day. He and the village priest had grown accustomed to celebrating a wedding just about every six months.

The next day, at a flower-adorned altar built outside the house, covered by a lace cloth, and with a rosary hanging on the wall, Geraldo married Mariana. After the wedding, she remained in her house while he stayed in the tent with the five men who were traveling with him. In the morning, they all left with the herd of cows. When they stopped for the night, they hunted for game, which Mariana then cooked for them. It was not until a month later that they slept together for the first time. This happened in the middle of a dark jungle of Rio Alto where Geraldo used to live.

Geraldo acquired something. Mariana modestly partook of his innocent intimacy. Surrounded by the savage silence of the jungle, on a wooden bed with a mattress made of corn leaves, they finally consummated their relationship. It was more a formality than a passionate union of joy and pleasure, and neither one of them completely undressed for it.

23

MARCH SHOWERS NORMALLY FELL sporadically, cleansing the air and moistening the earth. But something unusual happened in March 1871. For two weeks the rain did not cease day or night.

During this time little could be done outside. There was mud everywhere, and the smell of clay permeated everything. The residents of Claros remained trapped inside their houses unable to produce anything. They could only sleep, eat and wait for the rain to stop.

Jetulio went to the Pical Valley four times during the deluge. After the forth time, he decided to leave Fulgencio there to care for the animals and vowed not to return until the rain had stopped. The paths had become too muddy and slippery even for the animals.

During those weeks of rain, as usual, Jetulio sat on the veranda after dinner to smoke his cigar. A young man, only eighteen years old, he sat alone for long, melancholic hours, watching the rain fall. He did not have anything else to do or anyone with whom to talk because Geraldo was traveling with the troops and Fulgencio stayed in the Pical Valley with the horses. Bihato, Mariana, and the children were the only ones sharing the house with him.

Some nights when nine o'clock struck, Jetulio found himself still outside, alone, watching the rain and waiting for a train to pass, hoping that its noise would enable him to feel that there was still life in Claros, despite the rain.

As the weeks went by, and the rain persisted, Jetulio's sadness grew intensely and he felt a wild, suffocating anxiety in his heart. That was when he found he lacked the will to live. There wasn't anything worthwhile to think about. With no dreams and nothing to fight for, he resembled a lonely scarecrow and thought that if he continued like this, he would soon stop feeling his own soul.

One night, after the last train had passed, he went to the kitchen for some hot coffee. As he approached the stove, he saw the door to Mariana's room open, slightly. He quietly walked to the door and glanced inside. A washtub rested in the center of the room, and Mariana stood next to it completely naked, delicately unfastening her braids.

Jetulio stood there immersed in an immense sea of fresh fascination, selfishly watching her. It was impossible to stop. Slowly, his eyes shone brightly on her slender body, firm breasts and sensual gestures but Mariana was unaware of his presence. He watched in wonder as she curled her hair into a bun around the top of her head, then stepped into the washtub and sat down. With a clear view, Jetulio watched as she gathered water into her hands and softly let it stream down her body. Her gestures slowly stirred an unknown emotion in him and he found himself imagining how soft her skin would feel and how the warmth of her body could diminish the sadness he felt in his soul at that moment. Silently, he continued to watch until she finished bathing.

Thinking about what he had seen and felt, he returned to the veranda where he smoked another cigar, and another and another. The naked image of Mariana mischievously filled his thoughts.

Listening to the rain that fell softly from the sky, he willingly isolated his soul from its sadness and opened his desire.

The next morning, as she served his coffee, he impudently undressed her in his mind. And because Claros remained engulfed by the affects of the unusual March showers and kept itself lifeless, wet, and muddy, he spent the whole day thinking of her, dreaming of having her in his arms and feeling ecstasy as he let his mind play with this fantasy. Night fell once again, and after dinner he sat on the veranda, seeing the days and nights as eternal.

Around nine o'clock, tired of listening to the monotonous sound of the rain, he went back inside and sat down at the kitchen table with a cup of coffee. There were two plates on the table, one with cornbread and the other with white cheese. Distracted, he lifted the cloth that covered the food and cut a piece of cheese. With no interest in what he was doing, he bit the cheese and chewed. His eyes seemed to be lost and his soul full of sadness.

Bihato passed through the kitchen on his way to the pantry where he was still working. There was so much humidity that the sacks of food had to be moved daily from one place to another so they would not spoil. As Bihato entered the pantry, Mariana also came in to prepare water for her bath, and then she returned to her room with it.

Jetulio remained in the kitchen, imagining her as she bathed. From where he sat, he could hear the sounds the water made as she poured it over her body.

About that time the children concluded their activities and quietly went to bed. He, Bihato and Mariana were the only ones awake in the house—three, lonely beings with the entire night ahead of them. A night that seemed endless.

Because the plenitude of nothingness was so great and the absence of human warmth so overwhelming, Jetulio gave in to his desires, and suddenly appeared in Mariana's room. He stood in front of her entranced, inhaling the aroma of her delightful feminine scent.

When he entered the room, she had been drying herself, and

was startled by his sudden entrance.

Upon seeing him standing silently in front of her, she stood still holding the towel. To her, his action was beyond any explanation, but because he was the boss, she did not have the courage to utter a single word. Mariana felt that he should explain his bizarre behavior. She desperately needed to hear his words, and thought that he would utter them very soon.

Instead of saying anything, Jetulio came closer, sweetly held her face and kissed her. He embraced her firmly and prolonged their kiss until his entire body grew warm. Next, led by his own needs, he tenderly caressed her body with his lips. As he smoothly caressed her brown skin with his warm lips, his hands playfully tangled in her hair, and a passionate anxiety overcame them both. Lifting her in his arms, he placed her on the bed, undressed himself, and lay down next to her. Gently, he spread her legs and began to caress her most feminine parts. Mariana closed her eyes shivering with pleasure, allowing herself to enjoy this new sensation she had never experienced with so much passion. She had never been completely naked in her husband's arms, and Geraldo's hands had never touched the places Jetulio touched.

Later, satiated, they lay silently next to each other until the sound of the rain outside brought them back to reality. Then as he had entered the room, Jetulio dressed himself and left.

After that night, Jetulio continued his secret visits to Mariana. When Geraldo arrived home, Jetulio stayed away, but as soon as he left, Jetulio returned to her. They were consumed with a passion and need that was far greater than their fear of being caught. She would wait for him, naked after her bath, and gave herself to him, without asking any questions or demanding any promises.

In an innocent way, he started to enjoy her complicity and found himself completely possessed by the most singular desire he could ever imagine. Each night their being together turned into more than just sublime pleasure for them; it reconciled their feelings, needs and guilt. Through the dull hours of Claros, they found another reason to live.

Behind those enormous walls, they experienced all of the pleasures to be found in their bodies and did not worry about anything else. Bihato was left in the unenviable position of being a silent accomplice, the only member of the household who knew of Jetulio's clandestine visits to Mariana's room. He often saw Mariana take bath water to her room, and minutes later, Jetulio going in. He knew that this was not right. But he also knew that it wasn't his place to say anything. Jetulio was his savior, a good and charitable man, and the owner of everything in Claros. In addition to that, he felt that Mariana loved him. Bihato could see this clearly by looking at her.

During this time, Jetulio's business prospered tremendously. Geraldo was a very hard-working man and directed the activities with great interest, always cautiously selecting the horses to be bred, and as a tamer, he was unlike any other. Jetulio came to have the utmost confidence in him; Geraldo became the best employee he ever had.

Sometimes after a long trip they both sat at the kitchen table and talked until late in the night. Geraldo had the habit of narrating everything that happened on his excursions, always informing Jetulio of the business deals he had done, of the ones left pending, and with great pride, gave an account of each penny he spent. They drank cognac, smoked good cigars and had good, friendly conversations. As the years passed, the trust and friendship grew between them.

After coming to Claros, Geraldo and Mariana had one more child, a little girl. Geraldo watched his children grow up healthy, with clean clothes to wear, a roof over their heads, and able to read and write. In his mind, he had accomplished something very special and unique, and Jetulio Casimiro had helped him achieve it.

For two years Jetulio continued with his clandestine visits. Without fail, he visited Mariana's room each night while Geraldo was away. Even when a foal was to be born, and Geraldo was as close as the Pical Valley, Jetulio dared to go to her room.

One day, as December was approaching, Geraldo went on a short trip. He had to go to a small town not far from Claros to complete a business deal he had left pending. With him were Fulgencio and six other men. They had left Claros early in the morning after breakfast.

Late that night, just as Jetulio was leaving Mariana's room, Geraldo walked into the kitchen. The incident left them both staring at each other. Jetulio found no words to say for he couldn't believe his own eyes, and Geraldo, perplexed, stood silently looking at him. For an instant, Geraldo even felt embarrassed that he had arrived at that moment.

"Senhor Jetulio, what is happening here? Why are you coming out of my wife's room?"

Extremely displeased, Jetulio ran his hands through his hair and responded with his own question, "What are you doing here, Geraldo? Why are you back?"

"Because of Fulgencio. He is dead."

"What?"

"His body is outside. We decided to return because we were not far from here when it happened."

"How did it happen?"

"A snake bit him when we stopped to rest."

Jetulio and his men remained awake the entire night. All had admired Fulgencio and in addition to this, he had worked with the Casimiros for fifteen years.

Mariana came out of her room and made coffee. Bihato also rose to help. Meanwhile, Geraldo kept himself apart from everyone, and did not speak to Mariana at all. From a distance, Jetulio observed him as well as Mariana. She knew what had happened. From her room, she had heard what Geraldo asked Jetulio.

In the morning, they buried Fulgencio. After the burial, Geraldo mounted his horse and with no explanation of where he was going, urged his horse into a furious gallop and went to the

Pical Valley. There, he removed his shirt and went to a wild horse that was to be tamed. He placed the bit in the animal's mouth, took him to the center of the corral, and mounted him.

Jetulio, who had not lost track of any of Geraldo's movements, also got on his horse and followed him. He saw Geraldo with the wild horse and decided to stay near the back of the corral to watch him. Geraldo was very angry. Every time the animal threw him, he got up and mounted it again. The horse whined and jumped so many times it almost trampled him. After some time, Geraldo was scratched, bruised, and bleeding in so many places that Jetulio stepped in and grabbed the horse by the reigns, preventing Geraldo from mounting him again.

"What are you trying to do? Kill yourself?"

"That would be good, wouldn't it?" Geraldo responded.

"Geraldo, you are going to listen to me," said Jetulio. "In spite of the situation, I do have something to say. First, I did not want to harm you. To be honest, I don't know why this happened. Don't wait for an explanation because I don't have one. Do with me as your conscience dictates. Ruin my reputation if you want or kill me if you have the courage to do so. I deserve it. But, I will ask you for one thing, forgive your wife because she is not to blame. I started this. I went to *her*."

"How long has this been going on, Senhor Jetulio?"

"About two years, Geraldo."

"That long! You don't know the harm you have caused me. This woman and those children are all that I have in life. They are my wealth."

"I know, Geraldo," answered Jetulio feeling most wretched. "I did this to you and you are the person whom I admire most. I don't know what to say. I don't even have the courage to ask you to forgive me."

From that day on, Jetulio Casimiro lived in the Pical Valley. He had decided to stay away from Geraldo and his family. He found a cook for his house in the valley and spent all his time there. Though he still went to his other house next to the train tracks, he never slept there again.

Frequently during the day, Jetulio thought of Mariana and those nights in which they shared their passions. He remembered that he had never uttered a single word to her, as well as never heard a word from her. The need to speak had never mixed with their precious moments. What they felt for each other was stronger than words, and even though they were separated, these feelings would continue burning inside them.

To ease his pain, Jetulio habitually mounted his horse and galloped through the night along the rows of the train tracks. With his body bent over, whipping his horse without mercy, he galloped on until he felt as tired as his animal.

Jetulio's nightly passage became so common that no one even looked out the windows when they heard him pass. They already knew that this rider was none other than Jetulio Casimiro. However, they never knew he lost himself in this ritual while reconciling with his misery.

Geraldo often felt sorry for him, especially when he heard him ride past on his horse. Though he could never forgive him, he also knew that he would never meet another man as good as Jetulio. In time he forgave Mariana, and they remained in Claros working for Jetulio. Their children grew and everything seemed to return to normal.

Claros continued to be the same small town it had always been, cold and sad. Not even a hundred years of existence could destroy its melancholic aspect. Trains passed through endlessly, and rains fell often. Jetulio always ran his horse to diminish his unbreakable pain. No one, except Mariana, Geraldo and Bihato, could ever understand why he did this, or why he grew into such a loner.

Then after fifteen years of this, a miracle happened. In the chapel his father had built on the top of the mountain, Jetulio married. Nine months later, the cries of a newborn violently burst into the silence of the Pical Valley.

She was the heiress of Claros. Her name: Maria Catarina Casimiro.

24

IT WAS EARLY MAY WHEN Anthony stepped off the train in Claros, accompanied by Sergio Estrada, his interpreter. They waited until the train left the station before they walked down the ramp, crossed the tracks, and soon arrived at the Casimiros' house.

Out on the veranda, Catarina, dressed in her usual tight, white, riding pants, boots and jacket, waited for them. With a smile she greeted Anthony, "Good afternoon, Mr. Merlenes."

"Good afternoon, Miss Casimiro," he answered politely.

"How was your trip?" she asked.

"Fine. I am glad to be here. Thank you for the kind invitation."

"You are most welcome."

Catarina motioned for them to enter the house where they sat down in the living room. She graciously offered them a homemade fig liqueur. As she served the libation, she explained how she made it. After tasting the liqueur, Anthony smiled at her and said, "Delicious. The most delightful liqueur I have ever tasted. It's amazing that you made it from the leaves of a plant."

"That I did, Mr. Merlenes," she said proudly. "Here, in Claros, we often do things that people in New York don't usually do."

"I agree," he affirmed.

They remained silent for a few moments studying each other carefully.

"I was surprised when Mr. Estrada informed me that you speak English very well," commented Anthony. "I did not expect that."

"Nobody does because they don't expect to find a native of Minas Gerais speaking English in such a desolate place as this." Then smiling confidently, she asked, "Do you like surprises, Mr. Merlenes?"

"I love them," he said without hesitation.

"Then you will like my company...I'm very unpredictable."

"Oh, really?"

"I never lie," she said with a big grin.

That same afternoon, Catarina took him to see the stables located close to the house. As they walked side by side, she talked about herself and Claros. Anthony observed that her experience with running her own business helped her develop a sense of self-confidence that enhanced her presence. He was impressed by how knowledgeable she was. Soon, he realized she understood horses as well as his father did precious stones and he did not know enough about them to impress her.

As she confidently spoke, Anthony got the impression she had practical ways of obtaining what she wanted and she would always fight to protect what was hers. It surprised him that she had turned out to be more clever and perceptive than what he had expected. *She is quite an exotic woman...and very fascinating! I like being in Claros and close to her.*

Once horses were saddled for them, they rode to the Cipreste area where Catarina showed Anthony the boundaries of her property. On their way back, they approached the bank of the Pical River where cassiterite was being extracted. They dismounted from their horses and walked among the prospectors that were sifting through the dirt. Anthony knelt down and picked up a few pieces of the cassiterite. Silently, he examined them. He found it inconceivable that they came from the earth. He enjoyed this moment as much as a little boy with a new toy.

"Miss Casimiro, do you know what this is?" he asked.

"Please, call me Catarina. Only my employees call me Miss Casimiro. Yes, it's a mineral."

"This is composed of tin and oxygen. To be honest, it's exciting to see it being extracted from the earth."

Anthony remained crouched with the cassiterite in his hands as he watched the men sifting the soil. *A hard job,* he thought.

Catarina stood by his side quietly observing his youthful face with its prominent features. At the moment, his brown eyes held quite an intriguing hypnotizing look and an electric smile freely separated his thin lips. She found him very attractive. In fact, possibly the most seductive man she had ever met. *Quite an interesting gentleman.*

They mounted their horses again and left the prospecting area, continuing the trip along the river as Anthony, enchanted, gazed upon the beauty that surrounded them.

"Catarina, you still have not told me what motivated you to learn English."

"Oh, it was something from my childhood," she said. "I enjoyed talking to the gardener at the boarding school where I studied. He was a foreigner who spoke English and had a lot of patience in teaching me new words. Another reason was because of my father. I wanted to know things he did not, so that one day I could use it against him. A very silent war existed between my father and me.

"The warmth that flows between a father and daughter never existed between Jetulio and me. My mother died during my birth and apparently father could never forgive me for it. At the age of seven he placed me in a boarding school in Rio de Janeiro. After that, I visited Claros during the month of December when he only allowed me to stay for two weeks.

"During those fourteen days, I enjoyed the freedom I had dreamed about throughout the year. While here, I transformed myself into a happy child, forgetting the name Casimiro, the

Catholic school, and that I had a detestable father. Also during this time, I wore my favorite clothes, rode my horse alone through the valleys, walked barefoot in the rain puddles, took secret baths in the train station's water tank and crossed the Pical River on a tree trunk.

"Returning to boarding school meant a completely different lifestyle, one in which my father had no part. Actually, I found it very interesting. True, in school I lived like a prisoner, but I learned valuable lessons. I came to the realization that I could not learn what was in books while riding through the valleys of Claros and I needed to know things my father did not. Thus, learning became my safeguard against him.

"By the age of thirteen I had learned Latin, French and English. Around this time, a new gardener came to work for the school. When I realized he spoke English, I looked for him at recess time and would sit and talk with him. Finding I enjoyed conversing in another language, I decided to study English with much more dedication. Indeed, it became my favorite pastime.

"Every year when I returned from my two-week vacation, I would run to find the gardener and happily tell him all the things I had done while in Claros."

Touched by her story, Anthony asked, "What was this man like?"

"A very sweet person," she replied.

"Did you fall in love with him?"

"No, he was fifty-six years old," she said with a grin.

"Oh, I see. He was more like a father to you," Anthony commented.

"I never thought of it that way...but yes. Later, I brought him to Claros to work for me. This is where he died."

What she didn't tell Anthony was the rest of the story. When Catarina had still been at the boarding school, her father had died, killed by a bull that, according to him, had been his best friend. After his death, her father's lawyer had taken care of her inheritance and decided that Geraldo and his sons should be the administrators of the hacienda while she completed her education.

For two more years, Catarina remained at the school in Rio de Janeiro. When she finally returned to Claros, she felt as if she were a princess coming home to accept her throne. For the first time ever, she was proud to be a Casimiro. Suddenly her name gave her the privilege to gather the land, water, and sky, which surrounded her for hundreds of miles in all directions. She surely enjoyed her new life.

At that time her main ambition was to breed horses better than her father. With enormous determination and dedication she assumed her position as a horse breeder. Soon, she learned to negotiate fearlessly as she masterfully instilled her rules. Steadfastly she proved her ability. Her knowledge was so superior to that of all the men with whom she dealt with that she easily attained what she desired—their respect and willing cooperation.

Two months after she returned to Claros she traveled back to her school in Rio de Janeiro in search of the gardener at the boarding school. When she offered him a job and he accepted, she brought him back to Claros with her. Three years later, he accidentally discovered her mine.

25

CATARINA AND ANTHONY RODE for another twenty minutes until they arrived at the small wooden bridge that crossed over the river. The vastness of the Pical River in that area was approximately eighteen feet wide and at that time of year, the amount of water flowing between the two banks was about half the normal flow. About thirty feet from the bridge a huge, bark less smooth and uprooted eucalyptus tree lay fallen across the water.

Taking the bridge, they rode across the river. Upon reaching the other side, they again dismounted from their horses and tied their reins to a tree. They walked toward the eucalyptus tree and for a moment they stood silently contemplating the Pical River. The water traveled swiftly underneath the eucalyptus tree.

"Why this tree, Catarina? Don't tell me that before people needed it to cross from one side to the other."

"Correct, Anthony. For a long time people had to walk miles out of their way in order to get to the other side of the river. Then my father built this bridge. It was during my grandfather's era when some of his employees came up with this idea of using the eucalyptus tree."

"Why keep the tree now?"

"For some reason, the tree became very popular after the bridge had been built. There isn't much to do here in Claros, so the teenagers have taken to using it in a game—a game where they dare one another to prove their braveness. Through the years, during the summertime, the young people held competitions to see who could cross the river without falling into the water. Many people came and sat on both sides of the river to watch the event. Nowadays if you say that you are from Claros, you have to prove that at least once you did walk over this fallen tree."

Upon her saying that, Anthony decided to measure the extent of her brazenness and as the frenzied sound of the taunting water filled the air, he asked, "Are you from Claros, Catarina?"

She took an instant to study his face, for she had known that after her story he would ask her such a question. *Men are so predictable,* she thought.

"You can bet on it," she smiled.

"Really?"

"You have my word."

Displaying one of his biggest smiles, he moved his hands, solemnly indicating for her to lead the way.

She stepped back, sat on the ground, removed her boots and then returned to the base of the eucalyptus tree. Anthony, without any doubts that he wanted to witness her triumph, also prepared to watch. He approached the river, crossed his arms, and waited for the presentation.

At first Catarina spent a few moments enjoying Anthony's pretentiousness then straightened her body and steadily fixed her head. Next, using imperious gestures, she opened her arms in a flying position. As Anthony saw her do this, he decided to say something. He thought that showing some concern for her impending danger would be charming.

"Catarina, are you sure that you can do this?"

Without looking at him she answered, "Yes. I know how to

swim, Mr. Merlenes. Too late to be worried. I'm from Claros."

Anthony saw Catarina plant her bare feet carefully on the smooth eucalyptus tree. Looking ahead as if she would fly directly toward the misty horizon that rested peacefully behind the many mountains of Claros, Catarina skillfully began moving her feet. Like a ballerina, they held their positions in a graceful performance. She seemed so confident as she kept moving, that any spectator would have thought it was no challenge for her. His eyes followed her every step. *She is beyond expectation. I don't know how it would be doing business with her. Oh, gods of the world, help the Merlenes because we do want those diamonds.*

At the end of the eucalyptus tree, Catarina held herself on one foot, turned gracefully and began re-tracing her steps. One after another: right foot first, then left foot. She was walking toward Anthony. Every muscle in her face appeared frozen, almost lifeless in its concentration, as she was totally absorbed on the dangerous walk. Beautifully she moved, sustaining her arms in the free-flying position and her mind totally focused on the farthest point in the distant range of vision.

Anthony kept his arms crossed while he slowly moved a little bit closer to her destination. As she reached the end of the eucalyptus tree he extended his hand to hers and said, "An enjoyable performance, Catarina. I must admit, and also confess, that I had my doubts."

"I know. That is why I walked over the eucalyptus tree for you. It was to prove that I'm from Claros, and to show you something else."

"What?"

Walking away to get her boots she answered, "To show you it is the range of concepts already established in our minds that increases or decreases our courage. Sometimes a simple task like this one seems to be very difficult to carry out, but it's not. We establish the complexity of many things, Anthony. You saw what I did. It was easy."

"Whatever you say. You did prove to me that you are from

Claros, and I don't think what you just did can be called a simple task. Every time I remember what you just did, I will applaud your daring."

"Thank you. Now, come with me."

Immediately he added, "Of course."

He assumed that she would now be taking him to see the mine and as they crossed over the river on the bridge to the other side, he looked one more time at the water below them. It traveled swiftly.

"Who taught you how to do that, Catarina?" he curiously asked.

"One of my father's employees. His name is Bihato, and he has taken good care of me ever since I was a little girl. For many years he watched over me, and turned out to be like a father and mother to me. He never said no to me and many times, just to entertain me he crossed over the river on that tree. Delighted, I would clap my hands when he finished his performance and he would bow to receive my thanks. He promised to one day teach me to do that, and he did.

"When I was eleven, we started my lessons. First, he found a big log and put it on the grass. Every day during my vacation, he taught me to walk over it. I would go to bed without eating, so happy because I knew that what I was learning would irritate my father. It took three vacations for me to get ready. When I crossed the river for the first time, the excitement so overwhelmed me that I forgot everything else.

"Bihato is a good man. He taught me simple things and also how to respect my father."

Many times Anthony turned his head to look at her. After seeing her majestically flying over the river water, he paid more attention to her genuine beauty. Her black hair flowed loosely over her shoulders and was as stunning as her sparkling green eyes, which constantly held a shrewd, confident, and intense look. Adding to this allure, over her lips remained a visible state of softness mixed with an enticing smile which she could summon upon her face at a moment's notice. In Anthony's mind, she owned what men would call a ticklish combination.

"Catarina, I can see that the differences between you and your father made you very strong. It helped you prepare for whatever would come into your life."

"Perhaps. But besides the differences between us, I was born intelligent and my ideas never flourished in a scarcity of a great imagination. Meeting the opportunity to work toward my enlightenment only made me more secure. Through reading I learned that we need persistence in order to accomplish knowledge. I easily grew addicted to my lessons and began to learn things with an enormous appetite in every aspect of my life."

"Really?" said Anthony.

"Yes, I learned to understand the concept of patience. Rushing to meet the future means engaging in a dangerous journey for which we cannot only arrive at the wrong time, but also without enough erudition."

"You are really a young woman with a solid character. I have the impression that all your wishes were always close to some actions; and in a frantic fruition they helped you undo every step of the unpredictable course of your life."

"Indeed. A lovely way of thinking."

Instead of saying what breezed through his mind, Anthony looked around to enjoy the quiet afternoon. *A woman with pride. She doesn't dance for fun. Instead, music allows her to perform.*

He kept his thoughts to himself and Catarina was the center of them. She could be great company for any man on earth and also the most dangerous gift. None of her words were spoken without making sense. For the first time, Anthony was next to a beautiful young woman who was in full control of her abilities, and with so much richness of spirit. He was not quite sure of his usual charm any more. *She seems to hold the spirit that can meet the many paths life may offer— the conviction to select one—and the ability to tear herself apart for the many she would never know.*

"Do you ever experience fear, Catarina?" he asked to try her answer.

"Who hasn't? Of course, Anthony, it was when I discovered there was a lot to learn before I have a lot to say. That scared me more than death."

"How did you feel when you lost your father?"

"Indifferent. When alive, he never gave me anything that I would miss if he suddenly died. So his absence only brought to the surface what I already expected. Nothing scared me when he died."

"Of course, you did not waste your time. You had grown up prepared to take over when the time would come, and we all know that persistence forges good results."

"My father would have never empowered me to succeed him in the business because he never expected to see a girl at the head of the table. But you are right. I prepared myself."

"My father is one of my teachers," said Anthony. "He constantly advises me about everything. He thinks, for example, that we should only concern ourselves with those things we can control."

"He is a man of good will, isn't he?"

"Yes," replied Anthony. "We have a good relationship."

"Tell me...how is it?"

Urging his horse into a faster gallop, he called back, "Wonderful!"

Anthony left Catarina behind and approached the entrance of a narrow path that led deep into the woods. He guided his horse through it and looked up, fascinated with the size of the trees. The view and the chirping of the beautiful birds singing different tunes mesmerized him. In order to enjoy the sights, he walked his horse slowly for it was his first time in a forest. What he saw caused him to experience many new emotions. *How amazing life is! Here I am, a man born and reared in New York, suddenly finding myself among giant trees filled with different kinds of birds as they sing their songs.*

Quietly and slowly Catarina followed him, as she wanted him to enjoy the vibrant life all around them.

Anthony imagined this was the way to the diamond mine, and expected to see it soon. The moment carried much significance for him. *Historic afternoon for the Merlenes*, he thought. In his mind, the precious stones already belonged to his family and just lay somewhere, waiting to be seen by their new owner. *I want to always remember this. The first time I walked through this forest to see the diamonds that the whole world will soon know. My father will be very proud. Our destiny swiftly traced an incredible journey. These diamonds will cross from one America to the other.*

After walking for some time and allowing himself to sink in deep communion with his enchantment, he stopped his horse and turned to wait for Catarina. Her horse trotted slowly in his direction, as she had no intention of rushing the moment. When she reached his side, he looked at her quietly. The soft look in her eyes was simply irresistible.

Anthony held back from saying anything, for he wanted to hear something from her; but she remained silent, contemplating the birds on the branches of the trees.

"What do you call this, Catarina?" he broke the silence.

"What, the sound of many birds?"

"Yes."

"A serenade."

"I have never seen or heard anything like it."

"Of course not. You are a Broadway man."

"Oh? Anything against Broadway?" he said with serious look in his eyes.

"No. Contrary to what you may think, I dream of seeing it one day."

As he turned his head up to look at the birds he concluded, *I will probably invite her to come to New York.*

Excited to continue his journey to the mine Anthony said, "Please, Catarina, go first because you know the path better than I."

"This will lead us nowhere, Anthony. We need to go back before darkness catches us here."

"This leads us nowhere?" he asked surprised.

"Yes."

"I thought..."

"Anthony, don't be so anxious. Learn to give things their proper time. Enjoy expectations. Time is always with us."

"Women and their fancy way of thinking," he muttered.

"Are you annoyed?"

Keeping his true answer to himself he said, "We shall concentrate on our way out. It's getting late."

Catarina rode in front, and the only sounds they heard were from the birds as their songs mingled with the steps of their horses. To Anthony, places like this belonged only in the books he had read in school. Never had he thought that one day he would walk inside their pages. He felt like a man swinging back and forth from his childhood science class—trees, the age of trees, leaves, photosynthesis, birds, and forests.

When they left the forest, Anthony's horse once again trotted next to hers and he commented, "My father would love Claros."

"Why do you think he would?"

"He enjoys quiet places."

"Sometimes I love it too."

"Do you like it here?"

"No," she answered curtly.

"No? Your answer surprises me."

"I know it does. You are the first person who has heard me say that. However, I do enjoy being a part of Claros but long to live in another place. I have a fine taste for the arts and the theater. Any big city like New York would please me very much, I think."

"Really?"

"Yes," she replied. Then added, "Why are you so surprised?"

"I don't know," he answered honestly.

"Do not forget, Anthony, I received the best education money could ever buy. I have read about almost everything. For many years, and even today, I considered books as my dearest friends."

To see if she would say something about the diamond mine, he asked, "Did you ever read about gemstones?"

"You can bet I did."

"For example?" he prompted.

"Do you know that legend says the devil created colored gems? He saw how much people loved colored flowers, so he colored gems to gain power and control over mankind."

"I have learned from different sources, Catarina. Books spoke to me when school rounded out my days, but after that, I stopped reading them."

"That is probably because in New York you have many things to do. You have more places to go and girlfriends to take care of."

Silently he agreed with her.

"Do you have a boyfriend?" he asked.

She grinned at him and answered, "No. My ideal man still belongs in books."

"Do you believe in feelings like love?"

"Yes, I do," she readily said.

Anthony eyed her solemnly. Then he decided to fulfill his curiosity and said, "Since you are a fine woman, just give me an idea of what you know about love."

"Why? Did I give you the impression that I have no heart?"

"Definitely not, but you are so full of surprises that I cannot tell for certain."

She laughed joyously and Anthony enjoyed the absence of words and for a moment only his thoughts spoke to him.

"I think love is the most sublime feeling our hearts can hold," she finally said. "Yet, I haven't found the man who would know how to convey it to my heart. But I believe in it strongly. I like to play carefully with this matter for I'm not a lucky person, Anthony. The first man who should have taught me about feelings was my father, and he failed. Since I was raised without my father's affections, emptiness filled my heart. I learned the meaning of life by reading books—not by exchanging feelings. Thus I allowed my life to crush hastily into the hours and permitted the days to guide every event swiftly. To survive, I attached my precious dreams to the most significant hope existence could find. This helped me discern right from wrong and to persuade the curiosity which enticed my taste for knowledge."

"I should have imagined that," he commented.

"I don't want to give my most sublime feelings to a man who wants to be rich in the blink of an eye. My life, Anthony, is full of what people seek most—*money!* However, I'm not going to use it to buy what I missed most—*love.*"

"I can honestly say I am definitely going to learn much from you. You are indeed very sophisticated for your surroundings."

Genuine as stone, brilliant as diamonds.

26

UPON RETURNING TO THE TRAIN station, Anthony momentarily stopped in front of the tracks before Catarina motioned for him to turn left. They rode up a dusty road until they arrived at the entrance of a small chapel. In fact, it was the only chapel that had ever existed in Claros.

"This chapel was built a long time ago by my grandfather," she explained. "The old people say that twice every month a priest would come to celebrate mass. After the mass the priest would stay to eat with the Casimiro family. Events like that made for a momentous day for everyone. But then they stopped. "

"For what reason?"

"I don't know; maybe because of my father. As I remember hearing, he kept the tradition for some time, then instead of twice a month, he changed the priest's visits to once a month and then the visits stopped completely."

Quietly, Anthony walked to the edge of the chapel square and glanced from the train tracks to the Casimiro's house.

"Spectacular view," he commented.

"From here you can see the tracks going up and up, wrapping

themselves around the mountains like a serpent."

Just then, a train approached the station and they watched until it arrived and stopped.

"Look, there is a train at the station!" Catarina said. "Let's wait until it leaves so you can see how far we can watch it go."

They listened to the hissing of the locomotive and remained quiet as they looked at it. After a short time, they watched it leave the station and soon go all around the mountains, its smoke spreading in the air. From that distance, Anthony had the impression that the whole train was floating between the valleys.

"What a difficult job it must have been to build train tracks at that height," commented Anthony.

As soon as the train disappeared from view, they walked toward the small but cozy chapel. They found the door open. Anthony and Catarina entered and walked up to look at the altar. A beautiful crucifix hung on the front wall.

Anthony stopped in front of it and did what all Catholics would do when they enter the church. He made the sign of the cross on his forehead and on his chest. Then he said, "What a beautiful crucifix."

"It's pure, twenty-eight carat gold," she informed him.

"It's splendid."

"Yes. My grandfather bought the gold and had it commissioned."

"And nobody steals it?"

"Here, even the thieves believe in God, and this belongs to God. No one will touch it."

"In New York, this wouldn't survive thirty minutes inside a chapel or church. People there do believe in God, but also in gold."

Leaving the chapel, Anthony asked, "Why did you stop the services?"

"I didn't. We have it once a month. My employees deserve to see their children grow up with the opportunity to start a relationship with God. That way I help harvest their faith. Also, I believe that faith branches out like education. We are not born with it, we acquire it."

"That's true."

"I was seven years old when my father sent me to the Catholic boarding school," Catarina added. "We had three uniforms: One to use from Monday through Friday, another for the weekends, then the gala uniform we wore to church on Sundays. Every Sunday morning at 10 o'clock sharp, we entered the school's church to hear mass. Outsiders enjoyed coming to the school's church on Sunday morning just to see the students dressed in their beautiful gala uniforms. Our entrance was the school's most outstanding performance."

"So you must have a strong faith," Anthony stated.

"I define faith as a spiritual energy which is our lively portion. Each one of us carries that vigor in them. We should use it to fortify our intellectual aspirations."

"Catarina..."

Turning to look at him, she responded, "Yes?"

"You forget that I'm a product of a different society."

"Wrong. I didn't forget that at all."

Her lips ceased moving and his eyes locked on them. Anthony would have tasted her lips if she hadn't been Miss Casimiro.

"Perhaps I should say that my future is killing the time I could have to analyze my dreams and my faith," he said.

"Can I give you some advice, Anthony?"

"Sure."

"Take good care of your present. Learn today for tomorrow."

"I will try not to forget that," he said. "I like what I have heard, and I hate to face unfinished tasks, but I have to be honest with you. New York nightlife owns a huge part of my heart, so I only use half of my time to do my homework."

"You are still young and life brings surprises."

"Indeed."

Following a moment of silence, Anthony asked, "Has life already surprised you?"

"It certainly has. That is why New York City provided me a

gentleman for an afternoon ride."

Anthony smiled quietly, looking at the train station—thinking mostly about her diamonds and imagining the mine. *Is it true that she had one?* He wondered.

Since it was turning cold and dark outside, Anthony rode ahead as they hurried back to the house.

Soon after crossing the railroad tracks, they arrived in front of her house. Two of her employees came to take their horses back to the stable. Then, together, they climbed the stairs to the veranda.

Side by side they entered in the dining room and found Sergio Estrada reading a book by Eça de Queiroz, one of Catarina's favorite writers. She had a collection of his books on the shelves of the dining room.

As she removed her coat, she asked, "How was your afternoon, Sergio? How was the hammock?"

"Excellent. I never slept as wonderfully as I did this afternoon."

"And you will never know if the cause was the hammock or the fig liqueur," commented Anthony, "Am I correct?"

"Yes, Mr. Merlenes. I should say it was a combination of both."

Anthony also took off his long coat and left his slender, elegant figure exposed. Enjoying his masculine presence, Catarina glanced at him. In fact, if she had taken a moment to analyze her emotions, she probably would have discovered something interesting about those quiescent feelings hidden deep inside her heart. But no, she just let one of her best smiles easily spread across her face.

"Sergio," said Anthony, "I walked thirty feet inside a forest. I found it amazing."

"In this cold weather? You both must be insane." Sergio commented.

"No. It was a remarkable experience."

Moving closer to Catarina, Sergio asked, rather snidely, "How did you know he would enjoy that?

"It happens. He had never owned a forest before," she replied.

"And does he own one now?"

"I never answer questions to please people, Sergio, and you know it," she replied. "But, I am sure he enjoyed the experience."

"Catarina is a woman with many endowments, in spite of having her own trees and birds," commented Anthony.

"Sure, sure," replied Sergio with a suspicious look. Then he added, "Are you sure you are the same man that came from New York City?"

"I really am," Anthony assured him.

As they enjoyed a moment of laughter, Catarina turned toward them and said, "Make yourselves at home. I will go and have your bath water prepared because it is too cold at night to leave it for later."

Immediately after she left the room, Sergio commented as he poured some brandy for Anthony, "I see you two are getting along very well."

"She is very intelligent," Anthony replied.

"Clever, Mr. Merlenes. She likes to catch the birds while they are in flight because she knows that otherwise no one would call it hunting. Do not stray, however. Stop contemplating forests and birds. Remember, your journey here is to catch diamonds," Sergio reminded him.

"I know. We just had a good time getting to know each other."

"I hope you are thinking straight, Mr. Merlenes, because I have no explanation to justify how you both could tolerate being outside in this cold weather. And I think you will need more than—just having a good time—to grab those diamonds. Where did she take you, beside the forest? Did you go to the mine?"

"No. She did not even broach the subject. What do you make of that? Does she really have a diamond mine?" Anthony speculated.

"Yes, she has one," answered Sergio. "I have never seen it, but I know it exists. And I can assure you of this; you will not step foot into that mine unless she wants you to. Do you remember what she did at the meeting? That is the way she is—never asking for advice and she *always* gets her way. Use your head and knowledge to presume the best, but don't let your guard down. She is neither a bad person nor an angel."

"Thank you for your advice. I do appreciate it, Sergio. And let me tell you something–I can't waste my time. If I don't step foot in that mine tomorrow, I will leave."

"Do as you wish. However, if you want those diamonds, you will have to be patient. And another piece of advice, do not make her angry."

27

SINCE CATARINA HAD MOVED into the Casimiro house in Claros, it had undergone a tremendous transformation. She renovated the wooden floors, changed all the windows, added two bathrooms, and redecorated the entire interior to suit her personal tastes. She converted the game room into a formal dining room and furnished it with a large table that could easily seat twelve people. A huge rug, made from white and tan pieces of cowhide that had been creatively stitched together, covered the center of the floor. Floor to ceiling bookshelves lined all the walls except one, which was occupied by a massive fireplace.

That particular evening, Catarina sat at the head of the table with Anthony and Sergio seated to the right and left of her as dinner was served. It had been prepared by Raimunda and served by Jacira. Although Mariana, Geraldo, and their children still lived in the house, Mariana no longer cooked the meals. She now managed the small household staff and twice a week made pastries, as had her mother. Geraldo now spent the entire day inside because he was blind, and their sons and grandsons worked there at the hacienda.

Catarina and her guests dined sumptuously that evening. They enjoying delicious pork ribs, beef, and chicken, along with white rice, red beans, and macaroni topped with tomato sauce and two kinds of green vegetables.

After dinner Sergio joined Geraldo's sons in another room to play cards while Catarina and Anthony remained in the dining room drinking coffee. When they had finished their coffee, she moved two chairs closer to the fireplace and invited Anthony to join her there.

"I think it is time that you tell me about the Merlenes family," she said, as she added wood to the fire.

"What would you like to know?" he asked.

"Tell me about your father. How did the Merlenes become involved in the industrial world?"

Anthony looked at her, not understanding why she had asked that question. *What does this have to do with my purchasing the mine?* Anthony asked himself.

"Fine, Catarina, I will tell you," he answered politely. "But remember, I am here for business reasons, not to tell stories about my family."

"I have not forgotten. My interest in knowing more about the Merlenes is greater than anything else precisely because of our impending business. I have not told you yet, but your offer was inferior to my lowest expectations."

"Really?" he replied. "You should have realized that the reason for that was because I had not seen what you were selling. I have no idea of its size. Would you offer a fortune for something you had not even seen?"

"No," she agreed.

"Ah, you see. Now, explain one thing if you will. If my offer was so inferior, why did you invite me here?"

"Curiosity," she said.

"About what? How high my final offer would be?"

"Perhaps."

Anthony could not think of a way to steer the conversation in the direction he wished, and ended up telling her all that he knew about Charles Merlenes, his father. Modestly he related to her the same story that had been embellished for his mother many years ago.

Calmly, Anthony said, "My father was born in a modest town in France, and after receiving a small inheritance, came to New York. While in New York, he met a woman, my mother, and married her. Soon after that, with an influential partner, he opened his first jewelry store in Manhattan."

"What was your mother's name?" Catarina asked.

"Ana," he answered. "She died while giving birth to me."

"What a coincidence! My mother also died while giving birth to me! My father never forgave me for that."

"Oh, how terrible for you."

"No. It's okay. But you have something I did not have—*luck*. Bless your good fortune, Anthony. I think luck is worth more than forgiveness."

Curiously he asked, "Why?"

"Because with luck one can find forgiveness, but forgiveness does not lead to luck."

Anthony sat quietly, looking at her with a wondering smile. *What is she leading up to?*

After her comparison of luck and forgiveness, she abruptly stood and said, "Obviously only the eyes of a lucky man could touch my diamonds. Tomorrow we shall see the mine. We will leave at nine in the morning. Good night, Anthony," she said, bringing the day to an end.

"Good night, Catarina," he responded happily.

The next morning they left for the Pical Valley to see the diamond mine. They rode on horses through the dense and low-lying fog. Anthony could not see more than ten feet beyond his horse's head. He thought that the clouds had descended from the heavens and they walked in the midst of them.

They traveled on a dirt trail until they stopped in front of a rocky and steep path that descended in a zigzag route down into the valley. From there, silently, they enjoyed the spectacular panoramic view which nature exposed to them.

The old house was located in the center of the valley and on one side of it were the stables. Toward the back, deep inside the property, almost at the foot of the mountain was an equally old brickyard. The Portuguese settlers had made the bricks for the house there, and later the Casiniros had used it to make bricks to build the stables.

Albino, the overseer, met them as they approached the house. He greeted them and Catarina handed him the reins of their horses and told him their intentions.

While Albino stayed busy taking care of the horses, Anthony followed her into the house, through the living room and dining room, and then into the kitchen. Filomena, Albino's wife stood by a table grinding coffee. Catarina approached her and repeated what she had told Albino—their intention to descend into the mine.

It was important to inform Filomena of her plans because inside the kitchen pantry was the entrance to the mine. And whenever Catarina went down into the mine, Filomena kept the door closed so no one could enter the pantry.

Albino arrived a moment later and handed her a lit kerosene lantern. Then with Anthony close behind, she walked into the pantry and silently closed the door.

Attentively he watched as she went to a corner of the room and skillfully pulled up the old cowhide floor mat and exposed a trap door cut into the floor. She lifted it up and a wooden ladder leading down into its depths was revealed. Carefully they descended into an oval-shaped underground chamber with a floor composed of densely compressed earth, and walls reinforced with lumber. On the far side stood a sturdy door with an iron padlock. As she stood in front of it, Catarina removed a large black key from her pocket and unlocked it.

When she opened the door, Anthony was almost overpowered

by the strong, putrid smell escaping from the opening. "I'll go first since I am carrying the lantern," Catarina said. "You must remember to breathe slowly and shallowly. At first it will be difficult and you will feel as if you aren't getting enough air. A person can die from breathing too much mold and mildew in the air down here."

As soon as Anthony entered the passageway, he began to feel uncomfortable. The stinking humidity felt as if it would suffocate him. It was almost unbearable.

They followed a footpath cut alongside a steep bank leading to another set of wooden stairs that went down five steps before the path continued, taking them deeper into the bowels of the earth. After walking approximately three meters, they reached the opening to a narrow tunnel where they could barely stand upright. Its walls brushed their sides as they made their way through it. Anthony felt short of breath and slightly light-headed. But before he could say anything to Catarina, they came to the end and emerged into a small man-made cavern. As they came to a halt, Catarina raised the lantern so Anthony could have a better view. He looked around and saw shovels, hoes, and picks scattered over mounds of loose dirt. Several wooden containers of various sizes sat on the floor, filled until almost overflowing. Amazed, Anthony went closer, and bent to look at their contents.

"Diamonds! Oh, there are thousands of them!" he exclaimed.

"*Claros* is what the Portuguese called them, Anthony."

Silently he picked up a small stone and held it up to the light. "Beautiful...and genuine! How long have these been here?"

"For more than a century," she replied.

They continued deeper into the mine until they reached another large and more open passageway. This one had more curves and ended in the deepest and least explored part of the mine. Just before they got to this point, they turned to another opening to the left, and Catarina signaled for him to follow her. They walked about four meters and stopped in front of a towering stone wall.

Now, with a determined look she grasped the handle of the lantern tightly, and deftly started to climb up the wall. As she slowly moved upward, rock by rock, Anthony silently followed her. They arrived at the top in another cavern. There Anthony heard the rushing of water, which was the source of the Pical River. He realized they had ascended once again to the level of the valley.

"This is my favorite place, Anthony," Catarina said. "My grotto under the mountain. In the summer, rays of sunlight enter from a crack between the rocks, and reflect off the walls onto the surface of the water, which shimmers with beautiful colors. It is truly indescribable. I love the mystical silence that exists in here."

Anthony was so awed by their surroundings that he did not even notice she had spoken. He would never have imagined a place like this could exist under a mountain. "Man could never create a place like this," he observed. "This is the creation of a god...an amazing creation."

Observing how the river water flowed rapidly over large, smooth rocks, Anthony walked over and began to cross, stepping from one exposed rock to another, delighted by his experience.

Lifting the lantern high into the air to facilitate his view, Catarina cautioned, "Be careful, Anthony, place your steps carefully, this place has many *panelas*."

"What are those?"

"Deep pools of standing water, hidden among the rocks. Anything that falls in them disappears."

Anthony looked down carefully and saw many possible *panelas* around him. "Thank you for the warning!" he exclaimed.

After walking around the grotto and examining it with great curiosity, he returned to where Catarina waited, and they initiated their descent back down to the mine. Anthony climbed down after her, enchanted by the inexplicable sensations that the mystical beauty of the grotto had inspired in him.

When they stopped once again in front of the wooden troughs full of diamonds, Anthony bent over them, and stayed still for a moment, contemplating the precious stones. He gathered some with his hand and examined them carefully—both the small and medium sized ones.

Catarina placed the lantern on the ground and stood quietly next to him. She didn't want to disturb him while he inspected the diamonds. After a few minutes he said, "Very well, Catarina, let's talk business. I want to know your price for the mine."

Breathing slowly she looked at the diamonds almost casually then said, "You heard me at the meeting, Anthony, the mine is not for sale any longer."

"What?"

"I changed my mind. People do that all the time, don't they?"

"Yes, but why then did you bring me here?"

"Oh...call this an extravagant wish."

"Extravagant wish?" he repeated, while experiencing a bitter sensation in his throat. "That is not an answer." He was quite angry, quite incredulous, and at the same time, curious. "Why so much mystery, Catarina? Show your cards if you want to play a game, so I know how to defend myself. I like to play fair."

"Hmm...brave man!"

"Yes, and let me tell you more. I came here to do business. Obviously, I have a difficult person to deal with–you. But, if you tell me just what you have in mind... You must certainly have thought it out, haven't you?"

After prudently analyzing the intent of his question, she explained, "God's creation that you see in front of you, Anthony, is also the treasure of the Casimiros. It is something of great value which few people have the privilege of possessing. I can never part with it. Once, I thought I could, but I can't."

"Wonderful!" said Anthony, clapping his hands wildly surprised. "Do you realize you are being extremely difficult? Your thoughts and actions seemed to run in separate directions and your final words only change the matter that pleases you most. However, Catarina, not this time. I have crossed a great part of the Atlantic to come here, and I demand a more logical explanation. The truth, now. Why are you showing me the mine if you don't intend to sell it?"

Carelessly she said, "Oh, I have my reasons. It could be because you were the most attractive man at the meeting...or perhaps, because you are *lucky*; while the others were just buyers."

Oh, I am going to hate you, young lady. I can feel it coming, Anthony fleetingly thought.

He remained silent for a few moments while his eyes remained attracted by the many diamonds resting carelessly in front of him.

Catarina observed him with a benevolent look. Then she deliberately put her pride aside and tried to explain. "I have no man to protect me or my diamonds from the greed of outsiders. The only things I really understand about diamonds are that they are precious stones, everyone wants them and that I must be very careful about whom I trust. The last man who saw these diamonds did not see them more than twice. I had to kill him."

Shocked by her casual statement, Anthony croaked, "You what?"

"I killed him," she repeated. "He managed to come here by himself, and no one, Anthony, *no one,* enters this mine without me!"

Wanting to doubt her words, he asked, "And how did you kill him and get away with it?"

"I shot him with a rifle. It was simple, just two shots."

"Here, inside the mine?"

"Yes."

"And did you bury him?"

"No, I threw his body into one of the *panelas*. Nature took care of the rest."

Carefully he studied her for a few moments before saying, "You want me to believe that you climbed that rock wall with a body and threw it into a *panela*? Impossible."

"I was not alone," she said. "And don't be too impressed by my actions, Anthony. You would do the same if you owned these diamonds."

He glanced at her, shaking his head with disapproval.

"Do you know something, Catarina? You are undoubtedly the strangest woman I have ever met."

"Sure...and also the only one with a diamond mine."

Laughing at her practical and presumptuous words, he slowly pushed the sides of his trench coat back, put his hands in his pockets and turned to look at the diamonds one last time. *Yes, the only one with so many diamonds,* he thought to himself.

Despite having just met her, Anthony suspected that in her clever mind she was secretly plotting something.

Standing beside the lantern, Catarina also contemplated the wooden troughs filled with diamonds. When Anthony looked at her in the flickering light, he saw the ruthless look in her large cat-like eyes, and became hypnotized by the feline appearance of her face. Her lustrous dark hair shimmered with every movement of her head. When she was serious, she displayed a subtleness that only hinted at the possibilities of her beauty. And when happy and smiling, she resembled an adorable, playful child.

"Catarina," said Anthony. "Why don't you tell me what you are planning in your mind? I want to know because I need what you have here. And perhaps, we can agree upon a mutually beneficial arrangement."

"We need each other, Anthony," she said very quickly.

"Right," he answered. "You don't know what to do with your *claros* and—"

"And the Merlenes do know," she finished the sentence for him. "Right?"

"Exactly. Finally we are talking business. Aren't we?" he asked.

"Apparently," she replied. Then, still facing the diamonds, she told him her plan. "Anthony, if you want to take these diamonds to New York, you will have to marry me."

"I...I...what?"

"Marry me," she repeated. "It is the only way that I would trust you. It does not have to be a real marriage. I only need a husband to help me protect the Casimiro's treasure."

"Damn you, lady!" exploded Anthony. "Damn you!"

"No, don't feel miserable. This is just a conversation. I know that my terms may cost more than any amount of money you could offer, but it is the most logical one for me. You asked for my price, and I gave it to you."

Stunned into silence by his frustration, he came to a conclusion. *There is nothing more I can do here in Claros— I must leave.*

"Catarina—"

"Wait," she said. "Come, let me show you something else we have to offer here in Claros. Pure *aguardente*. You must try some before you leave. It is from the Alambique João Soma Vasto, the most famous distillery in the area."

She went to the wooden barrels standing in a corner, took a small wooden bowl made from a squash plant, poured some *aguardente* into it, and handed it to Anthony.

After tasting it he exclaimed, "Good! What is it made from?"

"Sugarcane."

"Strong drink."

Before tasting it again, he lifted his bowl in a toast, "Cheers to you, Catarina, and to your diamonds. I must say, it was a pleasure meeting you. Catarina Casimiro...indeed, a very intelligent woman and I think that, as the owner of the mine, you have the right to ask anything you want."

"Thank you for easing my guilt. It seems you do understand how much these stones mean to me. I see them as my...treasure... something that a good god must have decided to save for me to find. My father bought this valley, and yet he never found the mine. Destiny brought it into my possession. The legacy my father never knew he was leaving for me. After finding it, this mine became an essential part of my existence. Therefore, I can never separate myself from it."

For a moment they looked at each other without speaking. Catarina reached down and picked up three very small diamonds then said, "I want to continue to excavate the mine and take the diamonds out of Claros. But, I have found that this will not be easy, because wherever they go, I wish to go as well. Perhaps they will be the cause of my misery, the stones of my birthright."

She came closer and showed him the three diamonds that she held in her hand.

"Look at these little stones. They are small but when cut and polished, they will shine with the same intensity as the larger ones. These diamonds, Anthony, are my *claros*."

She then quickly threw the small stones into her mouth and said, "They taste good. I have the courage to swallow them to prove to you how much they mean to me."

"No!" Anthony exclaimed, frightened by her actions. "Don't do that, please." He grabbed her and cupped his hand around her jaw to keep her from swallowing. "It could be very dangerous. You do not have to prove anything. I believe..."

Once again, he saw that feline, ruthless look in her eyes. He thought she might be playing. "Oh, women's trickery!" he said as he gripped her jaw more tightly. His fingers pressed so hard that she couldn't speak. Her green eyes stared at him, silently begging him to release her. But Anthony didn't understand their plea. Humbly, he sank into the warm and seductive look they held, finding he did not want to stop gazing into them. Loosing all sensible thought, he leaned down and kissed her.

Anthony tasted the most unusual kiss he had ever experienced. He could feel the three tiny stones moving in her mouth—the sensation was exquisite. But the exquisiteness came from Catarina Casimiro, not the diamonds.

Abruptly, she pushed him away as she angrily said, "Don't you ever try to do that again! I am not like the women from New York or any other women you may know."

Silently he looked at her; the stones now in his mouth. Slowly he removed them, one by one, and held them in his hand as he answered her in his mind, *I know that. That is exactly what is now making everything appear so much more interesting.*

Aloud he said, "Very true, Catarina. You surpass them all. No other woman would have thought of such an unusual trick just to get a man to kiss her. Yet, coming from any other woman it would have seemed insane. You are extraordinary. If you don't mind, I would like to know what is going to be next?"

Displeased, she raised her hand and as she slapped him she said, "This is next, a mad thank you for the compliment. Don't think you have impressed me, Anthony. Yes, you are an attractive man, but it does not mean you qualify as my type. Rid yourself of the idea of a romance."

"Oh, I am so sorry! I forgot that. Now, where were we?" he asked sarcastically.

"Where we left off is you taking the train back to Belo Horizonte. Today, preferably."

"One moment. I have not spoken *my* final words yet."

"And I should wait for them?" she haughtily asked.

"Yes, you should. I made this trip to get the diamonds and I will not return without them."

"Oh?" she said her eyes widening in surprise.

"I accept your proposal. Let's get married. After all, business is business."

"Listen, Anthony. I am not playing games, so don't waste my time."

"Catarina, I want the diamonds and the mine. So do you. Yes, marriage is a mutually beneficial decision. It's a deal. You get to keep them shining for the Casimiros, and I will get to do the same for the Merlenes. What do you think? A happy ending, after all?"

Turning her cat-like-eyes on him, she gave him a most peculiar look as she said, "You mean... Are you sure?"

"Why? Aren't you?"

She gave a penetrating look as she said, "Of course, I am. But you must know one more thing. If we do this, nothing should be more important than—"

"Than the diamonds—I promise you that. Their brilliance will be first...always."

28

THREE DAYS AFTER MEETING, Anthony and Catarina were married in the chapel the Casimiro's had built on the mountainside. The only witnesses were Sergio Estrada, Mr. Castanheda, and Father Raul, who presided over the ceremony.

They all dined together that evening and a short time later, after Father Raul departed, Mr. Castanheda and Sergio decided they should also retire for the night, since they would be leaving early in the morning for Belo Horizonte.

Immediately after they left, Catarina stood up, looked at Anthony and said, "Good night, Anthony."

But, rather than return her farewell, Anthony said, "I don't think I will be able to sleep tonight. I'm still not used to the idea of being a married man."

"Don't make a big deal out of it, Anthony," she replied. "You will sleep."

"No—wait. I would like for you to stay a while longer. Please, I need company. Since this is the first time I have ever been part owner of a diamond mine, I want to celebrate the occasion. I want to go down into it, sit on the ground, and drink *aguardente* while looking at those beautiful diamonds."

"Good night, Anthony," she repeated not looking at him this time.

"Very well. You don't want to go with me? Then I'll go alone."

"I told you, Anthony, no one enters it without me. Have you forgotten that?"

"But, I'm not just *anyone*, Catarina. I'm your husband. Whether you like it or not, the mine now belongs to me as well."

Anthony had already drunk too much wine at dinner and because of it his actions turned impetuously out of control. Taking her by the hand, he pulled her to the veranda, and instructed her, "Call one of the men to prepare a horse."

"It's almost eight o'clock, Anthony," she said annoyed. Then hoping to change his mind she added, "The freezing temperatures down there at night could kill us."

"You don't need to come with me," he told her. "I married you and your *claros*, and I want to have a honeymoon with them. What's wrong with that?"

"Nothing," she answered. She disliked his look and his words even more. Abruptly, she pulled her hand away from him saying, "If this is how you want to keep our relationship, I think I will hate you."

Next, showing her displeasure, she called for horses to be brought out for both of them.

About an hour later they arrived at the Pical Valley. As they entered the mine, their senses were almost overcome by a combination of the silence, smells, and numbing coldness. The silence grew intense and somewhat morbid, the smell of mustiness and darkness appeared thicker than usual, and the earth around them seemed to have turned to ice.

Catarina followed Anthony this time as he held the lantern. Their teeth chattered from the cold, and their fingers soon felt numbed. They stopped in front of the barrel of *aguardente*, and Anthony served himself. He poured the clear liquor, then walked over to the troughs filled with diamonds to make a toast.

"To the Merlenes! I wish my father and Gaspier could be here to celebrate with me." He turned slowly toward Catarina, and added, "Consider yourself welcomed into the Merlenes family. Choosing me as your husband was a wise decision."

"You should know that I didn't marry you because I believe in you, Anthony. Your father is the one who will appreciate the true value and beauty of my diamonds."

"Whatever you say, *darling*," he added sarcastically. "You are not going to drink a toast with me?"

"No, I don't like *aguardente*."

Her answer elicited a smile from him. "Do you want to know something? Neither do I."

Immediately, Anthony startled her by throwing his *aguardente* up into the air. Then he reached into the pocket of his trench coat and removed a bottle. "I prefer cognac," he announced as he pulled the stopper out and handed it to her.

Catarina hesitated for an instant then took it from him because she knew it would make the intense coldness surrounding them bearable. After taking a few swallows, she returned it to him.

"I want to go to the grotto," he said as he took it from her.

"What? Whatever for?"

"To drink with the spirits. What if one of those spirits is the soul of my adorable wife's lover? Such a spirit would be perfect for a night like this. Wouldn't it?"

"Oh, you are so despicable. I see that I don't know you at all."

"Yes," he answered, "But don't rush yourself. We both have plenty of time for that in the future."

He walked toward the tunnel at the back of the mine, carrying the cognac with him, determined to go to the grotto. Catarina picked up the lantern and carefully followed him when he began climbing up the rock wall, drinking as he went.

Upon reaching the grotto, Anthony stopped and peered into the darkness. He couldn't see anything. The intensity of it seemed to magnify the murmur of the flowing water that echoed continuously. When Catarina reached him, the dim light of the lantern was barely bright enough to outline their silhouettes.

"Catarina, I like this place. The breath of the gods blows under these rocks. Man can commune with nature here."

She set the lantern on the rock and said, "I think it is time for you to stop drinking, Anthony. Don't forget that we have to get back down that wall to leave this place."

"But I'm having a good time. Don't ruin my night. I want to go to the other side to feel the darkness and see if there are spirits there."

"No. You should not even think of trying that. It's too dangerous. Remember the *panelas* and you are drunk."

Anthony paid no attention to her advice. He wanted to go to the other side and he would.

Walking over, he stepped on the first rock that led across the water. When Catarina saw he intended to make the attempt, she quickly grabbed his arms and pulled him back toward her. The unexpected incident caused Anthony to lose his balance and lean against her. The bottle of cognac fell from his hand crashing against the rocks, breaking noisily, and they fell together.

"Do you see what you did?" he said.

Lying entangled on the rocky ground, with the strong smell of alcohol surrounding them, she felt the weight of his body on top of hers. Roughly, Anthony started to kiss her as his hands fondled her breasts in a frantic way. Catarina closed her eyes in abandon. She never would have initiated something like this, but she would not stop it either. Suddenly, all that she desired at that moment was being there, in Anthony's arms. Serenely, she allowed him to undress her. They lay naked, on top of their clothes as if the coldness of the grotto, magically, had disappeared. That night, she welcomed and savored the pleasure of being a woman.

The next morning when Anthony opened his eyes, he found himself in a strange room, and immediately, he tried to get out of the bed. He sat up and his head felt as if it weighed more than all the rest of him. "Oh, my head!" he exclaimed, and fell back on the pillow once again.

He lay there thinking and trying to remember in detail what had happened in the grotto. "Oh, no! What did I do?"

With great effort, he rose from the bed and opened the window. He had slept in the Pical Valley. Quickly, he dressed and walked out of the room looking for one of the servants. He found Albino.

"*Bom dia, senhor,*" said Albino.

"*Bom dia,*" Anthony repeated.

Albino, speaking in Portuguese, signaled for Anthony to follow him, and showed him where he could wash up and find some coffee. After he freshened up and drank his coffee, Albino indicated that Anthony must return to Catarina's house next to the train station. Anthony did not understand a single word that Albino said but sensed that he was following orders.

Some time later, when he arrived at her house, Catarina came out and greeted him, "Good morning, Anthony."

"Good morning, Catarina," he responded meekly.

For a moment, he looked at her. *Oh, no! She will probably send me to hell.*

"Can we go inside and talk?" he asked.

"Of course."

They walked inside the house and went directly to the dining room. Before he said anything, he closed the door behind them.

"I would like to apologize for what happened last night, Catarina. I drank too much, and I had no right to do what I did."

She didn't say a word, only looked at him. Anthony seemed worried and embarrassed, and she loved it. That's when she decided to let him do all the talking.

"Why didn't you stop me? You stopped me from crossing the water."

She remained silent, observing him. *He is everything I've dreamed of.*

"Answer me, Catarina," he demanded, taking her by the arms

and shaking her. “Why didn’t you stop me?”

“Because I did not want to,” she said calmly.

“What?” he asked in disbelief. “I thought you would hate me for what I did.”

“I should, but I can’t. I like you too much.”

Her eyes furtively met his and Anthony sank once again into her intense and ruthless look. He found her lips more desirable than ever and leaning forward, gently kissed them. Next, he embraced her and whispered in her ear, “I’m beginning to enjoy this marriage after all.”

“Me too,” she whispered back.

29

FELIPE CASTANHEDA SPENT MANY weeks preparing the necessary documentation for Catarina and Anthony to submit so the Merlenes could begin operating in Brazil. For the first time the diamond mine was legally registered, and they obtained legal permission from the government of Minas Gerais to continue its exploration. Catarina's immense fortune was now under the name Merlenes Casimiro.

The horse breeding stock, which for years had been the Casimiros' most important business, expeditiously moved away to a new owner. Claros would no longer specialize in raising fine horses. Very soon, the Pical Valley would become the center of active excavation. The only horses would be those pulling wagons full of diamonds from the valley to the train station.

Anthony hired Sergio Estrada to be the administrator of this new company in Brazil. Sergio would remain in Claros overseeing the mine operations, and Anthony and Catarina would sail to New York with the first cargo of diamonds, the diamonds that had been excavated by the dying Portuguese settlers. The stone they had named *claros*.

Anthony and Catarina sailed from Brazil near the end of October. They arrived in New York during the second week of November and were immediately met by Gaspier, who was waiting for them at the port when they disembarked.

Catarina felt overjoyed. Being in New York exhilarated her spirit to the highest level of blissfulness, and experiencing that in the company of Anthony intensified the effect. She loved him as much as she loved her diamonds. For a woman like her, who had grown up in a Catholic school in Rio de Janeiro to then return to a desolate Claros, just breathing the air of New York released happiness beyond her expectations. It was the most momentous occasion of her entire life. She wished to enjoy this special time as she had never enjoyed any other.

When they arrived at the house, they met Charles and Isabella who appeared elegantly dressed to receive them. After greeting each other, Anthony introduced Catarina.

"Father and Aunt Isabella, this is my wife, Catarina. Catarina, this is my father and my Aunt Isabella."

They welcomed and hugged her, and discreetly, admired her exotic and unique beauty.

Charles kept himself silent for a moment observing her. He had never seen a woman so remarkably different. Instantly, Isabella classified her as a sensual type. Catarina had a perfect body, a beautiful face that fit a peculiar decisive look, and a cheerful smile. She was the type of woman who would be every man's dream.

Gaspier, also held back his words, impressed with her appearance. After carefully studying her black hair and deep green eyes, he concluded that the god who had created her must have been thinking of providing a mate for a tiger.

They all sat and conversed for a while. Then Isabella showed Catarina the room that had been prepared for them. While she dressed for dinner, Anthony remained downstairs to have a drink with his father and Gaspier.

"Tell me, why did you get married so suddenly?" Charles asked as soon as the drinks were served.

"Because diamonds spout their brightness in our destiny, father. And she came with them. This young woman, whom you just met, owns a diamond mine. It belongs to her alone. You have never seen so many diamonds in one place as I have. And you could never imagine the experiences I submitted to in these past few months. Any man who ever had the opportunity to possess such an incredible treasure would not be able to pass it up, nor ever rid himself of it, including myself. That's why I got married. I think that neither one of us could have ever afforded what those diamonds are worth."

"Do you love her, Anthony?" asked his father.

"I don't know. But I sense that I cannot live without her."

"I think you made a great decision, Anthony," commented Gaspier. "This will begin a new era for both families. Everything has a price. The important thing is being able to pay it. I am proud of what you have accomplished."

* * * *

That evening, before they sat down for dinner, Charles asked everyone to stand while he made a toast. From the head of the table, he raised his glass and said, "To the Casimiros and the Merlenes. And to everything else that shall come our way. May God bless us. Welcome to New York, Maria Catarina."

She thanked him and, as everyone proceeded to sit down, she spoke up unexpectedly saying, "I also have something to say. I want you to know that, even before meeting you, Mr. Merlenes, I already admired, respected, and trusted you."

"Catarina, please, call me Charles."

"Thank you," she said and continued. "The man who worked for me and who consequently discovered the mine, died two years ago. His last words were, 'Do not sell the mine, Catarina. Go to New York and find Charles Merlenes. He knows everything about diamonds. He might help you and you can trust him.' You knew this man, Charles. He was known as Saporo."

Her sudden revelation brought on a moment of silence, which only continued to grow. There was an expression of astonishment on everyone's face. Even Anthony hadn't known about that.

So, he followed my advice and left Colombia, Gaspier thought happily.

After dinner Anthony and Catarina sat and chatted with everyone until late that evening, enjoying the warmth of their family. Charles took advantage of a moment when he was alone with Anthony and Gaspier, as he prepared drinks for them, to ask Anthony the question of the century.

"She made you marry her, didn't she?"

"Women should not be clever, father," explained Anthony, thoughtfully. "Because besides being sure of what they want, they know how to get it. And, as we know, they are also indispensable. Catarina had something we wanted very much. That gave her the right to name her price. Gaspier taught me how to become a businessman. I simply could not let this slip through my fingers. The entire arrangement, in *every* aspect, is very attractive."

Reminding Anthony that he had yet to tell her about Brazil, Isabella called him over to sit with her. Quietly, Charles watched him walk toward her with a drink in his hand. "What is wrong with the men in this family, Gaspier?" he asked. "There is always someone else who decides who they should marry. Do you think that is normal?"

"No. But charming. Yes!"

* * * *

Catarina wanted her first night in New York to be perfect and unforgettable. She planned to spend it passionately in Anthony's arms, until morning brought it to an end. This was how she had imagined and hoped it would be.

The room, which had been carefully prepared for them, displayed extreme elegance, and Catarina simply loved its decorations. Isabella's feminine touch left its evidence throughout every square foot of it. The fine black furniture, contrasted with the expensive white drapes, which hung from the ceiling to the floor, and a beautiful green Persian carpet covered the floor. The bed was equally decorated with exquisite taste. In fact, the whole room pleased Catarina in every way.

Midnight passed before they all decided to retire. Anthony and Catarina went up to their room after Charles had excused himself for the night. As soon as they entered the room, Catarina began to undress. She gestured slowly, hoping to inspire Anthony to assist her. But no, instead, he took his coat off and angrily threw it onto one of the chairs.

"Why didn't you tell me that you knew Saporo?" he asked coldly.

"Why talk about him if you never met him? He left New York before you were even born."

"Right! But I knew about him. I had heard that he had killed my great-grandfather."

"Then I suppose you know that he also saved your father's life by killing Celino."

"Who was Celino? What are you talking about?"

"You see, I know more about the Ferboninis and Merlenes than you do. Saporo told me everything, Anthony. Don't forget that I practiced my English with him. Celino wanted to kill your father, and Saporo killed him before he could do that."

"Oh, Saporo was the gardener?"

"Yes, the school gardener."

"Now I understand," said Anthony. "And he also helped you dispose of the dead man's body in the grotto?"

"Yes."

"I can't believe that you met that man and knew so much about my family, yet never told me about it. Do you know what I think of all this? That you used me to get to my father because you never trusted me. Under no condition did you intend to put your diamonds in my hands! Right?"

"Anthony, at the time, we joined our interests in business together. Why should we have mixed family matters in with this?"

"I don't know, my darling. But if this was merely business, why did we end up sleeping together? What do you call this? Diamonds?"

"Oh please, stop before I start to think that you are the last man on the face of the earth whom I would wish to have for a husband."

"Too bad if you think that way, my darling, because I *am* your husband. And, like your diamonds, our marriage will shine forever in spite of the fact you don't trust me."

"Why do you have to spoil my first night in New York?"

"You started it," he replied brusquely, while grabbing his coat to leave.

"Anthony, if you close that door between us now, you might as well never open it again."

"Don't worry, Mrs. Merlenes, I will not stop being a gentleman."

Then, feeling a great sense of joy at her suffering, he quietly closed the door behind him, leaving her alone.

"Damn you, Catarina! Damn you!" he said in anguish as he walked away.

30

IN LESS THAN TWO WEEKS, Anthony returned to Brazil. Since walking away from Catarina that night, he had avoided her and kept himself busy with other matters. He felt she had betrayed him, and decided that the only way to handle this new development would be to treat their marriage as they had originally agreed upon—as a business arrangement.

Although he wished things to remain that way, nature quietly spoiled his plans. When he left New York, Catarina was already pregnant.

Catarina gave birth on July 16 at ten in the morning. And that afternoon, Charles arrived at the hospital to meet his grandson. He stood in front of the semi-closed door and knocked softly.

"Come in, Charles," she said from inside.

"Hello, Catarina! How are you?"

"I am fine."

"I heard that my grandson is a beautiful boy. Is it true?"

"What would you expect his mother to say? I brought to life the most beautiful child I have ever seen. I am bursting with pride."

Her nurse came in, and Catarina asked her to bring the baby. When Charles saw his grandson for the first time, memories of the circumstances of Anthony's birth emerged.

Charles had not experienced the joys of being a new father because of Ana's unexpected death. For many days after Anthony's birth, Charles could not bear to touch him. But now, looking at his grandson, he knew he would savor what he had once been denied.

This restored an abundance of new feelings in his heart, and he greatly enjoyed this great moment. The baby in his arms symbolized the beginning of a new generation, a union of the blood of the Casimiros and the Merlenes. Saporo, without knowing it, had caused the two families to unite, and Charles knew that one-day, their names would be recognized around the world.

"I sent Anthony a telegram," he told her.

"Yes, I know," replied Catarina. "Gaspier told me."

"The last letter he wrote me indicated that he would return in a few months. He wants us to buy our own ship for transporting the diamonds, as he believes this would be far more advantageous than paying for a freighter to do it. Gaspier has spent a great deal of time hunting for used ships, but so far, he hasn't found one in good enough condition for a fair price."

"How are things in Claros?" Catarina asked.

"Anthony said that in some ways, everything flows quite well; however, he needs more men to work the mine. He has been working almost twenty-four hours at a time without sleep just to keep everything running smoothly."

"But why? What about Sergio Estrada? Isn't he doing his job?"

"Yes. But according to Anthony, besides the exhausting job of supervising the workers, he must deal with everyday occurrences that demand his full attention and seem to consume his every moment.

"Also, we are encountering some problems in Rio de Janeiro. It takes too long to load our cargo onto a ship. And in addition to that, it appears difficult to find a ship that sails straight to North America. Most of them stop at other ports on the way."

"Do you also think that buying a ship is a good idea?" she asked.

"We already know this would be the best solution, but we should discuss the idea carefully when Anthony returns. He said he had prepared a report of the actual operating expenses so we can see it on paper and then we can review the whole situation in detail. We will make our final decision after that."

"So he will be here soon?" she asked.

"Yes, Catarina. Maybe in September or October. But I think, with the news that he is now the father of a son, it will be in September."

"Do you think he will feel happy about our son?"

"Of course. The word *father* never departs from a man's achievement. We all sooner or later desire it as much as we love prosperity. And he is no different."

"Anthony hates me, Charles. He thinks I used him to get to you."

"And, is this true?"

"Yes, the Merlenes' name provided the excuse to invite him to Claros. But afterwards, everything changed."

"Do you love him, Catarina?"

"Yes, I do."

"Then, don't worry. Love triumphs over all. Be patient. As men, we always fall at either extreme. When a woman means everything to us, she is the center of our attention. If we can hate her, this means we can still love her. Anthony is young, and he has a lot to learn. Give him time."

She remained silent going over his words, thinking, *he talks like lovers do*. Then to fulfill her curiosity, she asked an indiscreet question.

"Charles, did you love Ana?"

Wondering why she had asked such a question, he said, "Ana was someone very special in my life, Catarina. She loved me with all her heart and gave me a son. No other woman can ever take her place. Sometimes I think I was her destiny, but she was not to be mine. Nothing can refute this. I believe that God decides our happiness and the devil our miseries. People bear their happiness easily because it's painless. However, they need strength to face their miseries. She only met what blossomed blissfully."

"Perhaps you are right."

"I am, Catarina. Life taught me these things."

After a brief pause he added, "Now, I have to go. I hope to see you at home. When will the doctor allow you to leave?"

"In two days," she answered.

He leaned over and kissed her on the forehead. "Thank you for my fine grandson."

After Charles left, Catarina sat pondering his words: *God decides our happiness and the devil our miseries.* Then she whispered aloud, "Anthony, what is our misery, love or these diamonds?"

Two days later, after dressing for dinner, Charles walked downstairs to the bar. He was in the process of preparing himself a drink when Gaspier entered the room, extremely excited. It seemed that he had discovered a lost relic.

"Charles, you will not believe what I have to show you. No. I'd like to rephrase that. You have no idea what the gods have placed on our path."

But Charles paid very little attention to his words. He wanted to concentrate on the joy that strongly pierced all his heart's chambers. Catarina and his grandson had come home, and the pride he felt from being Charles Merlenes blasted out like a giant explosion. For the first time in his fifty-seven years of life, he let himself indulge in such a spontaneous pleasure. He felt like running, skipping, and singing around the house to express the joy he felt from becoming a grandfather.

In spite of being fifty-seven years old with gray hair, he still had a youthful appearance.

That evening, without even showing a small hint of curiosity about what Gaspier had to say, he handed him a drink and commented, "I have accomplished something else, Gaspier. I have a grandson. The evidence of a new generation!"

"Charles, I have something important to tell you. Something that will make you just as happy."

"I am already happy."

"Charles..." insisted Gaspier, "you cannot imagine what I have discovered. Would you please let me tell you about it?"

"No, Gaspier. I don't want to hear anything you have to tell me. I don't want to discuss business today. This is an important day for this family, and I want to enjoy it."

"Charles, you have to listen to me because depending on your thoughts I may have to travel to Portugal."

"Portugal?" repeated Charles.

Quickly, Gaspier went to his briefcase and removed a page from a newspaper. "Would you like to read it, or do you prefer..."

"You read it."

"Cargo ship for sale."

"Oh, no," Charles interrupted him, "wait until tomorrow."

"No, let me finish. At least listen to the ship's name...*Serenata*."

"*Serenata*?" replied Charles, surprised.

"It must go into dry dock for repairs," explained Gaspier.

"And Captain Alejandro Alvares?"

"He happens to be the person shopping for a buyer. He does not own the ship, but apparently, he does not want to lose it. May I send him a telegram saying that I wish to see it?"

Gaspier's questions rushed in unnaturally and raised an unexpected silence. For a few minutes, Charles paced the floor thoughtfully, his mind swiftly traveling away to hunt for lost events, somewhere in the past. When he spoke again, it was to say, "No, send a telegram saying that we want to buy it."

"Without seeing it?" Gaspier asked promptly.

"Right."

"But Anthony wants—"

"If Anthony dislikes the *Serenata*, let him pay for a freighter, as he has been doing. I keep my promises, Gaspier, and I promised myself that, some day, I would repay Captain Alejandro for all he did to help me. I think the time has arrived. The *Serenata* will sail the oceans for us as the Merlenes' first ship and Captain Alejandro, our leading captain."

31

FALL HAD ARRIVED AND THE orange chrysanthemums of many different sizes and shapes bloomed everywhere, adorning the streets and the gardens. Anthony was expected to arrive from Brazil with their third shipment of diamonds from the mine and finally, on the second Sunday of November, he disembarked in New York City. His son was already four months old.

Charles and Gaspier had eaten a late lunch together before going to the port to meet Anthony.

After the ship docked, they had decided Gaspier and Cafeno, another of Charles' employees, would stay at the port to wait for the release of the cargo while Charles took Anthony home.

On their way home Anthony asked, "How is my son doing?"

"He is wonderful," Charles answered.

"And Aunt Isabella?"

"Very well. Extremely happy for having the presence of a baby in the house."

"Tell me about the ships you have seen. Has there been anything we could buy?"

"Anthony, you haven't asked about your wife," commented Charles with a disapproving look.

"Oh. How is she?"

"Fine. But worried about you."

"And why?"

"Oh, Anthony. At least presume that I get around. Since you left for Brazil, you have not written her once, not even when you found out about her pregnancy. What is going on with you?"

"Nothing," said Anthony. "I am perfectly fine. Catarina's identity converts her into a rare woman. She ran over my expectations, father. You may believe she fulfills my dreams but...I have a different opinion about that. You also think that you know her, but you don't. Catarina reveals only one side of her personality. Skillfully, she places herself far from any ordinary concept and turns on every action that favors her desires. I refuse to be her pawn."

"You better make this marriage work, Anthony. Aside from diamonds, now there is my grandson's future to think of. Whatever the cost might be, you will respect her as your wife and the mother of your son. It is too late to do anything about the discovery that she failed your expectations. You accepted her conditions, didn't you? You placed yourself in this position without asking for my opinion first. Now, be a man about it."

Not looking at his father, Anthony asked, "Is there anything else?"

"Yes. I want you to return to New York permanently."

"Impossible. We cannot afford to have the mine operating without my supervision."

"Well. We will have to have a further discussion about this, but now I need you here to work with Gaspier. The diamonds speedily increased our production and gave rise to diverse obligations. A large-scale operation must start soon. We need a bigger place to work in, better equipment, more jewelers, and connections with the rest of the world. We must find someone to take your place in Brazil."

"Fine. We can discuss these matters, but I still need to stay in Brazil for at least another year."

"No. A year is too long."

"Then eight months."

"Eight months is almost a year. No."

"Damn it! Why don't you go there and see for yourself how it works. That way you may understand why we cannot leave this operation in the hands of strangers."

"I agree, Anthony. We will go together after Christmas."

"Are you crazy? I cannot spend Christmas here. I simply came to close the deal with the ship, and as soon as we take care of it, I plan to return."

Charles remained silent. He did not want to tell Anthony that he had already bought a ship, and that the *Serenata* was costing them a fortune in repairs. He decided not to anger him so soon after his arrival.

"So, you plan to spend your son's first Christmas away from him?"

"I did not plan on it. Obligations did. I refuse to spend more than three weeks in New York."

"Three weeks?"

"Yes, father, three weeks."

A few hours later, they all came together for dinner. Charles sat at the head of the table, with Isabella, Gaspier, and Cafeno to his left and Anthony and Catarina to his right.

Gaspier and Cafeno had returned from the port just before dinner, and as soon as they had been served, Charles asked, "Is everything in order, Gaspier?"

"Yes, Charles. It took so long because—you know how things are at the port. Anthony picked a busy day to dock, and unloading the ship took much time."

Isabella had ordered shrimp *crepes* for dinner. She wanted to serve Anthony's favorite dish, and Carmen, the cook, had prepared them to perfection.

Initially, Anthony paid no attention to the conversation, seeming too preoccupied with eating *crepes* and drinking the wine, which also pleased his taste. He enjoyed these with a voracious appetite while Charles and Gaspier spent some time talking to each other. When he had finished the last bite of his crepe, he decided to talk. However, the response to his questions spoiled the rest of his dinner.

"Gaspier, tell me about the ships you have found. I am eager to see them."

"Oh, you still don't know about it?" answered Gaspier with a bewildered look.

"Know? What is it that I don't know?"

Instead of answering him, Gaspier turned toward Charles. Only his eyes spoke at that moment. *Go ahead, tell him what he has to know.*

Quietly, Charles realized that the time had come when he must deliver the news about the *Serenata*. He calmly settled himself more comfortably in his chair, and after wiping his mouth said, "We have already bought the ship, Anthony."

"What?"

"I bought the *Serenata*."

"The *Serenata*? An antique?" Anthony asked incredulously.

Everyone looked at him, yet no one said a word.

"It could cost us a fortune to repair it. You both know that!"

"The ship is already in Massachusetts being repaired," said Gaspier.

"I cannot believe it!" he exclaimed. "I simply do not know what to say. I have been in Brazil, stuck in a mine alongside the miners to ensure that everything goes well, and...and at the end, I receive no consideration. You both completely disregarded my opinion. And beyond that, you went out and bought a piece of junk!"

"The *Serenata* is not a piece of junk, Anthony," said Catarina. "That ship means a lot to your father."

"Ah, you find what they did to me fair? Let me tell you something that you do not know. I have been dreaming of this moment—of buying our first ship. When I was a boy, I heard stories of ships, pirates, and brave captains, but I never imagined that one day I would need to own my own ship. However, here we are. See why I expected to be a part of this decision?"

A deep silence filled the room after Anthony spoke. He looked at everyone sitting around the table, searching and hoping to hear something encouraging. But no one broke the silence, and no one dared to continue eating. They just sat and looked at him mutely.

"Aunt Isabella, what about you? Do you also agree with what they did?"

"I admit that Catarina found the right thing to say," she explained. "The *Serenata* is not a piece of junk. It may qualify as an antique as you said, but one with a lot of memories for your father."

"Very well!" exclaimed Anthony. He stood up and threw his napkin onto the table. "I just lost my appetite!" he said as he pushed himself away from the table and walked out of the room. He paused long enough to grab his coat, and then left the house.

After his departure, Charles spoke again, "Let's continue with our dinner."

Anthony returned late that evening. When he entered the house and saw his father smoking a cigar alone in the family room, he knew that Charles had been waiting up for him. Tonight had been the first time he had ever left the dinner table and walked out in anger.

Walking into the parlor, he went directly to the bar. Silently, he poured himself a drink and sat down patiently waiting for his father's words, which he knew would come soon.

"Don't you think that you are drinking too much?" Charles asked in a normal tone of voice. "You have been out drinking and then when you come home, you continue to do so."

Carefully contemplating his glass, Anthony replied, "Yes, you could be right. I drink far too much cognac in Claros. If it weren't for the cognac and the *aguardente*, my body would not resist the cold."

"Oh, is that the case? One more reason for you to hasten your return," said Charles. "I was waiting for you because I want to tell you a couple of things. The first one is that, *never* during dinner will you leave the table as you did tonight. Secondly, I bought the *Serenata* because I owe Capitan Alejandro a favor. I'm still the head of this family, so I can make decisions like that."

"Sorry, father. I really thought that my opinion would count. I still think that it was unfair of you to exclude me."

"Good night, Anthony," his father said. "When you are in better condition and able to speak clearly, come see me." With that, Charles left the room.

Anthony remained seated, gazing into the depths of his cognac. *Yes, we shall speak again. But you will only tell me the same things I have heard since I was a child. The Serenata was a big ship and Captain Alejandro Alvares—a brave captain. He has been sailing the oceans since he turned twelve years old. He was a man of strong faith. As a child, I only had to listen to these stories, but now as a man, I have to understand them. Saporo, Captain Alejandro, Serenata, and diamonds are not only childhood stories...they outline Charles Merlenes' legacy.*

He gulped down the last of his cognac and went upstairs.

Anthony walked toward his room with the intention of going to bed, closing his eyes, and falling asleep as quickly as possible so he could forget his frustration. But when he passed the door to Catarina's room, he hesitated a moment, turned, and stood in front of it. He saw a thin line of light running from underneath it.

Damn it! I have to get her out of my mind! Would she still love me? Surely not. She could not even love her own father, he thought as he resumed walking to his room.

As he approached the door, he realized that he still had not seen his son. *Should I go see him now? Of course I should, he is my son.*

Swiftly, he walked back and knocked on her door. When Catarina opened it, he asked politely, "May I see my son?"

"Yes, Anthony. He is almost asleep. I was wondering when you would come."

He walked in and stood near the crib. Leaning over, he gazed silently at the sleeping baby.

Suddenly, he realized how incredible it was to be a father. He felt overwhelmed with such a strong emotion that his previous anger could not penetrate.

Catarina pensively observed him while sitting on the bed. She noticed he had grown thin, his face turned weary, and he showed pronounced bags under his eyes. He had lost all his handsome appeal and looked like an exhausted miner who had grown tired of the cold and the smell of the dirt. *The mine is consuming him,* Catarina thought.

The baby slept soundly, as he sucked his thumb. While Anthony covered him gently with a small blanket he asked, "What is his name?" So far, he did not know anything about his son.

"I was waiting for you so we could decide that together," answered Catarina. "I thought of Maximilien, your French grandfather's name. But I don't know if you would like the idea."

Her eyes held his firmly as she spoke, and he willingly drew nearer and sat next to her.

"Maximilien would make my father very happy," he said. "Does he already know?"

"No. I wanted to talk to you first. Anthony, I am only the mother."

Why do women love to remind us of things like these? Anthony thought while he observed her beauty. And as he looked into her eyes, he experienced a strong desire to stay with her.

Gently, he placed one of his hands over hers and began to ask, "Would you stop me if—"

"I could never do that before, Anthony," she said her eyes full of passion. "I have never been strong enough to resist you. You should know already that diamonds are not the only things between us. I love you."

Silently and without stopping to look at her, he brought his lips close and with his ever-delicate manner, kissed her. Slowly, they lay down on the bed, and his hands slid under her nightgown, over her soft skin and between her legs.

"I love you, Anthony," she whispered. "I love you more than my diamonds."

"No, you don't. Don't ever say that again, Catarina. Say that you love me as much as you love your diamonds. Be truthful."

He lay still as she undressed him, and because his need for satisfaction was great, he possessed her with a crazed and exquisite passion. "I love you, I really do," he whispered as he embraced her. "I love you as much as...I love your diamonds. As much as I love my own life. My entire being is already addicted to you."

Anthony never left her room that night; and when they awoke in the morning, their naked bodies demanded more caresses, and they made love once more.

32

THE TIME SEEMED TO PASS quickly. Anthony was so filled with the joy at having Catarina in his arms every night that he did not even notice how quickly the next three weeks went by.

He spent the days with Gaspier, planning the future operations of the Merlenes Industries. Gaspier had decided they should promote their name in a very distinctive fashion. He wished to appeal to ninety-nine out of every one hundred women in the world, to create a desire in them to possess a piece of Merlenes' jewelry. "We have everything we need to make this a reality," he stated at one of the meetings. "Prestige already adorns our image here in America, so we can reach the rest of the world in the same manner."

Anthony guaranteed his father and Gaspier that the Merlenes would have a diamond supply for many decades to come, enough for their own creations, and also to sell to other jewelers. "The mine can be classified as significant, and much of it still rests untouched," said Anthony. "We can fearlessly go along with the realistic idea that we have virgin ground. Because of it, I see that no other time would bring a period more perfect than this one for us to develop our forthcoming position in the world. We have the option of being able to use the diamonds in our own designs or to sell them in different sizes to any jeweler anywhere in the world, cut with our unique precision and ready to be mounted. And it will not matter, whether it is the *jewel* or only the *stone*s—they will carry our name, MERLENES."

At the last meeting they had before Anthony returned to Brazil, they finalized their plans. Attending that meeting were Cafeno, who by then, had advanced as a sales director, Ruben Galego, director of finance and Charles' second-hand man. Charles also had Paul Volati and Roberto Coroneli, both directors of promotion, Luiz Dejaviro Leplon, the designer, and Aichan Nanichin, the Merlenes' topmost craftsman at the meeting.

Charles had already employed all those men for more than six years. Some of them had worked in the industry for over twelve years, and it was due to their talents and outstanding dedication that the Merlenes had become THE TOP OF THE LINE as jewelers in America, and that they were branching out into France and Italy.

At that same meeting, Gaspier presented the synopsis of his plan of expansion. He believed that every last detail required their full attention because he definitely wanted to raise their prestige in more than one country. They must spread out to achieve world recognition, and to grow with an image of dignity and honor. The Merlenes would arrive at the right place at the right time. According to him, they must keep one thing in mind—that whatever they did should have an explosive impact.

"We have a virgin diamond mine in Brazil and a name already known in parts of Europe," Gaspier rephrased at the end. "Our product is unquestionably one of the best, so TOP OF THE LINE is still our slogan."

After Gaspier, the next person to take the floor was the vice-president of the Merlenes Industry, Anthony. He began by saying, "I am leaving for Brazil in a few days, and I do not know when I will return to New York. But before I go, I want to share some of my ideas with all of you."

Thoughtfully, he walked around the table, and as he did, he looked in the eyes of each one sitting around it. He knew that none of them expected to hear what he was about to say, except for Gaspier. Gaspier, once in Africa, had stepped foot inside a diamond mine and probably could describe the coldness and smells found inside it. Anthony thought that it was specifically the *coldness* and the *smells* of their mine that would establish the superiority of their diamonds over all other diamonds in the world.

His audience knew from the beginning that Anthony had not prepared his speech. But, because of the look in his eyes, they understood that he felt confident about what he intended to say.

The words flowed from his mouth easily giving rise to his first experience speaking at such great length to a group. His speech recital contained revelations, even to his father and Gaspier.

Anthony's principal concern was to put an end to the Merlenes old era and start a new legacy. He pointed that out by saying, "Now that we have our own diamond mine, we also possess a new chance of enticing opportunities and, therefore, new responsibilities. Without much effort we simply arrived in a position to stand up and audaciously demonstrate our superiority with an effective yet dignified approach."

"However, before we launch the course of actions into a new orbit, we definitely need to operate with more sophistication. TOP OF THE LINE symbolizes one of our goals. Now we must seek other ambitions, for our position within the industry has changed completely. We have a lot more to offer and also much more to expect.

"The main objective now is to refine our image, and consequently attract women to our exquisite styles and techniques. Women's inspiration and imagination swirl around our products, and each woman has a unique personality. This extraordinary quality they possess is precisely what makes them so striking. Likewise, we may do the same. Let's give a new touch to our image and secure our position with—*eye-catching, extraordinary details.*"

He paused and calmly waited to see if any questions would follow his last words. He also stopped pacing the room and poured himself a glass of water, which he drank thirstily. Since the silence persisted in the room, he proceeded, "I honestly believe that women will love it. Our jewelry is finely crafted and the diamonds are like no others—totally genuine. We must emphasize our differences by describing the source of our gems. And we certainly have something to say about that. They are not just diamonds they are *claros.* Unlike other diamonds, they do not come from Africa. They blossomed from the womb of *South America's* underground, beneath the mountains of a place called the *Pical Valley in Minas Gerais, Brazil.* Can you see how, with just a few words, I have made them glamorously more attractive? This can generate the excitement that we need. I think it would be enticing to include, with each of our pieces, a small card engraved in gold letters disclosing their origins."

As Anthony's last words floated in the air, he returned to his seat. He did this with a great deal of expectation, anxious to hear some feedback on his ideas. But, it seemed that no one intended to say anything. They remained quiet impressed by his transformation. In very little time, he had become another person—a sophisticated businessman. The concept he had just proposed was absolutely brilliant. They witnessed the change and wondered how it happened so quickly. Strongly thinking about it, certainly, his unexpected marriage and the diamond mine that came with the package were the reasons.

Charles finally broke the silence around them by saying, "Anthony, I believe we are all impressed. Your presentation was remarkable and your proposition has caused an avalanche of intriguing new concepts. Where did you get this fantastic idea?"

"I think from the Pical Valley, from the spirits that live there. You should see this place, Father. It's eerie. And the people who live there also seem peculiar for they grow up with such strange beliefs. Claros is a sad place with nothing more to offer the world than its diamonds—all that we need."

"I see," Charles replied. "I loved what I heard," he continued. MERLENES as a synonym for exclusivity? Wonderful. Gaspier hasn't given his opinion yet, but if I know him as well as I think I do, he too, finds your proposal—outstanding."

"Yes, Charles, you do know me," said Gaspier taking the floor. "Anthony, let me put it this way. You have found the angle that brings light to our project and effortlessly converts a vision into a reality. I never thought that your ideas would be so remarkable. You have a wonderful imagination, the one that delivered exactly what we need. We will make sure that these little cards will carry words of our subtle differences all over the world." Then with the smile of a rascal, he added, "Do you know something? You have become quite thorough. That's terrific. If you continue this way, the world really will be in danger!"

At that comment, everyone in the room laughed.

* * * *

To officially set the start of this new era, and obviously, to mark it as their debut into the international market, Charles planned a dinner party. He made reservations at the best French restaurant in Manhattan, the Le Bistro Restaurant, for the night before Anthony's departure.

Approximately sixty people attended the event. They were directors, supervisors, and jewelers who worked with Aichan Nanichin. Seven of them came from nearby cities to join the festivities. Isabella and Catarina, at Charles' request, also attended. This was Catarina's first public appearance since she had arrived in New York City. Of those invited, only Gaspier, Cafeno, and Mr. William Ugany had the opportunity to meet her.

The gown Catarina wore for the night displayed her exquisite beauty. It was of a rich green hue that complimented her skin tone and highlighted the color of her eyes. Its sleeves and neckline, adorned with very delicate embroidery, was the handiwork of a talented seamstress in great demand from Belo Horizonte. Every detail of the dress showed the hard work used to sew it. And Catarina's unique beauty simply gave to the art the finishing touch.

"I have never seen such a magnificent dress!" Isabella exclaimed as Catarina and Anthony descended the stairs.

"Thank you," Catarina answered as Anthony smiled at her.

Le Bistro Restaurant had reserved their large dining room for the Merlenes' private party. The guests were already there when Anthony and Catarina arrived. As soon as they stepped into the room, everyone stopped talking and looked at them. They all had longed for this moment, to meet the woman who had the good fortune of owning a diamond mine and of having married Anthony Merlenes. The moment had finally arrived. Maria Catarina Casimiro unpretentiously stood in front of them revealing her distinctive beauty.

Everyone stood speechless, evidently, because none of them had ever encountered a woman as exotic as Catarina. As all of them were captivated with her beauty, Anthony leaned over and whispered in her ear, "Darling, I think they are overwhelmed. They did not expect a woman with cinnamon skin, shiny black hair, and such beautiful green eyes."

"You mean they never knew anything about your taste in women?"

"Something like that."

She looked at Anthony thoughtfully. Then, smiling at the group, she delicately tilted her head and said, "Good evening everyone. It is a great pleasure to meet all of you."

"Good evening," they answered in unison.

After that, Anthony made the formal introductions.

* * * *

Dinner was served punctually. Afterwards, Gaspier stood to speak to them about the significance of this day in the Merlenes' future plans. He briefly explained that this event marked the beginning of a future without limits, and concluded by saying, "The world is waiting for us."

They all applauded him warmly as he returned to his seat. And when they finished, Charles rose before them. He looked at all the expectant faces around the room and began to speak, "We are here today to celebrate the beginning of a new era, maybe the most significant of them all as we are preparing to enter the international market. Luis Dejaviro Leplon, Aichan Nanichin and I have started to work on a new project. We collaborated on an extensive collection, the largest we have ever created, which will be presented for the first time in Europe. We intend to introduce ourselves with a quality of jewels and a style of craftsmanship which has never been seen before.

"And now, Luis Dejaviro Leplon wishes to have the opportunity to describe the new collection to you. Mr. Luis Dejaviro, please."

Murmurs of speculation spread throughout the room as Luis Dejaviro rose and took Charles' place before them. The room fell silent as he looked around and smiled at the group. "Good evening, my friends," he greeted them. He held out his empty hands and said, "First, I would like to apologize for not having a sketch-book of this collection with me tonight. The reason is that I just returned from Italy, where I spent some time surveying the jewelry market for Charles, and the second, leads to Anthony's insistence that he must return to Brazil soon after his arrival here. None of us expected that. He caught us unprepared. We had so many plans to finalize that it made it impossible to have everything ready on such short notice. So, I would like to at least present the concept of what the collection is all about."

After a short pause, he continued, "As Charles said, this will be a very extensive and sophisticated project. It will be called the *Claros Collection*, one hundred and fifty distinctive pieces of jewelry made with combinations of diamonds, emeralds, and rubies. Since we decided to use emeralds and rubies with the diamonds, I suggested dividing the collection into two parts, and

Charles agreed with my idea.

"The pieces with diamonds and emeralds will be introduced as the *Casimiro Style*, and the pieces with diamonds and rubies, the *Pical Style*. Charles and Aichan Nanichin have developed a new cutting technique to increase the amount of facets in the stones, which consequently enhances the radiance and sparkle of the gems. We have introduced this cut in all our new pieces. And now, Aichan will stand to present his masterpiece."

Aichan Nanichin joined Luis Dejaviro who held a beautiful jeweler's box. Without a word, he opened it and removed a black velvet pouch with a black satin ribbon tied around it. As he silently untied the ribbon and consequently opened it, Luis Dejaviro resumed speaking, "Aichan is unwrapping the most magnificent piece of jewelry ever crafted by the Merlenes Industry. The most stunning—the centerpiece of the *Casimiro Collection*. This necklace sparkles with Brazilian diamonds and carries the new cutting technique."

Aichan removed the necklace, which glittered under the many lights in the room, and held it up for them to see. Then Luis Dejaviro said, "It is a five hundred thousand dollar jewel, and it is *not* for sale."

The combination of the effects of the necklace, its radiant beauty and its exorbitant value, elicited an astonished gasp from everyone in the room. And as they all admired it, Charles joined Aichan and Luis Dejaviro.

"This is one of my later designs," Charles explained. "I am not usually as creative as Mr. Luis Dejaviro, but sometimes I can even surprise myself. I designed this necklace with two objectives in mind: as a family heirloom and as a special gift from the Merlenes family to Maria Catarina."

With a look of great satisfaction on his face, Charles took the necklace from Aichan and approached Catarina and Anthony. He held it out to Anthony and said, "Would you please place this around your wife's neck as a token of our esteem for her?"

Anthony stood up and held it for a moment, admiring its

beauty, and then he gently draped it around Catarina's neck and fastened the clasp. The diamonds and emeralds sparkled as they reflected the matching green of her eyes and her gown, and when she looked up with a dazzling smile, the result was breathtaking.

After this special dedication, everyone spent the rest of the evening approaching Catarina, eager to examine this fine necklace and its owner close-up. They welcomed her to New York and complimented the beauty of the jewels.

When Aichan Nanichin had the opportunity to speak with her, he said, "Mrs. Merlenes, I want you to know that I used all my expertise when selecting the stones for this necklace because I knew it was for you. Now that I have met you, I feel very glad that I selected the stones carefully. You are as beautiful as they are."

"Thank you," she said gracefully. "You did a wonderful job. I am very pleased with your choices. Let me tell you a secret. These are the first diamonds that I have ever worn."

"Really?" he said, quite surprised.

"Really," she answered. "When they lay peacefully in the mine, I could only look at them."

At the end of the evening, Anthony opened the velvet pouch as he said, "Darling, let's take off your necklace. I do not want you to leave the restaurant wearing a half million-dollar worth of jewels. You are not in Claros but New York. It can be dangerous."

At home, before going to bed, Anthony went to the family room to speak with his father. "Father, the night was wonderful," he said. "Very meaningful. Dedicating the necklace to Catarina was a beautiful gesture, which neither of us expected. I will always remember this. Tonight you reminded me of important things that I had forgotten—things that I have learned from you. Like the values that should always lie at the heart of every family. I hope that I will be able to endow these values on to my children as you have endowed them on to me. I am very proud of you."

"Sometimes I think that I do not deserve all the good fortune that has come to us, Anthony. But surely you do. I am proud of you, too."

Anthony went to Charles and hugged him for the first time in many years.

"I'll see you soon in Brazil—you and Captain Alejandro. Speaking of him, forgive me for not easily seeing the significance of the *Serenata*. I am no longer angry."

"Thanks," replied Charles. "I knew that you would understand. That is why you are my son."

It was almost midnight when Anthony went upstairs to his room. Catarina was waiting for him wearing only a sheer, white nightgown. This would be their last night together before his return to Brazil. Immediately after Anthony entered the room, she came closer and hugged him. As their hug turned passionate, effortlessly she let her nightgown slide and fall to the floor. Anthony stepped back to marvel upon her beauty and sensuality. He reached into his pocket and removed the velvet pouch. Slowly, he opened it and placed the necklace around her neck once more.

"Do you know something, Catarina? You were absolutely right when you said that I am a lucky man. I am the only one who will ever see you like this–dressed in nothing but diamonds and emeralds."

She answered him with loving kisses. Anthony kept her beauty in his mind. *If Aichan Nanichin could see you right now, he would find out that the diamonds, which he so carefully selected, are still quite ordinary when compared to your beauty.*

33

THE WATER IN THE BAY moved choppily, churned up by the continuous arrivals and departures of the vessels using the port. Charles and Gaspier were standing on the dock, quietly observing the activities. The winter buzzed over its last dying days while the next season rested silently behind them, waiting for its chance to come. No other time of the year provided the same optimism as the upcoming season—spring, the most beautiful and romantic season of our time. Through it, the bright days fused the ambiance with gentle winds, which carried the sweet fragrance of budding and blooming flowers.

The *Serenata* was one of the largest ships entering the port that afternoon. Her repairs had been completed, and she looked like new, painted blue and white, with her name embossed in black. As Charles watched her from the dock, he felt a great satisfaction. Although he had never dreamed of owning the *Serenata*, he felt it was like a dream come true. The *Serenata* sailed through the water as gracefully as he remembered from all those years ago. As she approached the docks, Charles recalled the soft, fast, and constant sensation of balance he had experienced when he sailed away from

Port Cherbourg—the unforgettable movement that had separated him from France.

He then thought about everything he had left behind in France, especially his mother, the sweetest memory he had. Also, he remembered how he felt when he was sailing toward his unknown future that frantically transformed into his present life. France supplied the stage for his first deceptions, and America the scenery for his dreams.

Then these thoughts brought to mind his friend Antoine. *Oh, it is so sad that Antoine could not be here with me to see the Serenata entering the port.*

As soon as she docked, Gaspier said enthusiastically, "Let's go, Charles. It is time to welcome Captain Alejandro."

"No," responded Charles. "I am not ready to meet him. You go first. I want to stay here and look at the ship."

"All right! I think I understand. I know how much this means to you. Don't worry, I'll bring the captain here."

Gaspier walked away toward the ship, and Charles watched him until he disappeared.

The Serenata will be sailing again, Charles thought. *I did help the captain fulfill his dreams. If someone had told me that this would happen one day, I would have walked away in disbelief. This must be his fate or our fate intermingled.*

Sometime later, when Charles saw Gaspier and the Captain walking toward him, he put aside his memories, and prepared to greet the captain. After twenty-nine years, the encounter would surely be another unforgettable moment in his life.

They stopped in front of Charles, and Gaspier said, "Captain, may I introduce the man who saved the *Serenata*, Mr. Charles Merlenes."

"Good afternoon, Captain Alejandro," said Charles extending his hand. "Welcome to New York. It is a pleasure to have you here."

"Good afternoon," answered the captain. He then remained silent because he suspected that Mr. Merlenes had more to say and ask than he did himself.

"Don't you remember me, captain?" asked Charles, knowing what the answer would be.

"No, sir. Did you expect me to?"

"Of course not. I know I have changed a lot."

The captain was now fifty-nine years old and had changed very little physically. In twenty-nine years, his face only gained a few wrinkles, and some gray hair appeared discreetly, delineating his age. His eyes still held the same peaceful look that never feared anything and they went along with a spirited smile that seemed to be a gift. His body showed a well-toned physique for his age, and consequently revealed his lack of ailments. Silently, Charles concluded that the captain's life on the ocean undoubtedly, fostered his good health.

"Captain, I am Charles Merlenes. We have met before. I was the Frenchman..."

"Wait..." the Captain interrupted, "you are...you lost your friend during our trip."

"That's right," affirmed Charles. "You gave me my money back. So you do remember."

"Yes. And it's wonderful to see you again." Then, to express his pleasure, he hugged Charles like an old friend. Next he looked at Gaspier and asked, "You said that he is the man who bought the *Serenata*?"

"Yep."

"Then you must be very rich, Charles."

"I am."

"I knew it. I knew that you would get what you wanted. I would have bet on it."

"Faith, Captain. Apparently, I have mine."

* * * *

Charles and the Captain enjoyed an extraordinary evening in each other's company. He treated the Captain like an old friend who hadn't changed, despite their years apart.

After dinner, they sat in the parlor and continued their

conversation while enjoying delicious liquor and smoking expensive cigars. They talked for hours without getting bored or running out of topics, determined to relate all the events that had occurred during their years of separation. The Captain had much to ask, and Charles a whole life to tell.

Easily one could see the Captain was curious, and anxiously desired to know what had happened to Charles after he had left him in the port of New York with his suitcase in one hand and the envelope of money in the other. Since he knew Charles had many interesting things to reveal, he attentively listened.

Charles felt the same way and was eager to share his experiences with the Captain.

Confidently, Charles told him everything about Andre, the Italia Campibeli Restaurant, Don Prieto Ferbonini, Isabella, Saporo, Gaspier, and Juan Carlos Catarel. He spoke of Ana, Anthony, and Catarina, only hiding the inconsequential incidents for fear that they would maliciously diminish his dignity.

The Captain met Isabella and Catarina during dinner. His perception of Isabella was that she was an authentic female, the kind that truly has a heart capable of love and yet able to display a feminine softness. She surely exhibited a flawless character that could fall in love, cry, suffer, betray, and yet feel sorry for everything she had done wrong. Her dear soul acted like a deep well of water that nourished all who were thirsty that came to it.

In contrast, he saw Catarina as a tenacious woman. When he met her and she looked at him, unexpectedly, he caught a strange force emanating from her eyes. His life on the ocean had taught him about things of legends, superstitions, and the power of the gods and goddesses. Silently, Catarina demonstrated the headstrong person she was. A woman with a tenacious spirit, a lady of strong words—a dominant female. Her heart and soul fused together to a deliberate vitality. Tactfully, she could go as far as loving with the strength of hate, and to hating with the strength of love.

She was three months pregnant, and her lips held a divine smile when she had entered the dining room. Walking boldly in a loose dress, Catarina reminded him of the Greek goddesses who towered over the ancient temples—she could easily be one of them. The weaknesses of the heart and the insensibilities of the soul would never shake her structure. She had been born to guide others with her power. And later, when Charles had mentioned her diamond mine, the Captain finally understood the connection that existed between her and the strange forces of the universe. Only a god could give a diamond mine to a person. She was the chosen one.

After bringing him up to date on everything, Charles decided to talk about their trip to Brazil, the *Serenata*'s first voyage under the Merlenes' ownership.

He had just started when Isabella walked into the room to inform them that the guest bedroom had been prepared, and that the butler would escort the captain to it whenever he was ready. She then politely bade them goodnight, and left.

Before reaching the door, Charles asked her to wait. He mutely stood up, went to her and whispered in her ear, "Come to my room tonight. I am happy and I want to be with you."

She gave him a sweet look that Charles knew meant yes, turned and left the room.

Discreetly, Charles smiled in anticipation as he returned to his seat. "What were we talking about, Captain?"

"The trip to Brazil. But before we continue, I have a question, if I may?"

"Certainly," replied Charles.

"Do you love that woman?"

Caught by surprise, Charles replied, "Do you mean Isabella?"

"Yes."

"I... Actually..."

Charles encountered so much difficulty in answering the question that the Captain said, "I am sorry. You don't have to answer."

"No, I should. Yes, I love her. Like you Captain, she also

became very special to me. We have...we call this a *discreet relationship*."

"Why? Feelings between a man and a woman keep the life-giving progress in our planet. What is wrong with being in love?"

"Nothing," said Charles. "But things are not as simple as you think. She is the mother of my dead wife, and the aunt of my son. Complicated no? Have you ever heard about cases in which a person's heart double-crossed them? That is my case."

"Listen Charles, I should have never asked. I am sorry."

"It's okay, Captain. As my friend, I don't mind your knowing about this, but don't waste your time trying to understand. Avoid solving impossible puzzles."

"I liked you Charles from the moment I met you," said the Captain. "Life provided me all that I didn't have plus a lot of experience, and I know that to rise from nothing sometimes means to mess with things that certainly pave the roads against our will. I want you to know that I am very grateful that you saved the *Serenata*. I never pictured you as a failure. The bad things that may exist in your life will never change my affection for you. I strongly believe that you are the same good man I met a long time ago. I do not measure people by their faults, but by the good deeds they do."

"Thank you, Captain. I know you mean that."

Sometime past eleven o'clock, they ended their conversation and went to bed. The butler showed the Captain to his room, and a few minutes later, Charles went to his.

Thinking that he had never received such pleasure from a guest as he had from Captain Alejandro, he climbed the stairs experiencing a great sense of peace and joy. Upon entering his room, he calmly unbuttoned his collar, removed his tie, and sat down in his favorite chair, where he liked to smoke his last cigar of the night.

Peacefully, he took a cigar from the box on the table beside him, lit it, crossed his legs, and relaxed as he exhaled. Thoughts of Isabella playfully filled his mind, anticipating the pleasure she would bring him that night.

Moments later, when furtively she entered the room, he looked at her tenderly. She was still what he loved most in this world. The serene look in her eyes mesmerized him and he gazed into their depths as she walked toward him. Mutely, she stopped in front of him, humbly enjoying his presence.

Charles put his cigar in the ashtray, pulled her onto his lap, gently brushed her hair aside and kissed her neck softly. He placidly closed his eyes, and abandoned himself to the pleasures that only she could give him.

"Oh, Charles! How much more could I love you?" she asked in a whisper.

"Not much more," he murmured. "Not much more," he said his eyes still closed and his lips caressing her skin.

34

HIRING A CAPABLE CREW TOOK longer than anticipated, and the launch date for the impending voyage, more than once, had to be postponed. When they finally completed all the preparations to leave the port of New York, it was near the end of April.

Once they were underway, Charles and Captain Alejandro spent many hours in each other's company playing chess and talking endlessly. The Captain entertained Charles with vivid descriptions of the fascinating adventures he had during his lifetime of traveling the oceans.

However, when the Captain's duties called him away, Charles occupied himself by meditating, calmed by the forceful presence of the ocean surrounding him. The combined vastness of the sky and water made him ponder the magnitude of God, feeling minute and ordinary.

For some reason he thought of his brother and sister, and how, long ago, innocently they shared their lives. But now, every detail of St. Denis belonged to a dormant past. Then he suddenly saw the past as a fearless passenger that he had overcome. All the mistakes he made and rights he had given up rested motionlessly inside of a big, old trunk. He had won. He now portrayed the fearless passenger.

They anchored in Rio de Janeiro early one Saturday morning, and Anthony was at the dock to greet them, exited by their arrival. After his trip to New York, he had playfully visualized this moment—the day in which he would be walking on the dock to receive his father and Captain Alejandro Alvares, and especially to finally meet the *Serenata*. He thought of it as a memorable occasion, a historic moment for his entire family.

As Anthony desparately wished for them to acquire their own ship, the *Serenata* emerged as a gift from the heavens. Life brought him something from his childhood stories—the *Serenata* and Captain Alejandro. Many years before, this ship had brought his father to America, and he now was standing where his father once stood.

Anthony, Charles, and Captain Alejandro spent the morning on the *Serenata* and in the afternoon they boarded the train to Minas Gerais. Charles remained quiet as Anthony described the points of interest, engrossed by the natural beauty of Rio de Janeiro. When Anthony referred to the residents as *Carioca,* it caught Charles' attention and he asked, "Why are they called *Carioca*?"

"I do not know as much about Rio de Janeiro as I do about Minas Gerais," answered Anthony. "But I asked Sergio Estrada the same question once, and he told me that French explorers once established a colony here on the bay and that some Portuguese explorers later arrived and drove out the French settlers. They then built a fort, homes, churches, and stores. When the local Indians saw the Portuguese buildings for the first time, they called them *Carioca*, which means the house of the white man in their language. Since then, the people here have called themselves *Carioca*."

"Hmm...the house of the white man," Charles repeated.

They arrived in Claros late, ate a light dinner and went to bed.

The next day Charles found himself fascinated by what he saw of Claros. He glanced around and rested, entranced by the serenity of the surrounding mountains. Calmly, the memories of the past overpowered his soul and as a result he was magically transported back to St. Denis. For some time, he was lost in his recollections, as if almost impossible to separate the past from the present.

From the veranda of Catarina's house, he could see the train tracks, the station, the small houses, and the chapel on the mountain. As he looked at the mountains, trees, and the vast, empty spaces that made up the town of Claros, he felt a connection to something deep within himself. The peace he experienced as he gazed upon the scene before him was unlike any he had ever felt before. In an unexpected way, it aroused a quiescent part of his soul, sensing an unknown mysticism that opened his mind and he saw how shallow his life had been. It seemed as if everything he had seen, thought, and said throughout his life had been wrong. In an instant he discerned an understanding that he existed for a reason. And in this same philosophy was not only his ancestry, but his entire being, and that of succeeding generations.

Charles realized that this fabricated an ambiguous concept, which most people easily pushed aside for not having the full understanding of existence, in a simple way, he saw it. In a blink of an eye, God appeared to be wise and compassionate. Many of the things that had once threatened his ego lost their importance. The mysteries had been revealed to him with a clear and concise logic that he had never known before. He felt foolish for not knowing the answers that had been so obvious and free of complexities.

What a delightful joy he experienced! The serenity of Claros' ambiance peacefully inspired his awareness of a totally new dimension of his life. He recognized that his enlightenment arrived as a gift of which he had just become aware, but surely, it existed in the universe before man. "Thank you," he said to no one but the universe.

The strident blare of the train's whistle brought him back to reality. *I would like to die here*, he thought with great conviction. The memories of that afternoon were like a storm of happiness flooding his soul.

In the afternoon, Anthony took them to the Pical Valley. Charles and the Captain found the valley a most inappropriate place for a diamond mine, nothing like they had envisioned. As they descended the steep trail into the valley, Charles thought that they must have been going to the ends of the earth. The seven mountains, which formed the valley, towered in defiance of the gray sky surrounding them. Innocently and harmlessly, their eyes touched the seven mountains that had been drawn on Juan Carlos Catarel's old treasure map. From long ago the pieces of the puzzle had passed from one hand to another to finally comply with their destiny. Some god or goddess in the universe had used their dexterity to keep everything moving for Charles before he had even left France.

Sergio Estrada was waiting for them when they arrived, and Anthony made the introductions. "Sergio, this is my father, Charles Merlenes," he said. "And this is Captain Alejandro Alvares."

"I am pleased to meet you," Sergio answered in French. "Welcome to Claros."

Anthony was anxious to show the mine to his father and went directly to it. He knew that Charles had never been inside one before, and he was eager to see what his reaction would be.

They stopped inside the entrance to put on heavy jackets. When Charles took his first breath of the odorous and humid air within, he remarked, "It is unbelievable that diamonds come from a place like this."

As they went deeper they saw miners at work. They all worked dressed in heavy clothing to protect them from the cold. Deep inside the temperature was minus ten degrees centigrade.

"A person exposed to the elements down here could die of hypothermia," Anthony explained. "From time to time, they must drink some *aguardente* just to survive. They also must be very well fed. We give them everything they need, from the clothes they wear to a place to sleep. They are good men, lack ambition, and find happiness easily. I have learned much from them. Sometimes we sit together and drink *aguardente* while playing cards. I enjoy their simplicity."

When the miners saw the visitors, they stopped working to look at them. Anthony introduced Charles, and they shyly bowed their heads to him. Charles noticed the contrast between the healthy young men with white teeth and the tired old toothless men. All had the same look of resignation.

"Look at their hands, father," Anthony said while holding one of the employee's hands. "Look how callused they are. I have learned something new while sharing my life with them. I realized that their misery easily crafts my glory and my glory effortlessly diminishes their needs. One sets the other and neither one would ever exist if the pain in misery didn't determine the happiness in glory. Mankind has no power over the power that establishes this contrast. No one knows why...then misery itself becomes as big as glory, too."

When they reached the stone wall, Anthony invited them to climb up to the grotto. Anthony and Charles went ahead of Sergio and the Captain, and they continued talking as they climbed.

"Anthony, how much longer do you intend to stay here?" asked Charles.

"Maybe three more months. Cafeno has learned a lot, and I believe he could manage the operation smoothly. And Sergio is excellent at his job—efficient and quite trustworthy. I estimate my departure to New York before the end of the year."

"Catarina is pregnant, Anthony. You should be there now."

"I've thought about that. *This* is her second pregnancy and like the first one, I am here. But right now business affairs that I started cannot go into the hands of others. You and Catarina must understand that."

"She does understand because she loves you, and love gives her the ability to accept the difficulties," Charles said gently.

They had reached the grotto and his words faded into its depths. Anthony did not respond. He just lifted up the lantern he held and then asked, "Have you ever seen anything like this before?"

Looking around him with admiration, Charles answered, "No, I have never seen anything so stunning in my entire life."

His voice echoed loudly throughout the grotto, and they all waited until it died in the distance. Then Anthony explained to them that the grotto was at the same level as the valley, underneath the junction of two mountains. He told them Catarina's story about the deep holes of water called *panelas*, and that the water flowing past them was the source of the Pical River. They stood silently, fascinated by the uniqueness of their surroundings.

The Captain wished to examine the walls more closely, so he and Sergio headed toward them, leaving Anthony and Charles standing beside the flowing water.

"I have a secret to tell you, father," said Anthony. "When I received the news about Catarina's second pregnancy, I wished more than anything to be in New York, to hug her and to tell her how happy I was. To lessen my frustration I came here. Catarina loved this grotto. It used to be her favorite place when she lived here. Once here, I sat on that rock next to the water. I thought about the new life we would be bringing into the world and realized that time flies. It seems like just yesterday I was a single man and now a father-to-be for the second time. I envisioned having a baby girl as part of the new generation Catarina and I started. Even though I didn't plan this, I felt happy. Then before leaving I leaned over to wet my fingers in the water, something I do every time I come here. This time, though, I saw a small green stone lying under the water. Curiously, I picked it up and examined it. It was an emerald."

"Do you mean emerald as in the gemstone type?" Charles asked surprisingly.

"Yes, a real emerald," replied Anthony. "I came back the next day with a better light, but I did not find any more. I do believe that there are more somewhere in one of these mountains. I feel it."

"Are you serious?"

"Of course. Why else would I be telling you this?"

"I would like to see the stone you found."

"I'll show you when we return to the house. I haven't told anyone else about this. I almost wish that it wasn't true, because to get to them we would have to dynamite the mountain and that would destroy both the grotto and the source of the river. The valley would have no water."

"It would be a sin to destroy the source of the river," said Charles.

"Yes. So, we must continue to keep it a secret. We are not in a position to do anything about them anyway. It would take a lot of money to prospect the mountain, and we must concentrate on first things first. We can wait, can't we?"

"Of course we can," Charles answered with a smile.

Charles had planned to spend only two weeks in Claros. During that time, he wanted to meet with Felipe Castanheda, their attorney. So, they used the next few days to travel to Belo Horizonte to pay him a visit.

After their return to Claros, Charles and the Captain went on a carriage ride with Geremias, the man who oversaw the cassiterite prospectors along the banks of the Pical River. Charles had not yet seen the process by which the cassiterite was extracted.

Many small shacks made from clay and wood surrounded the area of the river giving the impression of a small Indian village, but they were the miners' homes. As they stopped, Charles and the Captain saw women working outside sifting beans and washing their clothes in the river. The children and elderly people of the camp sat quietly, contemplating the life around them.

Charles and Captain Alejandro followed Geremias through the

camp to where the men were mining and watched them as they went about their work.

While they walked behind the row of shacks as they returned to the carriage, Charles saw a very old man with a long beard sitting on a log. He kept a blanket wrapped around him and held a cane with one hand.

Charles looked at him and felt weird. The old man's fierce look sent a chill up Charles' spine. Very aware of the unusual experience, Charles stopped and said to the Captain, "Please ask Geremias who that man is."

After speaking with Geremias, the Captain said, "Macael. He is one-hundred years old. Everyone comes to him to be cured of his or her illnesses, or simply to ask for advice when they need it. He is a spiritualist."

"Very powerful man," said Charles. "I feel strange as if he draws me toward him. Do you believe in such things?"

"I have spent my life going from port to port, Charles. I believe in everything."

"Come with me; I want to meet him."

They walked toward Macael, and when they approached him, Charles and Macael looked at each other strangely. The look in Macael's eyes was eerie.

"Someone will soon die," Macael said unexpectedly. "And I see a child who will never wake up from its sleep."

When the Captain translated this for Charles he asked, "Who is going to die? And what child?"

The Captain repeated Charles' questions to Macael, who responded that he did not know.

Silently and quite disappointed, Charles analyzed the old man's words but he did not understand them either.

The next day, Sergio returned from Rio de Janeiro and reported that everything streamed swiftly toward a perfect course, so Charles and Captain Alejandro could plan their trip back to New York if they wished. The cargo they were planning to ship had been inspected by the authorities, and had received the approval to leave the country. They would begin loading the *Serenata* the next day.

Sergio's news left everyone in good spirits, and Charles began to plan his return to New York. After some discussion, they decided they would sail two days later.

Anthony and Charles spent the rest of their time together. They went out early in the morning for a horseback ride so Charles could see the boundaries of Catarina's extensive land, which was now their land as well. They had lunch in the Pical Valley, and in the afternoon, descended into the mine once more.

When they returned to the house, they found the Captain smoking a cigar on the veranda, already bathed and ready for dinner. They greeted him, and then Charles left them to bathe and change clothes. While they waited, Anthony poured some cognac for the Captain and himself. After all, Anthony was greatly enjoying the old sea captain's company.

They had just begun to drink their cognac when Sergio came in with a telegram in his hand. He handed it to Anthony saying, "Bad news, Anthony."

Anthony read it, and exclaimed, "Oh, no! This is terrible!" But Anthony decided he would not deliver the terrible news to Charles before dinner.

They sat down to eat and because Charles was immediately involved with the delicious stuffed duck that had been served, he didn't notice Anthony's lack of appetite. Only after realizing the deadly silence around him, Charles saw that Anthony had hardly touched his food.

Worried, he asked, "Why are you not eating, Anthony?"

"I am not hungry."

"You look very sad. Is there something wrong?"

"Yes, but let's finish dinner first."

"No," said Charles firmly. "If there is something wrong, I want to know what it is, right now."

Not quite sure whether he should do as his father wished, Anthony said, "I received a telegram from New York."

"What happened?"

"Something terrible. Aunt Isabella died from hepatitis this morning."

Stunned, Charles sadly closed his eyes as he felt a wave of pain wash over him. In an instant, everything inside of him died as well. He had lost the woman he loved most in this entire world.

Someone will die soon. Macael's words haunted his mind. "It was Isabella."

35

DURING THE FOLLOWING SPRING Great Britain, Australia and New Zealand were fighting in the Gallipoli Peninsula of Turkey, an incident which cost the British 200,000 lives. Around May, a German submarine sank the ocean liner Lusitania forcing Italy to declare war on Austria-Hungary. In the summer of that same year, in a hospital in New York, a doctor was busy helping a woman deliver her baby.

"Push...push," the doctor said. "Good. Let's try again."

When the doctor first saw the baby's face, he grabbed it and gently pulled the rest of its body out. "Welcome to the world little girl," he said but seemed concerned.

Catarina closed her eyes, exhausted with the ordeal of delivery, and fell asleep without learning that she had given birth to a baby girl.

Dr. Bareli, cradling the infant in his arms, asked the nurse to give the news to the father who anxiously waited outside the delivery room, then took the baby to the pediatrician.

The nurse stopped, surprised by this request. Normally the doctor spoke with the father and the nurse took the newborn to the pediatrician. Yet she complied at once, and hurried out of the room with a worried look on her face. Although she didn't understand what had happened to change the routine, she suspected that there was something wrong with the baby. Dr. Bareli had found it necessary to pull the baby out of the birth canal instead of her coming out naturally, and she hadn't cried after her birth, as newborns usually do.

In the waiting room, the nurse smiled at Anthony and said, "Congratulations, Mr. Merlenes! You are now the father of a baby girl!"

"A baby girl?" repeated Anthony with a proud smile lighting up his face. "How is my wife?"

"She is fine. She is sleeping now. Dr. Bareli will be out to see you in a few minutes."

"Thank you."

She left the room, and Anthony sat down again, elated by the news. *Yes, we have a baby girl. Her name will be Ana, the same as my mother's.*

Thirty minutes later, Dr. Bareli and the pediatrician, Dr. Rudel entered the waiting room and greeted Anthony. They asked him to follow them and silently escorted him to an office nearby. After they were seated Dr. Bareli began to speak.

"Anthony, I'm very sorry, I must give you some bad news."

"What happened to my wife?" asked Anthony, alarmed.

"Nothing is wrong with Catarina," said the doctor. "I'm afraid it's your daughter who has a problem. She was born comatose, with no brain activity or control of her body. Beyond breathing, she is lifeless."

"No! Not my baby girl. It's a bad dream, isn't it?"

"Anthony, how I wish that was the case. However, it is not. Dr. Rudel will explain her condition to you. We want you to know that we intend to do everything in our power to help her, but you must face reality."

"Oh, heaven!" Anthony moaned, fighting the truth and at the same time sinking into a state of despair and resignation.

Dr. Rudel spoke slowly, choosing his words carefully while he described the medical aspects associated with the problem. Next, he explained the critical steps they must follow attentively, and that Anthony must know. He assured Anthony that he would dedicate himself to learning all that concerned the child's disorder, and to do whatever he could to provide for her well being. At the end he added, "I know this is difficult for you, but telling the truth complies with my duty. It would be unethical of me to let you see her before you had been informed of her condition. We couldn't let that happen."

"Thank you, Dr. Rudel," said Anthony. "I think that all you have done, and all you will do in the future, will be useless as far as easing my pain. However, I agree with you, it would not have been ethical to hide this from me. My greatest concern right now is meeting my daughter and then, finding the appropriate words to use when I deliver this terrible news to my wife. Would you both help me?"

"Of course."

A few minutes later they took Anthony to see his daughter. He held her in his arms and silently studied her. He found her as beautiful as the girl he expected to have. Then to satisfy his curiosity he lifted an eyelid and looked at her eye. It was green! Dark green. Catarina's eyes. Anthony cried helplessly, his tears streaming down onto the baby's face. *Oh, Catarina, this pain will last forever.*

* * * *

World War I harshly progressed soaking the earth's surface with blood, and at the same time, the circumstances of Ana Merlenes' birth cruelly filled her family with pain. Anthony, who intended to remain in New York permanently, soon changed his mind. In addition to growing upset by his daughter's condition, he was submerged in a miserable frustration by the effect the war caused on their plans to expand the Merlenes Industries. In fact, there was little to do in New York, and much to be done in Brazil.

Like Anthony, Catarina did not accept her daughter's condition easily. She found herself crying frequently, and at night she began having nightmares. Sometimes, she screamed in rage at the silent walls, refusing to believe that her daughter would never live a normal life. From time to time she refused the reality entirely and vigorously denied her child. Along with her distress, she cultivated all the reasons available to blame herself for Anthony's pain. He wanted so much to have a baby girl and instead, she had given him a lifeless child.

The fact that a stain stigmatized their blood and obviously increased the possibility that their future children might also be like Ana, suddenly became too harsh a reality for Catarina to bear. She promptly saw their other children as part of this unsuitable lineage, and this obliterated her common sense. Sadly, she drowned in her grief without any hope of redemption. Her anger and her pain possessed her soul so thoroughly that this madness separated her from her son as well.

Little Ana's condition caused her to withdraw from all those she loved. Her well-known strength seemed to be diminishing as she lay down, consumed by this wretched state of mind, listlessness and agony. What she feared most was losing Anthony's love.

Alone with her own thoughts, she remembered something Charles had once told her, *God is responsible for all our happiness, and the devil for all our miseries.*

When the time came for Anthony to depart from New York once again, Charles called the Captain for a private conversation. Since the Captain's arrival, it had become quite typical for Charles to ask for his advice. They sat together over tea and Charles said, "That old man we saw in Claros, do you think that he has some kind of power?"

"What man? Macael?"

"Yes."

"I would not call it power, Charles. He is a good spiritualist. He saw the death of someone that you loved and also the condition of your granddaughter before she was born."

"So, do you believe in him?"

"Listen, Charles, a simple man like Macael may surprise us all."

"I want to take our little girl to him. What do you think?"

"Miracles happen," answered the Captain. However, secretly he remembered that Macael said—that the child would never wake from her sleep. But he simply chose not to make any comment about that. "Hope tenderly revives the spirit, Charles."

"Do you think that it would be a good idea to take Ana to Claros?"

"How much worse could it be?"

As a result of their conversation, in February Catarina and little Ana also sailed to Brazil. Anthony made this voyage without any hope of a miracle, but Catarina urgently needed to go. A strong force drove her back to Claros.

Catarina had been born in the Pical Valley and on the night she came into the world, heavy and violent rain burst unexpectedly from the skies, frightening even the animals. The only persons with Sara, Catarina's mother, were Mariana, Bihato, and Malvina, the midwife. Jetulio Casimiro was away on a trip to Bahia.

After the birth, without even cleaning the newborn, Mariana wrapped her in a white sheet and took her to the kitchen. She opened a drawer and removed a large knife. Then she approached Bihato, who stood close to the stove tending the fire, and held out both the child and the knife.

"Take this child into the forest, kill and bury her," she instructed.

"Why?" asked Bihato, his eyes wide open with disbelief.

"She must not live," said Maraina. "Go and do as I say."

Obediently, Bihato left the house to perform this task. He took a shovel and quickly walked through the rain toward the forest. Deep inside the woods he placed the baby on the ground and firmly held the knife poised over her chest. However, his action hung frozen for an instant, while a series of thunder and lightening bolts filled the night. They came in rapid succession, illuminating the entire forest, shattering trees with loud crashes, and shaking the earth with their force. On the ground the baby instinctively cried out because of the rain and the noise. She fiercely kicked and waved her arms in fear.

Bihato looked at the infant, and then at the knife he held in his hands. His own thoughts terrified him. He realized how horrible it would be if he went through with such a crime. His eyes could never abandon the baby and humbly he listened to what his heart told him was right. Decisively he threw the knife into the dirt, picked up the baby, and returned to the house.

He entered the kitchen visibly shaken and soaking wet, yet trying to shield the innocent newborn within his arms. When Mariana saw this, she quickly expressed her happiness and thanked God that the baby was alive. Extremely concerned about the child's condition Mariana took her from Bihato and held her once again. Next, she did what she should have done the first time. She bathed her with warm water, dried her with a soft cloth, and wrapped her in warm blankets.

Malvina, the midwife, remained kneeling next to Sara's body when Mariana returned to the room with the baby. Malvina had been through her most difficult experience as a midwife. Sara had suffered through many hours of hard, fruitless labor, lost a great amount of blood after the delivery, and had died moments later. During those endless hours of labor, Sara's terrifying screams frightened even the midwife. Malvina worried that evil spirits would be attracted to them by the shrieks of anguish.

At the same moment when Sara drew her last breath, the horses in the stable whined and stirred about uneasily. Then a loud bellow from a donkey filled the air. The direful sound had terrified the other horses, and they quieted almost immediately. Malvina shivered with cold chills as she watched shadows moving across the room, swirling diabolically, and appearing to be laughing. Instantly, she was filled with dread, and made the sign of the cross repeatedly while she said to Mariana, "This child is not a gift of heaven, but of the devil. It must die."

When Malvina learned that Bihato had returned with the child unharmed, she understood that he could not do what had been asked and neither could she or Mariana. Soon after the infant was bathed and wrapped warmly, Malvina did what a woman with her beliefs would do. She lit a candle and held the baby's hand wrapped around it, while she prayed aloud. Then she told Mariana that they must take turns watching the candle for the rest of the night—its light must not die.

Early the next morning, Bihato went to get Geraldo and his sons. They returned to the valley with some of Jetulio's other employees, dug a grave for Sara, and prayed for her soul as they buried her. A short time later, they all left the valley and returned to the house near the train tracks, bringing the child with them.

Jetulio did not learn of the news until three weeks later when he returned from Bahia. He never cried for the loss of Sara, and did not know why he never did. He stood at the foot of her grave, removed his hat, and respectfully dedicated one last prayer to her. And after that the Pical Valley seemed a very sad place to Jetulio. He could no longer live there, so he moved back to his old house.

For four months, Jetulio kept his distance from his daughter. To him, she had brought no happiness to his life. He recognized her as his daughter, but considered her to be like his land and fine horses, just another one of his possessions.

Jetulio decided to name her Maria Catarina, after his mother. Resurrecting his mother's name from the grave indeed became the only happiness the fatherly decision brought him. He knew the love that should embrace father and daughter would never exist between them.

To him, having a daughter was just as strange as his choice of Sara for his wife.

36

CATARINA'S ARRIVAL CREATED A break in the monotony of life for the residents of Claros. Many of her old friends and neighbors came to the house to visit and see her new baby. With a brave look on her face she met and greeted them amicably, smiling to conceal her misery. Since she did not want the people of Claros to know of her tragedy, she told them her daughter had the best doctors in the world, and that one day soon, she would be fine.

The next afternoon, Catarina mounted a horse and rode out to the cassiterite miner's camp by the river. When she stopped in front of Macael's small house, his sister came out to see what she wanted. Catarina greeted her as she dismounted and tied her horse to a tree. She then told her that she had come to see Macael.

Graciously, the woman showed her in and then went into a small room where Macael lay sleeping in his bed, obviously very ill. Upon seeing him in this weakened condition, Catarina knew that it would be impossible for him to either speak with her or to answer her questions. Upon placing her hand on his forehead, she felt that he had an extremely high fever.

"He has been like this for three weeks," his sister explained.

"He needs a doctor," said Catarina. "I'll go and send a telegram asking Dr. Fonceca to come and help him. Meanwhile, please take good care of him. I need him to get well."

Then Catarina immediately left the camp and returned to town, where she sent an urgent message to the doctor.

Dr. Fonceca arrived in Claros the next morning. He was a short, heavy-set man, with gray hair, and a big mustache. He had successfully treated ill people for many years. Upon doing an examination, the doctor determined that Macael was suffering from a severe infection. Calmly he treated him, prescribed the care he would require for the next several days and before leaving, assured Catarina that the old man would be fine.

A week later, Macael felt better and was well enough to talk. Catarina, who had visited him daily to monitor his progress, finally said, "Macael, we must speak. You know that I have never believed in what you do; however, you spoke of my daughter before she was even born. Please, tell me how you knew about my child."

Instead of answering her, he asked her to help him to the small table in the corner of the room. She seated him on a chair and then sat down on the other.

"I did not know about your daughter," he said. "The spirit that spoke to me did."

"Macael, I need to know if she can be cured."

"No, she will never get well," he informed her.

Then before Catarina could speak again, he picked up some small shells which lie in front of him and cast them onto the table. While looking at them he proceeded to speak in a peculiar voice. "You are a daughter of darkness. The devil's spirit celebrated your birth." He continued to toss the shells and to say strange things to her. "Your blood is impure. It is full of mildew, which will taint all of your descendants. Your mother used spirits of the darkness to obtain the man she loved.

"She went to see Serda, a witch who used Jurupari, an evil

spirit, as her guide. Serda taught your mother witchcraft so she could trap your father. The witch instructed her to use a cloth that was stained with the blood of her menstruation to brew the coffee for your father to drink. Jurupari blessed the deed, and she possessed the man she desired.

"Jurupari is a very powerful spirit. Tupã, an Indian god, and the father of all gods expelled him. It was Tupã that wished you dead, for the good of your race. But Jurupari became a storm, and you lived. Now Tupã, as well as Jurupari, are with you. Tupã makes you strong, and Jurupari makes you beautiful."

He paused and Catarina was spellbound by the look in his eyes. She wanted to say that she did not believe a word he said, but his look of conviction was so persuasive that her thoughts wavered, and she did not say a word.

"Three children will come to you as a gift," he continued. "They will not have the mildew in their blood. You will accept them. A woman with blue eyes will give birth to the first child and—"

Macael was unable to continue because his body was taken over by a strong seizure and he fell to the floor.

Frightened, Catarina called for his sister to come immediately. It was obvious that Macael was dying. The end of his life had come upon him suddenly and mysteriously. He lay serenely, stretched out on the floor with his eyes and mouth closed. When he fell, he suffered no injuries. It was as if a spirit had taken him from the chair and carefully arranged him on the floor. Suddenly, the unpleasant smell that accompanies old age was gone. His skin tone became normal and his face held a look of tranquil peace.

Macael was buried that afternoon and afterwards, Catarina rode to her home in the Pical Valley. Soon after their arrival in Claros, Anthony had left for the valley and had not returned since.

She urgently wanted to speak with him; to tell him that she must return to New York with Ana as soon as possible. That it had been a mistake to believe that Macael could cure her.

Alone, she arrived without anyone seeing her, tethered her

horse, and entered the house. Once inside, she soon wished she had never come. An unsuitable surprise awaited her in the dining room. She found Anthony kissing a young girl, the daughter of one of their employees. Catarina's sudden presence shocked them both and the scared young girl ran out of the room.

It had meant nothing to Anthony. However, to cover his embarrassment, Anthony cynically asked, "What brings the tigress of the valley here?"

In response, Catarina slapped him across the face then said, "Do not disrespect me, Anthony! Do not make me hate you, because if I do, we will suffer together!"

She observed that he had been drinking heavily. His eyes were blood-shot, his body moved unsteadily, and he reeked from the smell of whiskey. "When you sober up, come see me. It's important," she said to him as she spun around and stormed out of the room.

Catarina left the valley in a rush. She mounted her horse and urged it into a gallop as she fought to hold her emotions under control. The horse raced down the path, and she paid no attention to which way they traveled. Her chest felt heavy, her heart pounded fast, and her fear of losing Anthony surfaced once again, terrifying her. He was the only man she had ever loved or desired. If she lost him, it would be worse than dying.

Consumed by her panic, Catarina whipped her horse mercilessly. It had never been so difficult to control her emotions. Once again she blamed her frustration and fears because she had had a defective child. In her heart, she felt that Anthony would never forgive her.

As the horse sped across the countryside the wind blew against her face, cooling her flushed skin and ruffling her hair. The sound of the whip quickly striking the horse and the pounding of hooves alerted the small creatures ahead of them, and they scurried away to safety. On this day, just like her father did for many years ago, she rode her horse at breakneck speed.

Undoubtedly, Claros would always be the setting for the

Casimiro's miseries and riches. The enigmatic forces that emanated from the nearby mountains held the mysterious shovel that dug all the elements and forces that greatly influenced the creatures of strong passions. Before beginning this trip, Catarina had fought these forces but they drew her back to Claros. She had experienced unusual feelings when she was actually leaving New York, strongly sensing that she must make the trip, yet at the same time, reluctant to do so.

It was early evening before Catarina returned, breathless and tired, to the house in Claros. Still feeling miserable, she took a hot bath and sat down to dinner. In spite of the many delicacies served to her, she had only a small bowl of soup for dinner—and she dined alone.

After dinner she stood in front of the window contemplating life outside her house. She saw the train station and the people who silently waited for the next train. Vaguely her father's image came to her mind and she remembered how he had loved to sit on the veranda to watch the trains passing. Suddenly, against her will Macael's words penetrated her thoughts. In her mind she visualized herself circling backwards in the center of a vortex and strange images swirling recklessly around her, over and over. Unexpectedly, Macael's voice sounded close and she heard the words clearly. *Your blood is impure. It is full of mildew. Your blood...full. Impure...mildew.*

Strangely her eyes moved to the train station once again and thoughts of her mother disturbed her greatly. She told herself, *I want to know more about her. It's strange that no one ever spoke of her. Sara...her name, the only thing I know.*

Aroused by curiosity, she turned from the window and went to the kitchen in search for Bihato, assuming that he would be able to tell her about her mother.

Instead of Bihato, she found Mariana seated at the table, half asleep with her head down upon it. In her old age, Mariana had developed a crippling affliction in one of her legs that prevented her from walking alone. Her leg was very red and needed medicinal wraps to reduce the swelling and heat. Geraldo, her husband, had died in his sleep soon after Catarina had gone to New York, and now Mariana relied on Bihato and her sons to help her move about each day.

As soon as she realized Bihato was not there, Catarina turned to leave the kitchen as quickly as she had entered it. But just as she turned around, she stopped. A thought caused her to change her mind. *Mariana must know as much about my mother as Bihato. She has worked for the Casimiros her whole life.* With that thought in mind Catarina walked to the table, sat down, and gently called, "Mariana!"

"Yes," responded Mariana, lifting her head to see who had called her name. When her eyes met Catarina's, an unusual expression came over her face. This was the first time in their entire lives they had been so close.

"I want to know about Sara, my mother. Mariana, please tell me everything you know about her."

The old woman looked at Catarina for a moment and then asked, "Why have you waited so long to ask about her?"

"Because, it is only now that I feel the need to do so."

Unknown to Catarina, nothing could take place in Claros that had not already been preordained by her mother, even before she had been born. The dark spirits of the universe had never ceased working toward this moment. Those same spirits were neither good nor very powerful, but they moved tirelessly with no concept of time. When they arranged for something to happen on full moon, it could be ten thousand full moons away, or it could happen during the next one. The spirits' biggest concern toward the activities of evil made under their sponsoring was that they were always obligated to somehow make them happen.

Slowly, Mariana adjusted the black shawl covering her shoulders and with her eyes fixed on nothing in particular said, "Your mother, Catarina, was my daughter."

Apparently, Mariana had waited many years for this moment. Meekly she proceeded telling Catarina all the secrets she had hidden in her heart most of her life. She told Catarina what had happened between her and Jetulio, speaking about their love with such emotion that tears rose in her eyes and flowed down her face. As she humbly advanced digging into the piles of secrets she had kept sealed in her mind, Catarina found herself listening to the most disgraceful story she had ever expected to hear. Clearly Macael's saying about the mildew in her blood made sense—evil and love had surely mixed together to shame her name.

Evidently Sara very much resembled her own mother at the age of fifteen; she was tall and shapely, with remarkable green eyes, and every eligible man around wished to marry her. But she had fallen in love with the one man who never noticed her—Jetulio Casimiro, the solitary man who ran his horse every night as some sort of personal ritual.

Innocently, Sara fantasized as she stood at her window each night, watching her nightrider. She found him completely different, quite impossible, and secretly she impelled all her actions toward this silly greed of hers. Like a wild animal full of strength, she fed her mind with all the sights, sounds, touches, smells and tastes that could possibly help her possess him.

Because through the dull days of Claros things happened in very strange ways, people did not question events that usually would have been considered bizarre. To de residents of Claros, anything that urgently spun in the air and seemed beyond any comprehension landed peacefully as a normal episode. So it was that one day, Jetulio asked for Sara's hand in marriage.

Yes, Jetulio had noticed Sara standing at her window every night watching him; and strange as it seemed, shortly afterwards he decided he should marry her and have a son to inherit his fortune. It was as simple as that. He awoke one morning with the crazy idea stuck in his mind and accepted it submissively without question or hesitation. The dark spirits had swiftly prodded his secret wishes and promptly deflated his arrogance–foolishly he dove into this new infatuation and the rest came about naturally.

His reason for doing it quickly, led to the fact that he had to leave on a trip, which he had been planning for months. He was going to Bahia with four of his employees and had no desire to postpone the trip just for his marriage. Therefore, he decided they should marry before he left.

The ceremony was held on a Saturday. The windows and door of the chapel were opened wide to celebrate the occasion and a nearby priest came to marry them. At the time, Sara was sixteen and Jetulio thirty-five. After the wedding they went to his house in the Pical Valley and the next day he left for Bahia.

While on that trip, Jetulio encountered many setbacks. Since they were traveling by horseback, it took them months to reach Bahia. During the long journey, one of his employees became ill and died. The same illness spread through the rest of the group, and Jetulio also spent two months in bed sick. By the time he felt strong enough to start his return to Claros, Catarina had already been born and Sara was dead.

Strange as it may seem, Jetulio could not recall why he had decided to marry the young girl, as he had never loved her. And his trip to Bahia—it also remained as vague in his memory as his marriage to Sara.

He finally accepted his baby daughter and named her, Maria Catarina. Since Mariana, as usual, was very busy running the household, Bihato became the person in charge of the little girl. He bathed, fed, and put her to bed at night. In time he learned to love her as if she were his own daughter. When Catarina started to talk, he taught her to say goodnight to her father. Every night, before she went to bed, Bihato took her by the hand and stood her in front of Jetulio. And because Bihato addressed him as "Senhor Jetulio," she also learned to call him that as well. "Senhor Jetulio, *boa noite*," she would say. Her father, without even looking at her, would respond, "*Boa noite*, Maria Catarina."

A few years later on one of those nights, Jetulio raised his head and looked at his daughter. Upon observing her, his eyes opened in surprise. At the time she was seven years old. That night it finally sunk in that she was his only heir, and therefore, needed a good education.

After that he became concerned about her schooling and went to Belo Horizonte to speak with his lawyer. A month later, he took Catarina to the best school in Rio de Janeiro where she spent the next eleven years of her life.

When Jetulio died, his lawyer went to Rio de Janeiro and brought Catarina back to Claros for his burial. Afterwards, she returned to the school and remained there until she was graduated at the age of eighteen.

Jetulio had been killed by his Dutch bull, Cobalto, which had gored him in the stomach. He had adored that animal and personally groomed him daily. When the accident happened, one of his employees took his shirt off and pressed it against the wound to stop the bleeding. Cautiously, they carried him into the house and called for Geraldo and Mariana.

Geraldo immediately ordered a man to go to the train station and send a telegram for the doctor to come. Then he jumped on his horse and hurried to find Elias, the only person in Claros who might be able to handle such an emergency.

After Geraldo rode away, Jetulio had motioned for the others to leave the room, and for Mariana to sit on the bed beside him. "I am dying, Mariana," he gasped, as he pressed the blood-soaked shirt against his stomach. " I want to know the truth about Sara. I woke up from a dream one morning with a vague awareness that she could be my daughter. You are her mother. Please tell me that I am wrong."

Full of grief, she answered, "No, you are not wrong," she replied.

Mariana watched helplessly as pain engulfed him. She was greatly distressed when she saw that her words had touched an innermost and sensitive part of his soul. It broke her heart to watch him going down with pain and the shame of this situation. He crouched over the bed and in disgrace let his blood drain out in his last moments. Instinctively, Mariana knew he had given up his will to live.

As she watched in horror, Jetulio closed his eyes and with the last of his strength, pushed his fist completely into the wound. He screamed savagely like a wild animal as his blood flowed freely onto the bed. Only death would stop his pain.

After hearing this story, Catarina was numb. Now, ashamed of her own existence, she felt that Mariana had caused this humiliation. A long silence hung in the air of the kitchen, and as it grew, a huge wave of resentment and rage swept over Catarina.

Angrily she grabbed Mariana's arms and as she shook her roughly shouted, "How could you have let this happen? How could you let my father marry his own daughter?"

At that moment, Bihato entered the kitchen through the back door, carrying a load of firewood. Frightened by the look on Catarina's face, he quickly threw the wood down and ran to them. In her eyes he saw a strong, eerie expression and they were glazed over and distant. She did not say anything when she saw Bihato, but he was sure that if she had, it would have been with the voice of whatever evil spirit had possessed her.

He grabbed Catarina and struggled to pull her away from Mariana, who had fallen to the floor. While Bihato bent to help Mariana up and into a chair, Catarina grabbed a knife and quickly ran out of the kitchen. She headed straight to her daughter's room, stopped next to the bed, raised the knife into the air, and then plunged it into Ana's chest.

"Go after her, Bihato. She is possessed by an evil spirit," Mariana instructed him, confirming her fears at the same time.

Terrified, Bihato ran after Catarina, and found her in the bedroom, still stabbing poor little Ana's body. Quickly he grabbed her by the arm and forcibly removed the knife from her hand. She stepped back from him and leaned against the wall, breathing heavily. Catarina let her body slide down to the floor, where she remained, dazed and exhausted; now with tears streaming down her face.

There was blood all over her, and Bihato as well, and they looked at each other with haunted eyes, like two phantoms who had known that this would happen one day. Suddenly, it seemed that for this precise moment Bihato had been compelled to stay in Claros—Jetulio's dog had sensed it many years ago. The animal had detected Bihato's kind soul, and it had also bitten the porcupine, which was taken as a bad omen.

The things Fulgencio had predicted finally had happened—disgrace, pain, and blood unmercifully covering the Casimiro's ground.

Suddenly, Mariana and Anthony appeared in the doorway. Anthony, after sobering up, had decided to come and speak with Catarina. When he entered the house, he found Mariana dragging herself across the floor and she had told him something terrible had happened. He helped her to his daughter's room and there they stopped, appalled by what they saw.

Anthony stared in disbelief, motionless, hoping that he was trapped in a nightmare, hoping that at any moment he would open his eyes and the whole scene would disappear. Cautiously, he approached the bed and looked down. His eyes opened wide, as if seeing something beyond human comprehension. Then he turned his head toward Catarina and saw her sitting on the floor crying softly. Next he looked at Bihato, who still held the knife in his hand.

"*Alguém pode me explicar o que passou aqui*? Bihato, *por que você matou a minha filha*?" "Would someone explain what happened here? Bihato, would you tell me why you killed my daughter?"

Bihato quickly looked at Catarina. Her beautiful face was filled with fear and pain. She would always be the little girl that he had raised with so much love. No one else could understand and love her more than he had.

"*Eu não sei senhor, eu não sei.* I don't know sir, I don't know."

Book 3

Satin, Passion, and Tears

37

New York, 1938

SOMETIMES THINGS THAT BOTHER us the most are suddenly taken away, just like dry leaves on the ground. We hear the crackling of the leaves under our feet with every step we take. Then, the wind softly blows them away, leaving behind a clean ground and bare branches that will be adorned with new green sprouting leaves—evidence of a new beginning.

Catarina hid her pain in a remote corner of her heart allowing the rest of her humiliations go as dry leaves do. She still had what she loved most, Anthony.

* * * *

"Good evening," said the young lady.

"Good evening," responded the attendant at the door.

He took her invitation and quickly verified it. Politely, he asked for their names, which he wrote down. She was Elizabeth Sfeel and he, Giovani Doneli Cassarete.

"Miss Sfeel and Mr. Cassarete, please follow me," said the attendant.

Elizabeth Sfeel and Giovani Doneli were introduced to the others in the big salon and then were immediately seated at a table.

The salon was elegantly decorated. White linen tablecloths covered the tables displayed one after another behind the enormous pillars surrounding the dance floor. Fresh flowers colored the ambiance spreading their intoxicating sweet aroma among the guests who enjoyed themselves dancing, smiling, and some just talking while drinking fine champagne and eating hors d'oeuvres.

This was the first time Elizabeth and Doneli had participated in such a lavish reception. They were seeing New York society's most extravagant event. Never had they dreamed of the luxury that loomed in front of their eyes. Even the sparkling chandeliers, which hung from the ceiling and the silverware used to serve the food and drinks kept them captivated.

The stylishly dressed women moved from one side of the salon to the other, their eyes gleaming with simple smiles on their lips. They appeared to be nymphs at a god's party, while the gentlemen jubilantly walked between them, exhibiting their charm.

Elizabeth Sfeel was perhaps the simplest and most innocent young girl in that salon, and for the occasion she wore a long blue dress with some silver decorations. She had bought the dress just for that evening and was the most expensive one she had ever owned.

When the waitress walked by with a tray of drinks, Elizabeth picked up a glass of champagne and then looked around, impatiently.

"Where are they, Doneli?" she asked.

"I don't know, Elizabeth," answered Doneli. "Like you, I only know them from the newspapers. I'm not sure I can recognize them today."

"It would be impossible not to recognize her, Doneli. She is very different. No one can be in the same place without noticing her presence."

"Really? I didn't know that."

"Ah, there she is!" said Elizabeth. "Can you see that table next to the orchestra? There they are. That lady must be Catarina."

Carefully, Elizabeth observed them then said, "That man sitting in the center must be Charles. He is the oldest man at the table. The one next to him could be Maximilien, his grandson and the other, Anthony, his son." Slowly sipping the champagne she added, "It's true what people say about Catarina. Look at her, Doneli. She is one of the most envied women in New York...beautiful and rich. I think we will never have the opportunity to meet someone as rich as her."

"You are probably right," answered Doneli.

The orchestra started playing another song as a handful of couples walked on to the dance floor.

Max rose from his chair and invited a girl to dance with him. Quietly, Elizabeth contemplated them. *What a wonderful man! He is gorgeous—like my father and Doneli. The kind of man I wish to have as a husband.*

"Doneli, what should a woman do to allure a man like that?" she asked.

"Like whom, Elizabeth?"

"Like Max. Like you and my father."

"I don't know, Elizabeth. I'm not good at that. I think this is a question a woman should answer. Besides, I don't know Max."

"Oh! You men are so naive. I only want to seek his attention. I don't need to know a handsome and rich man to win him over. The reason I asked you is that I failed to acquire the first handsome man I fell in love with—you."

"That's a dead subject, Elizabeth. Even you buried it already. Let's not talk about it. We're good friends now and I'm a married man."

"Of course! I don't know why I even brought it up. It must be the champagne." With a smile, she said, "I'm sorry, I'm sorry, I'm sorry."

Giovani Doneli was in a very interesting profession. He was a thirty-two year old FBI agent of Italian descent, married to an Italian girl named Luzia Badoleti.

Elizabeth had known Giovani for about six years. He used to buy his clothes in the Imperial, a men's clothing store located in Manhattan in front of the Merlenes' Jewelry store. Her father owned the Imperial.

The first time she spoke with Doneli, her heart had skipped a beat, a new sensation for her. Her blood suddenly ran hot, and millions of imaginary ants seemed to hasten crazily inside of her stomach. All of him disturbed her peace—his voice, gestures, smile, and look. In less than a second, her mind had etched every detail of his image. She sensed that a hundred years could go by and she would still be able to close her eyes and describe him perfectly. Tall and thin, with a tiny face, short nose, long eyebrows, deep green eyes, and shiny black hair.

From that day on, Giovani Doneli had remained in her mind and without any hesitation, entered her heart taking control of all her thoughts. It was Giovani Doneli, Giovani Doneli until the day he married.

Elizabeth was an Irish-American girl who had inherited her strong Irish features from her mother—light complexion, a sweet round face, and bright blue eyes with an ardent celestial look. And her lips always carried an expressive faithful smile.

When she turned seventeen, she invited Doneli to her birthday party. She did it with an ulterior motive in mind. She wanted to tell him that she was in love with him, and did so while dancing with him. "I'm in love with you and I want to be your girlfriend," she blurted out.

Doneli, who already suspected as much, found her attitude funny. He never thought she would have the courage to declare her feelings. After all, he was ten years older and he had always thought of her as just a lovely young girl. Careful not to hurt her feelings, he said, "I'm afraid that what you want is not possible, Elizabeth. I'm too old for you. I can't be your boyfriend."

"If you can't be my boyfriend, then we will be enemies. I'm

not going to speak to you anymore and if you want, you can leave. Thanks for coming."

Doneli took all that she said as a joke. He did not get angry with her nor did he leave as she asked. Instead, he sat with her father and they spoke all night long. To him, what she did was a normal reaction of a young girl in love.

However, Elizabeth decided to keep her promise and did not talk to him again.

Three years later, Doneli married. When Elizabeth saw the wedding invitation on her father's desk, she cried like a baby. Her tears ran down her face for hours, and she refused to accompany her father and Sophia to the wedding.

Sophia was her father's second wife. When barely eleven years old, Elizabeth had lost her mother, and exactly a year after her mother's death, her father met Sophia, a Spanish girl, and married her. That made Elizabeth's life unbearable and she could only hate that woman.

The day of Doneli's marriage, she remained in her room crying without consolation. When there were no more tears to be shed, she finally realized she had to remove him from her heart. Like she had years before when she had to compromise and accept Sophia in order to make her father happy. After that, everything between Doneli and her became purely platonic and it would remain so.

Before leaving her room that day, she had looked submissively at herself in the mirror and concluded that she would always have to accept things. She loved her father very much and she had to share him with someone else—a strange woman who used cheap perfume. It was hard but she would also have to get used to her smell—and she did. It hurt, it left a scar, but she survived. So, with effort, she could erase Giovani Doneli's image from her mind.

Her father died when she had turned twenty-one. During his stay in the hospital, Doneli went to visit him and she was there. That was the first time she spoke with Doneli since the day she had declared her love for him. As a mature woman she treated him politely, not forgetting that she loved him very much, but also accepting that he was no longer single.

The death of her father brought them together. During his illness, Elizabeth met Luzia, his wife, and they became good friends. When she felt how sincere Doneli and Luzia's friendship was, Elizabeth swore to herself never to remember that once she had been in love with him. She realized then that this must remain in the past.

After her father's funeral, Elizabeth moved in with one of her aunts. It would only be until she became used to the idea that she had lost the one man she most loved, and also until his lawyer settled everything regarding his will.

A few months after Frederick Sfeel's death, Mr. Malfonso, his lawyer, called her. Elizabeth was the sole heir, and owned four hundred thousand dollars in shares of Merlenes Industries. Her father had bought those shares before Charles had grown powerful. Her father and Charles used to talk about business frequently, but never became close friends. Many times they exchanged favors and Elizabeth's father once told Charles, "I like the name Merlenes. It does not sound too strong when pronounced, nor does it sound fragile. It is just perfect to be associated with jewels."

Frederick Sfeel sensed that Charles would go far with his jewel business, and it happened. The name Merlenes stayed forever and eventually the Merlenes controlled the jewelry business around the world. They had jewelry stores in almost every country and supplied diamonds to thousands of small jewelers. Their ships, which now numbered two, the *Serenata* and *Maria Catarina*, sailed from one ocean to another. A great part of their diamonds and semi-precious stones still came from Brazil. The Pical Valley had turned out to be the richest valley in the world.

Through the years, Anthony had established excellent relations with the governor of Minas Gerais, and this helped him to easily keep control of the Merlenes Industries' interests in Brazil.

Besides that, his kindness and honesty had created an aura of trust and distinction around his image. This led to his gaining a widespread reputation, which no other industrialist had ever accomplished before him.

Soon the whole world started to do business with the Merlenes. Anthony became an icon of prestige everywhere he went. All doors seemed to open instantly for him, no matter in which country he arrived. Whatever Brazil's soil could not supply, he had the power to acquire from Colombia, Africa, or any other country. His intelligence and charisma helped him build such a vast rich empire, that no one in the world could or would ever destroy it. The Merlenes—there was no one better behind them and no one superior in front of them.

The reception tonight was to celebrate Charles' eighty-first birthday and also to officially dedicate the Merlenes' new building in Manhattan. Their investors and friends arrived from different parts of the world to participate in this important event for the Merlenes Industries, and among the shareholders was Elizabeth Sfeel.

The opportunity to participate in this reception simply blew her mind. For the first time she would be involved with such sophisticated and rich people. She thought this would be an unforgettable experience.

When she received the invitation, she felt frustrated for she had no one to escort her to the event. Attending the reception alone would be very distasteful for her, and besides that, the invitation was for two. At the moment Giovani Doneli happened to be the only male friend she had and also the most qualified person for the occasion. He portrayed the experienced and charming image of a perfect gentleman.

She started thinking seriously about asking him to go with her, and one evening she finally worked up the courage to go to his house and speak with both, him and his wife. To Elizabeth's surprise it turned out to be the easiest thing she had ever done. After she explained the purpose of her visit, Luzia quickly said

Doneli would escort her to the reception with great pleasure. “That is what friends are for,” said Luzia. “I’m glad you thought of him.”

Between the two women deciding what he would or would not do, Doneli ended up in a tuxedo accompanying Elizabeth Sfeel to the reception.

38

THE MERLENES HELD THE GALA event in a large room of their building, located on the first floor. People spent their time mingling, enjoying the champagne, having conversations, and listening to the music. When dinner was served, everyone withdrew to their tables and busily started enjoying the delicious Brazilian and French dishes on the tables.

After dinner, the orchestra, which had ceased to play dance music, began to play again. As some couples walked to the center of the dance floor, Elizabeth got up and looked determinably at the other side of the room.

When she rose abruptly, Doneli asked, "Where are you going?"

"There," she replied as she motioned her head at the Merlenes table. "I'm going to say Happy Birthday to Charles Merlenes. What do you think about that?"

Pensively Doneli looked at her, then at the table where Charles was sitting.

"If you say so, you will."

"You know me quite well, don't you?"

"A little, Elizabeth."

After crossing the dance floor, she arrived at the other side of the salon and stopped in front of Charles' table. Cheerfully she smiled as she said, "Good evening, Mr. Merlenes! And happy birthday."

"Thank you," answered Charles politely. He extended his hand to hers. "With whom do I have the honor of speaking?"

"Elizabeth Sfeel. I never had the opportunity to meet you before, but my father did."

"Sfeel? The daughter of Frederick Sfeel?"

"Yes," she replied.

"You don't know how happy I am to meet you. Sit down, please," said Charles. "It is so delightful to have you here today. I heard about your father. I'm deeply sorry."

"Thank you, Mr. Merlenes."

"I only found out about it months later when Anthony informed me that your lawyer had come to see him."

"Yes, everything happened very unexpectedly. I didn't even know he had those shares, as he never told me about them. Our relationship changed a great deal after he re-married."

"Your father was a wonderful person, Miss Sfeel. I admired him greatly and I want you to know that I followed some of his advice. Would you please join me for a drink?"

"I'd be honored."

Charles poured some champagne and made a toast: "To the Sfeels."

"To the Merlenes," she returned.

Before they could say another word to each other, Catarina approached the table.

"Catarina, please meet Miss Elizabeth Sfeel," said Charles. "She is the daughter of Frederick Sfeel, one of our shareholders."

"Nice to meet you," said Catarina graciously.

They stared at each other like two statues frozen in time. Elizabeth was struck by Catarina's exotic looks and Catarina was surprised by the intensity of Elizabeth's bright blue eyes.

Catarina had just turned fifty, and yet did not appear to be a year over forty. Her beautiful green eyes were still intense.

That evening, she experienced a strange feeling upon meeting Elizabeth, a feeling quite difficult to explain. It was the kind of glimpse that disrupted the quiet peace of her soul. Her mind went blank, yet she felt as if she could hear the snapping of fingers trying to awaken her memory of something extremely relevant. But she failed to remember what it could be.

"You said Sfeel?" Catarina asked.

"Yes."

"It is an English name, isn't it?"

"My father was English."

"He was?"

"Yes, he passed away recently."

"Oh, I'm sorry."

"Thank you."

"And your mother? Is she also English?"

"No, Irish. She died when I was eleven years old."

"What a spectacular combination. You must be a fine, sweet girl."

"What makes you think so?"

"Because English girls are fine young ladies who have a queen serving as a good example and the Irish...just happen to be the sweetest ones in the world."

Elizabeth had never heard such a comment before and found it amusing.

Their conversation would have gone further if Anthony had not come looking for Catarina. He wanted to introduce her to some investors from Egypt. However, before following Anthony, Catarina presented Elizabeth to him.

"Anthony, first meet this young lady, Elizabeth Sfeel."

"Elizabeth? It is a pleasure to finally meet you. I'm glad you came. In the last few months I have spoken a great deal with Mr. Steve Malfonso, your lawyer. We only knew about what happened to your father months later when Mr. Malfonso got in touch with us."

"I understand," she said, "Everything happened quite suddenly."

"I would like to continue our conversation," said Anthony, "but at this moment I have some investors waiting for me. They want to meet my wife. I hope we can speak again. Please come and visit our offices soon. Your father invested his money in us when we were nothing. That makes you a very special shareholder. My father admired him a great deal."

Before leaving the table, Catarina added, "Do not go away, Elizabeth. I need to speak with you."

Catarina didn't have the slightest idea why she had said that. In reality, she did not have anything special to say; it was only that she sensed some urgency in establishing that their encounter would not end just yet.

As soon as Catarina left in the company of her husband, Elizabeth also got up to leave. She knew that Doneli was alone and like her, did not know a soul in the salon. She spoke a few words to Charles and then walked back to her table. Sitting next to Doneli she commented, "Incredible people. I'm very glad that I spoke with them."

"I'm happy you did too," replied Doneli.

At eleven o'clock the music stopped, and two waitresses brought out to the center of the salon, a table on which sat an enormous cake. *Happy Birthday*, *Charles* was written on the cake.

At that moment, Charles quietly walked to the center of the salon. In spite of celebrating his eighty-first birthday, he maintained his erect posture and good spirits. His face held a serene, confident smile and his white hair only enhanced the delicate lines around his eyes. Intellectual vigor radiated from him effortlessly.

When he reached the center of the salon, the orchestra started to play Happy Birthday and those present sang along as they clapped their hands. The waitresses replaced the empty glasses with full ones while the guests remained expectantly awaiting for Charles' words.

Calmly, Charles ran his eyes from one side of the salon to the other. About three hundred people had come to join him on this special day, and at that instant, everyone was standing and looking at him.

"Dear friends," he said moving his head slowly, "first I want to thank you all for your presence here today, celebrating my birthday and joining me in dedicating our building. This is a big event in the history of the Merlenes Industries. A couple of minutes ago, I asked myself if I had dreamed it all. Yes, my friends, I did."

Everyone applauded and then the room went quiet as he continued.

"Please, excuse me as I remember three people that can't be forgotten on a day like this. Sadly they have all passed away. The first one is Fairboyvan Gaspier, the genius who worked tirelessly to make moments like this possible. His loyalty can never be forgotten. Second, is Captain Alejandro Alvares, who helped me at the most critical moment of my life. He taught me many valuable lessons and I will never forget him. Lastly, one of our shareholders that passed way recently, Mr. Frederick Sfeel. Today, we have the honor of having his daughter present with us."

Looking around the salon he said, "Miss Elizabeth Sfeel, please join me. I would like to introduce you to my friends."

Nervously, Elizabeth left her table and walked towards the center of the salon. Everyone quietly looked at her. She had not expected to be called. When she drew close to Charles, he held her hand and continued his speech.

"The father of this young girl once told me, 'I like the name Merlenes. It does not sound too strong when pronounced, nor does it sound fragile. It is just perfect to be associated with jewels.' Mr. Frederick Sfeel was a great man and a valuable shareholder of our industries. Let's make a toast in his honor and also, a toast to Fairboyvan Gaspier and Captain Alejandro. To them, to all of us, and to our dreams and faith!"

The applause filled the room and continued on for some seconds. Charles and Elizabeth remained in the center until the waitress came and helped him cut the first piece of the cake, which he gave to Elizabeth. Charles offered the next piece to Catarina, then one to Anthony, Max, and finally his own. After that, the waitresses began serving the guests.

When Max approached the table to receive his piece of cake, he cordially introduced himself to Elizabeth.

"Miss Sfeel, it is a pleasure to meet you. I'm Max."

"Nice to meet you, Max," she said smiling.

"I bet that you are Irish," he said with a smile.

"No. I'm American. But yes, I had an Irish mother."

"I knew it! Only Irish girls have eyes with a blue color so bright that..."

"That what?"

"That daze every man on earth," he finished.

Happily she smiled at him but no words came to her lips. Max's self-confidence had instantly perturbed her very much. She had the most desired young man in New York society there speaking to her.

"I know what you are thinking," said Max.

"Oh, really? What?"

"That I'm trying to impress you."

"No. Actually, I did not think of anything. You did not give me much time to do so."

He laughed but gave her a puzzled look. Then the music began once again and some couples started to dance.

"You are wonderful. Would you like to dance?" Max asked.

They danced more than one set and Elizabeth experienced a forgotten childhood pleasure while in his arms. As the music played, she felt drawn into her old dream—that of being loved by a man like this, handsome and rich.

Going along with her fantasy, she thought she could dance with him forever and step into his life without a second thought. In her imagination all that a woman could ever dream of could reach reality in his world. Allowing her body to sway with the rhythm of the music, she thought to herself, *I lost Giovani*

Doneli...and now I'm dancing with Maximilien Merlenes.

Later that evening when they said good night, she gave Max the softest smile her lips could ever give.

"Miss Sfeel. You are the most beautiful girl I have ever met. Would you have dinner with me, tomorrow?" he asked.

Her intense, celestial look quickly diminished as she asked, "Is this an invitation?"

"Yes."

"Have you ever found a girl who said 'no' to you?"

A little bit embarrassed he answered, "No."

"Then I have no intention of being different. I would love to."

* * * *

The next evening they met again. The same occurred on the following one and the one after that. Happily she accepted his invitation to visit their offices. After spending some time with him, she became interested in knowing more about the shares she held and suddenly, to her surprise, he invited her to his home to have dinner with the whole family.

Little by little she acquainted Max with the workings of her business, the clothing store her father had left her, The Imperial. Max advised her repeatedly regarding her business decisions. More and more, they felt the need to meet in the afternoons for coffee or for dinner. Then as their relationship blossomed, Elizabeth began to tease Max, sometimes giving him anything he wished from her, and other times withholding her favors from him. As a result, Max desired her more than anything he possessed and soon was deeply in love with her.

Nine months after meeting, they married. She was already two months pregnant. On September 6, 1939, exactly three days after France and Great Britain declared war on Germany, she gave birth to twins—two boys: Maximilien Junior and Anthony, named after his grandfather.

That was the beginning of the third generation of the Merlenes and the end of a peaceful era. World War II had just begun—

39

SINCE THE END OF WORLD WAR I, the social and economic status of the Merlenes family had grown tremendously. After the war ended, the Merlenes once again concentrated on their plans to make their name known all over the world. It was then that they began to make business deals with many European countries.

During that time, Anthony had to stay out of the United States for such long periods of time doing business with European countries. He decided to buy a chalet in Paris and bring Catarina and Max with him. Catarina took advantage of this by traveling, improving her French, and enjoying Anthony's company. Little Max was enrolled in one of the best schools in Paris where he simultaneously studied French, Portuguese, English, and music with a private tutor. At home, he had Gertrudes, his governess, who taught him etiquette lessons. She also had custody of him when Anthony and Catarina traveled together.

Once Anthony's business deals began to increase, he took Catarina along with him wherever he went. It didn't take long before her charm was known all over Europe, making her quite popular. She became an object of attention at the social gatherings in every country they visited; the social columnists focused on her and loved her. Her exotic appeal when she entered a party on Anthony's arm caused everyone to turn and look at them. The women among the guests silently envied her and the men, as politely as possible, enjoyed what her presence offered—temptation and ecstasy.

With such prestige they smoothly penetrated into the high society of Europe and found they were never excluded from any gathering. Their presence grew so indispensable in European circles that they even participated in private parties given by the monarchs. They had dinner with princes and dukes and sometimes, they were the guests of honor.

In spite of all their social activities, Anthony never lost sight of his goal and kept his attention on his purpose for being there. He believed that persistence meets tomorrow before tomorrow runs away. Rigidly he kept himself focused on his ambitions. After four years of dedication and hard work, he reaped what he sowed. The family name controlled the gemstone market in every country in Europe. The Europeans knew the name Merlenes stood simultaneously for diamonds, Anthony, and Catarina. This information was imprinted upon everyone's mind once their image had been established.

At the end of those four years they discreetly closed up the chalet and sailed back to New York. On the trip, Anthony felt content and immensely proud of the work he had done. Now the Merlenes had the authority to control the diamond enterprises all over the world and in the process, Anthony was given the opportunity to learn what Gaspier and his father could not teach him. He had accomplished what all industrialists dreamed of doing.

They had not been back in New York very long before Anthony had bought a mansion on Long Island. Catarina brought Ivan Cupe from Europe to decorate her new home in the French style. He did exactly what she had pictured. The evidence of her good taste appeared in every corner of the house and cost was never a concern. The furniture, Persian carpets, draperies, chandeliers, and even the statues in the garden, had all been imported. The paintings on the walls were carefully selected. She brought from Europe authentic pieces and also expensive copies of works by French Rococo artists such as Jean Antoine Wotteau's, "A Pilgrimage to Cythera," which she hung at the entrance of the main hall, and another by Francois Boucher, "Venus Consoling Love," which decorated one of the walls in the music room. The amount of money that Catarina spent on the paintings alone was four times more than what the *Serenata* had cost and the work Ivan Cupe did for the mansion was simply breathtaking.

* * * *

Five years after Ana's death, Catarina traveled back to Brazil in order to get Bihato released from jail. He had become very sick and she wanted to take him back to Claros. She went to Belo Horizonte and used every influence that Anthony had with the politicians he knew to free Bihato. After three weeks of intense negotiations with influential people, she acquired a signed letter by Arthur Silvano Bernardino, governor of Minas Gerais at the time, authorizing Bihato's release.

Bihato returned to Claros where he lived the last part of his life. Nothing had changed within him as he continued to cultivate his main gift—kindness.

Before Catarina left Claros, Bihato asked her, "Catarina, do you really think that I killed that child?"

"No, Bihato, you would never do such a thing."

She walked toward him and gave him a kiss on the cheek. "*Eu amo você. Adeus* Bihato." "I love you. Good-bye, Bihato."

"*Adeus*, Catarina. Please ask your husband for my forgiveness."

Without turning to look at him, she said, "He has already forgiven you, Bihato. Despite the fact of not understanding how it happened, he never hated you." That was the last time they spoke.

In Claros, though, no one ever forgave Bihato because he had murdered an innocent child.

Bihato died a year later.

* * * *

About a year after his twin great-grandsons had been born, Charles left New York to live in Brazil. He wanted to spend the last years of his life in the peaceful valley where Claros was located. To him it had become like St. Denis.

He was almost eighty-three years old when he made the trip and it was the first time he had sailed on their ship the *Maria Catarina*. It was during the month of January that he left New York and while sailing, he had much time in which to think about the three people who had proved great significance in his life—Isabella, Gaspier, and Captain Alejandro. Thinking about them made Charles realize that he had lived too long.

In Claros, Charles stayed in the big house close to the train station. Anthony and Catarina, who had made the trip with him, took care of everything in order to leave him as comfortable as possible. It was arranged that Henry, his new butler, would also stay in Claros with him.

Despite the great distance between Claros and New York, Anthony and Catarina felt confident about Charles' decision. They sensed he was fulfilling another of his dreams.

To Charles being there and enjoying the peace that existed in the valleys around those mountains was a gift from heaven. Especially, since at that moment the world was once again engaged in another war.

A day before leaving Claros to return to New York, Catarina sat with him and they spoke for a long time. Holding his hand she said, "I hope you will be all right here, Charles."

"Don't worry. I will be," he responded. "And you Catarina take good care of this family. Be faithful."

"You are talking as if you are going to die."

"I would not wait until I die to have this conversation with you. I'm an old man—a happy old man. Destiny put us together. After me, you are the strongest person in this family. Keep in your heart dreams and faith—always Catarina—always. There will be a generation like you desire—with clean blood. You will see it. Sometimes God works in a strange way."

* * * *

A month later, while sitting in the library in New York, Catarina was surprised to remember that conversation. She then realized that what Charles had passed on to her was exactly what he had held inside of his heart for so many years. He had spoken of God, dreams, and faith and had intended for those words to be strong and hoped that their meaning would be even bigger. Serenity had come as a gift during his last days because he dreamed his dreams and kept his faith.

That same night, Catarina's concentration was broken by Elizabeth's screams. Elizabeth wanted someone to call Dr. Rudel and the chauffeur because the twins had to be rushed to the hospital.

Joseph, the butler, immediately went after the chauffeur while Florinda, the nanny, ran up the stairs to meet Elizabeth. Max, who was in the gambling room playing chess with his father, also came out. Anthony took the initiative to call the doctor.

In spite of perceiving all that was happening, Catarina stayed quietly in the library. She decided not to move. Twice she saw Joseph pass in front of the library, then Florinda, Max, and finally Anthony. No one thought about her and no one looked for her at that time. Only a few minutes later when the chaos had passed and the mansion became silent once again, Joseph found her as he was returning from closing the front door.

"Mrs. Merlenes?" he said when he saw her. He found it strange that she was downstairs and had not come out to meet them.

"Yes, Joseph," she responded.

"Do you know what happened?"

"Yes."

Not knowing what else to say, the butler asked, "Would you like some coffee or tea?"

"No, thank you."

The twins were just nine months old and ever since their birth they had been back and forth between home and the hospital a number of times because of respiratory problems. Not even Dr. Rudel knew if they would survive.

Tonight, as the family faced this difficult moment with the children, Catarina remained silent in the library, alone with her thoughts and also without hope. In her heart she knew it was the mildew of her bloodline that would shape the Merlenes' pains and she lacked the power to change it. Her husband, son Max, and Elizabeth, all had their hopes tied together—but not her. She knew that hope does not last forever and she chose to live close to her pain in order to build the strength she might need to help keep her family strong. Knowing her blood carried the shame that stained the Merlenes' name, she determined it would be her secret. Her heart would need to be hard as diamonds so she would be able to keep the phantoms of her past in check so they could not wipe away all the goodness of her delightful present.

As Joseph left her and she stayed alone thinking about all the things that money couldn't fix, she became deeply engrossed in her thoughts. Suddenly, she remembered a peculiar smell—the smell of older people. Then Macael's image appeared in her mind and she whispered aloud the words he had told her: "A woman with blue eyes will give birth to the first child—"

Instantly, she clearly saw that the woman was Elizabeth. She realized that Macael had said "child" not children so obviously he hadn't been referring to the twins. For the first time she connected Elizabeth with his predictions and had an explanation as to why she experienced such a strange feeling when she had first met her. *For some reason this Irish girl has come into my family.*

Catarina also remembered Charles' words. He had assured her that the Merlenes would have a generation like she wished—with clean blood. She took a moment to enjoy the good fruition of the spiritual energy that visited her soul. *Now I have pains disturbing my soul but there will be happiness uplifting it—someday. If it were not because of one, I would not meet the other, and tears establish the difference between pains and happiness. Pain soaks our faces and happiness moistens our cheeks.*

Then she let her past tiptoe over her present, as nothing worse would come to fill her eyes with tears. She let her wishes mix with her thoughts as tears ran freely down her face.

"Dear God, what could be next for this family?" she whispered aloud.

40

ELIZABETH SLOWLY OPENED HER eyes and lazily observed the details of the beautiful chandelier that hung from the high, white ceiling. She was lying in the middle of the expensive and comfortable bed she shared with Max. After rearranging her hair to one side of the pillow, she took in a deep breath. The lovely lavender scented smell of satin heightened her feeling of the luxury around her.

She lay there for some time viewing everything around her when suddenly, she remembered the children. *Oh, God! The children! Why do I always have to suffer?*

To her it seemed she had been suffering ever since her mother's death. As a young girl she frequently used to lie down on her bed and speak with God. Sometimes she did it because she was happy, and sometimes because she was angry. When she loved Doneli she would linger in bed for hours imagining she was in his arms. At the time, it was a comfort to have him to think about and she thanked God for it. However, when Doneli married, she felt betrayed and became quite angry with God and saw Him as her enemy.

Now as Max's wife, she still had a conflict with God. Lying on the satin sheets she said, "God, each day that passes by makes it harder for me to understand You. My mother taught me to love You, but You do things Your way and it hurts me constantly. Look at me, Elizabeth Sfeel, no, Elizabeth Merlenes. Max and the children are all I have left. You took my mother and my father away from me, and now...You are threatening my children."

She closed her eyes in an attempt to feel the presence of God inside her but instead, she felt even more miserable. Angrily she threw one of the pillows against the wall and muttered, "I'm suffering, and I don't like to suffer. I'm tired of believing that You are everywhere and that You see everything. You don't see my pain!"

Before marrying Max, she had thought the Merlenes' world couldn't be otherwise but perfect and she loved the idea of being a part of it. Indeed, she only saw the lovely side of it. Now, she could draw a different opinion. Even in their world there were things that money couldn't buy. She had entered this new life only to experience another kind of pain. And of course, who could be better than her to carry that cross? She already knew how to cry.

Slowly she rose up from her bed, dressed herself in a robe, and stood in front of her mirror to brush her hair. "I love my children," she whispered as tears flowed freely from her eyes. "Please, God, help us!" she pleaded.

The day was Sunday and everyone was home except her twin boys. Elizabeth finished combing her hair, wiped her tears, and went down to have breakfast. While going down the stairs, she saw Joseph escorting Doneli across the living room.

"Doneli?" she called as she hurried down the stairs in order to reach him. "The children again, Doneli. We have them in the hospital. We don't know what to do anymore. I don't know how much longer I can hope."

"We will find a solution," said Doneli. "There has to be one. You must have faith."

Oh, faith sometimes seems so distant...

She simply ignored Doneli's comment. "Come," she said drying her tears and pulling him by the hand through the hall. "Let's have coffee."

As soon as they entered the dining room, Max, Anthony, and Catarina stood up to greet Doneli. Emma, the servant, brought more coffee and another cup to the table.

"I came as soon as Luzia told me," said Doneli. "How are the children doing?"

"The news is good," answered Max. "I just spoke with Dr. Rudel and they are doing better now. I'm leaving in a few moments to go to the hospital."

While Doneli and Max occupied themselves by talking about the children, Elizabeth sipped her coffee. Then she cut a piece of cheese and spoke with Catarina.

"Catarina, where were you yesterday when we took the children to the hospital?"

"Sitting in the library."

"And you didn't hear what happened?"

"I did," she said curtly.

Surprised by her mother-in-law's answer, Elizabeth prompted, "And?"

"I decided not to get involved, Elizabeth. My presence wouldn't have changed anything, would it?"

"I can't believe you!"

"Sorry, Elizabeth. I do not have hope for the boys."

"Oh, no! Please don't say that," said Elizabeth crying and hugging her husband who sat next to her.

"Mother, please don't talk like that. You will cause her emotional state to get even worse," Max said.

"I think it's time that we all face reality," insisted Catarina.

"What reality?" asked Elizabeth now rather angry. "They are my children and I want them to live! That is *my* reality."

"They are my grandsons and I want them to live as well. But there is no hope, Elizabeth. Not in those children."

"Stop this nonsense, Catarina," Anthony demanded.

Anthony sensed that for some reason, Catarina was becoming aggressive, and he hated to see that. He hated to see her blaming herself for the problem they had with their bloodline. It seemed to be a form of punishment for her. Usually she was successful in keeping her pain inside her, but she did not always succeed. When it did surface, that was when she acted irrationally. Anthony remembered well Catarina's reaction to Ana's sickness and knew Catarina could never forgive herself. Of course, Elizabeth could never understand that.

To prevent the argument between them from escalating, he said. "I think we have to be happy at this moment because the children are doing much better. What we need to do is find a better way to help them. I want opinions from other doctors and we will go wherever we have to and will pay whatever is necessary to see they are made well. Though Dr. Rudel is an excellent doctor, and I trust him completely, I want other doctors to work with him. We must try everything possible to save our precious little boys.

"Now, let's change how we feel and let's fight together to be rid of this pain we are all suffering. I promise that my grandsons will not continue to live this way–going back and forth from their home to the hospital. That way of life just ended."

Everyone listened without making any comment, and looking at their faces, Anthony knew that they understood what he had said.

* * * *

Besides the children's problems, the Merlenes/Sfeel union had brought into the family another issue—the Imperial. Right after Max and Elizabeth's wedding, the clothing store became more and more a part of the family's conversation. Max and Anthony suggested that Elizabeth sell the store, while Catarina and Elizabeth had a different opinion about the matter.

When they first talked about it, Catarina had asked, "Why sell it?"

In response Anthony had said, "Because we don't know anything about selling clothes."

"Anthony, my darling, selling clothes is something that can be learned," she assured him.

"Oh, no! Don't come to me with strange ideas because in business, mistakes can cost a lot of money."

"True. But I don't see this as the reason for you to view it in a negative light. I think that selling clothes is a good business; maybe as good as selling jewelry. Remember, that clothing store was Frederick Sfeel's whole life and purpose for living," Catarina reminded him.

At the time of that conversation Elizabeth was five months pregnant and confidently she participated in the discussion. She was a designer and spoke about clothing as if it were her life. In a lovingly way she let them know that whatever Max decided would be okay with her, but she also said, "Being a well-known clothing designer has always been my dream. Fine clothes and exquisite jewels go very well together," she said cleverly. "In my opinion one can be the charm of the other. Of course, I'm talking about elegant and exclusive clothing for men and women, designed with taste." She spoke freely and with conviction because she understood as much about clothing as they did about jewelry.

When she had finished speaking, everyone remained quiet, just looking at her. No one knew about her design expertise. Then Charles, who had until now just listened, decided to give his opinion. "I just heard two very interesting things—first, that Elizabeth's father did this for a living and second, that she is a designer. Am I right in thinking that this has surprised us all?"

"Let me give my opinion in this matter. If she has dreamed about becoming a well-known designer, who else better than us to help her? Perhaps what she said about clothes and jewelry makes more sense than what we don't know about clothes. One can be the charm of the other."

An intense silence filled the room and Anthony had nothing relevant to say. He thought that the head of the family had spoken and did so in Elizabeth's favor. Therefore, he decided to keep his final opinion for later. He could wait and see in what direction things would go.

Following Charles' words, Elizabeth saw her idea taking shape. Max, for example, quickly became very concerned about the matter. And to show his interest, he commented, "Suppose we begin to design and make fine and expensive clothing. What name would be on the label? Merlenes would not be right as it stands for jewelry."

"My name, Max," answered Elizabeth, sweetly. "Madame Elizabeth Sfeel."

Charles was the last one to speak on the subject that night and he did so calmly. To his son he said, "Anthony, before parting, let's give this some thought. After all, it is Elizabeth's dream. You know me, I like to respect everyone's dreams." After that, the issue moved from the dining table to the conference room of the Merlenes Industries.

The Merlenes' dining room was located at the end of the second longest hall in the mansion. On the left side of the hall was the parlor; and to the right the gambling room. Next to the gambling room were the music room and the library. The dining room table was made of white marble and seated twenty-four guests. Suspended from the ceiling were two, large round chandeliers that looked like a cascade of cut crystals flowing over the table. A rectangular Persian carpet on the floor was wine-colored and matched the seats on the chairs. Hanging on one of the walls were two, very large, gold-framed photographs. In one of them Charles Merlenes was sitting in a classic pose looking serenely at all who entered the room. Catarina, Anthony, and Max as a child were in the other. Catarina appeared seated in a high-backed chair, with Anthony and Max standing next to her. They all posed elegantly dressed in navy blue, and Catarina wore the diamond necklace Charles had given her.

It was in the dining room where the family talked the most. During dinners they talked about business as well as discussed family problems. Around this big table they had bought ships, sold shares of the company, faced their miseries, and enjoyed happy occasions together. Sitting in those chairs each one of them had the right to be his own person—common human beings in touch with their emotions and bereft of their status. The walls of this room guarded their pain and their secrets. It was the family tabernacle and the most private spot in New York City. In it, not even the *New York Times* could hear them.

Since Giovani Doneli had become an intimate friend of the Merlenes family, he had the privilege of frequenting this sacred tabernacle at will. Often he came to their family celebrations, and regularly participated in their poker and chess games.

Max had chosen Giovani and Luzia Doneli to be the godparents of Maximilien Jr. One night, after consecutively losing two chess games to Doneli, Max had come to that decision. When playing together, Doneli had said, "I know that Elizabeth went to see the doctor and that everything is well. She said she has just begun her ninth month. Congratulations, Max! Luzia could never get past the third month. She has not been able to carry a baby to full term."

"Oh, I didn't know that," Max commented.

"Yes, we have lost any hope of having a child."

Later on in the privacy of their bedroom, Max hugged Elizabeth and asked, "Who will be the godparents of our child?"

"I don't know. I haven't thought about it."

"What about Doneli and his wife?"

"Doneli and Luzia?"

"Yes."

"Are you serious?"

"They cannot have children. I think this will make them very happy."

"Oh, that is a wonderful idea, Max!" exclaimed Elizabeth. "You don't know how happy that makes me."

From then on the fondness that existed between the two families was established forever.

41

ANTHONY DID AS HE HAD promised at the table. He spoke with Dr. Rudel about the children and explained to him that they couldn't go on living as they had as everyone in the house was under a tremendous amount of stress because of the children's problem. "Seriously," he said, "we need to find another way to help them, Dr. Rudel. Please use your influence as a doctor and help us."

Dr. Rudel drove home that afternoon thinking about what Anthony had asked of him. He really wanted to do more for the twins and he had already asked other doctors for their opinions. Actually, Dr. Rudel had done more than what Anthony knew, but in medicine, things are not solved from one day to the next like in business. The fact was that the boys had been born with a serious problem. Their tiny lungs were undeveloped, thereby not enabling them to take in enough oxygen to sustain them. That was why they had to stay in the hospital for two months before coming home. Even then, they remained under the care of a nurse twenty-four hours a day.

For nine long months Dr. Rudel worked with an exhaustive

dedication to keep the little boys alive. As a doctor he had seen some positive results with his treatments. But he also understood how Anthony and his family felt about the problem and he began considering what Anthony had suggested.

Anthony had been reaching out for help and he wanted Dr. Rudel to work together with other doctors in order to find out if a new treatment might not help. Every afternoon, while on his way to see the boys in the hospital, Dr. Rudel thought about this matter. One day, like a miracle, a doctor's name suddenly came to his mind; an old college friend, Dr. David Scarshiner.

Dr. Scarshiner was a Jewish doctor who built an excellent reputation as a pediatrician and had also done research work in laboratories, conducting experiments related to many kinds of diseases. At the time, he was living in Boston. Dr. Rudel contacted him as soon as he could.

Upon hearing about the twins, Dr. Scarshiner became seriously interested in their case. He had read about them in the newspaper and felt very sorry for the Merlenes. At Dr. Rudel's request, he rescheduled his agenda in order to go to New York to see the boys.

As it turned out, Dr. Scarshiner became the children's savior. He designed a new treatment for them and made arrangements to spend blocks of time in New York every other week so he could see them. He believed that as the children grew older, they would become strong, and eventually would overcome their problem. But until that happened, he wanted them to remain in the hospital. Whatever Dr. Scarshiner asked, the Merlenes did without hesitation.

* * * *

While in New York, the Merlenes' most important concern was to save the lives of the twins; at the same time in London, the *RAF* fighter force confronted the Luftwaffe pilots. Day and night the two forces met each other in the air. It became useless to describe the terror to the civilians, and only the fighting spirit of the *RAF's* fighter force brought some hope for the English.

In a short time, all the people in the world were interested in turning on a radio to hear about the war. In every country, the most common conversation on the streets, in bars, restaurants and cafes was about Hitler. That man of small stature and funny mustache had turned the entire world's attention toward him. People relished saying, "Austria gave the world great composers and also an unforgettable bastard!"

In July 1941, American marines were sent to Iceland to protect the English flotilla and two months later, President Roosevelt announced that the Americans would respond to any attack from German and Italian ships that interfered with U.S. ships. This declaration made the world understand that the war had taken a new twist in the field of combat—Roosevelt, Hitler, and Mussolini.

That day in the Merlenes' house, Max commented, "Finally, President Roosevelt found something interesting to say. My God, why did he take so long?"

"Goodness, Max!" said Elizabeth. "Why do you think that getting involved in this war is something interesting?"

"My darling, it is not interesting to remain useless at a moment like this. It is obvious that we have to be in it if we want to live in peace. And I'm going to go help the Americans fight."

"What?" asked Anthony in surprise.

"I want to go to the war," repeated Max.

"Are you crazy? I do not want to hear this nonsense again. We have a war *here*—the problem with the children."

"What purpose will it serve to save their lives if we will not understand the language they might speak? I do not want to learn German. Not today, not tomorrow, not ever!"

After that, Max kept his eyes and ears open as to what President Roosevelt did, and followed the news on a daily basis. He knew the Americans had to enter the war for the sake of the world, and they had to do it with the same fervor as Hitler. Max hungered to be part of a naval combat, to express his hatred for

Hitler. In his opinion, every country that was not an ally of the Germans should enter the war to fight against them. And he saw this happen. Without any problem, Max was accepted into the Navy. Instantly his qualifications designated a place for him because he had studied navigation as a complement to his education.

* * * *

In the past, Max's interest in navigation had not surprised his father or his grandfather. As a child, Max loved to ask Captain Alejandro questions about ships and oceans, and often stood next to the Captain at the helm of the *Serenata*. How many children had a grandfather like Charles who owned a ship called the *Serenata*? And how many children had the opportunity, like Max, to meet a captain who was part of the family? So as a child, Max's biggest dream was to grow up as fast as he could and learn to sail his grandfather's ships. And because the dreams of rich children can sometimes become a reality, he learned navigation as he learned music, painting and fencing. Diamonds paid for whatever he decided to pursue.

Max graduated with a major in geology and during his studies he visited Africa and Brazil in the company of Dr. Selesque, his geology professor. Of course, it was a privilege that Dr. Selesque gave only to Max because no other student of his had a private diamond mine, and even for Dr. Selesque this turned out to be an extremely attractive trip.

The good professor had never been to Minas Gerais before but had heard a lot about it. For example, he heard the gold that the Portuguese had taken from Minas Gerais during colonial times would have been enough to cover the walls of Coimbra University many times over.

Max and Dr. Selesque spent more than a month in Brazil. When they returned to New York, they gave Charles and Anthony great news. Max told them there were emeralds in one of the mountains in the Pical Valley. But of course Charles and

Anthony were not surprised with the news because Anthony suspected this already.

What had been surprising was Anthony's unsuitable answer: "No one will destroy that mountain while your mother is alive, Max. No one. Do you understand?"

Max had never before heard his father speak like that. He responded, "Yes, I understand."

Even though Max felt somewhat disappointed with his father's response, he was proud to be a Merlenes. That day he discovered how much his father truly loved his mother and that brought him more joy than the news about the emeralds. He felt happy and thankful about everything he had—including those forbidden emeralds.

* * * *

Anthony was fifty-four when Max enlisted in the navy in order to fight in the war. The sadness and uncertainty he felt cost him even more gray hair. Everyday it weighed heavily on him and he couldn't lightly accept Max's decision. He felt that the Merlenes could have helped in some other way—either by sending their ships or in some monetary fashion. But Max hadn't seen it from his father's point of view. He wanted to be part of the war both in body and soul.

Elizabeth cried day and night, not knowing what to do to change Max's mind. But her tears, the children's problems, nor Catarina or Anthony's pleas could dissuade him from his decision.

On the day Max left, as he said good-bye to his family, he told them, "There are some things in life that a man must do. For me, going to this war is one of them."

42

MAX JOINED THE MARINES, WHICH was a branch of the Navy during WWII, and went to boot camp for six months of training. Immediately after that, he took part in the operations of the North Atlantic and his first mission was sailing on their own ship, the *Maria Catarina* that was being used as an escort in a convoy.

At the time, convoys were the best defense against the German submarines. To diminish the possibility of being attacked, a flotilla of more than sixty merchant ships navigated around them. Joining the flotilla were both the Merlenes' ships. Max felt extremely proud when he saw how the Merlenes contributed in the struggle to stop Hitler and even though he sensed the danger in which he was engaged, he also knew that he was doing the right thing.

* * * *

Anthony grew accustomed to spending long hours at home. He didn't mind it because of the war situation. Going to the office once a week was more than enough. In Claros their operations did not change and the daily routine remained the same. The diamond mine wasn't as prosperous as it used to be, but the company still had it under exploration, and other natural stones also began to be mined in the valley. Aside from that, the cassiterite prospecting beds along the river grew in an unexpected way. Every square meter dug in Claros brought a surprise to the Merlenes. Not even Catarina had imagined she owned such a rich land.

Besides the operations in Claros, Anthony also acquired, through his political influence, participation in two other mines—a diamond mine in Diamantina and a gold mine from the surrounding mountains of Ouro Preto.

In spite of being in good health, Anthony was very sad at this time and many wrinkles lined his face. His sadness came mainly from the fact that he just could not accept the idea that his son was in the war and therefore, in obvious danger. Since Anthony greatly feared that Max might not come back alive, it caused him to lose his appetite. Besides not eating well, he also avoided the company of his friends. No one, not even Doneli, could convince him to get this idea out of his mind.

Anthony began spending countless hours alone in the library, submerged in his thoughts. He sensed he lacked the strength to go on with life and every day his pain increased and silence became his only consolation. Constantly he needed to think, remember, pray, and hope for a miracle.

One night while he was in the library, Catarina came and sat next to him. He looked so sad that she said, "Anthony, don't be like this. He's not going to die."

"Perhaps he will not," he uttered embracing her.

She also hugged him, and for a while she cried without saying anything. Over the years she had become more softhearted. Her relationships with Charles and Captain Alejandro helped refine her character and in the midst of this she had her son Max to fortify her faith. As he grew from a child to a man, he renewed the feelings of her heart. She chose to believe he was a gift from God.

After Ana's death, she experienced one more pregnancy but

suffered a miscarriage. Something horrible came out of her womb—deformed flesh, which reminded her of the *mildew* in her blood, and only her gynecologist and Dr. Rudel saw it. When the miscarriage occurred, Anthony happened to be in Africa.

That day, while crying in Anthony's arms she whispered, "I also am afraid of losing Max. He's our only son. Can't we do something?"

"No. There is absolutely nothing I can do," he answered gently caressing her hair. "You heard what he said before he left: 'There are some things in life that a man must do...' He is a man, Catarina. We need to respect his wishes."

Quite frustrated she commented, "At this moment we have a son and two ships in the North Atlantic. Oh, Anthony, I hope America does not ask more of us."

* * * *

In July 1942, Charles returned to New York on a ship called the *Doce Bahia*. Henry, his butler, who had stayed with him in Claros, had earlier sent a long letter to Anthony in which he informed him of Charles' health. The weather in Claros had turned cold. It hadn't been good for Charles and he became very sick. Henry ended the letter saying, "Mr. Merlenes, if you don't authorize me to return with your father to New York, I'll do it under my own responsibility. Your father needs to be under medical treatment."

As soon as Anthony read the letter, he sent a telegram to Araujo Farcante in Belo Horizonte and he also sent one to the governor in Rio de Janeiro. Anthony could not use their ships to bring his father back to New York because they were with the American Navy in the Atlantic. So in desperation he contacted the governor for help. Forty-eight hours later, Charles and Henry traveled to Rio de Janeiro to board the ship, *Doce Bahia*, for their return home.

It took almost a month for *Doce Bahia* to reach New York. Captain Pedro Santos had never sailed this route before. In addition, he had been confronted with a difficult voyage. If it hadn't been for the help of a Greek ship, they would never have arrived safely in New York.

Once in New York City, Charles was immediately taken to the hospital. His doctor, as well as Dr. Rudel, did not want to give Anthony any false hopes. When Charles finally arrived, he was unconscious and had a very weak pulse. When his doctor saw him, he exclaimed, "One more hour in this condition and he would have been dead!"

Anthony, who did not accept the seriousness of his father's critical state, thanked God for having him back. The delay at sea had been no one's fault. They all knew Captain Santos did what he could and Anthony felt so grateful to him that he invited the captain and his crew to have dinner at his house. Even Henry sat at the table with them. After dinner, Anthony and Catarina returned to the hospital. They found Charles' pulse was still quite weak, but they had hope. At least he was now in the hands of good doctors.

The *Doce Bahia* didn't stay in New York City very long. After hurriedly taking on supplies, it left for Brazil the next day. Before parting, however, the captain received directly from Anthony's hand, an envelope with a small gift inside—a sum of money that was to be divided between the crew and him. It was impossible to refuse the generous gift. And for an instant, Captain Santos thought that Jesus Christ had returned to the earth; and that this time, he was performing miracles in New York City instead of Jerusalem.

That same day, in Rio de Janeiro, a messenger carrying two packages from the Merlenes' jewelers entered the governor's residence. In one package was an emerald and diamond pin for the governor's wife and in the other, an ivory and gold pipe for the governor.

The enclosed card read:

With all of my gratitude,

Anthony Merlenes.

Charles left the hospital two weeks later and was taken home. In spite of being physically in stable condition, he did not recognize the people around him nor his surroundings. In his mind he thought he was still in Claros. Sometimes he spoke about the trains he heard and of course, this was all a figment of his imagination.

Anthony was so worried that he called Henry and asked, "Henry, how long has it been since my father lost his memory?"

"Since he read the letter you wrote telling him that his grandson, Max, had gone to the war."

"Oh, I see." Anthony commented, thoughtfully.

"Have you ever seen your father cry?" asked the butler.

"No."

"I did—on the day he read that letter."

A month had elapsed since Charles' return to New York. During this time he never came out of his world. In his mind, he remained in Claros.

One day when Catarina approached to kiss him goodnight, he said, "I saw her."

"Who, Charles? Who did you see?"

"Isabella. I saw her. She was calling me."

With tears in her eyes, Catarina looked at him. She understood his time had come. Isabella would be the last person he remembered and Claros the only place he couldn't forget.

Immediately, she went to find Anthony. Crying she said, "Anthony, your father is dying. We should stay with him tonight."

They asked for some tea and then proceeded to sit next to Charles' bed. Some time later, Catarina became tired and rested her head on Anthony's shoulder, quickly falling asleep. Then Anthony also dozed off. At dawn, as they slept, Henry entered the room and found that Charles had died.

Many people attended Charles' funeral. He was buried in the

family tomb where years ago Ana, his wife, and Isabella had been laid to rest. The burial and Anthony's words made the front page of the *New York Times*:

> **"God allowed my father to fulfill all of his dreams. Even the last one, which was to die in Minas Gerais. He died in New York thinking he was still in Claros. We lost a great man."**

43

A MONTH AFTER CHARLES' DEATH the twins turned three years old. Dr. Scarshiner had saved their lives and for everyone it was a moment of great happiness and celebration. It seemed like a miracle to have seen them live this long. Because of the circumstances, their birthday was the only thing that made sense at the moment—the only reality that brought some joy to the house.

After dinner, they sang happy birthday to the little boys and cut a beautiful cake that had been baked by the Merlenes' cook. Only the family, the children's doctors, nurses, servants and their godparents attended the celebration.

Maximilien Jr. and young Anthony were dressed alike; and while being held by their nannies, they blew the candles out. "Happy Birthday, Max and Anthony," everyone sang.

The last people to leave the house that day were Doneli and Luzia. And before leaving, Doneli said, "I have some news. Tomorrow I'm leaving for France."

"What?" asked Elizabeth. "Don't you know that everything there smells like Hitler?"

"That's why I have to go. We must know everything about the perfume he uses," answered Doneli jokingly.

"FBI mission?" Anthony asked.

"Yes."

"Oh, no! I think that everyone will eventually go to this war," commented Catarina. "Can't you just say no?"

"To my country? No. I would never do that. Especially in circumstances like these," Doneli replied.

Moments later, Elizabeth was in Doneli's arms crying while hugging him and saying good-bye. When Doneli felt her tears wetting his neck, he knew it was worth it to go to war.

* * * *

For a long time Doneli had secretly fought against his wild feelings for suddenly, he had fallen in love with Elizabeth. At the time she was eight months pregnant.

One night he had passed by the house to play chess with Max and as Max poured some cognac for them, Elizabeth entered the room. She had come close to Doneli as she always did, said hello and gave him a gentle kiss on the cheek. But that time, without knowing why, he had seen something new in her. She was a woman who had emerged from the tender body of a girl. For the first time, without being modest, he had erased the innocent and sweet image of that seventeen year old child who had once danced in his arms.

Her beautiful blue silk dress had buttons down the front. When she had kissed his cheek, she misjudged the size of her belly and Doneli had felt the buttons of her dress between them. Instantly he closed his eyes to enjoy her sweet smell, and in the intimacy of his mind, it had become irrelevant that she was pregnant. From then on, he had imagined her exactly as he wished her.

He couldn't ever stop desiring her, and even though he knew the idea was insane, he hadn't been able to stop his feelings. The new sensation and desires circling his soul and filling his imagination day and night had become unbearable. He began living in his own hell in which only God and he knew how much he was suffering. Unexpectedly, she had become his every fantasy.

When Doneli had found out that he and his wife would be the godparents of the child she was expecting, he felt extremely happy. He felt so happy that he vaguely anticipated it was her idea. However, he was wrong about that. Max had brought up the subject first, and Elizabeth had agreed with it.

To everyone's surprise, Elizabeth gave birth to twin boys. Doneli used this as an excuse to prolong the hug he had given her that day. Later, they all had to deal with the news about the twins' health problems, for the doctor wasn't sure if they would survive. Since Elizabeth was suffering and constantly crying, to remain close to her seemed to be Doneli's obligation. Sometimes she cried in Max or Anthony's arms, and even in his. It had been impossible for him to stop loving her.

Something of that young girl had remained within her and it still haunted him. Saying good-bye to her and leaving for France was indeed another joyous moment for him. Doneli not only delighted in her tears wetting his skin, but also while kissing her cheek he had enjoyed the sweet taste they left behind.

"Goodbye, Elizabeth."

"Goodbye, dear Doneli. I hope God is with you as he is with Max. I will pray for both of you."

Doneli left and not much out of the ordinary happened after that. The Merlenes' daily routine kept the same course, and the stable condition of the twins captivated their full attention. They finally started to enjoy some happiness as the war continued.

In France, while Doneli spent his time searching for secret information for the FBI, Max was assigned to an American convoy. During that terrible time Elizabeth was the most precious person on both their minds.

In early December the *Serenata* made a trip to New York. On this trip, Stalke Normiro, the ship's captain, brought Elizabeth a letter from Max. He asked her to go to France to meet him for Christmas as he had received a week's leave.

In the beginning, Elizabeth had found the idea to be a crazy one—completely out of the question. But after she read Max's letter again and again, things became quite clear in her mind and she grew more concerned about what her husband wanted. And even though she thought Max had lost his mind, she decided to speak with the captain regarding the trip.

Captain Normiro told her that there wasn't a single place to call safe at the moment. However, Paris was no longer Hitler's target because he had already acquired it. The captain also told her that Max had contacted Doneli for help. He stated firmly that no one better than he could make her trip safe. Because of his job, he knew for sure what goes on behind the walls. So against everyone's opinion, Elizabeth packed and got ready to leave New York with Captain Normiro.

"Catarina," she said on the day she left. "Please look after the children for me." Then approaching Anthony she added, "I'm sorry, Anthony. I have to go see him. You understand, don't you? If I don't go and something happens to him, I could never forgive myself. I would have to die as well."

"I think that everyone is losing their minds," commented Anthony. "Not only the Germans, but everyone else."

Elizabeth entered Paris at nighttime. Doneli came to meet her and escorted her to the chalet where Max was waiting. Max had already been in Paris for two days and as soon as she entered the chalet, he ran forward and hugged her, keeping her held tightly in his arms for what seemed to be forever. They both were oblivious of Doneli's presence.

"Oh, my darling! I have missed you so much."

"Max, my dear, why are you doing this to me? Why are you in this war? What would I do if something happened to you?"

"Please, Elizabeth, let me hug and kiss you. Don't make me waste my time trying to answer something I cannot." Then holding her face between his hands he added, "I had to overcome so many obstacles to make this moment possible, and you had to have a lot of courage to come here. So don't waste time asking silly questions. Let's make believe the war has ended. I love you."

She smiled and cried while he kissed her face, neck and lips. Following this, they looked around and remembered Doneli. But he wasn't there anymore. He had gone elsewhere carrying his misery. Elizabeth had already given him his kiss when they had met that night. And incredible as it seemed, he left—after all—miserably happy.

Max and Elizabeth closed the door of the chalet and forgot about what was going on outside it. They made love for hours. That night, they did not even remember to eat. In the morning she walked through the chalet and discovered the kitchen.

Because it was Christmas Eve, she planned for all three of them to dine together. They waited for Doneli until past midnight, but he never came. While waiting, they drank some wine and talked about the children and Charles' death. Elizabeth told Max how Charles had lost his memory and how he had died thinking he was in Claros. Max listened to her, preferring to remain silent; remembering the good moments he and his grandfather had spent together. At half past midnight, they decided to sit down and eat. Dinner consisted of rice, peas and some roasted meat. They did not have presents for each other, but they did have the rest of the night for themselves.

The next two days passed quickly and once again, Max had to leave for the Atlantic. Doneli returned that same day to accompany him to his ship. When he entered the chalet, Elizabeth ran toward him.

"Doneli, where have you been? We waited for you on Christmas Eve because we expected to dine together."

"I'm sorry but I didn't want to disturb anyone. I thought it was better not to come."

"I don't understand why you did that!" said Max. "During the holidays no one should be alone, especially knowing friends were waiting. I will not forgive you for this, Doneli."

"I'm sorry, Max. We are not in New York and this Christmas belonged to you both."

Doneli had brought Juliet, a young English woman, with him to stay at the chalet with Elizabeth and keep her company. He had arranged for Elizabeth to return to New York in two days time on a military flight. At 10:00 p.m. Max said good-bye to his wife and with Doneli walked to the car where a French chauffeur awaited.

"You don't have to come with me, Doneli. Luis knows where to take me," said Max.

"I know," answered Doneli. "But I will go with you anyway to make sure you leave Paris safely. You don't know what is happening here or what could happen and I do."

"Thank you, Doneli. Thank you for everything."

After being assured that Max had left Paris safely, Doneli returned to the chalet where he informed Elizabeth that Max had safely left and promised to pass by the next day to see both Juliet and her. He felt responsible for her while she remained in Paris.

For the next two days Elizabeth waited patiently for the day of her return to New York. But, things did not work out as smoothly as Doneli had planned. Some complications arose. Namely, the military flight that Elizabeth was supposed to take back to New York was rescheduled for two days later. Under the circumstances, Doneli couldn't do much and she had to remain in Paris until then.

That small change of plans gave rise to another problem. Juliet was scheduled to return to London and could not stay any longer. Doneli did not have enough time to find someone else to replace Juliet, so against his will, he remained in the chalet to make sure Elizabeth was safe until she went back to New York.

Though the chalet's decor was very simple, the furniture seemed expensive. It had a wooden floor, red carpets, and brightly colored pillows spread all over the sofas and on the floor. The room with the highest ceiling in the chalet was located beyond the dining room, and in one of its walls was the fireplace.

The day Juliet left, Doneli arrived at the chalet about 7:00 p.m. when Elizabeth had just finished preparing a dinner of leftovers. They dined together and then spent some time talking, speaking about so many things that for a while, it was possible to imagine the world without a war. They exchanged ideas regarding simple things they were never given the opportunity to discuss before. For example, "Burgundy is my favorite wine," Elizabeth revealed.

"Funny," he commented. "I also love Burgundy. In my opinion the best wine comes from the Pinot Noir grape."

She smiled sweetly at him.

"Our life in New York never allowed us to discover these things, isn't it true?" he asked.

"Yes," she agreed shaking her head.

They also discussed serious topics. Elizabeth said, "If we win this war against Hitler, what do you think will become of the Germans? We all hate them."

"This, Elizabeth, will be the hardest part of the war—to combat that hatred. If we don't change a bit after this war, why are we fighting it then? We should be concerned about that from now on."

"Right. I never thought of it in that way," she agreed.

"It is not your fault as it has not been necessary to think about these things before."

Silently she observed him as they talked. He looked as she always imagined him—a calm and profound man, always right in his way of thinking and quite intuitive on matters of great importance. He observed and listened well. It was past 11:00 p.m. when they went to their separate rooms to sleep.

"Good night, Elizabeth," was all he said.

"Good night, Doneli."

The next day, once again he arrived at 7:00 p.m. This would be the last night she would spend in Paris, as she had to leave the chalet around 3:00 a.m. in order to catch the military flight that was to take her back to New York City.

As Doneli entered, she greeted him, "Hello, dear Doneli."

"Hello, Elizabeth," he responded closing his eyes to enjoy the kiss he felt he had the right to receive.

Doneli had brought some bread pudding for their desert. She took the pudding and they walked together into the kitchen. "Umm, it smells good. Fresh food?" he asked.

"Yes, I cooked it. I did what I could with what was here. I made a stew and white rice."

While talking, Elizabeth had not taken her eyes from him. Deep inside she wanted to see if he would appreciate her efforts. And yes, Doneli thanked her for being so kind.

"I never imagined, not even jokingly, that one day I would be in Paris eating bread pudding," she said happily while placing the pudding on the table.

"Oh, life always brings surprises," he replied. "Bread pudding is not what I would pick if I had the choice. But to be honest, I was lucky to have found it."

"Pudding is also not my favorite dessert," explained Elizabeth. "But being in Paris during a time of war isn't my dream either."

Doneli took off his overcoat and placed it on a hanger. Then he confidently stood in front of the wine collection that Anthony had acquired, and carefully chose a bottle and walked into the kitchen to open it.

"Look what I found, Elizabeth, a bottle of Chambertin. The best Burgundy wine I have ever tasted. The fame of this wine dates from Napoleon's era. It is said that he took solace in being able to have a regular supply of this extraordinary red wine during the long and hard battle on the Russian front. Did you know the Chambertin is the top-of-the-line of great wine aristocracy of Burgundy? We have to allow it to breathe for a while. Do you mind if we wait?"

"Of course not. I still have to prepare the table."

Doneli was ten years older than Elizabeth. However, he looked thirty-six. His sensual, intriguing appearance and his Italian traits discreetly enhanced his charm.

Elizabeth placed everything on the table. Afraid of disturbing their moment together to go into the kitchen for something, she concentrated on each detail as she set the table for the special occasion. When the wine was ready to be tasted, Doneli poured two glasses and handed one to her. After savoring the fine wine, she served their dinner.

In the beginning, the silence between them filled the whole room. Then Doneli held up his glass and said, "To you, Elizabeth."

Smiling she repeated, "To you, Doneli."

At that moment it appeared so simple to leave everything else behind, that they were not even surprised by the intimacy of their words. Only peace existed inside of the chalet and they seemed to enjoy it.

When dinner was finished, they ate some of the bread pudding.

"Umm...delicious," she said totally forgetting that bread pudding was not her favorite dessert.

"It is the best I have ever eaten," he added. Doneli had not eaten a bread pudding since he was a child.

They got up from the table, took the dishes into the kitchen, washed and cleaned everything. The rest of the food and the pudding went into the garbage, as they would not be there after that night.

Following this, they sat in the family room holding their glasses of wine as they sipped its wonderful flavor.

Looking closely at her, Doneli said, "Thank you, Elizabeth. I..."

"I do love bread pudding, Doneli," she quickly interjected.

She did not know why she said that. Maybe for fear he would never find the word for which he was searching. They had not noticed it, but since he had brought the bread pudding, to them it had become like a gourmet dessert.

Doneli smiled without taking his eyes off her.

"Why is it that sometimes everything runs perfectly...like now?"

She sensed that he was going to kiss her. She closed her eyes without thinking of anything else. Once in his arms, she discovered his kiss tasted as she had always dreamed.

The solitude of the chalet in a magical way allowed them to forget about the rest of the world for a brief moment. They ended the night like two innocent children playing a delightful game on the red carpet. Elizabeth gave in to what she couldn't have in the past and Doneli for what he now missed.

She had to leave by 3:00 a.m. so they did not have time to talk about what had happened. Everything remained as if it had been a dream.

"Goodbye, Doneli, and good luck," she said as tears came into her eyes.

"Goodbye, Elizabeth."

44

ELIZABETH FELT RELIEVED TO be back in New York. "Home sweet home," she said as she entered the house. She hugged Catarina and added, "Oh, Catarina, I love New York."

"You didn't have a chance to see Paris like I did," replied Catarina. "New York is great, but Paris...is Paris."

"Not anymore, Catarina. Now it's like Berlin, believe me. It is not nice, not good at all."

During dinner Catarina spoke about the children and Elizabeth about Max. And of course, Elizabeth had much more to say. After dinner Catarina asked about Doneli.

"He is fine," Elizabeth answered curtly. For the first time she had difficulty speaking about him.

Later, she walked upstairs and spent some time with her boys. She was extremely tired. After that she went to her room to rest. As she lay on her bed with her eyes closed, Doneli's image suddenly appeared in her mind. She saw him in the middle of the chalet's kitchen with the bottle of wine in his hand. She remembered the popping sound the cork made when he opened it. Then there was that great smile on his face. Her thoughts drifted back to how much she had loved and desired him in their younger years.

No matter how fatigued she was, she carefully went over everything that had occurred in Paris. *Oh, no! What have we done?* Once again, as it had so many times in the past, tears filled her eyes. But now the tears were for Max, Doneli, and herself.

By the end of January, bad news came to Doneli's ears. Max's convoy would be going to Scotland, and going to Scotland caused him sheer terror. The convoys that would go to Scotland would continue on the run to Russia, which was extremely dangerous. Doneli knew that of the last forty ships assigned to the mission, only fifteen safely completed their trip. The purpose of the trips was to bring supplies from Murmansk. However, the entire route happened to be exposed to the naval and air attacks from the bases that the Germans had in Denmark and Norway. Those ships that suffered an attack and the crew that jumped into the ocean, died almost immediately because of the freezing temperatures. Going to Murmansk to get supplies was like setting forth on a trip to your death.

Doneli worried about Max going on that mission, sensing that he could die if he went, and more than anybody else, Doneli knew this would be devastating to Max's family. Besides that, Max was his friend. He grew so concerned about the matter that he thought about the possibility of avoiding this incident. He spent some time analyzing the entire situation and cleverly developed quite an interesting plan to get Max released from going on that convoy. Furtively as he could, Doneli made some important contacts and got his plan in motion.

During the war, no one really knew what was going on. Soldiers in those convoys lived very isolated lives. Skillfully, Doneli took advantage of this situation, and with the help of another FBI agent, made arrangements for him to go to the Atlantic to board Max's ship. Using his FBI credentials, he informed the captain that Max Merlenes had been assigned to another mission and he had to move to a Brazilian ship that was helping the US Navy. After Doneli presented Max's transfer signed by General Benclock, they left. The officers never knew that a General Benclock never existed. The next day Max's former ship left to bring supplies from Murmansk. That ship never came back.

Weeks later, Max went to the Pacific, where he remained until the end of the war. The time he spent on the Brazilian ship turned out to be the best moments he had during the war. The food was excellent and the officers very cheerful. They immediately recognized Max. Max Merlenes, the rich man that owned a diamond mine in Minas Gerais. Max ate with the high ranking officers and the captain. He found out that even a war can have its good moments, and those were his.

* * * *

The month of March arrived bringing a lovely surprise for the Merlenes. One morning as Elizabeth entered the dining room, the butler said, "Good morning, Mrs. Merlenes."

"Good morning, Joseph. How are you today?"

"Very happy, Mrs. Merlenes. Very happy."

"And why is that?"

"My sister and niece came today from Iowa. They just moved to New York."

"Then that explains it."

"Yes. She is my only sister and the mother of my only niece."

"I see. How old is your niece?"

"She is a two year old, adorable child. Like a beautiful blonde doll. You have to meet her."

"Of course I will. What's her name?"

"Victoria."

"Beautiful name, Joseph."

"Yes, but I think it's a strong name for a little girl. My sister wanted to name her Victoria in honor of her late husband, Victor Alexander. He was a train conductor who died tragically in a train accident. He never met his daughter. The sadness of his death almost caused my sister a miscarriage. But thank God it did not happen."

Catarina and Anthony were also at the table having breakfast. Joseph brought more coffee and started to pour some for Elizabeth.

"No Joseph. I would prefer tea."

"Tea?"

"Yes."

Silently, the butler studied her for an instant because she never drank tea. Then to convince himself he had heard her correctly, he commented, "I thought you did not like tea, Mrs. Merlenes."

"I don't, Joseph. But the smell of coffee makes me sick this morning."

"Yes, Mrs. Merlenes. I'll get you some tea."

As soon as the butler left the room Catarina, Anthony, and Elizabeth started to talk.

Anthony seemed to be in a very good mood. He had received the report of the research he had asked for regarding clothing designs and the prospects were excellent. He thought Elizabeth would be delighted in hearing the news. They would keep the Imperial. Taking the opportunity to share this with her that morning, he promised he would plan everything, and when Max came back, if he made it back, everything would be ready to begin production.

"What wonderful news," Elizabeth said. Then she added, "Max will return, Anthony. We should never doubt that."

She started to drink her tea when suddenly Anthony and Catarina blurred in her eyes. Then, everything around her turned dark and she fell.

Quickly Joseph and Anthony lifted her and took her to the sofa in the next room.

"Alcohol," Catarina cried. "Bring alcohol, Joseph."

The butler rushed out and returned with a bottle of alcohol, which he gave to Catarina. She wet her hands with the alcohol and made Elizabeth smell it. Instantly, after smelling the alcohol,

Elizabeth moved her head and opened her eyes.

"What happened?"

"You fainted," answered Catarina.

Feeling queasy, Elizabeth moved, attempting to sit up.

"Don't do that," said Catarina. "Anthony is calling Dr. Rudel."

Dr. Rudel, besides being the pediatrician, had also become a close friend of the family. He baptized one of the twins—Anthony. And after that, he came before any other doctor.

When Dr. Rudel arrived that morning, his face showed the concern he felt. He immediately opened his bag and pulled out what he needed to examine Elizabeth. He took her blood pressure, temperature, listened to her heart, and checked her throat, as well as her chest and eyes. Everything seemed normal.

"I don't see anything unusual. Were you feeling well before?"

"Yes," she answered.

"Not even any headaches?"

"Not even a small one."

"How is your appetite?"

"Very good."

"When was your last period?"

That stopped her and she took an instant to study his question. "I'm a bit confused about it. I have been so worried about Max, this whole war, and my trip to France, that I might be...a month late...or maybe two...?"

Dr. Rudel made a funny face and gently held her hand between his. Then he softly said, "Elizabeth, I think you are pregnant."

Undoubtedly, the doctor's unexpected words produced a wonderful smile upon her lips.

Catarina, Anthony and the butler looked at each other in order to share their surprise as well as their happiness. Afterwards, Joseph left the room saying he would announce the news to the other servants.

"One moment, Joseph," said Dr. Rudel. "I think we should wait. I could be wrong about this."

"In these cases, doctors are never wrong," replied the butler.

"And let me tell you something that you don't know, Dr. Rudel. This morning, the smell of coffee made her sick and she drank tea instead. Believe me, she *is* pregnant."

Elizabeth felt extremely happy about being pregnant. At the moment, being pregnant seemed wonderful and everything around her gained a new meaning. She thought she would stay busy taking care of herself and stop thinking about the war for a while; and when Max returned, life would be just great.

When her pregnancy was confirmed, she thought about writing to Max and telling him the news. She planned to start the letter by saying, "Max, I have wonderful news for you. You are going to be a father again." However, her thoughts ran fast and sunk in an ocean of questions. Instead of having Max on her mind, what came to her mind quickly was Doneli's image. As before, she saw him in the middle of the chalet's kitchen, with the bottle of wine in his hand. Elizabeth's happiness disappeared in a flash when she realized that Doneli could be the father of her child—as well.

Terrified and panicked by this horrible possibility, she ran down the stairs to the library looking for Catarina.

"I can't have this child, Catarina! I do not want to have this child. You must understand."

"What?" replied Catarina moving closer to her, and completely clueless.

"You heard me. I *can't* have this child."

"Why not?"

"Because he could be..."

"Could be what?"

"He could be..." the last of her words were unspoken. Instead she hugged Catarina crying like a child in pain. "Oh Catarina, I'm afraid."

"You are very nervous, Elizabeth, and I understand how you must feel."

"Do you?"

"Of course. After all that you have experienced with the twins, it's logical that you feel like this."

Catarina's words ceased her tears. She knew that no one would understand her pain—no one.

"I think you're right. I'm too nervous."

* * * *

Elizabeth spent the last seven months of her pregnancy drinking tea and dreaming of Doneli. He became the focus of all her dreams and by the end of her time, she had no doubts. She sensed strongly that the child inside of her was his, and that she still loved him.

Once born, the child was named after his great-great-grandfather, Charles. And to everyone's joy, he was a healthy child. His arrival brought an extraordinary atmosphere to the house. And the family began to treat him as if he were a prince. Finally, they could enjoy a newborn as they had dreamed—without doctors and nurses around.

Like everyone else, Catarina felt very happy with her new grandson. She saw Charles as the child that the Merlenes had always expected to have—the blessed child. Humbly, she thanked God and prayed for his well-being.

Certainly, Charles' existence brought a great serenity to her heart and soul, and while she was enjoying this wonderful gift, unusual thoughts began to invade her mind. And those thoughts shaped a series of confusing ideas, which started to puzzle her. *Why was this child born with no evidence of mildew in his blood?*

She spent hours after hours thinking about what the answer might be until she couldn't suppress her suspicions and decided that Elizabeth had secrets—secrets that she should know about.

So, in order to understand what was happening around her, Catarina went to see Dr. Rudel and after he confirmed Charles' good health, she faced this new reality—that something unusual had happened in Paris.

Back at home Catarina prepared herself to have a serious conversation with Elizabeth so that her mind would not be consumed by her own thoughts. She had lived enough to know that not all truths should be acknowledged. However, she determined that not one truth concerning her family would be kept a secret from her.

They met in the afternoon at the library and Catarina spoke first.

She calmly said, "Elizabeth, please forgive me for what I have to ask you. I don't want to hurt your feelings, but I feel that you carry secrets that I must know. I promise you that I'll do my best to understand whatever they might be. But I want to know the truth. I must know what happened in Paris. I have to know about Charles...he cannot be my grandson."

Despite accepting what was happening, Elizabeth had never imagined having this conversation with Catarina. She had believed she could keep the secret to herself. Not even vaguely had she thought such a meeting would happen one day. Now facing the moment, she realized she did not have the courage to lie.

Looking into Catarina's eyes she said, "Before I tell you what you want to know, I have something to say. I would like to inform you that I will be with Max until the day I die. He is the best thing that has ever happened to me, and nothing can interfere with our relationship. And I mean it. I did not plan what happened. It just happened."

"Tell me who is the father of this child? That is all that I want to know."

Holding her head up high, for she believed she had nothing to be ashamed of, Elizabeth said, "Doneli."

"Oh, for heaven's sake! Max's best friend," exclaimed Catarina with her eyes wide open.

"He's still Max's best friend, Catarina. I don't know how it happened. You said you would understand. For the sake of the children, let this remain a secret. Secrets, Catarina, avoid shame. And besides that, they diminish the curiosity of our neighbors and give our friends less questions to ask. I'm already suffering from it, and nothing will diminish my pain. I never had the intention of being unfaithful to Max. I have accepted it by blaming it on the war."

"Very convenient, no? If I forgive you, I can still blame the Germans."

"I love my husband and my children. I'm not asking you to forgive me, but to do what you promised, to accept it. Forgiveness is not to be given everyday, but rather to offer it as a gift. Doneli does not belong to me, and we both know it. Our children are our treasure. Let's bury the pain that all of this has caused us and raise them with love. Together we can do that."

On that afternoon, Elizabeth left the library feeling, in some way, relieved. Now, Catarina would help her bear her cross.

Catarina stayed for a while thinking about this new reality—her clandestine grandson. It became difficult to imagine how a serious man like Doneli could fall into a situation like that. And at the moment her feelings remained like a cliché. She was not mad. And she knew why she wasn't. Charles was the child she would accept—he would be the jewel of her family. What Macael had said just happened. As some tears ran down her face, she uttered, "Oh, Lord, make me strong."

* * * *

Charles had been born in September 1943, and two years later the war ended.

After the war, Max and Doneli returned home to their families. Doneli arrived first, and on the same day he set foot in New York, he and his wife Luzia went to the Merlenes' house.

That evening turned out to be an unforgettable moment for both families. They sat together in the parlor talking for hours. The twins, now six years old, were running through the house talking and laughing without tiring. Elizabeth had intentionally left Charles upstairs in the nursery until she decided that the time was right to invite Doneli to see him.

They walked upstairs side by side. They had so much to say to each other and yet they did not utter a word. There would not be enough time. Upon entering Charles' room, Elizabeth politely asked the nanny to leave them alone. She went to the child and picked him up to introduce him to Doneli.

"This is Charles, Doneli," she said looking at the child. Then, in a normal tone of voice, she added, "He is your son."

Evidently Elizabeth's revelation left Doneli stunned. If he had the slightest idea what fate held in store for him after the past three years, he probably wouldn't have been as surprised as he was now. But he had eliminated this possibility by giving himself some peace of mind. After Elizabeth left Paris, he convinced himself that nothing unusual had happened between them. The war was real and that night in the chalet—a dream.

Had Charles not existed, he would have died thinking that way.

Speechless he extended his arms to the child and as he hugged him he said to himself, *I have a son. Nothing else in the world could make me happier.*

Before they returned to the family room to meet with the others, he said, "Thank you, Elizabeth, for having made me a father and forgive me for not having loved you when you were seventeen."

"That girl ceased to live a long time ago," she explained. "A woman took her place. A woman who discovered that this love never died and yet would never belong to her. Max should never know the truth about this child. He will be raised as his son. This is how Catarina and I want it."

"I understand. So, Catarina knows?"

"Charles is a healthy child, Doneli. I couldn't hide it from her."

"I want you to know that no matter what happens, I will love you, always."

A week later, Max arrived in New York. He had Elizabeth waiting for him as well as the three children. He felt as if he were opening a new chapter of his life. He felt proud and happy of being Max Merlenes and having Elizabeth, the twins, and Charles. One day he would sit with his children and tell them of the chapter he had just closed.

A special dinner had been prepared to celebrate his return. Doneli, James Ugany, their lawyer, Dr. Rudel, and Dr. Scarshiner, who now lived in New York, participated in their celebration.

During dinner Max talked about the war and commented about the time he had spent on the Brazilian ship. He told everyone what Doneli had done to save his life. He confessed to them that he was alive because he never went to Murmansk. Everyone noticed the sadness which veiled his face when he mentioned that incident. All his shipmates died on that mission.

That evening, Max took the opportunity to thank Doneli for what he had done for him. He put his arms over Doneli's shoulder and said, "I will never forget what you did, Doneli. You are the best friend I have ever had."

45

LIFE IS THE MOST PRECIOUS gift we possess, until we find out that the art of knowing how to live is what is most precious. That was the idea that Doneli and Elizabeth worshiped. They took every precaution not to fall into the same situation as in Paris. Even though they didn't stop loving each other, they were not foolish. Their souls shared the same pains. And one day, they would find out that this was more beautiful than all the pleasures they could have had.

The Imperial turned into a sewing center that created design lines for both men and women. The sign outside said: Merlenes & Sfeel. All the clothes made there had *Elizabeth Sfeel* written on the label. As the years went by, the good taste for fashion of Madame Elizabeth Sfeel began to gain popularity. Other shops began to open across the country and later in Europe, South America, and Central America. She became famous.

As it happens sometimes, when money is no object, everything is possible.

* * * *

The twins were already seventeen and Charles thirteen when their Grandfather Anthony died at the age of sixty-nine from a heart attack. Every day for a month, Catarina went to the cemetery. She looked like an adolescent experiencing her first heartbreak and her family knew her grief would last for a long time. Lombard, the new chauffeur, was always at her calling. Her trips to the cemetery were so frequent that Max felt it was ridiculous and had a talk with her.

"Mother, I want you to stop this. You have to understand that he is dead."

"He will never die for me. He will always be alive in my memory."

Max hugged her and said, "I know, mother! He will never be forgotten, but you have to understand that he is no longer with us. What you are doing is not good for you, and you know it. Please don't do this to me. I'm very worried about you."

"Don't be, Max. Let me mourn my loss. I'm strong."

The next day Max made a remark about this to Doneli, and Doneli advised him, "Give her some time, Max. Time is the best medicine. It diminishes every feeling that exceeds its proper limits, cures our pains, proportions our happiness and decreases the whim of our passions. Time always defeats our strength."

What Doneli said turned out to be correct. The day came in which Catarina understood that Anthony was no longer among them, and ended her almost daily visits to the cemetery. She reduced her visits to twice a year.

* * * *

Catarina grew old as well. Her hair was now the color of snow. In spite of all the years that passed, her eyes held the same unique green color they always had. At seventy, her image was still very genuine.

Max Junior, young Anthony, and Charles, became three handsome and popular men.

Anthony and Max kept the French/Brazilian appeal and the

Irish perceptive charm. Their light brown eyes easily held a peaceful look and their faces depicted attractive features. At the age of sixteen, they left for France to complete the first part of their education, and when they returned—three years later—Catarina gave a big party in their honor.

That day they were officially introduced into New York society.

At the party Max developed an interest in Jacqueline, Dr. Scarshiner's daughter. Without a care, they spent the evening in each other's company, talking and smiling at everyone, as happy as two lovebirds. On that evening no one paid much attention to this. However, later on, both families began to worry because Max was Catholic, and Jacqueline, Jewish.

It was almost a year after that party when Catarina met with Dr. and Mrs. Scarshiners to discuss the possibility of a marriage between Max and Jacqueline. Sitting in front of three cups of tea, Catarina openly spoke of the subject.

"I would like to have your opinion regarding the children's relationship. I see this getting serious and I do not want them to suffer if there are any objections from both of you."

For the first time Dr. Scarshiner and his wife Helen expressed their opinion about this. Surprisingly, they drew different opinions about the matter.

"We can't let this happen," said Dr. Scarshiner.

"Why not?" his wife asked.

"You know why. He is not Jewish."

"Dear David," said his wife. "You are not any god to decide what is good or bad for our daughter. I don't want to discriminate against this young man because he is not Jewish. Please don't justify what Hitler did to us. When two people are in love, anything that bothers you will not bother them. They will fight against us, if necessary."

Calmly, Catarina also expressed her opinion.

"Dr. Scarshiner, I admire you very much and I will never forget that you saved the life of those children. I will respect your opinion regarding this matter, but you should know that I think exactly as your wife. Their happiness is my only concern."

Never again did Dr. Scarshiner give his opinion about the matter. He clearly understood that if they were in love, he would have no power to stop them. After all—he liked Max very much.

In October 1962, after dating for four years, Max and Jacqueline were married and traveled to Europe on their honeymoon. Their wedding left Max's father in awe. He could hardly believe that he had a son who was already married.

That same week, while playing chess with Doneli he commented, "Oh Doneli! How fast time flies! One day they are born and then...they are getting married."

"Almost unbelievable," said Doneli. "It seems like only yesterday I saw them playing happily in the garden. We are getting older, Max. That's what is happening."

"Absolutely true," responded Max with a smile.

* * * *

At the time of Max's wedding, Charles had been away. Two years before he had left for France and had to stay one more year in order to finish his studies. But he arrived in New York just in time for his brother's wedding.

Catarina had insisted that all her grandsons, at the age of sixteen, would spend three years studying in France. And of the three, Charles was the only one who rebelled when his turn arrived. When his grandmother called him to discuss the matter, he told her steadfastly that he would love to visit France, but not to live there for three years and especially not study there. Freely, he explained to her what he wanted, and of course, she told him what he would do.

Until then he hadn't known her wishes were like her diamonds—hard and inflexible.

She told him, "All of my grandsons will go to France to study, and they will speak French as well as Portuguese. You are no different, Charles. So good-bye and good-luck."

Humbly, Charles had returned his eyes to his plate and said, "Yes, grandmother."

That had been at his sixteenth birthday dinner. Three weeks later he left New York City.

* * * *

Max and Jacqueline's wedding celebration had been beautiful. About six hundred people came to the reception and they all enjoyed it as much as the Merlenes and the Scarshiner families.

The wedding took place at the party salon in the Merlenes' building. When Jacqueline entered the salon on her father's arm, she was a radiant bride. Through her smile, people could only see the happiness of a lovely and pure young girl. And she was walking down the aisle for Max Merlenes—one of the richest young men in the world.

No religious service was held. A rabbi spoke beautifully and blessed them in the name of God. After that, the music, champagne, and caviar, ushered in the celebration of that significant evening for Max and Jacqueline.

That evening when Charles arrived at the building for the wedding, a limousine entered the driveway and stopped almost in front of him. An attendant approached the car, opened the door and out stepped a beautiful young girl. At a distance Charles stood observing her. She had long, blonde, curly hair, and wore an exceptional red dress. Her singular beauty left him astonished. He knew who she was, yet this was the first time he had seen her since she had become an adult. She looked like a delicate doll with dancing crystal eyes and skin made of porcelain. Getting out of the car, one of her gloves fell from her lap. Quickly, Charles approached and picked it up for her.

"Thank you," she said smiling sweetly.

"You're welcome," he responded. Then extending his hand, he added, "I'm Charles Merlenes. It is nice to see you."

"Charles?" she exclaimed. "Oh! The last time I saw you, you were ten years old."

"Incredible, isn't it?"

"Yes," she replied sweetly. "Apparently life keeps us very busy, no?"

While Charles smiled in order to agree with her, she excused herself and walked toward the reception.

She was Victoria, the butler's niece. Charles had just seen the most famous model of the Merlenes & Sfeel's shops, Victoria Pelbeck. To the world, she was heaven's divine creation and Elizabeth Sfeel's masterpiece.

Thoughtfully, Charles watched her walk away. *If Leonardo Da Vinci would have met her, the Mona Lisa would surely have had her face. She is simply divine!*

46

CHARLES WAS NINETEEN YEARS old when he saw Victoria at his brother's wedding. Before that, he had seen her twice during his childhood, the last time when he was ten and she, thirteen. Later, he heard his mother was paying for her education, and then he started to see her in the newspapers and magazines. She became a very well- known model. People just loved the innocent look that sparkled from her eyes, and her marvelous sensual body. The combination marked her singular, sharp beauty. Famous clothing designers saw her as the most tempting figure the world had ever seen and the columnists simply adored writing about her.

It was at the wedding reception that Charles first really spoke with her and her beauty captivated him. He spent the whole night thinking up ways in which he might approach and speak with her again. However, he did not succeed in doing so. Getting close to her that night turned out to be a difficult task because so many of the other men at the reception wanted to do the same. And to make it more complicated, his brother Anthony happened to be one of them.

Anthony had a great personality and simply got the best—always. He had good taste in girls and a wonderful sense of humor. It seemed that wherever he went, girls surrounded him. There was no woman in the society circle in which he frequented that did not enjoy his company. Even the married ones sometimes provided him with entertaining moments.

Exactly as Charles had expected, Victoria caught Anthony's interest and was the next in line. As soon as she had entered the room, Anthony approached her and with a big smile said, "Victoria, it's nice to see you in person. I thought you were in Mexico."

"I was, Anthony."

"When did you arrive?" he asked in order to keep her from walking away.

"Oh, it's not really important. Is it?"

"No. Of course not," he answered.

From a distance Charles stood observing them. *Damn you, Anthony! Damn you!*

Anthony talked and managed to keep her attention while she smiled at his every word. The way they were conversing made Charles think she would probably end the night with him. Many of the other men there felt the same as Charles—eager to get close to Victoria but not sure how to do so. It seemed they were not quite ready for the competition. The only one secure and confident enough about his tactics appeared to be Anthony.

The night reached its end, and Charles had not spoken to her again. To his surprise, Victoria left as she had come—alone. Apparently, even Anthony could not charm her enough to change whatever she had in mind. He ended up like the others—without Victoria.

On Sunday, the day after the wedding, Elizabeth, Charles, and his father went to their country house to spend the afternoon. They called the place "Bolevar" and it was located approximately two hours from New York City. There they had acres of land, stables, and even small lakes.

At noon they left New York City with Sebastian, Max's chauffeur, driving their limousine. The air was crisp and cool, perfect for riding. Charles wanted very much to visit Bolevar before returning to Paris. It had been a while since he was there, and he heard his family built new stables and bought more horses.

As soon as they arrived, Charles and his mother took a walk so Charles could see the changes his family made to the place. When they returned to the house, they sat on the veranda sipping glasses of orange juice while they waited for their horses to be brought to them.

While waiting, they talked about Charles' studies and the trip all over Europe he wanted to take. Once, his mother had promised it as a gift, but it seemed they never had an opportunity to discuss it again. That day they intended discussing it and planning his trip in more detail but they were interrupted by one of their limousines entering the driveway. When the car stopped, Lombard, the chauffeur, stepped out to open the back door. Charles saw the most unexpected thing happen—Victoria getting out of the car.

For a moment Charles held his breath as he tried to hide his immediate excitement. He remained on the veranda while watching his mother as she walked down to greet her. His first assumption was that his mother invited her to join them that afternoon because he noticed she wasn't as surprised to see Victoria, as was he.

How nice it is to be here, he thought to himself as he continued to watch Victoria's arrival. *Dear Anthony, when the fairy godmothers decide to wave their magic wands, everything becomes perfect.*

Now he knew there was no doubt that for him, this particular Sunday would be very interesting. He would have the whole afternoon alone with the most beautiful woman he had ever met. He felt as if he had won a lost battle; definitely a significant victory for his ego.

Charles and Victoria enjoyed riding across the countryside on two beautiful horses. She was wearing her riding habit with red pants, her favorite color. He remembered that at the wedding she had also worn red. It seemed hot colors had a lot of influence on her personality.

As they rode, they happily spoke about important things like careers, work, and the future. They also talked about ordinary things like card games, summer, wine, and Coca-Cola. After their ride, they spent a great amount of time sitting on the lawn next to the lake. Gracefully, she lay on the grass and for a while, as she talked, looked up at the sky.

Charles enjoyed this time as he had never before. It would have been spectacular if he would have the courage to kiss her. However, he couldn't do that. He knew Anthony would have done it easily, but not him. He was shy, cautious, and lacked self-assurance to take risks. Kissing her was on his mind, but he decided not to spoil the day.

"When do you return to Paris?" she asked still contemplating the clouds.

"In two days," said Charles.

"So quickly? This means you only came for your brother's wedding?"

"Yes. Only for that."

"It was a beautiful wedding."

"Yes, it was," he responded.

A brief silence stretched between them but apparently neither of them noticed. She seemed absorbed in contemplating the sky and Charles enjoyed looking at her, delighting in admiring her beauty. It took some time for the enchanted silence to end.

"And you? How long will you stay in New York?" he finally found a question to ask.

"One week. Then I have to go to Rome."

"Italy!" exclaimed Charles. "And for how long?"

"Only for the weekend. We're presenting a small collection. It's your mother's last-minute idea. Something simple and convenient for the end of the year."

"My mother! She always has those ideas, no?"

"She is exceptional. All of her ideas work very well."

"What are you going to do after this weekend?" he asked.

"I will return to New York City where I will have a week to rest before flying to Hong Kong with your mother."

"Don't tell me that...?"

"Yes. She's opening a store there, and she has an incredible collection for the grand opening."

Victoria's words remained as silent butterflies in the air. Charles did not have anything to say. He wished he could have had some of Anthony's expertise.

"Have you been to Rome, Charles?" she asked.

"Once," he responded.

"I love France," she added.

"Really? Have you been to Paris?"

"Only for a weekend but I wish I could have seen more of the city."

"Then, why don't you come to France instead of returning to New York on your week off? If you do, I promise to show you the best of Paris. You may stay with me at the chalet."

Now, it was his words that remained floating in the air like silent butterflies. Even he surprised himself with his abrupt yet wonderful idea.

"Is this an invitation, Charles?" she asked sweetly.

"Of course, and I very much hope that you accept. No one except for my mother visits me in Paris. It would be a nice change."

"Are you sure this would not be an inconvenience for you?"

"Absolutely not."

Extremely happy, she said, "Then I accept."

In the evening they dined with Elizabeth and Max and afterwards, they all returned to New York City. Victoria's last words that evening were addressed not just to Charles, but also to all three of them, "Good night and thank you."

* * * *

Back in Paris, Charles had so many things to plan for their time together, that the rest of the week flew by without notice. Besides planning their activities, he made sure everything in the chalet was in order. Esmeralda, the housekeeper, had to plan a menu for the week. Charles asked her to cook something typical and of course, for her not to leave out the delicious shrimp *crepes*—her specialty.

Shrimp *crepes* were a favorite dish with the Merlenes men. They could eat them almost every day. What puzzled Charles was how the Merlenes had always found someone to cook them so well. Once, his brother Anthony had said after eating many of them, "This is better than sex!" And of course, everyone knew that Anthony was not serious. It was just his sense of humor speaking.

The Monday on which Victoria was to arrive in Paris, Elizabeth called. Charles hadn't known that she was also in Rome.

"Hello, Charles."

"Mother?"

"Yes. I'm here in Rome. How are you?"

"Fine," he answered.

Charles adored being in the company of his mother yet he did not want her to be in Paris this week. Not now that Victoria was coming.

"Mother, are you planning on coming for a visit?" he asked fearing her answer.

"No, Charles," his mother said. "I just finished seeing you. Did you forget that last Tuesday you were in New York?"

"No," he answered happily. "I did not forget it."

"Then, since we have already rid ourselves of the sadness of not seeing each other, I will return to New York City without going to France. I hope that you understand. You know that your mother would never do such a thing if she hadn't seen you recently."

"Of course, mother."

"Excellent, Charles. I'm happy that you understand. Good-bye. I will see you in December in New York City."

Feeling relieved, Charles said good-bye and hung up the phone. Victoria had already called to let him know her arrival time.

In the evening, when her flight arrived, Charles was at the airport to meet her. He took care of her luggage, which consisted of only one small piece, and side-by-side they walked to his car, which was a two door, red Alfa Romeo, a gift from his grandmother. It had been his reward for going to France for three years. Victoria was delighted with the car's black interior. She loved the color combination of black and red.

"How was your trip?" Charles asked.

"Fine."

"I spoke with my mother today," he said. "She called to tell me she would not be stopping in France to see me. She was worried about that."

"I know. I was next to her when she called you."

"Did you tell her that you were coming?"

"No. I kept it a secret."

"Any special reason for that?"

"No. I simply did not want to tell her. What I do in my free time is no one else's business."

"Of course. I also didn't mention anything either."

That evening they dined at the chalet and afterwards they drove Esmeralda home. When they returned, they sat and had some tea and talked for a long time. Victoria seemed happy and content. They enjoyed each other's company so much that neither one wanted to go to sleep early.

She spoke about love and herself. "I believe in love," she said, "but so far I have not found it. As an adolescent I never dated and have never had a serious boyfriend. The younger boys around me kept their distance, seeming afraid to receive a 'no' for an answer. Because of that, I was always alone. While my friends had a great time dating, I stayed at home envying them."

Charles not only believed what she had said but also felt sorry for her. He knew that young boys and men feared being rejected by a beautiful girl more than dating a girl that wasn't so gorgeous. Therefore, it was very common for the *beautiful ones* not to be approached and thus were forgotten.

Victoria also revealed to Charles that one time, someone had invited her for dinner. It happened only four hours after they had met. Furthermore, he had asked her to marry him! This occurred in Greece. She was only eighteen at the time and the man who had proposed to her happened to be sixteen years older than she. Charles listened to her attentively and found her story charming.

For an instant he remained quietly thinking about himself. He was three years younger than she and thought about his fairy godmother who had made it possible for him to spend a wonderful Sunday at Bolevar, and a magnificent time in France with her. If the fairy godmother had not intervened, Anthony would have won over him.

The next day, while Victoria spent the whole morning sleeping, Charles attended his classes. At noon, they visited the places Charles thought she would like to see. That day he dismissed Esmeralda early for he planned to take her out to dinner.

Paris automatically triggered Victoria's aspirations and she called it a dream city. France had been the stage for the most extravagant queens about whom she had read. Having the opportunity to visit the city in the company of Charles Merlenes, elevated her joy—as much as receiving an expensive diamond in a piece of soft, black velvet for a gift. This simply energized her ambition.

In the middle of the week, Charles skipped his classes in order to dedicate the entire day to her. She wanted to visit Versailles, and he did not object. Victoria grew very excited about the trip. Louis XIV's fame, power, and luxury always set her soul aflame. The pretentious declaration of Louis the XIV, "*L'etat c'est moi,*" *I am the state*, stirred a lot of feelings inside her. She could hardly wait for the moment when she would walk into the palace and admire its solid design. In her opinion, France could never destroy Versailles because of the power felt deep inside those walls.

Charles spent the whole time listening to her talk about the palace and the Louis' of France. He learned more about them than in his humanities class. Returning from the palace, she thanked Charles for the tour and her contentment gave her the courage to kiss his cheek.

"Thank you, Charles. I don't remember having a more pleasant day than this one. You are such an adorable person. I never thought that you would be so nice."

Her happiness was so contagious he instinctively held her hand.

"You're welcome. You deserve it. I'm glad that you came."

The soft breeze of the afternoon blowing through the windows of the Alfa Romeo created a steady, relaxing sound as it touched their faces, cooling the warmth of their skin.

Charles did not let go of her hand, and she did not complain nor try to release her hand from his.

As soon as they arrived back at the chalet, each went to their room and bathed. In Europe, one bath a day was more than enough, but most Americans did not seem to understand it. After they dressed for dinner, Charles and Victoria then sat down to dine on the shrimp *crepes* which Esmeralda had prepared for them. They dined at 9:00 p.m. The warm and delicious *crepes* came from the oven to the table.

They sat across from each other at the table as if they were Adam and Eve in the Garden of Eden. Absent, of course, were the apple and the serpent. They sat completely dressed, each sipping a glass of white wine.

"Esmeralda cooks deliciously," Victoria said after she tasted the food.

"I agree with you," responded Charles. "I don't know the Merlenes' secret, but we always have a world-class chef as a cook."

After dinner, they walked to the kitchen with the intention of preparing some tea. In order to help, Victoria began to open the high-reaching cabinets looking for sugar. Charles approached and raised his arms to reach out for the jar. Accidentally, he pressed her against the counter and together they grabbed the jar, causing it to fall and break.

"Oh!" she exclaimed.

"Did I hurt you?"

"No...," she answered. Absorbed in his green eyes.

Instantly her look grew intense. She was so dazzling that Charles finally did what he figured his brother Anthony would have done under the circumstances—he kissed her.

Victoria savored his lips with the desire of a teenager. After all, she was experiencing her best kiss ever. She found his lips so warm and delicious, that when she looked into his eyes once again, she asked, "Why do you kiss like that?"

"Why, do you like it like that?" Charles replied, sweetly.

"I don't know...Do you believe in sex before marriage?"

"Right now, Victoria, I only believe in what you believe."

They never drank the tea that night, and the sugar was left spilled on the counter and floor. They were not superstitious. However, there are those who would say that spilling sugar brings bad luck, especially in the beginning of a relationship. But Charles and Victoria had so much to share they didn't even think of such things as superstitions.

It wasn't long before they found themselves in the bedroom. The desire reflected in their eyes removed all of the doubts which could cloud their minds. Charles breathed in the soft fragrance of her skin, and kissed the most pleasing parts of her body.

It was the first time for her and she closed her eyes offering her beautiful body to his undeniable desires. Humbly, she let him teach her all she wished to learn. Sinking into a solemn silence, she eagerly gave herself up to the delightful sensations that his kisses brought to her skin. In his arms she discovered the amazing secrets of his hand and met the heavenly taste of his lips. He awoke a universe of feelings that had been sleeping within her. The end of it submerged them into a pleasure beyond their expectations. It resembled a galaxy dissolving inside of them and all the planets and the stars were exploding at the same time.

Wonderful seemed such an inadequate word to describe what they had shared.

47

ON VICTORIA'S LAST DAY IN Paris, Charles skipped classes once again. After all they had experienced so far, it became impossible for him not to dedicate another day to her. They had coffee at nine, and then went to visit another interesting place Charles wanted to share with her. At 4:00 p.m. they returned to the chalet in order to prepare for dinner and the theater.

When Charles entered the living room dressed formally in a gray linen suit, silk shirt and tie, she was speechless. She found him extremely handsome and could not resist his charm.

"Is this from—"

"Yes, Victoria," he interrupted, "it has my mother's name on the label. It was her gift."

"I like it," added Victoria. "The colors are perfect and go so well with your eyes."

"Again, she made a good choice?"

"Well, I would say that."

They had a marvelous evening and everything flowed smoothly. The restaurant was cozy and the play, *Constantine and Her Lovers*, was spectacular. Soon after the theater they returned to the chalet, and once the door closed, Charles took off his jacket and his tie and poured some liqueur for them. He placed a gentle kiss on her lips as he handed her one of the glasses. Gazing into each other's eyes they tasted the liqueur. Then he proceeded to kiss her again.

"Are you going to make love to me tonight?" he asked with the face of an innocent boy.

"If you don't mind, can it be all night long?" she impishly replied.

"It can be until tomorrow noon since your flight leaves at four. I told Esmeralda not to come tomorrow."

"You did?"

"She needed a day off, and I thought we would probably be busy anyway."

The next afternoon they arrived at the airport and held hands until the very end. When the moment to say good-bye came, Victoria looked straight into his eyes and asked, "Would you marry your butler's niece, Charles?"

Surprised by her question, Charles frowned and asked, "Why are you asking me that?"

"Why shouldn't I?"

Sweetly he said, "Please don't spoil everything now."

"What do you mean by that, Charles?"

"That I would never—"

Hearing the last call for her flight she interrupted saying, "Good-bye, Charles." Then she reached up to kiss his lips one last time, preventing him from finishing his words.

"Good-bye, Victoria." He had wanted to add, "Call me from Hong Kong," but she did not wait.

* * * *

The month of November seemed the longest month of the year for Charles because he missed Victoria very much. Though he was in Paris, his thoughts were with her in a distant part of the world.

Victoria never called him. However, Charles tried to get in touch with her and all he heard was, "She is in Hong Kong." "She is now in Canada." "No, we don't have any way to contact her." For the first time, he hated his mother's business.

Because of Victoria's absence, he started to visit brothels. He didn't want to sit at home alone and scream like a hungry wolf. He wanted her, and his need of her started to drive him crazy. In time he admitted to himself that he was in love with her, and began to think about marrying her.

Charles even formulated his plan, which in his imagination would be very simple. In December, he would return to New York City and talk about it with his family. He knew he still had to finish his studies but that shouldn't be a problem. His family had lots of money so he could afford to get married before having a career. Charles just hoped his family would understand and felt this was what Victoria expected from him.

* * * *

Meanwhile, Victoria kept herself busy traveling from one place to another, fulfilling the demands of her career. She came back from Hong Kong and went to Texas. After that, she went to Canada.

The last Saturday before her trip to Canada, she went to the Merlenes' home where she had coffee with Elizabeth. While they were at the dining room table, Anthony arrived.

"Victoria, what a surprise!" he said kissing her hand and holding it between his for an instant. "You are the last person I expected to see today. Mother never tells me when you are coming."

Elizabeth noticed how much he enjoyed Victoria's presence that afternoon. But she also knew how he liked to woo women and he never took anyone seriously.

Without further thought, Anthony sat with them and enjoyed their company. Later, when Victoria was about to leave and Elizabeth was going to get Lombard to take her home, Anthony immediately said, "No, mother. I will take Ms. Pelbeck home. It will be my pleasure."

Studying Anthony's face, Elizabeth asked, "Is that okay with you, Victoria?"

"Yes. I will gladly accept his offer."

Ingeniously, Anthony managed to keep Victoria company for the rest of the afternoon. He usually got his way, so it became almost impossible for Victoria to refuse his invitation to have dinner and go to the theater. Then it also became quite complicated not to accept spending the next day with him at the family's country house.

In Bolevar, after breakfast, Anthony gave her a quick kiss on the lips. He also kissed her while helping her mount and dismount her horse. By lunchtime, he had kissed her face, her lips, and her neck. He kissed her at every opportunity he found in the garage, on the grass, next to the lake, and while on the bridge. When he took her home that night, he pulled her into his arms and kissed her on the lips as if she was already his "official" girlfriend.

While in his arms, she looked straight into his eyes and asked him the same question she had asked Charles, "Would you marry your butler's niece, Anthony?"

Cheerfully, he answered, "Without hesitation."

From that day, their relationship blossomed. Victoria loved Anthony's answer and Anthony found it all very appealing. He figured that marrying her would be wonderful. She was very pretty and together, they could have lovely children.

* * * *

In early December, Charles called home. He was planning to be in New York City by the middle of the month. However, he couldn't speak with his mother, as only the servants happened to be at home whenever he called. *Christmas! Of course, they are very busy shopping.*

When Elizabeth finally returned his calls, he said anxiously, "Mother?"

"Yes, Charles. I'm sorry—?"

"It's okay, mother."

"Joseph told me you wanted to know about your trip?"

"Yes, mother. That's exactly it."

"Good, Charles. I will make the necessary arrangements. I need you here before the 20th. I have some wonderful news. Your brother Anthony is going to get married!"

"Anthony?" Charles asked making sure he had heard correctly.

"Yes. You know how twins are. If one is sick, the other is also. So one got married and now so is the other."

"I never thought that this was true."

"Neither did I, but it's happening."

"Mother, who will be my lovely sister-in-law?"

"You know her. It's Victoria."

At that instant Charles had the feeling that Paris was being hit by a strong earthquake and that under his feet, the floor had opened up to swallow him.

"Charles," Elizabeth said. "Are you there?"

"Yes, mother. I'm listening."

"Your brother is very happy! He's walking on clouds."

"How nice, mother," added Charles. Intentionally changing his plans he said, "Mother, tell Anthony that I wish him the best. I will not be able to be in New York City for the wedding. The trip I was going to talk about is the one you promised me I would take through Europe. You do remember it, don't you?"

"Of course I remember, Charles. But—"

"Well, mother, I want it now."

"Are you going to miss your brother's wedding?"

"He will understand. After all, he's walking on clouds."

"Yes, but he will be sad."

"With Victoria? You must be kidding!"

"Are you sure that you can't change your mind?"

"Yes, mother. I'm sure. I'm dreaming about this trip."

"Okay, Charles. Take your trip. How much money do you need?"

"I trust your generosity, mother. I will take whatever you think is necessary. Oh, one more thing. Send me a copy of the itinerary of our ships the *Serenata* and the *Maria Catarina.* Who knows, perhaps I can enjoy the company of one of our captains during my travels."

"Fine, Charles, I will take care of everything. Do not forget your mother. Call me. Kisses to you."

"Good-bye, mother."

After Charles hung up the phone he muttered, "I don't think this world is big enough for us, Anthony." Then he remembered Victoria's question, "Would you marry your butler's niece?"

Playing a game with himself, Charles tried to guess his brother's answer. He said aloud, "Without hesitation."

48

ANTHONY AND VICTORIA'S WEDDING was celebrated on the last Friday before Christmas. Since she wanted to be married on a Friday, Anthony did as she desired. To him, being ready to carry out her wishes would be the most important thing in his life. If she wished to have their wedding in Africa in the middle of the jungle with the gorillas around, it would have been fine with him. Likewise, on a small canoe in the middle of the Amazon River, with a school of piranhas watching the ceremony waiting for the bouquet to be thrown. He was so much in love with her that her ideas would always have a special meaning.

Approximately three hundred people were invited to their wedding and none of them missed seeing Victoria Pelbeck walk toward the altar. Events like that only occurred once in a lifetime. They just knew Victoria would be the most beautiful bride New York City would ever see, and besides that, all the women invited were dying of curiosity to see the wedding dress that Madame Elizabeth Sfeel had created for her future daughter-in-law. All of them imagined something beyond expectation—spectacular, a wedding dress to be remembered. And they were not disappointed. It was exactly as they had imagined it. She appeared at the church dressed in a beautiful white gown topped by an exotic veil with more than thirteen intricate patterns made of lace and pearls.

For the rest of December and part of January, Victoria and Anthony became the center of attention for many newspapers and magazines from all over the world. Her dress and her beauty were the topic of a never-ending story.

After the reception, the newlyweds went to a hotel, and the next day they embarked on the *Vernice De Pion,* an Italian yacht, that took them to Rio de Janeiro. Victoria chose to spend her honeymoon in Brazil. One of her dreams had been to walk inside of the Merlenes' mine in Minas Gerais. She had a strong desire to see, in the rough, the diamonds that had shaped the family's business. Anthony agreed with her, because under the circumstances, he wanted what would make her happy.

However, Claros was the last place he would have chosen to go with her if it had been up to him because he simply detested Claros. Actually, all three of Elizabeth's sons never developed any special feelings toward the place. To them Claros was the end of the world; the worst place a person could desire to be. Silently, Catarina respected and understood their opinions for she also refused to live there. Claros only held sad memories for her. But she established a tradition that all of her grandsons, at least once, must visit Claros. They had to see Claros and the Pical Valley and breathe the humidity of their mine. And they all had done it.

Now that Victoria was part of the family, she reveled in having something in common with Catarina. Likewise, she felt she couldn't die before setting foot inside that mine and holding in her hands some of the diamonds. In fact, no one knew the scope of her ambition, for it was delicately veiled behind the sweetness of her face. Since a child she had believed she was born to become part of the Merlenes' family. And as an adult, she hoped to see the world turn around her hands in the form of diamonds—lots of diamonds.

Surprisingly she still loved Charles with all her heart even though he had failed to answer her question. She was determined not to lose Anthony. Charles was young, so he could wait and she had plenty of time. In her mind, first things should come first. Anthony happened to be the sword in the stone for her—the beginning of everything.

* * * *

In December when Anthony and Victoria had celebrated their wedding, the Merlenes spent Christmas Eve only with Dr. Rudel's family and with Doneli Cassarete. Doneli had come alone because Luzia, his wife, had died of cancer at the beginning of the year. The doctors had done everything possible to save her, but it was all in vain. Luzia had died knowing that for some unknown reason, she had lost the love of her husband.

Charles had telephoned from Italy to wish them all a Merry Christmas. He planned to spend a few days in Milan and then the following week he would travel on to Florence. He spoke with his family and casually ended up speaking with Doneli as well.

"Hello, Charles," said Doneli.

"Hello, Doneli. Merry Christmas."

"Thank you, Charles. Merry Christmas to you, too. I heard your mother say Florence. Are you in Florence?"

"No. I will be there next week."

"What wonderful news! I will be there next week myself. I do not want to interfere in your plans, but perhaps we can meet and have dinner."

"Excellent idea," said Charles.

Quickly, Doneli made plans with him, and when he hung up the phone, Elizabeth said, "I didn't know that you were going to Europe."

"Neither did I, Elizabeth," replied Doneli. "Sometimes my job offers these kind of surprises."

Doneli had lied. Charles was the reason for his trip to Europe. Catarina had asked him to do that because she was worried about

Charles. First of all, it seemed as if Anthony's wedding didn't matter to him. Then, he decided to spend Christmas away from home. She needed to know what had caused these sudden changes.

* * * *

The following week, Doneli arrived in Florence and stayed in the same hotel as Charles. That day they got together and had dinner. During their meal Charles talked about the career he had finally decided to pursue which was to study law. Charles told Doneli his grandmother seemed pleased with his decision. Of course, she would be. Max graduated with a degree in economics, Anthony with a degree in business, and now Charles would be a lawyer. They were all competent to handle the Merlenes' business needs.

In reality, Max and Anthony never worried about their career choices. They always thought like a Merlenes, felt like a Merlenes, and never set their aspirations beyond the family expectations. They understood at an early age that they were meant to sit behind conference tables, making important decisions for the Merlenes Industries.

However, this was not the case for Charles. He had wanted more exciting things for himself. The idea of having a career as a racecar driver started to shape his ideas and ambitions at a young age. He dreamed of Grand Prix racing. Before he could understand what being a Merlenes meant, he really thought this would be possible. It was only after he shared his wishes with his father that he encountered the reality that he had no right to be what he wanted. His father made him see the complexities of being a Merlenes, so his decisions should not interfere with the family business. Instead of being behind the wheel of a racecar, Charles Merlenes would have to spend his life inside a conference room making decisions about jewelry and clothing.

On that day, for the first time, he saw the family business shattering his happiness.

"Charles, don't dream of impossible dreams," his father had said. "Pretend that you never said this to me. That would be better. Your grandmother would never allow it. For some reason you are her favorite grandson and the most obvious choice to occupy my place. Don't pursue this idea because it will only cause a war between both of you. And in a war with her, you will be the one to lose."

"How can you be so sure? And if I'm her favorite grandson, my chances should be greater. Besides that, what do you think she would do to stop me?" Charles innocently asked.

"Oh, Charles, what a question! Why don't you go and find out for yourself?"

"Good idea, I will."

"Then good luck, my son."

Not long after this conversation with his father, Charles worked up the courage to talk with his grandmother about his dream. In advance he prepared how he would approach her, hoping that it would convince her. He looked for her and found her in the garden drinking tea in the company of her memories. Charles went close, leaned over and gently gave her a kiss. He sat next to her and began his small talk. For a while they enjoyed each other's company, chatting happily and laughing occasionally. Then Charles eagerly spoke about his dreams.

"Car racing?" she repeated after him. "Oh, Charles, that is simply impossible. I can buy you as many race cars as you want. I can even have a track built in Bolevar for you so you can drive your cars, much like the others ride their horses. But you cannot be a racecar driver."

"Why not, grandmother?"

"Cars have nothing to do with diamonds, Charles. Is that so difficult to understand?"

"No. But what about me and my choice?" he insisted.

"Charles, in this family, men cannot make their own choices. You can choose on which floor you would like to have your office and how it should be decorated. However, you can't choose to stay out of it. This is as far as you can go."

Silently, he went over everything she had said. Her words seemed to be irreversible, and to fulfill his curiosity, he asked, "If I insist on this matter, what can you possibly do to stop me?"

"Everything, Charles. Absolutely everything you can imagine. And you have no idea what I'm capable of. I think it is better for us to drop the subject."

Evidently the echoes of her strong will came harshly across his mind and obliterated all the words he had planned to say. Charles just did what she suggested—he dropped the subject. His father was right. It would not be worth it to engage in a war with her.

But when he calmly got up to leave, she answered his question by saying, "If you were to become a racecar driver and a corporation sponsored you, I would not only buy that corporation and shut it down, but also make sure that no one else sponsored you."

Only by the expression in her eyes could Charles easily understand that she was capable of going that far.

* * * *

During his dinner with Doneli, Charles lamented his impossible dream and Doneli sensed how sad he felt about not being able to become what he wanted, and no one could fix that. Then to diminish his sadness, Doneli explained to him that his grandmother loved him very much. It was precisely because she adored him that she tended to be more restrictive with him than either of his brothers.

Following that, Charles also confessed that he loved her very much and could not imagine the Merlenes without her rules and her decisions. Then, because Doneli had brought up the subject, Charles decided to ask him for a favor. He asked Doneli to try and convince her to allow him to continue studying in France.

What he didn't tell Doneli was that after his disappointment with Victoria, he wished to be away from home for a long time.

"I can't believe that you don't want to return to New York

City," commented Doneli.

"People change their minds when they grow up."

"What makes you think that I can help you?"

With assurance Charles said, "You have a lot of influence over my grandmother. I have noticed it. In fact, above everyone else in the family, including my father and my mother."

"Charles, I don't think that's true."

"Yes. They all listen to what you have to say. And I believe that if someone can help me, you are that person. Please, try. I would be very grateful if you did."

"Why don't you want to return to New York City?" Doneli asked, now very curious.

"I like France," was Charles' quick reply.

"No, you don't. You did not want to come to France. Remember?"

"That was before."

Charles' words brought forth a silence which extended far too long. When the tension reached its climax, Doneli spoke again.

"I sense that you are not telling me the whole story. And if you expect for me to help in this matter, I must know the real reason. 'I like France,' is not enough."

"But then what else could it be?" asked Charles.

Calmly Doneli leaned forward and said, "A woman."

"Wrong," insisted Charles.

"Not so. And I can prove it."

"Really?" replied Charles.

"Tell me about Victoria. Why did she come to visit you?"

Surprised, Charles asked, "How do you know that?"

"I spoke with Esmeralda."

"Oh, Lord! Are you investigating my every step?"

"Yes, and no," replied Doneli.

Again another silent moment filled the space between them. Charles began to shake his head from one side to the other.

"Now, I see how convenient it is to have a detective as a friend. Did my grandmother pay you to do that?"

"No. I'm the only one who knows it, Charles. I called Esmeralda before Anthony's wedding. Don't forget that I recommended her to your mother. Esmeralda's mother cooked for me during the war. But I did come here to see you at Catarina's request. She wants to know why you suddenly changed your plans about coming home for Christmas. You failed to have a good reason for not coming to your brother's wedding. Right now, there are two main questions circulating in your house: 'What is happening with Charles?' and 'Is he all right?' "

"Do me a favor, Doneli. Tell my grandmother that she can sleep in peace because I'm going to become a lawyer. I haven't changed my mind about that. Everything will be as she wishes. And as far as Victoria, we spent the day together in Bolevar and then she came to Europe and happened to visit me in France. That was all."

"If you say so."

"I prefer not to talk about it."

"It's all right with me. I'm beginning to understand."

For a few moments Charles didn't have anything to say. Thoughtfully, he looked at Doneli—realizing that Doneli had not bought what he had attempted to sell.

"Fine. You win. I lost her to Anthony. But it was not love."

With a grin on his face, Doneli got more comfortable in his chair. Then he said, "Let's talk about this idea of staying in France. Do you really want that?"

"Yes. Tell my family that this is important to me. Tell my grandmother that agreeing with me this once could make the difference in our future relationship. Tell her to think about that."

"Fine, Charles. I will give her your message."

* * * *

Doneli left Florence two days later and went to see Catarina immediately upon his arrival in New York. They sat outside in the garden while drinking tea.

"Charles is all right, Catarina," Doneli said. "He did not come for the holidays because he truly wanted to explore Europe."

"So there is nothing wrong with him?"

"No. But he asked me to talk to you about something that seemed very important to him."

"What?"

"He wants to remain in France and finish his studies there. He said you never agreed to any of his wishes. He expects this to be the first."

"But why does he want to stay there? Does he have a reason?"

"Yes, he does. He's in love with Victoria, and he lost his chance. We have two brothers and one woman. Let him stay in Europe. It will be better for him and better for all of us."

"Do you see what a problem beautiful women can be?"

"Rich men as well, Catarina. They are very desirable. Every woman wants to have one."

Due to the circumstances, Catarina allowed Charles to stay in France on two conditions. The first: He must come to New York City once a year for Christmas and New Year's. Second: He had to travel twice a week to the Merlenes Industries in Paris to learn from Carlos Lardie, their lawyer, what would be impossible to learn from his professors.

Charles agreed with his grandmother's conditions. After all, they seemed fair enough.

When he had heard the news, he called Doneli to thank him. Charles knew he had made it possible.

49

FIVE YEARS PASSED AND DURING that time, Charles' elder brother Max died suddenly, leaving his wife Jacqueline a widow. Max had died a little over two years after his marriage. Evidently he developed a blood clot in his neck that then moved to his brain. Not even Dr. Scarshiner could help him. He left behind a three-month-old-daughter who sadly had been born with muscular dystrophy and it was understood that she would never walk but spend her life in a wheelchair. Jacqueline and Max had proudly named her after his grandmother, Catarina.

The same friends who attended Max and Anthony's weddings came to the funeral. They saw Elizabeth and Jacqueline crying without being able to find solace for their pain. Catarina was there as well and with a steady look in her eyes, she demonstrated that she would always be present in both the joys and sorrows of her loved ones. Her matriarchal image became a tradition among the Merlenes and would symbolize the strength of the family from one generation to another.

After Max's death, Victoria also gave birth to a child. She named him Alexander, after her father, Victor Alexander.

Fortunately, little Alexander seemed to be a healthy child. He slept and breathed well and moved his hands and arms without any difficulties. He reminded everyone of Charles' birth—a perfect child everyone enjoyed.

Despite bringing much happiness to the Merlenes, his arrival marked the beginning of a lifelong battle between Catarina and Victoria. As Catarina began to know Victoria better, she noticed that Victoria had unpleasant qualities ingrained in her personality that she expected to see manifested very soon. For some reason, Catarina was never wrong.

On the other hand, Victoria acted as if she knew very well the ground on which she stood and that she would ultimately get what she wanted. In her vocabulary, negative words like incompetence, inexperience, and inability did not exist. Instead, diamonds, diamonds, and diamonds seemed to provide a radiant light inside of her mind. Every night, like a religion, she consciously desired them. Her idea now was to destroy Catarina's firm image. She wanted New York City to forget that woman because she–Victoria–wanted to be the one representing the Merlenes.

Unknowingly, baby Alexander sowed seeds of hatred between his mother and great-grandmother. While Anthony was extremely happy at being a father, Catarina sunk into deep misery. Without a single word from Victoria, she knew that Alexander was *not* Anthony's son. When she looked into the baby's eyes, she instinctively knew that he was the second child that she would have to accept. Suddenly, she saw it clearly.

Since long ago, Catarina had understood she had a cross to bear, and she swore to herself that she would do it humbly for the sake of her family. Her madness quickly exceeded its level of tolerance and triggered her attention toward Victoria. To her it became impossible not to perceive that *pretty Victoria* was waiting for the precise spot and the right moment to start playing her muskrat game. And this, of course, left Catarina extremely upset.

A few days after Alexander arrived home from the hospital,

Catarina demanded Victoria's presence upstairs in her reading room. They spoke for less than fifteen minutes, and this was enough time for Catarina to discover that she had underestimated the woman. What Victoria did had been beyond any forgiveness.

Catarina said, "Victoria, I learned throughout my life that the best way to find peace is to fight for it when we are losing it. So I want to have a conversation with you, but before we start, I would like to inform you that you don't have to be so impulsive. We can go over our differences. After all, I believe there is still time to have decent thoughts."

"I know that you want to ask me about Alexander's father," said Victoria. "Don't worry. I selected a healthy man for I wished to have a healthy child. We all wanted that, no?"

"Of course," replied Catarina. "And—"

"Don't waste your time with me Catarina," she interrupted, "because I always know what I want, and I'm used to getting it easily."

"May I ask what it is that you want?" asked Catarina.

"Right now, that is none of your business."

"Are you having an affair?" Catarina asked.

"With whom, the father of my son? No. I paid that man to get me pregnant."

"You what?"

"Listen, Catarina. I know that there is a problem with the blood of this family. Dr. Rudel advised me that you would call me for this conversation. He knows you pretty well. Anyway, I have nothing more to explain. What I did is done. As far as everyone knows, Alexander is my husband's child. I don't think you will have the courage to destroy Anthony's happiness. Will you?"

"No," answered Catarina. "Count on that!"

"Of course. A grandmother's heart never fails."

Quietly, Catarina admitted being defeated. Victoria's first move was simply remarkable.

"Victoria, you can leave," Catarina said calmly. "You have won for now. I do not have the courage to tell Anthony what you have done, but be careful with what you will do from now on. You got what you wanted and I am very unpredictable. Maybe the combination of both could harm one of us."

"In this case, that person will be you. I am young and ready for anything."

"We will see."

"Of course."

After that, Victoria walked out. *I will kill you, Catarina, because I hate you!*

Catarina remained in her room, lost in a vast, dark space crowded with unsuitable old memories. Her soul sank deeply into an awful and sardonic misery. She kept pondering, for a long time, Victoria's role in their lives and saw her as a strong, spiteful enemy. Again she thought about the three children that Macael had told her would come, and once more felt sorry for the Merlenes.

The wisdom of humankind must be the consequence of pain not happiness. Otherwise what would build our strength and what would shape our faith? Charles was right, God does work in strange ways. He takes care of our happiness while the devil—of our miseries. God needs the devil to refine our souls and we need God to understand what is evil.

Then Catarina whispered, "You will lose this battle, Victoria. I don't know how, but I have faith that it will happen."

* * * *

During the past five years, Charles remained in France studying. Upon his graduation he was to return to New York City and incorporate himself in the administrative body of the Merlenes Industries. Everyone was waiting anxiously for him to come back, and among them Catarina seemed to be the proudest of his accomplishment. Her contentment was so great that the entire family, little by little became caught up in her expectations. To her, Charles' graduation and his return to New York City was not some simple event. She saw it as a new beginning.

As her blissfulness grew, her imagination started to work hard in order to create lots of fresh ideas for the new era. The hopes inside of her heart and the sounds of her pulsing desires crashed inside her mind, forcing away the sadness of the past and bringing in new happiness. She felt full of vigor and ready for the Merlenes to turn over a new leaf.

* * * *

Back in December 1967, one year before Charles' graduation, she had made a statement that had surprised even her son Max. They were in the dining room celebrating her seventy-ninth birthday. Except for Charles, everyone was present that evening. With her head held high, she walked downstairs wearing an understated gray dress and the necklace which was the symbol of her family. Before cutting her birthday cake she rose, and said, "Today, I have something very important to say." She paused to take a breath and then calmly she proceeded. "Next year, Charles will come home."

They had all expected she would start with him because they knew that Charles occupied first place in her heart and no one better than he had ever been born. Everyone had the impression that he had hatched from a Faberge egg and had become the most valuable thing she had ever acquired.

Confidently she continued, "The moment to make new decisions has arrived. I don't plan to go to Claros ever again. I'm too old to make that kind of trip. Claros is too cold, and I don't want to die of pneumonia. I know that Anthony never started mining the emeralds because he did not want to destroy the grotto that holds such significance for me. That is no longer the case. Without my Anthony, I can't step foot inside it. The emeralds belong to all of you. And to mark Charles' homecoming, I decided to begin mining them."

As her words traveled around the walls of the vast and luxurious dining room, everyone around her held an expression of surprise upon their faces. They all seemed to express both astonishment and happiness. Finally, they would get their hands on the forbidden emeralds and Charles' homecoming from Paris had made it possible.

Max, who had spent his entire life dreaming about mining those stones, after recovering from this pleasant and yet unexpected news, arose from his chair and went to her. Happily, he embraced his mother and kissed her cheeks many times. Then he proceeded in opening a bottle of champagne to make a toast for this great moment in the lives of the Merlenes.

While they engaged themselves in the celebration, Catarina sat down. From the head of the table she saw the spirits of Charles, Anthony and Gaspier walking around them. They too also appeared to be celebrating.

Charles' spirit came close and whispered in the ear of his daughter-in-law, "Dear Catarina, no other moment could be as perfect as this one. God bless you."

Book 4

Shadows of a Legacy

50

"É noite de São João!
São João! São João!
Opague a fugeira do meu coração."

CLOSE TO THE BONFIRE, the accordion continuously played June songs in the chapel plaza. In the huts, the ladies were selling *quentão* and *canjica*. The adults moved around speaking to each other, drinking and eating, while the children played happily around the fire. It was June 24, São João's Day.

Everyone in Claros commemorated this special day. In the chapel, the priest prayed the rosary with the local people; a majority of them were miners who worked for the Merlenes. After praying the rosary, they drank *quentão*, a typical beverage of this celebration and ate *canjica*, also a typical dish made of white corn.

Elizabeth, who had arrived two weeks before in Claros, came to the chapel to enjoy the festivities. This was indeed the first time she had visited Claros, and despite the fact that she could not speak Portuguese, she was having a wonderful time. Next to Max, in the chapel plaza wearing her mink coat, she also ate *canjica* and drank *quentão*.

Usually this type of celebration lasted through the early hours of dawn. Everyone waited until the fire extinguished itself. After that the people started enjoying the best part of the São João celebrations. Everyone present approached the bonfire and solemnly took off their shoes, and while barefoot, they tried to cross the hot coals. At that time, everyone, adults and children alike, came closer to the hot coals to witness the traditional event and find out who really had the courage to do it.

According to the very religious people, only those who had strong beliefs could cross the hot coals without burning themselves. It was all a matter of faith. Participants in this type of event ended up having a wonderful time because lots of people did not hesitate to try. Enthusiastically, they kicked off their shoes to undergo the ritual, but as soon as they started, most regretted their actions. The ritual seemed more painful than faithful. This was surely most common among the ones who drank too much *quentão*.

Every year a man known as Preto Rá would come to participate in the celebration. He was famous for being the one who never failed to cross the hot coals. Preto Rá was the auctioneer in charge of the bidding of the various items people donated for that night. Besides being a very religious man, he also had the gift to cure the sick with herbal remedies.

Customarily, when the great moment to walk on the hot coals arrived, the music ended and all the huts ceased to sell food. Everyone came to the center of the chapel plaza to watch this extraordinary event. As in years past, Preto Rá did the opening walk across the red-hot coals. Silently, he took off his sandals, clasped his hands at his chest, closed his eyes, and miraculously walked over them without burning his feet. Looking at him, all the women present made the sign of the cross and prayed the Creed.

Elizabeth watched his performance like everybody else, very

quietly. Astonished, she exclaimed, "Oh, heaven!" She admitted to herself that she had faith, but certainly not that strong. Seeing this was something outside her world.

Like the others, Max was very happy that night. First of all because of the next day's impending activities—he would dynamite the mountain and finally start mining the emeralds. And second, the six cups of *quentão* he had drunk.

Soon after Preto Rá demonstrated his devout faith, other volunteers stepped up to the coals. This was quite an amusing sight since there were many burned toes and cries of pain. Among the volunteers appeared Dona Amelia, a very religious woman, who like Preto Rá could always carry out the difficult task.

Everyone enjoyed the celebration without paying any attention to the coldness of the night. They laughed and clapped at those who failed and prayed for those whose faith carried them across. Max and Elizabeth enjoyed themselves as much as two teenagers experiencing something new.

"Elizabeth, would you have the courage to try it?" Max suddenly asked.

"No," she answered quickly.

"Don't you have faith?"

"Yes, Max. But, I don't think my faith is strong enough."

Smiling he kissed her on the cheek.

"Do you love me, Elizabeth?"

"I do. Why do you ask me that?"

"Because I know it's true. If I had any doubt about it, I would have never asked."

She looked at him. *Yes, I love you. Of course I love you.*

"I know you would not walk across the hot coals to prove your faith, but I know that you would do it to prove your love for me," Max said excitedly.

"Would I?"

"Yes. And because I'm sure about that, I will try to do this for you." Quickly, he kissed her again. "Look at me, Elizabeth, I will walk across the burning coals because I love you."

Determinably Max walked to the center of the plaza, took off his shoes and socks, and rolled up the bottom of his pants. As he did this, everyone's expectation quickly mounted into a state of profound emotion. *Would Senhor Max actually walk across the hot coals?* Every mind inquired.

With hope Max began to emulate Preto Rá. He stopped in front of the hot coals, clasped his hands to his chest, closed his eyes, and began to walk. His first step showed no hesitation. After the second step all the people's expectations fell upon this quite unearthly moment. Miraculously he did not burn his feet. In an almost fantastic slow motion he kept going and going until he reached the end of the hot coals. Then, proudly he looked at his wife. All the women in the chapel plaza once again made the sign of the cross and prayed the Creed.

Elizabeth looked at her husband in disbelief. Her mouth fell open and her eyes bulged, as if in a state of stupefaction. Obviously everyone around noticed her. Still, she could not accept what she had seen. Many questions filled her thoughts. *How? Why? Max was able to do it!* And because she failed to understand it further, she presumed that the saints might allow it to punish her. Perhaps she would do that for Doneli.

Indeed, after his heroic act, Max declared himself triumphant. He walked toward his wife and then hugged and kissed her happily. Then he moved away to drink *quentão* with both the faithful and faithless ones.

Long after the celebration reached its end, they returned home. Max spent the last hours of the dawn making love to Elizabeth. He could not remember another occasion in which he had been as happy as this one. He would certainly remember this evening as a very unique and enjoyable one.

Despite all the *quentão* he had drunk, he woke up in the morning feeling extremely well.

The *quentão* was a natural drink and usually did not cause a hangover. So, as soon as his eyes opened, he knew he was in Claros and remembered that this day would be a special day for the Merlenes—the day in which they would officially mine the emeralds. With that thought he jumped out of the bed, quickly dressed, and before leaving the room, reached for Elizabeth and lovingly kissed her lips.

"I love you, my Irish girl."

Luciano, one of the employees who happened to be Cafeno's son, had already brought the Jeep to take Max to the Pical Valley. In the past, Cafeno had worked for Prieto Ferbonini and later for Charles. He had come to Claros years before to take Anthony's place. In Claros, he married a girl twelve years younger than he and together they had four children. He had died a couple of years after Anthony. Everyone in Claros had loved Cafeno.

As was expected, Luciano greeted Max in the dining room.

"*Bom dia*, Senhor Max," he said. "I have the jeep ready outside."

"Wonderful. We can leave now. I'm ready and I do not want to waste any time. This will be a historic day for the Merlenes. I want to oversee it myself."

In fact, Max was a few hours away from fulfilling the one impossible dream he had ever had—finding the emeralds. Before his father's death this had been completely forbidden, but now his son Charles had made it possible. Max strongly wished to have the opportunity to hold the first green gem beryl from that mountain. He had always sensed that they were there.

While traveling to the Pical Valley, Max and Luciano enjoyed their conversation. Enthusiastically Max said, "Luciano, have you ever held an emerald in your hand?"

"Never, Senhor Max."

"Then prepare yourself to hold one very soon. Emeralds are crystals that form naturally in metamorphosed rocks called mica schists, which have a restricted growth. They are very beautiful. Despite their fragile state, they symbolize immortality and faith."

As the jeep bounced from side to side on the rocky soil, they continued to talk. Luciano enjoyed Max's accent very much. His Portuguese was amusing.

Max was already in his fifties, and as a matter of fact, his age did not bother him at all. Only a few gray hairs lightened his head and no evidence of aging touched the skin of his face. He still had an attractive and healthy appearance, which matched his contagious outgoing personality. His peaceful look quietly enhanced the serenity of his eyes. Everyone in Claros enjoyed his presence and Cafeno's sons even more.

"Luciano, did you know that emeralds were extracted in Egypt from Cleopatra's mines 2,000 years before Christ?"

"*Não*, Senhor Max," responded Luciano. "I don't know who Cleopatra is."

"Oh, she was a beautiful woman."

"Was she more beautiful than Senhora Victoria?"

"I don't know, Luciano. I didn't know Cleopatra either."

The jeep stopped in front of the house in the valley, and they both stepped out of it.

Thoughtfully Max glanced at the mountain range. He seemed very excited about what he was about to do. And even though he loved the valley and its beautiful view, he was determined to go on with his plans and dynamite the smallest mountain located precisely over the grotto.

"Luciano, I'm going to climb the mountain one more time. I want to check the work that was done yesterday."

"Yes, sir," responded Luciano. "I'm going to tell Mr. Rios that you are here."

Laurindo Rios was the man in charge of the whole operation. It had taken him months to prepare the mountain to be blasted, and for two weeks Max had closely supervised his work. Now the big moment had finally arrived. A new era was to begin for the Merlenes.

Max pictured the headlines:

EMERALDS FOUND IN THE PICAL VALLEY!

Gemstones for the Merlenes are gifts from the gods.
They are never depleted.

As Max climbed the mountain, the idea of those lines on the front page of the newspapers excited him. Suddenly, the thought of his grandfather and father came to mind. How wonderful it would have been for them to be alive and see this moment.

Among the seven mountains that surrounded the Pical Valley, the smallest one wasn't as steep. So during those two weeks that Max had been in Claros supervising Mr. Laurindo Rios' work, he had become accustomed to climbing it without any hardship. Because of that, this morning he easily reached the peak. However, on his way up, he made short stops to check the work that had been done the day before. Max needed the assurance that nothing would go wrong.

Upon reaching the top of the mountain, he took a moment to contemplate the valley one last time. *Pical Valley, the Merlenes' richest land in the whole world!* Max carefully memorized the picturesque view which extended magnificently in front of his eyes. He breathed in the cold air of the morning and briefly lost himself in the gentle breeze of his fantasy. In his mind he could almost see the green emeralds in his hands. Their brilliance...as bright as the sunrays on a summer morning and their green color, as deep as his mother's eyes. The first one found would be given to the woman he loved most—Elizabeth.

Soon after, he put away those thoughts and started down. He walked slowly down the same path he had climbed, and once in a while he looked at a distance to feel the mysticism that enveloped the valley. After being informed that Max had arrived, Luciano went outside, sat on the veranda of the house and quietly observed Max's descent. From their previous conversation Luciano knew that Max would be extremely happy when he held the first stone in his hand. And while Luciano's mind rested peacefully on these simple thoughts, his eyes suddenly opened wide and his face filled with astonishment. Max began rolling down the mountain together with what appeared to be a dense, black cloud. At the foot of the mountain, Max attempted to stand and run, but the black cloud repeatedly stung him to the ground. They were killer bees, hundreds of them. They covered Max's body as they swarmed and viciously attacked him.

The rockiest part of the mountain was situated precisely on the side Max had climbed. And in between two rocks was a small gap from which a ray of light reached the grotto. The beehive happened to be inside the grotto close to the gap. While descending, Max had accidentally slipped and rapidly took hold of a branch, which gave way, and its long roots pushed out the hive that had been there for years.

Luciano had never seen anything like it. The shock of the scene paralyzed him. There was absolutely nothing he could do to help. Only when the black cloud lifted itself and flew away did he run to see Max. His eyes froze with terror, for he saw the worse thing he could have ever imagined.

Max's body kept swelling until it was unrecognizable. Blood poured from his eyes and mouth as fast as water flowing over smooth rocks. Immediately his skin, riddled with bites, reddened and broke out everywhere. His eyes could not be seen because of the blood and the swollen tissue around them. Luciano had the impression that if Max's body continued to swell, the skin itself would rupture. No one could have imagined such a gruesome scene.

His body was wrapped in sheets and brought to the house. Immediately Luciano rushed to his jeep, drove back to the other house and telephoned Mr. Eduardo Medeiros, the Merlenes' formal lawyer in Belo Horizonte. At this point no one knew what to do. They were all in shock.

Three hours later, Mr. Medeiros arrived in Claros and rapidly drove to the Pical Valley to see Max's body. He also could not believe his eyes. He had never seen something as horrifying as this. Then after drinking a strong cup of coffee in the company of Luciano and Mr. Laurindo Rios, he felt capable of taking care of the situation. An hour later he sat with Elizabeth delivering the sad news.

Until this time, everyone in Claros had known, except her. As Mr. Medeiros' words filled the air, she opened her eyes in disbelief and fainted. A few minutes later, at Mr. Medeiros' request, Preto Rá arrived at the house. He made some herbal tea for Elizabeth that made her sleep for more than eight hours. The next day, when she opened her eyes, Mr. Madeiros told her in detail how the accident had happened and that Max had been buried.

"No!" she screamed lifting her head and trying to leave the bed.

"You would not have watched," said Mr. Madeiros. "I couldn't let you. Please understand it. As his lawyer, it would be inhumane to allow anyone to see him in the condition he was."

Crying hopelessly, she said, "Oh my God! A man who went to war and ends up like this! I don't know how to take the news back to New York City."

The day she was to leave Claros, Preto Rá came to see her again. He asked Mr. Medeiros to serve as his interpreter. Preto Rá told her that Max had walked across the burning coals as his final farewell to this world. Many people, he said, do things like that before their deaths. Then Preto Rá told her a story of his own father. One morning before mounting his horse and leaving the house, his father did something very peculiar. His father reached down, picked a red rose from the garden, and handed it to his wife. Under other circumstances, this would not have been out of the ordinary, except for the fact that his father had never done that before. Four hours later, a terrible storm reached Claros, and a lightning bolt hit and killed him.

Preto Rá held Elizabeth's hands as he said, "Mrs. Merlenes, your husband sensed his death. He walked over the hot coals because he knew you would never erase that scene from your mind. This is how he wanted you to remember him. He said good-bye to you in a very mystic way. You should never forget that."

51

THE NEWS OF MAX'S SUDDEN death covered all the front pages of the major newspapers around the world and once again, in the minds of everyone, came the familiar sequence of names, Claros—Pical Valley—diamonds. It seemed that never before had there existed better-known gemstones with so many stories attached to them than those from the Pical Valley. Neither the diamond of 3.106 carats found by Frederick Wells in Africa, nor the famous French Blue found by Tavernier in India, could have been more talked about than those from Brazil. Possessing a Merlenes diamond meant inheriting not the simple but rather a multi-faceted legacy of a gemstone.

Jarlaz Coberck, a columnist from New York, grew fascinated with the Merlenes. Following Max's death, he compiled all the major events in the Merlenes' history. With that article, Maria Catarina, once again, easily won the sympathies of the entire world.

Shortly after Max's death, Catarina conducted a meeting in the Merlenes' building. The first one she had ever called. She arrived around eleven o'clock in the morning and went directly upstairs to the spacious conference room where all the men responsible for the day-to-day operation of the Merlenes Industries were waiting for her.

When she entered the room, she walked straight to the head of the table—the place once occupied by Charles, her husband Anthony, and finally, Max. Calmly, she sat and ordered everyone to do the same. Anthony, her grandson, occupied the chair to her immediate right. They all knew this was strictly an informative meeting.

"Good morning, everyone," she said.

"Good morning," they replied.

"This will be a brief meeting," she explained. "I have three things to say and I intend saying them in a simple manner."

Despite the fact she was more than seventy years old, she did not show hesitation about her actions. That morning her mere presence reminded everyone that she stood for an unyielding sense of will.

"The three things I have to say are indeed very important. First of all, in relation to all pending business, no important decisions are to be made until December. However, we will continue with our regular operations as well as honor our agreements. The second is in reference to the emerald explorations in the Pical Valley; they have been postponed until next year. And lastly, it is my wish that my grandson Charles take this chair as president. I trust all of you and hope to have the full cooperation of our shareholders. That will be all. Thank you."

None of what she said surprised anyone. They knew that Charles would be the one to take Max's place. Even the Statue of Liberty, if it had a brain, would have known.

* * * *

In December, five months after Max's death, the family flew to Paris for Charles' graduation. Catarina chose to take her doctor's advice and wait for him at home. He had told her, "You may do everything, Catarina, for you are a strong woman. However, don't exceed your limits because no doctor is ever one hundred percent right."

In Paris everything went well. Elizabeth could finally bring a smile to her lips, something she hadn't done since Max's death.

Charles now twenty-five years old, was a rich and handsome lawyer and would become, besides the head of his family business, the youngest powerful man in the whole world for the next decade. His handsome face, which displayed a pleasant and mature expression, also held a delightful, calm, and confident look. Certainly it would be covering the front pages of numerous important newspapers throughout the world.

At his graduation reception, Victoria congratulated him with a hug and to everybody else it looked very formal, except for her. She hugged him lovingly, insinuating that she had never forgotten him. And for an instant Charles felt that if he closed his eyes, he would probably not let her go. Her scent still held the power to awaken his desires. Her astounding beauty was still fascinating to him. She walked, smiled and talked like an angel.

He approached his mother, and hugged her tightly. As she quietly sobbed she said, "I'm so proud of you, Charles, and your father was also."

The only person who saw Charles immediately after Max's death was Doneli. He flew to Paris to give Charles the terrible news while Elizabeth was still in Brazil. How ironic, Doneli delivering the news when in reality, he was Charles' real father! When Charles hugged him, crying for Max, Doneli thought that he was being punished for not being able to diminish his son's pain.

Charles arrived in New York exactly one week after his graduation. The early snowflakes floating lightly in the air seemed like dancig musical notes, filling the empty spaces between the skyscrapers. He rejoiced immensely as the first winter chills refreshed his face.

Lombard, the chauffeur, went to meet him at the airport. Upon arriving at the house, everyone came outside to greet him.

Parked in front of the house was a beautiful white Ferrari.

"Congratulations, Mr. Charles Merlenes," said Catarina alluding to his new title as a lawyer. "You don't know how happy you make me! The Ferrari is your graduation present. I hope I picked the right color."

Surprised, Charles said, "Yes, you did. White is beautiful. Thank you, grandmother."

"I have another surprise for you in Bolevar. I built a racetrack which circles the lake and goes as far as the end of our estate. I'm sure you'll love it."

Charles shook his head as he gave a big smile and said, "That was not necessary."

"Yes, Charles. You wanted to be a racecar driver, remember?"

"Yes, but today I see that it was not meant to be. After my father's death I understood your reasoning. If I had become a racecar driver, I would have had to drop my career to come home and help Anthony. So it would not have worked out anyway. Once again, you were right."

Lovingly, she kissed and hugged him, thankful for his understanding.

"You made me do what was right. I love you. Thank you for the Ferrari and for my own racetrack. You have the prettiest green eyes I have ever seen and you are the beautiful lady who owns my heart." His words made Catarina feel proud of herself, proud of him, and proud of the Merlenes.

Charles accepted everything around him as part of his destiny. He knew now that the role he was playing was for real as he entered the world of responsibilities. It seemed incredible, but he sensed he had been born to be his father's successor.

On December 21st, he officially became the new president of the Merlenes Industries. The announcement was made and his picture appeared in all the national and international newspapers with the following words:

> Merlenes Industries, one of the most powerful corporations in the world, now headed by Catarina's

third grandson, Charles Merlenes.

After becoming president, Charles granted several interviews to the press. He encountered questions like: "Mr. Merlenes, in regards to your brother Anthony, don't you think he is rightly suited to occupy the head of the industry as president?"

"I will grant it to him whenever he wants it," Charles answered smiling.

"So he refused the position?"

"No, you said that," Charles added cleverly.

* * * *

Two weeks into the New Year, Anthony went to Claros. Catarina had decided the search for the emeralds should not be postponed any longer. They had already invested too much money in it and the diamond mine had reduced its prospecting greatly. Besides that, the employees had been hired for a set number of years. Time was running out and the project must go on.

Actually, Anthony loved the idea of being engaged in that operation. So he happily embarked on this trip to Claros. Like his father, he grew very excited about seeing and touching the first emerald—if they could find one. He dreamed about saving the first one for Victoria, his beautiful wife.

Anthony left New York in the middle of the week, and that weekend, as customary, Charles went to Bolevar. He enjoyed driving his Ferrari on the track his grandmother built for him, so almost every Saturday he left New York City in the company of Lobo, his chauffeur. However, on that particular week when Anthony embarked for Brazil, they weren't the only ones to go there. Charles and Lobo had arrived in the morning and then around 4:00 p.m. that afternoon, Victoria, Alexander and the nanny also showed up.

Alexander was now three years old and, thanks to his nanny, he spoke fluent French. Charles loved speaking with him.

"*Comment allez-vous*, Alexander?" asked Charles holding him up in his arms.

"*Tres bien*, Uncle Charles. *Merci*."

"Do you want to ride your pony?"

"Yes. Can you come with me to see him?"

"Of course."

They walked to the stables where a beautiful pony was ready for Alexander. After his ride, Charles took him around the track in the Ferrari. With great satisfaction, Charles spent the whole afternoon with him, and it seemed difficult to tell who enjoyed each other's company more. Alexander was in his child's "Why" phase. He asked about everything and as usual, questioned every answer.

Being in Bolevar when Victoria also visited was something that Charles always discreetly tried to avoid. Before going he would always check with the housekeeper before making any plans, but on that weekend his tactics apparently had not worked.

In the evening, they all sat together for dinner. It was an awkward situation as Charles and Victoria did not have much to say to each other and Alexander was very busy eating. After Charles finished his dinner, he wiped his mouth, placed his napkin on the side of his plate, and excused himself from the table. Then he calmly walked toward the coat rack next to the door, gathered his coat, and drove off.

He drove to the Alameda Country Club that was located four miles from Bolevar. Everyone who owned an estate in Bolevar frequented the club. It was an exclusive, secure, and elegant place to meet friends, have a drink, and also play cards.

Charles had never been a fanatic of card games or had developed the habit of drinking with friends. The reason he went to the club that evening was because he wanted to have a conversation with the senator from New York, Mr. Risley Ashford. Charles had just found out that the senator had, in an unknown manner, acquired a significant percentage of the Merlenes' shares. This caused Charles to focus his attention toward this matter. He could not understand how his father had allowed this to happen. And besides that, he disliked Mr. Ashford greatly.

When Charles had taken over the presidency of the Merlenes Industries, he felt his first responsibility should be to review the policies of the shareholders. In doing so, he discovered that Senator Ashford owned fifteen percent of the company's shares. Besides being surprised at the discovery, Charles grew concerned about the inconveniences that this could cause for their future transactions. In order to avoid further complications, he immediately froze all action on the sales of the company's shares. As a precaution, he wanted to investigate his father's previous negotiations.

Charles had frozen all sales the day before so the news would hit the newspapers by the weekend. The reason why he had driven to the club was because he figured Senator Ashford would be very upset.

Sitting at a small table and drinking some whiskey, they talked about the matter. As expected, the senator was not happy and had no intention of hiding it from Charles.

"I think that I should have been informed about this before you made your decision. Your father would have done that."

"I'm not going to run things the way my father did," said Charles.

"Yes, I can see that. I will try to accept that."

"I'm sorry if my decision caused you any problems. It couldn't be different because we are dealing with my interests."

Senator Ashford looked at Charles and firmly said, "I only want to warn you about one thing, Charles. Be careful. Having a problem with me is like having a problem with the state of New York."

"I will try not to forget it," responded Charles.

Then he finished his whiskey and placed the glass on the table. Without adding another word, he left.

At approximately 11:00 p.m., Charles arrived back at the house. He entered, placed his coat on the rack, and went straight to his room. Calmly, he undressed and walked toward the bathroom to take a shower. After preparing the water temperature to his liking, he began to relax. While the water rapidly ran down his body, his mind was engaged in his own thoughts. *Risley, you are merely the senator of New York...and I am Charles Merlenes. Many of the world's great transactions spin in my hands.*

He finished his shower, turned the water off, and with his eyes closed, reached out to grab his towel. The gesture was unnecessary because someone handed it to him.

Hesitantly Charles opened his eyes and to his amazement, Victoria stood before him completely naked. Her long, blond, curly hair hung over her shoulders, barely covering her breasts. Charles thought he was seeing a mirage but then realized that she was really there holding the towel.

Her dazzling image quickly replaced that of the senator. Charles had spent six years of his life without her. Six years making love to her only in his imagination. An imaginary body, imaginary caresses and imaginary orgasms. And now there she was, a gift, wearing an intense look and willing to please him.

Slowly he dried his face, arms, and chest and then walked out of the shower. He simply couldn't take his eyes off her. Instead, his hands and lips gently began touching her. Tenderly, Charles knelt down bringing his lips between her legs, tasting and searching. Charles' mind deliberately avoided everything that could forbid him from going any further.

Some time later, when Victoria prepared herself to leave the room dressed in one of his bed sheets, he asked her a question. "Why did you do this?"

"Because you still love me," she said.

Then wearing a lovely sensitive smile, she walked away.

You will never forget this night, Charles. I did this for two reasons. For love, and for diamonds. Your first child will be mine. And darling, this will be my next surprise for your grandmother...

52

ON FEBRUARY 12TH, ANTHONY returned from Claros to give his family the news about their latest operation there. Enthusiastically, he described in detail the blasting of the mountain. Then he said they had yet to find a single emerald; however, he affirmed they would soon do so, because the scent of emeralds was already lingering in the air.

As Anthony kept talking about Claros, Catarina became very sad because in reality, in searching for the emeralds, she had begun the destruction of the valley. Anthony said the grotto no longer existed, the river flowed less, and the birds, which once flew over the valley were no longer there. The only possible consolation that remained was the hope of finding the emeralds. For a while she let the memories of the valley fill her mind.

That evening they were all sitting in the family room listening to Anthony when Joseph suddenly came in and announced there was a long-distance call from Africa. It was their lawyer, Mr. William Dussant. Charles immediately went to the library to answer the call.

"Hello, Charles speaking."

"Hello, Charles," responded Mr. Dussant. Then he proceeded. "Charles, I have some bad news. A little while ago, about forty miles from the coast, an explosion rocked the *Serenata*. The ship has been destroyed and everyone on board is presumed dead."

In shock and disbelief, Charles sank down, silent, waiting for the terrible news to sink into his mind.

"Either Anthony or I will be there as soon as possible," he managed to say when he recovered from the shock.

"Yes, Charles," said Mr. Dussant.

Upon returning to the family room, Charles immediately delivered the sad news to the others. Quite upset and with his heart racing he said, "We have just lost the *Serenata* and its crew. It exploded off the coast of Africa."

"What?" replied Anthony in shock.

"We lost the *Serenata*."

"I had no idea that the *Serenata* was even in Africa," said Anthony.

"You should know, Anthony. You were the one who authorized that trip."

"Me?"

"Yes, you."

Withdrawing from his recent state of enthusiasm, Anthony added, "All right, I did. You just informed me of that. Now, tell me why it exploded."

"There could be several reasons. Don't you know that we have enemies?"

"If we have some, it is news to me, Charles. Everyone liked our father. He was always honest."

"Everyone liked him because lately, they were getting everything they wanted from him."

Shocked by the news Anthony added, "I don't understand what you are trying to tell me."

"Then let me explain it to you. We have a shareholder that is the owner of almost fifteen percent of our shares. If we close our eyes to this, he will no longer be a shareholder but another owner of our assets. Would you like to have the Senator of New York owning half of our mines, jewelry stores, and ships?"

"What on earth are you talking about?"

"A well-organized conspiracy. Did you know that one of our ships had been used to transport illegal armaments?"

"That's impossible!"

"No," said Charles. "Anthony, let me tell you a story that I bet you don't know. In the last three years our ship, *Maria Catarina*, had been authorized to go to Africa six times while we only bought gemstones from there four times. You authorized two trips, our father three, and Sidney Maskuitiz, one. There have been several times when our ships were sailing from one port to another, and neither you nor our father knew if they were going to Africa or coming from Colombia, sailing to India or returning from Brazil. Why couldn't any of you see this?"

Anthony had no answer. He seemed lost in a turbulent river of surprises.

"Charles," said Catarina. "Do you think that the *Serenata*'s explosion was sabotage?"

"I don't know. We have to find out."

* * * *

Unknown to Charles, on that same evening, the senator from New York also received a call from Africa. Actually he had been growing very impatient awaiting the call. He jumped from his chair when the phone rang.

"Hello?"

"Risley?"

"Yes," said the senator.

"I saw everything. The terrorists did an excellent job. I will be in my house in Greece awaiting further news. Good night."

"Good night, Hard."

* * * *

The next day, Charles turned on the TV to listen to the

evening news and saw a young journalist covering the incident in Africa. Indeed, it was the first time Charles had seen her. She reported:

"Yesterday afternoon, the *Serenata*, the first ship acquired by the Merlenes Industries, was destroyed forty miles from South Africa. Sergeant Franco Parke, the officer in charge of the case, declared that there were no survivors. Sergeant Parke speculated that this might be a terrorist act, and that the police have not yet pieced together the rest of the story. This is Rebecca Macklen for *NBC News*—from South Africa."

Exactly a day after this report, Senator Ashford received another telephone call. It was Hard Narquilet again. The same man who had called from Africa.

"Why did they send this woman to Africa?" he asked.

"I don't know. I believe for no special reason. It's her job."

"I don't like this. She could cause us a lot of problems."

"A simple journalist? You can't be serious."

"I am. I don't want her nosing into my business."

"What do you want me to do? I can't control who gives the news."

"Yes, you can. Find a way to stop her."

"Oh please! What can she possibly do to harm us?"

"I don't know, Risley, but I prefer to eliminate any chance she could have. I'm an old rat. I can smell when the cat is dangerous."

Hard Narquilet happened to be a man who possessed extraordinary power. Swiftly, he had become the head of a 'powerful refined Mafia,' and he cleverly used very sophisticated ways when making his deals. He had been born in Syria and raised in New York City. Nowadays he not only dwelled in New York City but also in other countries and owned as many homes as the months of the year—twelve in all. He was an attractive man—very tall, with dark hair and a well-defined face. Never had Hard experienced any problem in gaining people's trust. As an introduction, he always wore a perfect smile on his lips—typical of a sheik—very vivid and impressive. Intelligence and necessity made him astute, a combination that made him a dangerous man.

Frequently Hard traveled on his yacht or his private airplane that was always ready to take off at a moment's notice. Only a handful of people knew where he was at any given time. His life was connected to many activities so that he was constantly giving orders and making important decisions.

The CIA, INTERPOL, and the KGB, among others, knew as much about Hard as they did about their own organizations. And even though they knew Hard Narquilet pretty well, they never interfered in his business. Catching and imprisoning him would be of no use because he directed many important enterprises. Those who worked for him on small operations were more dangerous criminals than Hard himself. For many intelligence agencies around the world, a character like Hard represented the fabric which made up an intricate crime world that justified the existence of the intelligence entities. In other words, they needed Hard at the top of his game. And because of it, the most reasonable thing to do was play the game of cat and mouse. Sometimes the cat made them believe he wanted to catch the mouse, and sometimes the mouse let the cat run after him. There was no need to completely stop the fun.

In Europe, among the French agents, Hard's nickname became Tartuffe, a pleasant hypocrite who knew how to guard his interests very well. This comparison was raised among some fellow agents. Jokingly one of them said, "I will call this Syrian, Tartuffe. The CIA, INTERPOL, KGB, etc, etc, are like the ORGON'S house. Hard is the son-of-a bitch that does whatever he wants and we, the agents, play the role of Madame Pernelle. We repeat her phrase daily, 'I hear strange tales of very strange events.' We don't care, do we?"

"No!" the others answered.

53

WHEN VICTORIA CROSSED THE hall and entered the dining room it was 6:00 p.m. She was dressed somewhat conservatively but elegantly in a long-sleeved, high collared, gray cashmere dress with a scarf around the neck and to enhance the look, a short rabbit fur coat.

"Uncle Joseph," she said. She had never been able to get rid of the uncle part when addressing him. She had always called him uncle. Certain rituals are hard to break and to her this was one of them. When they had company in the house, she avoided addressing him directly in order not to remind the others about their relationship. Victoria suffered very much because of this and of course, her uncle did not know. If ever the day came when she would have to point out the person whom she loved the most, it would probably be Uncle Joseph. But unfortunately, he was an insignificant figure in the world she trod.

That afternoon she had asked him to call Lombard for her, and minutes later she entered the limousine and Lombard drove her away. While downtown riding down many busy streets, she carefully looked through the car window. She saw hundreds of cars honking their horns obsessively while collectively polluting the air. The people resembled ants rushing to reach a destination. She considered herself fortunate not being one of them.

"A good saint truly blessed that bitch," Peter Lacerda would have said if he would have had to cross in front of the limousine at that moment. Peter did not belong to her daily routine, but swiftly he had become part of her expenses. He believed she had fallen from the sky before she could earn her wings. That explained why she didn't have to walk on the streets of New York.

Lombard parked the limousine in front of the Merlenes building in Manhattan. At that time of day only a few people happened to still be working. She had come to see Charles.

Victoria stepped out of the limousine, exchanged some words with the guard outside the door, and headed for the elevator. She went to the seventh floor where Charles had his office. She walked slowly through the hall looking for the sign in gold letters that read Charles Merlenes. When she found it, she gently knocked on the door.

"Come in," Charles said without knowing whom it could be.

Slowly she turned the handle and entered the room. Charles couldn't believe his own eyes when he looked up.

"Hello, Charles."

"Hello, Victoria," he said politely.

At that moment the combination of the rabbit fur coat with her pale face seemed extremely powerful. And to enhance this impression, she kept her hair pulled back, arranged in a loose bun that appeared as if it would come undone with a single touch.

"Can you put aside your papers for a moment and listen to me?" she asked.

"Yes," he answered immediately closing the file on his desk. "Please have a seat."

Victoria sat down and with the best tone of voice she could find, she said, "Charles, I'm here to tell you something that you probably do not expect to hear."

"All right."

"I'm pregnant."

"What?" he gasped.

"You are the father."

"No!" Charles said as he quickly swallowed the sour taste of the news.

She just calmly sat there and dispassionately observed him.

"Are you sure, Victoria?"

"Yes."

"Isn't it too soon to know?" he asked in desperation.

With a smile she said, "I can see clearly that you are a lawyer and not a doctor. If we begin to feel the symptoms and the doctor confirms it, then it is true."

Charles walked to the window where he stared blankly outside. Suddenly, New York City appeared to have been a mistake. He felt that all the skyscrapers looked out of place and they had nothing to do with the city. Instead, he wished the Eiffel Tower could be out there in front of his window. *Why did I come back? Every time I get involved with this woman I lose.*

Turning from the window he said, "It is hard to believe this is happening. Did you plan this?"

"Why would I plan such a thing, Charles?"

"I don't know. Maybe to play with my feelings."

"Play with your feelings?"

"Yes, I think."

She studied him for a moment determined she would never lose him.

"Charles, you don't have to worry because I don't plan to have this child."

"You don't?"

"No."

"Are you going to have an abortion?"

"Yes."

"Why?"

"Because of the problem in the blood line of your family. I

don't want to take any risks. I feel that I was lucky with Alexander."

"I never imagined you had such a terrible mind," Charles, commented.

"Neither did I. But every time I see your niece, Catarina, I get scared."

"I see."

Simultaneously they ran out of questions and answers. Charles thought he needed something to drink in order to go on with this conversation. "Would you like to have something to drink," he asked.

"No, thank you."

He walked to the corner of his office, poured himself a whiskey, and began sipping it. Then turning to her asked, "If you were so sure about what you planned to do, why did you bother telling me that you are expecting my child?"

"I thought you should know."

"Of course..."

Thoughtfully, Charles started to pace the room. *This is unbelievable. You are a fool, Charles. She always gets her way,* he told himself.

Then he said to her, "I'm against abortion, Victoria."

"You can't force me to have this child, Charles."

"You don't have to remind me of that because it would be the last thing I would attempt to do," he said firmly without taking his eyes off her.

As his words slowly filled the room, he wished to do with her what he should have done a long time ago. For the first time he hungered to put her in her place. He felt ready to show her his way.

"What I have in mind is much better than that," he explained. "I'm going to make you a proposition. The best one you have ever had. I'll give you two million dollars to have the child and, if it really is mine, I'll give you three million more."

"What? You can't be serious."

"Why not? If all this is true I do not want my child aborted. I made a mistake and I want to handle it properly. You're the niece of my butler, so this can be negotiated. Don't you agree with me?"

"I knew that you were always aware of that."

"Wrong, Victoria. I would have married you because I was in love with you. My big mistake was not knowing that you were in love with my brother."

"I was never in love with Anthony."

"Then why did you marry him?"

"I can't explain it, Charles. I think differently. Don't forget that I'm the niece of your butler—lack of money makes people less sophisticated."

"No excuses. And let's not continue this conversation. It will take us nowhere. So will you accept my proposition?"

Instead of giving him an answer, she stood up and walked toward him. She came so close that her lips almost touched his.

"What will happen if I disagree with you, *Mr. Merlenes*?"

"You simply lose five million dollars."

Charles' green eyes at that instant held an exquisite, soft look. She felt lost in their serenity. Delicately she brought her lips closer and began to raise her arms to hug him.

"No, Victoria!" he said holding her arms back. "No more games. In my world we do not play when there are millions of dollars involved."

"Oh, you...you're exactly like your grandmother. Only money counts. I thought I knew you."

"My proposition, Victoria."

Displeased, she walked away from him, and searched for her purse. At the door she answered, "I accept it."

When the door closed behind her, Charles returned to the window. He now knew the extent of her ambition, and realized how much he missed Paris. Placing his hands in his pockets, he began to imagine the Eiffel Tower in place of the Statue of Liberty.

On one side of the window was Manhattan and on the other, a charming, young, rich man. Under his breath he said, "Victoria, we never belonged to each other." Now, he finally understood.

Charles returned to his desk and made a phone call to Doneli.

"Doneli?" he said when he heard his voice.

"Yes."

"Charles speaking."

"Charles, what a surprise!"

"Yes. I need to talk to you about something very important. Can we meet tonight?"

"Of course. Where are you right now?"

"In my office."

"Why don't you come and have dinner with me? Fettuccini. Do you like it?"

"I love it."

"Excellent. Call home and tell them you have changed the shrimp with *palmito* for fettuccini."

Charles glanced at the calendar on his desk. Friday. On Fridays the Merlenes had shrimp with *palmito* for dinner.

"Unbelievable, you know the menu by heart."

"I have known the Merlenes for many years, Charles. It would be silly of me not to remember what is for dinner on Fridays."

Charles simply laughed. "I'll be at your house in half an hour."

"I'll see you then."

Charles hung up the phone and called home to notify them of his absence that night. Immediately afterwards he gathered the papers on his table, grabbed his overcoat, and went downstairs to the lobby.

As he entered the lobby, he saw Ernesto Lobo, his chauffeur, talking and laughing with the doorman at the main entrance. Lobo was a Portuguese man born in Tapira and had lived in New York City since 1957. Lobo brought his sense of humor wherever he went. He was thirty-nine years old and had at least sixty-six different stories about his adventurous life. Also, he had one hundred twenty-two jokes, three divorces, and five kids. It was impossible to be bored in his company.

"Good evening, Mr. Merlenes," Lobo politely said.

"Good evening, Lobo."

Both of them said good-bye to the doorman and left the building. Half an hour later, Charles met with Doneli.

* * * *

"Charles, please make yourself comfortable," said Doneli as he led him into the house. "Dinner is ready. What would you like to drink, red or white wine?"

"Red," said Charles while taking off his coat, loosening his tie and seating himself at the table that Doneli had already set.

After handing him his wine, Doneli brought the salad, bread, and fettuccini to the table. Following that, dinner started.

"Now we can talk," said Doneli. "What's going on, Charles?"

"I need a detective to go to Africa to investigate the *Serenata*'s explosion. I must know more about this whole thing. Senator Ashford is now one of our biggest shareholders. I can't imagine how my father allowed this to happen. When I took over as president, I did something that made the senator and one of our vice-presidents, Sidney Maskuitiz, very unhappy. I froze the sale of our shares. A month later the explosion in Africa took place. Even though it was supposed to have been a terrorist act, I believe that someone we know is involved in this."

"Senator Ashford, the Merlenes' biggest shareholder?" asked Doneli.

"Yes. And there is still more to it. Our ships have been used to transport illegal arms."

"Who told you that?"

"Kamuka Imaka, one of our vice-presidents. This did not happen recently."

"And why didn't he tell this to Max?"

"He did, but my father didn't believe him."

"Oh please!"

"Apparently my father gave away his authority."

"Who did you send to Africa?"

"Anthony."

Silently Charles served himself another glass of wine. Meanwhile, Doneli observed him carefully and thought, *Catarina was always right. He was never meant to be a racecar driver. He belongs where he is.*

"Can you help me find a good detective?" Charles asked.

"Of course. You will have one tomorrow."

"Thank you. I knew I could count on you."

"Any time, Charles."

For dessert they had strawberries and cream. After their coffee, Charles left.

* * * *

He arrived at home around 10:00 p.m. Joseph greeted him with a cordial smile and in a perfect tone of voice said, "Good evening, sir."

Handing him his coat and briefcase, Charles asked for his grandmother.

"She is upstairs in the reading room," said Joseph. "I just took her some tea."

"Thank you, Joseph. That will be all."

Charles walked upstairs thinking about what he wanted to discuss with his grandmother. He went directly to the reading room and at the door he loudly cleared his voice to announce his presence.

"Charles!" said his grandmother, immediately closing her book and taking off her glasses. "Why did you work so late? Did you really need to? I know we are having some problems, but they can be managed differently, can't they?"

With a smile Charles sat down next to her and gave her a loving kiss as he said, "You worry too much."

"Because I love you."

"I wasn't working, grandmother. I went to speak with Doneli."

"About?"

"I would like to hire a detective to investigate the incident in Africa. Who better than Doneli to help me find a good one?"

"Very clever. You can trust him completely. Would you join me in a cup of tea?"

"No. Thank you. I ate too much for dinner."

While talking, she noticed a puzzled look on his face.

"You look worried, Charles. Is there something else that you want to tell me?"

"Yes. I have very unpleasant news to tell you. However, I can't go on with my decision without your approval."

"All right. I'm listening."

With a serious expression on his face, Charles stood up, moved his chair closer and sat immediately in front of her.

"Is it so bad that we have to be *this* close?"

"Worse than you can imagine."

Oh, God, help me! was her first thought. Then she said, "I'm ready. Tell me."

Charles then started.

"Grandmother, this is very ugly. But you have to know it because what happened can't be fixed."

"I see."

"Briefly, let me tell you what happened in Paris a long time ago, when I was nineteen."

"I know that, Charles. Victoria spent several days with you. You were in love with her when she married Anthony. That's why you decided to stay in France."

"So you knew all about it?"

"Yes. Otherwise, I wouldn't have allowed you to stay there."

"Of course."

"Go ahead, Charles. Say what you have to. I'm a strong old lady."

"Well, now things became more complicated. We were in Bolevar, and she came to my room naked. I lost my mind, and we made love. Today, she came to my office and told me that she is pregnant and wants to have an abortion. She wishes to avoid the chance of not having a *normal* child."

"Bitch!" snapped Catarina.

"Grandmother, I want that child."

Silently Catarina left her chair. She felt the need to move around in order to keep the circulation going throughout her body. Somehow the news wanted to paralyze her. For a while she kept walking from one side of the room to another.

"I never liked that woman, Charles," she said returning to her chair. "I knew that something like this would happen."

"I'm very sorry."

"Oh, I know you are. And I know that it is not all your fault. She planned it because she is no good, Charles. You and your brother could only see her beauty. But not me. I know how far she will go if we do not stop her. You are right. What happened can't be fixed. But I don't want an abortion either. So do you have an idea of what can make her change her mind?"

"Money. I offered her five million dollars, and she accepted it. That is why I'm here. I can't obtain this kind of money without your approval."

Quietly, Catarina looked at him. He meant a lot to her and his child, too.

"Let me ask you one thing, Charles. Do you still love her?"

"No. She is the most beautiful woman I have ever seen, but I don't love her."

"I think your brother should know about this."

"I agree with you. I will tell him myself."

Calmly Catarina tasted some of her tea. "You have my approval, Charles. You can have the five million, but I will need to talk to her. From now on, she will have to do things my way. And I guarantee you they will not be pleasant."

"It will be as you wish, but don't forget that I want that child."

"We will have it."

Kissing her goodnight, he added, "Thank you."

"You need a wife, Charles. Start thinking about that."

"I will. I promise."

54

TWO DAYS LATER, CATARINA asked Victoria to join her in the library. They met downstairs and Catarina decided to be polite with her because of Charles' baby. Under no circumstances did she want Victoria to suspect how valuable and important the child she was carrying was to her.

"Dear Victoria, congratulations for winning again," she said politely. "You sure are a lucky young woman."

"Really?" responded Victoria, expectantly. She knew Catarina would always uphold her family's interests. Therefore, she intended to file away anything she might say.

"Charles informed me of what happened between you two at Bolevar," Catarina proceeded. "Very bad, Victoria. You are heading in a very dangerous direction, but you just don't know that. I already have enough reasons to hate you. However, my patience hasn't ended yet, though I must confess that I'm fighting against it. You're young and sweet, and we have all known you since you were a little girl. Honestly, I truly desire to respect that. You deserve another chance. In my opinion, accepting Charles' proposal was quite fair, and I would like to double it. I want to make it ten million dollars."

Victoria, visibly astounded, wondered what would be next. After some moments, she moved ahead to satisfy her curiosity and asked, "May I ask what I have to do for the extra five million?"

Cut your veins after giving birth, was Catarina's immediate response, but she only said that in her mind. Out loud she replied, "After giving birth, I want you to sign divorce papers and leave this house forever."

"And my children?"

"Without your children. I'm buying them."

"You and your lousy money!" Victoria spat, not trying to hide her hatred. "You think that you can buy whatever you want, don't you?"

"You were the one who first showed interest in my money, Victoria. Under the circumstances, I'm only trying to cooperate."

"I love Charles, Catarina."

"Do you? I believe you then. Actually, we both love him. That is why we are here talking in terms of millions. Right?"

"You will not succeed in getting in my way," cried Victoria. "At the end, he will be mine!"

As if Victoria hadn't said anything, Catarina continued her stipulations. "You will have twenty-four hours to leave this house after giving birth. On that same day, ten million dollars will be deposited in your account. This is not a choice, Victoria. I never give people the right to make choices. If you do not do as I say, I'll simply hire someone to kill you. Remember, my 'lousy money' can buy good lawyers and also a respectable judge. Besides that, people die in accidents everyday. I have two things that you don't, Victoria—experience and lots of money. That's a dangerous combination. Now you can leave."

Impressed by the overpowering and straightforward manner with which Catarina handled the matter, Victoria walked out of the library. She departed very disappointed, upset, and totally confused. Catarina had surprised her in such a way that she couldn't even find the right words to use in order to fight back.

When she realized that the ten million dollars had more meaning than all those harsh words she had failed to use, she became furious. In the hall she walked right past Doneli and simply ignored his presence.

"Hello, Catarina!" said Doneli not quite sure if he had arrived at an inappropriate moment. "I saw Victoria in the hall and she seemed very upset."

"She is. Come and sit down. She is the reason why I called you."

"What happened?"

"She is pregnant again, Doneli. And this time, Charles is the father. Can you believe that?"

"You are joking."

"No. I'm giving her ten million dollars to leave the house without her children."

"Really? And did she accept?"

"Oh, Doneli, ten million is too much of a temptation for just about everyone. Also, she knows I would have her killed if she refused."

"My, my."

"The reason I called you was because I want her watched twenty-four hours a day until she gives birth. I would like to know her whereabouts and every person with whom she has contact. In other words, I need a private detective. Can I count on you?"

"Yes," responded Doneli without hesitation.

Their conversation lasted for a long time; and while Joseph was serving them tea, Catarina said, "Charles needs a wife, Doneli."

"How fast your mind works," replied Doneli. "Your comprehensive ideas quickly avoid any impossible mission. Yes, I agree he does need a wife, Catarina, but it is not up to us to find her."

"True. We can just give it a nice push by helping him meet a fine woman."

"No. That won't work. Charles wouldn't fall for that. Just let things happen naturally."

"Oh...all right! The subject is dead. Don't start lecturing me because I never thought about hiring someone to find him a fine woman. I'll pray for it instead."

Doneli laughed. "Better, much better. Catarina, you never change. I see you fighting for the Merlenes in every aspect until the day you die."

"They are my family, Doneli. Don't forget that my love for Anthony survives through it."

Before leaving the house that afternoon, Doneli asked about Elizabeth.

"She is fine," said Catarina. "She went to London for a week—finally taking up designing again. Time is helping her accept what happened."

"Good! I'm glad to hear that."

"Anthony is in Africa," said Catarina.

"Yes, Charles told me."

"Did you see what happened to the *Serenata*? What do you think about that? Are the Merlenes starting to sink? So many things have happened lately, Doneli."

"No, Catarina. I have learned a lot of things in life, and one of them is that everything has a purpose. It takes time for us to understand why they occur, but we come to know the real reason. For example, what would have happened if you didn't have Charles? Anthony would not have been able to go to Africa because he would have had to be here in New York taking care of other things. Tomorrow we will see something similar with Alexander, young Catarina, and this new child that Victoria is expecting. I compare life to a carousel—it never stops turning. Again and again chances and opportunities repeat themselves endlessly. The Merlenes are not sinking. The carousel just started another turn."

"I hope you are right."

"I am."

* * * *

Charles finally met Luis Demetrius, the detective Doneli had hired. Luis happened to be the son of Detective Ferdinando Demetrius, Doneli's close friend. Luis was thirty-six years old and had an excellent reputation as a detective. As an investigator he was meticulous, persistent, certain in uncertain situations, and full of shrewd ideas—undoubtedly, the right man for Charles.

Accompanied by Doneli, Luis Demetrius walked into Charles' office where the three of them conversed for more than an hour. Charles informed Luis of their transactions with Africa and provided him with copies of the *Serenata*'s travels within the last eight months. In fact, Charles handed Luis everything he had found that might be relevant to the investigation. Also, Charles spoke to him about Risley Ashford and Sidney Maskuitiz.

Luis carefully took notes of all the accounts, and when there was nothing more to discuss, the three of them went out for dinner. Since Charles extended the invitation, Doneli decided on the restaurant. He chose the China Inn, in Chinatown.

After ordering the best house wine, they began to relax and enjoy some pleasant conversation. Luis was a very talkative person, and evidently always had something interesting to say. Right away he began to talk about one of his father's adventures with Doneli during the war—the incident over the Atlantic, which had saved Max's life. He said that his father had loved to tell stories. Ferdinando Demetrius had died five years before in a car accident in the streets of New York City. According to Luis, the incident in the Atlantic was his father's most heroic achievement during the war.

"I didn't know you saved my father's life, Doneli," Charles commented.

"It wasn't exactly like that, Charles. We only helped transfer him from one ship to another."

"No," said Luis. "The truth is that he fabricated that transfer. And as far as I know, the vessel that your father was on never came back from the Barents Sea."

"Why didn't anyone tell me that story?" asked Charles. "Was

it necessary for me to meet Demetrius in order to hear it?"

Just as Doneli was ready to respond, a well-dressed young woman approached the table interrupting his train of thought.

"Excuse me," she said looking at Charles. "Are you Charles Merlenes?"

Politely, Charles answered, "Yes, I am."

Gently, she extended her hand out to him and said, "Nice to meet you, Mr. Merlenes. I'm Rebecca Macklen. I work for *NBC News*. I went to Africa to cover the story about the *Serenata*'s accident. I would like to hear the rest of the story, if possible."

"You're not the only one who wants to know it. Is it Miss or Mrs.?" Charles asked.

"Miss."

"Like I said, Miss Macklen, you are not the only one after the truth. I'm also searching for answers. Let me introduce you to Mr. Cassarete and Mr. Demetrius."

Cordially she nodded at them and repeated her name.

"Would you like to join us for dinner?" Charles asked.

"Thank you, but I can't. We are on our way to the airport—my cameraman, Roberto Delvalle and I," she said pointing to the young man with her.

"Nice to meet you Mr. Delvalle," said Charles.

While Rebecca spoke she held a fortune cookie in her left hand, and distractedly she placed it on the table in order to look for her business cards.

"Here's my card, Mr. Merlenes," she said. "Please give me a call so we can discuss the accident in Africa. I would appreciate it if you would grant me an interview."

"I'll see what I can do Miss Macklen."

Extending her hand one last time she said, "Good night," to the gentleman at the table. To Charles in particular, she added, "It was a pleasure to have personally met you."

After watching her walk away, Charles glanced at her card. Then he took out his wallet and placed it inside. While silently returning his attention to his glass of wine, he discovered that she had left without her fortune cookie. Smiling at her carelessness, he collected it as well.

When their dinner ended, the waiter brought them three fortune cookies. Doneli opened the first one and read aloud, "Everything you have is a blessing from God."

After Doneli, Luis Demetrius read his, "Listen to the words because they are significant." Then Luis exclaimed in amazement, "*Caramba*! Detectives learn these things on their first day of class. What I would like to know is how the Chinese manage to give the right cookie to the right person. It never fails."

Lastly Charles opened his and read: "Everything that belongs to you is on the way."

* * * *

Later on at home, Charles had a cup of tea with his grandmother. After briefly informing her about the latest events, he kissed her good night. Once in his room, while emptying his pockets, he found Miss Macklen's fortune cookie. For an instant he held it thoughtfully. Then for no real reason, he opened the wrapper, cracked the cookie, and softly read: "Everything that belongs to you is on the way."

"Hmmm! Nice coincidence."

55

JOHANNESBURG, SOUTH AFRICA, would have been merely another city for Luis Demetrius if not for the condition of the sky on the afternoon he arrived. The intensity of the red above the city made him feel that he had just walked into a red hole inside the planet Mercury. Though he was taken from the airport to the hotel in a taxi, sitting next to Inspector Sardine, who spoke with a funny accent, Demetrius could not stop looking at the red horizon. The more he watched it, the more fascinated he became. The sunset left in the sky—behind the clouds—traces of red, mixed with intense and bright orange shadows. Those hot flaming colors, far away, collapsing towards infinity, gave a picturesque touch to the city, making it quite unique. It displayed a phenomenal panoramic view.

At the hotel, Demetrius found Anthony waiting for him. Immediately after greeting each other, they sat in the reception lobby, close to a spacious window through which they could see the vast red and orange sky. Even if they were to travel to Cape Town, Port Elizabeth, or Mozambique, those intense, hot colors would be there in front of them over the Indian Ocean.

Anthony ordered two martinis for them. The drinks were served with a delicious *pâté.* That day was the first time they met. Charles had called Anthony and informed him of Luis' arrival. The two men spent that afternoon together talking and getting better acquainted with the *Serenata*'s accident. Also, they discussed how investigations in Africa were conducted in such situations.

"Luis, this is another world," said Anthony. "Here, whoever knows a lot, remains quiet and whoever knows a little, sells the wrong information. Do you see that sunset? It is spectacular isn't it? I assure you that you will never see one like that in New York City. Everything here resembles that sunset. You have just entered another world. I don't know what tactics detectives in the United States use, but here you will need to use the best you've got."

"Thank you for the advice," said Demetrius. "In my line of work, everything is valid. Even the wrong information."

Smiling at his sense of humor, Anthony asked, "What possible value could wrong information have?"

"More than you can imagine," said Demetrius. "There are times when the wrong information builds confidence and allows us to identify the truth when it does arrive."

"Interesting...very interesting," replied Anthony as he mulled that statement over a few moments. Then he said, "Inspector Sardine is a good person. You can rely on him."

Later on at dinner, Inspector Sardine joined Luis and Anthony.

By the end of the week, Anthony had left, returning to New York City.

* * * *

Upon his arrival in New York City, Anthony went directly from the airport to the Merlenes' building in Manhattan. It was late Friday afternoon when he entered the building and proceeded straight to his brother's office.

"Good afternoon, Charles."

"Oh, Anthony! Hello! How was your trip?"

"Terrible. I'm exhausted. Three weeks in Johannesburg is definitely too much for someone who enjoys New York City like I do. Don't forget I have been traveling quite a lot lately. When I returned from Brazil, I immediately had to go to Africa. Now, I need some time here to inhale the air of Manhattan. Can you understand?"

Charles moved his head in agreement. "Yes, you do need some rest. What if we spend the weekend together at Bolevar?"

"Excellent idea! I want to drive your Ferrari. It seems that each time I plan to do it, something happens. My weekends get so complicated that I end up not going to Bolevar. Therefore, tomorrow will be the day."

"I didn't know that," said Charles. "Please, take it for some laps this weekend. I know you're going to love it. Now, tell me about the problems in Africa."

"The *Serenata* is completely destroyed, Charles. If we recover anything, it will only be pieces of the ship—small pieces. Mr. Dussant and Inspector Sardine are taking care of that. The cause of the accident remains unclear, as it seems no one knows anything. Everyone kept saying the word terrorist as if they couldn't find anything else to say. And there was nothing in the midst of the gossip to suggest otherwise. Also, no one knows who kept contact with the terrorists, either."

"What did you think of Luis Demetrius?"

"He seemed to be a nice fellow...promising. He will enjoy Johannesburg as well as Inspector Sardine's company. But in all honesty, I don't think he will come up with anything relevant. You have no idea how ugly things become when terrorists are involved. Everybody talks and walks carefully because they fear everything, their gods and the devil. Only powerful people make deals with those guys. We are in the middle of something big, Charles. I don't want to scare you, but from now on, be careful with your decisions. They could destroy our lives."

"What do you want me to do? Do you want me to let someone

from the outside dictate our actions and run our business? Let me tell you something, Anthony. If that is the case, they will have to kill me."

"Charles, it's only advice. From now on just be careful. Perhaps we can find another way to solve the problems. I am with you in this war. However, I hate terrorists because they die for their beliefs, and that is bullshit!"

"All right, Anthony. I promise I will be more careful."

Soon after, Anthony left for home. Charles approached the window in his office. He enjoyed looking at the concrete structures of the skyscrapers. Sometimes he imagined the rhythmic noises from the streets rising between them until they reached the wide-open space, and then finally disappearing into the air.

How can I tell him what happened between Victoria and me? He does not deserve this.

The noise from the outside hardly penetrated Charles' office, but he could describe it if he wanted to. In his mind New York City was real. Then he went back to his thoughts. *Sunday...either Saturday or Sunday, I'll tell him. It will be terribly difficult...but I have to.*

* * * *

The next day at breakfast, Anthony asked his brother if he would go with him to Bolevar.

"No, you go on," said Charles. "I have to go to the office this morning to finish some paperwork that needs to be ready for Monday. I didn't have a chance to do it during the week. But I'll leave in the early afternoon so I'll be there by dinner time."

"All right. Fine with me."

An hour later, Anthony left New York City, alone, driving his black Porsche. When he arrived at the country house, Emmanuel, the caretaker, greeted him.

"Good morning, Mr. Merlenes!"

"Good morning, Emmanuel!"

As they entered the house together, Anthony told him, "Charles will be here for dinner. I think we will be the only ones here this weekend."

"I will notify my wife then. Would you like anything special for dinner?"

"Let me see...what about the traditional shrimp *crepes*? Is that possible?"

"Yes. I will take care of it."

Emmanuel had turned to leave when Anthony said, "One more thing, Emmanuel. I need the keys to the Ferrari."

"Yes, sir. I will bring it to you right away."

A few minutes later, Emmanuel returned and handed Anthony the keys.

Happy to be home from his travels, Anthony opened a bottle of champagne and drank one glass. Then he walked the distance to the garage near the track.

Located close to the track on the left side of the lake, the garage had the cpapcity to house five cars. Emmanuel followed Anthony halfway and then walked to the stables to check on the horses. Excited, Anthony crossed the track and arrived at the garage where he reached down to the handle and pulled the door open. The beautiful white Ferrari appeared—as usual—very clean and shiny. It had been washed and polished the day before. Anthony smiled upon seeing Charles' new, expensive toy.

He walked around the car checking it out and enjoying its beauty. He leaned over and touched it. "Hello, baby," he crooned, "You look great!"

Anxiously anticipating the rush of driving the car around the track, he opened the door and sat in the driver's seat. He took a moment to breathe in the smell of the finest leather. Then eager to finally experience the speed of the wheels going around the track, he placed the key in the ignition and turned it on.

"Okay, baby, let's go—"

Anthony probably heard something but felt nothing. He didn't have time to taste the sweetness of the Ferrari's performance because instantly there was a sudden and violent explosion that filled the air. From the stables Emmanuel turned, but only saw the black, dense smoke rolling up into the sky. Pieces of wood and metal flew fast and in all directions from the center of the dark cloud.

Emmanuel rushed toward the garage but stopped a few feet away. He could only stare in horror at the immensity of the fire. The flames spread fast, the heat intensifying around and devouring everything it could. Emmanuel watched in shock—unable to see clearly or do anything.

It took him more than a few minutes to utter, "Oh...my...God!" as Anthony finally came into his mind.

Trembling, he ran to the house. Upon entering the kitchen he was further shocked to find his wife unconscious on the floor. She had apparently seen everything from the window and fainted. Still shivering, he placed her on the bed and used some alcohol to revive her. After that, he called for help and telephoned the Merlenes' house in New York City.

The phone rang and Joseph answered. "The Merle—"

"Joseph, it is Emmanuel," he interrupted in a frightened voice. "I have terrible news."

Emmanuel's voice was so shaky that Joseph could hardly understand him.

"Emmanuel, calm down. What happened?" Joseph asked, moving the phone from one ear to the other in order to better hear him.

"Mr. Merlenes...Anthony...I think...he is dead. The garage is all in flames. I don't know how it happened! I heard a terrible explosion and when I turned, everything was in flames. Tell his brother to come immediately because I don't know what to do."

"Oh, my heavens!" Joseph said and then hung up and sat down. He broke out in a cold sweat and his hands and legs began to shake. Visibly shocked and fighting against his distress, he called Charles.

"Mr. Merlenes?" Joseph said shakily.

"Yes, Joseph," said Charles recognizing the weak voice. Charles happened to be alone in the office so he had answered the call.

"Oh, sir...I...I don't know...how to say this to you...I just received a phone call from...Bolevar. Emmanuel said...the garage is in flames and...and he thinks..."

"What?" Charles said, an ominous feeling creeping over him.

"Apparently, your brother was inside when it happened."

"No!" Charles exclaimed then couldn't utter another word. He took a moment, wishing that everything was a mistake, confusion or a misunderstanding.

Then Charles finally said, "Call Emmanuel and tell him I'm on my way... And Joseph, please don't tell my family anything about this until I find out what really happened."

"Yes, sir."

Immediately, Charles took his limousine to Bolevar. In his despair he made Lobo drive so fast that he even placed his own life close to the limits of death. As every minute went by, Charles grew terrified at what might be the truth.

The two-hour drive to Bolevar took them just over an hour. There, the mood was haunting. Charles found lots of cars in front of the house that belonged to their neighbors who had also heard the explosion and had come right away, the fire fighters who had finally extinguished the fire and the police.

Lobo couldn't approach the driveway because the number of vehicles and police blockade obstructed the area. So, before he could find a place to park, Charles stepped out of the car and frantically crossed the garden arriving next to Emmanuel, the police, and the fire fighters. Among the people he found Dr. Justino Carfeu, a respected plastic surgeon that owned the estate next to the Merlenes. Dr. Carfeu seemed to be the one in charge of the situation.

"Thank God you arrived, Charles!" said Dr. Carfeu.

"How is my brother?" Charles asked.

"I'm sorry... There was nothing we could do."

Charles covered his eyes with his hands, feeling the pain both in his heart and soul, in memory of his brother, for there was no other way to face such news. For a moment he forgot how to think and how to talk. He simply breathed without thought or reason.

Moments later, he walked toward the site to find that the garage no longer existed. Ashes and parts of burned metal replaced it, and in the midst of the burned objects remained pieces of his brother's cremated body. That scene would never be erased from his mind.

After talking with the police and answering their questions, Charles became aware of the stark reality—it was his life that was in danger! The bomb placed in the Ferrari had been intended for him and not for Anthony.

In the midst of everything, he entered the house to make a phone call. He needed someone to go to his house and deliver the news. Doneli was the only person he trusted to do this for him.

On the other end of the line Doneli answered, "Hello."

Charles just said, "Doneli...I need your help. I'm in the middle of something terrible. My brother Anthony is dead. Someone planted a bomb in the Ferrari and Anthony tried to use it. I'm at Bolevar right now, and I need someone to go to my house and tell my mother and grandmother what happened. I want everyone to know what happened before they see it on the news. Please see what you can do. Call Dr. Rudel and Dr. Scarshiner first. You're going to need their help."

"You can't be serious..."

"I am. Anthony is dead, Doneli."

After hanging up, Doneli sat down on a chair, stupefied. *What is going on? Someone has decided to play a tough game with the Merlenes. Poor Elizabeth...I think this will forever erase any smile from her lips. God has punished her—more than He has punished me."*

56

IT WAS FOUR O'CLOCK IN the afternoon when another car approached the Merlenes' residence in Bolevar. A tall man with hair down to his shoulders, wearing small glasses that just covered his eyes, and a slim, very well dressed woman, stepped out of the car and walked toward the entrance. They were from New York City and hadn't expected to see what they saw in front of them—fire trucks and police cars parked along the driveway. Surprisingly they walked to the gate where a police officer came forward to talk to them. Despite having identified themselves by showing their credentials, the police officer wouldn't allow them in.

Charles was speaking with Inspector Henry Mac when he saw them. Politely, he interrupted the inspector and called to Emmanuel. When Emmanuel went over to him, he asked him to tell the police officer to allow Miss Rebecca Macklen and her cameraman to come in.

That morning Rebecca had contacted the Merlenes' office and

luckily had spoken with Charles. Because of her good connections she had found out that Anthony had arrived in New York City from Africa the day before. She desperately wanted to be the first one to hear the "fresh news" if there was any. So she had called for the purpose of setting up an interview with both Charles and Anthony. When she had spoken with Charles, he had explained to her that they would be at their country house in the afternoon and that he would gladly grant her an interview if she didn't mind driving there. Promptly she had agreed and he then proceeded to give her their address.

Now she was there. Upset and quite shocked. "Good afternoon, Mr. Merlenes. I'm terribly sorry to hear about your brother," she said.

"Thank you. This is Inspector Henry Mac. Inspector, this is Miss Macklen and Mr.—"

"Robert Delvalle," said Robert.

They all walked into the house, and sat in the living room. Charles honestly told her what he knew and how everything had happened.

She asked, "Mr. Merlenes, do you think there is any connection between this incident and the explosion and destruction of the *Serenata*?"

"I don't know."

"Do you think that your brother's trip to Africa had something to do with his death?"

"Perhaps. But I don't think so."

Cautiously, Charles told her that his brother hadn't found anything in Africa that could be relevant to the *Serenata*'s case but that he couldn't rule out the possibility of a connection between the two incidents. They talked about Charles' latest decisions regarding the Merlenes' shares, and about Charles' security as well.

Following that, Inspector Henry Mac also answered some of her questions. He made sure that all he said were facts relating to the explosion. He didn't want to harm the investigation.

Later, Charles took Robert and Rebecca to where the garage used to be so that Robert could take some shots of the scene. They felt extremely sad upon viewing the site and suddenly realized that what they were seeing was more gruesome than harmful.

She and Charles stepped away while Robert moved around taking pictures. It was hard to witness such a dreadful, fiery scene with the body of such a young man still inside the burned Ferrari. The only crime he had committed was turning the car key.

Looking at the devastation, Rebecca imagined the explosion. The awful noise which had broken the peaceful silence and had exposed the last tenacious terror a person's eyes could ever frame. The debris lay on the ground mixing with the black fumes and permeating the air with a strong and uncommon stench. Everything now rested harmlessly behind black ash and in between hot pieces of metal. She realized that somebody had started a very dirty war with the Merlenes and that their enemy, besides being dangerous, was also skillful at killing people and burning the evidence. As she stood there contemplating the ashes of what should have been Charles' demise, Rebecca looked closely at him and saw that Charles was in the midst of someone's plan.

"I have no words to describe my feelings," she said. "I see fearful things every day but I have never seen anything like this."

"This scene will never be erased from my mind," Charles said. "He died in my place and I don't even know why."

"I hope you can find out why. Otherwise..."

"Otherwise, I will never have peace," he finished for her.

Rebecca had to get back to New York City for the evening news so she and Robert prepared to leave Bolevar.

"Thank you, Mr. Merlenes, for letting me in and for allowing me an interview at a moment like this. I would like to see you again if it is possible, to cover this story in more depth. Evidently, we haven't reached the end of it yet."

"I will keep you in mind, Miss Macklen. I have your card."

* * * *

In New York City, Dr. Rudel and Dr. Scarshiner met at the Merlenes residence. They entered the house worried, spoke to Joseph and then walked toward Doneli.

"What is it, Doneli?" asked Dr. Rudel.

"Anthony is dead."

"Dead? How?"

"A bomb in Charles' Ferrari."

The two doctors sat in silence in the family room thinking about the news and repeating silently whatever crossed their minds at the moment. *Dead. Why? How? Who?* Their thoughts were going every which way until reality allowed them to adjust themselves to their next course of action. After that they agreed to go tell the women the news.

Victoria fainted when she heard that her husband was dead. No one knows what caused such genuine stress. It could have been either because she was really in shock, and she was pregnant, or because she couldn't embrace the happiness of finally being free. Secretly she knew why she was crying, but her eyes seemed scared and full of questions. Following her first reaction, the doctors kept her under careful observation for fear she would miscarry the baby.

Jacqueline cried in the arms of her dear father, Dr. Scarshiner, and couldn't help thinking of things that made her remember her own husband and her handicapped child. How could she have known that the family was cursed? Their riches only seemed to attract misery. Like Elizabeth, she didn't know that her life was to be a life of tears. How could she?

After hearing the terrible news Elizabeth threw herself into the abyss of a nightmare where the cold wind blew violently and the bodies of her husband and sons elevated in the air swirling like flying objects and disappearing one after another. She remained strong as a scarecrow resisting the wind while rivers of tears ran down her cheeks.

Next to her was Catarina, still strong, still the Catarina of the cat-like eyes. She accepted Anthony's death quietly, then bravely and finally with indignation. She heard the news while holding Doneli's hands. She pressed them forcibly, while her body collapsed a little to the right and her cat-like eyes stared at images that weren't in the room. Totally lifeless spirits moved inside her mind. They were all familiar spirits arriving as if for a tea party. Like ghosts around a mahogany table waiting for the new guest. It was the astonishment of yet another tragedy.

Looking deeply into Doneli's eyes she screamed loudly. No one had ever heard her scream such a scream. She repeated it once, twice, and again for at least a full minute. Her pain and rage filled the air at the speed of light, bouncing off the walls and reaching the outside, traveling through the universe from inside her cocoon. Pain and rage, which had invaded God's sacred tabernacle with full strength; the echoes that would never die, in the name of her grandson whose life was swept away so unmercifully.

For this grandson of hers, part of her soul would depart from this world and part of her heart would survive in his name. She determined to resist. For so much love she would resist.

Dr. Rudel and Dr. Scarshiner remained in the house monitoring the family. They prescribed sedatives to help them through this difficult moment. This tragedy had happened only a scant eight months after Max's unexpected death, from which the Merlenes still had not yet recovered.

When night fell, Lombard, the family chauffeur, took Doneli to Bolevar. Doneli wanted to be next to Charles and to closely follow the course of the investigation. He knew there was nothing more he could do for Anthony, but there was a lot he could still do for Charles.

More than anyone else, he desired to find the son-of-a-bitch who was responsible for this horrible crime, and from then on he determined it would be his personal mission. He simply couldn't bear Elizabeth's pain at this time. He loved her dearly and having seen her lose her husband and two sons made him feel so powerless. Now, her tears were washing away the last drop of patience his soul could bare. It became impossible for him just to stop and just look. No. He would not take it anymore and like a mad fighter, he would fight for her last son.

Because Anthony's remains were merely ashes, Catarina decided to have a private funeral. Only their close friends came to the religious services that took place inside the funeral home chapel and it was during this service that Catarina stood up and said her last words to her grandson. Then on the following day, at the burial, she spoke publicly, "No one on the face of the earth could ever imagine how much pain I'm carrying in my heart. I feel that a great part of my existence died with my grandson. I have lost two Anthonys, but, still, I feel strong. If in the past I have survived for what I loved most, today I have to live for what I still love. We are a family and like a rock we are indestructible."

Then as expected, her words were printed in many newspapers, showing the world that like diamonds, her strength was also everlasting.

57

IN JOHANNESBURG, LUIS PROBED deeper into the sequence of events that had taken place before the *Serenata*'s destruction, trying to find a starting point for his investigation. He moved from one place to another and talked to the strangest and most important people imaginable, trying to dig up at least a small portion of what lay behind this tragedy. However, he didn't succeed.

While Luis was trying to dig something up in Africa, Doneli in New York City, concentrated on uncovering facts about Senator Riley Ashford's life. Doneli believed that politics and terrorists danced together when the music played mutually pleasant songs.

In his investigation, Doneli found out that Senator Ashford had been born in New York. His father was a lawyer and his mother a schoolteacher. Like his father, he had become a lawyer and at a young age had immersed himself in politics. Risley dreamed of being famous to prove to his friends and family that he could achieve more than they all could. For years he saw the world through his atypical vanity. His greed for power and fervent passion for money not only shaped the strength of his determinations and enlarged the core of his dreams, but also polished the cleverness of his character. This helped him learn to climb the mountain with the right stream. Then, because power and money always influenced his every decision, one day he woke up as the senator of the state of New York.

When Risley saw the possibility of becoming the center of political attention as the representative of such an important state, his ambition drove him wild. He couldn't think of anything else but that. To comply with his greed he eagerly invested some time researching the political field and knew then that he was the right man for this job. Skillfully he set the course and rowed his boat with those who would be part of his vanity.

He envisioned himself as a master puppeteer. He pictured himself making decisions for the state and for his bank account, simultaneously. He acted around people who admired him even without knowing him. He fulfilled the state's needs and walked a fine line between corruption and honesty for his own desires. Predictably his aspirations drove him toward the political field and his acute talents guided him down the convenient path, so he could win both ways, as a politician and as a thief.

He honestly believed in himself and thought he could handle any kind of event properly and intelligently. It eventually happened. He had an appealing and flawless face, a responsive look, and the most touching smile that lips could ever show, which is exactly what politicians needed to gain people's hearts. And when his marvelous image began to speak on his behalf, the state of New York began to drown in the midst of a glowing but dubious reality.

As a senator he concentrated on the people's welfare and used the best of his abilities as a politician to affect changes and accomplish what he had promised. He developed a great interest in the old projects that for years had been passed over because of the lack of better leaders, and he brought them to Congress. Then, these improvements suddenly became a reality.

In a short time, Risley accomplished all that many in politics never attempted even in a much longer term. He became a powerful political figure. Though he was not the man who promised much, at least he did the most. And to him, it was so amazingly easy to do what he had done, that he began to believe he really was born for it. He accepted the idea of being the right person at the right place. Spontaneously, his actions spoke for him and established his reputation as a good politician. Indeed, he gained the best—the heart of the people.

Perhaps his appetite for power and passion for money—worked like magic.

Doneli moved forward with his investigation. He pushed toward Senator Risley Ashford's quiet past. He began to climb the same steps the senator had climbed in order to get to the top. Doneli executed his work with discretion in order to avoid unnecessary speculation. Mysteriously, Risley had become one of the Merlenes' Industries major shareholders and soon after Charles' decision to freeze the sale of their shares, boom, the *Serenata* was blown to pieces!

Maybe the whole thing was just a coincidence, but exploring the circumstances, Doneli didn't think so.

Charles stopped the sale of their shares because he needed to carefully investigate his father's latest dealings with the shareholders. Evidently Charles' sudden move irritated Risley very much. The *Serenata*'s destruction caused enormous losses for the Merlenes Industries and brought to light many delicate issues that were discussed around Charles' conference table. In fact, lots of unexpected complications came together stemming from the beginning of a terrible season. Indeed, so terrible that Charles might not have been able to keep the sale of shares frozen for very long.

Besides that, the evidence of terrorists playing dangerous games with them would immediately drop the prices of the shares. Doneli believed that rather than being worried about the complications, Risley would be celebrating the new season. Always, one bad incident needed to occur to start a big mess.

It took time, but finally something popped up. Doneli discovered that one source of the money used in Risley's political campaign remained at the bottom of the sea covered by a coral reef.

Doneli traced Risley's whereabouts and deeds from when he became a lawyer and his past was spotless. There was absolutely nothing that stained his professional or political career. But Doneli continued his search because his intuition almost always proved right. He figured that if Risley could become a brilliant politician, he could also succeed in hiding his dirty laundry. So Doneli didn't give up on his search. He sought the help of two good friends who had spent their lifetimes involved with political campaigns, sticking their noses into old files.

"Hallelujah!" Doneli shouted. "Just what I predicted. The buried bone has been uncovered."

It turned out that a large amount of money used in Risley's campaign had come from an unkown source, and the evidence and inquires about the case had fallen into sealed files as though the information was not very important, which remained as such until that day.

Now, quietly Doneli analyzed the situation. *Perhaps in the beginning of his career as a senator, those people close to him had thought about tracking the origin of it, but then probably asked, "What for?" Risley rapidly won people's hearts, and one black spot on his political campaign would be just like a grain of sand in the desert compared to all the good deeds he had accomplished for the state of New York. So, it makes more sense to close the chapter with the thought that he did what he had to do, then to start a political scandal. And now it would be ludicrous to bring up his story. After all, he is a man of action and no one would stop to listen to old tales.*

In reality, Senator Ashford had acquired control of his territory very quickly and had managed everything so well that even Doneli and Charles found it difficult to criticize him as a politician. Charles had admitted that he was a good man for the role he was playing and would support him if necessary, but nothing further than that. Running the state of New York was fine with Charles, because it had nothing to do with cutting stones or making jewels. However, having him mixed up in the Merlenes' business—was hot water. By being a major shareholder, the senator could undermine Charles' decisions; however, under no circumstances would a politician have authority inside the Merlenes Industries. No one would tell the Merlenes how to run their diamond business.

But Charles' father didn't spend time watching Risley Ashford when, three years before, Risley aggressively began acquiring the Merlenes' shares. Max and Risley were good friends and golf companions. Max only saw the beneficial side things. He accepted the cheap philosophy that it would be valuable for his family and business to have a good politician aboard. Max had viewed their friendship as a kind of investment for his future accomplishments and never suspected the dangerous transactions that were happening behind his back. Ingeniously, Risley used their friendship as a green light to move and acted swiftly. He moved undetected from point A to B inside the diamond business.

Max hadn't seen the senator's movements in time to cut his rope. And when Max became so obsessed with the emerald search in Brazil, he inadvertently took his eyes off the family business for quite a while. Then the worst thing occurred—he died. So he never knew about the events he had allowed to occur.

Of course, his death brought no relevant concerns to Risley, since Risley had no intention, whatsoever, of stopping his treachery. In fact, Risley felt stronger after Max's death because he thought that everything would be much easier. Charles would return from Europe to take over the family business, but would lack the necessary confidence and experience. After all, Charles had spent his youth studying in Europe, not knowing much about the day-to-day operations. Besides, Risley had a strong insider, Mr. Sidney Maskuitiz.

In reality, the senator was accurate on many accounts but not all of them. While in Europe, Charles had always gone to their offices in Paris to learn the family business. And with one of their most remarkable lawyers, he had learned all that his grandmother expected him to learn—wise lessons. Life could always be counted on to surprise people. Charles might have lacked some things but not everything, and overnight Senator Risley had to face it in black and white.

As soon as Charles had taken over the family business, he immediately used his knowledge to run their industries with expertise. He was not in any way in the dark about making the right decisions.

Doneli, Charles' real father, began to follow Charles' every step. He was an Italian-American, sixty-three years old, with gray hair, now more silver than black, with a smooth clear-shaven face. He always arrived impressively on time with a tranquil look in his eyes. Doneli, an ex-FBI agent, was willing to use all his abilities and experiences to protect his only son.

* * * *

Exactly one week after the incident at Bolevar, Luis Demetrius returned from Johannesburg. After landing at John F. Kennedy International Airport, he went directly to see Doneli. He wanted to show him something he had brought back from Africa.

In Johannesburg Luis had met with Victor Corcega, an INTERPOL agent. They saw each other twice at the hotel bar. Mr. Corcega was a short man, extremely thin, and with a great sense of humor. He liked to meet people, have drinks with them, and talk about what men like most—sex and money. When he had seen Luis at the bar, he had been the one who introduced himself to Luis.

Since Anthony's departure from Johannesburg, it had been the first time Luis had time enough to stop at the bar for a drink. He did so because he was feeling frustrated with his investigation. Anthony told him the truth—Africa definitely had a different sunset.

When Luis sat down and ordered a martini, Victor watched

him from across the bar. Victor already had his drink, as he actually started half an hour before. He waited until Luis was alone and then came closer.

"Hi, I'm Victor Corcega." Then he leaned a little bit closer and whispered in Luis' ear, "INTERPOL agent."

Luis shook hands with him and also repeated his name.

"South Africa," Luis uttered. "Difficult, isn't it?"

"Very," responded Victor.

The martini arrived and silently Luis sipped it. Then he said, "I'm leaving soon. Going back to New York City. Apparently nothing has happened here."

"Only the explosion of the *Serenata*," added Mr. Corcega.

"Hmm, I see you are very well informed about me, Mr. Corcega. You even know why I am here."

"Who doesn't? Johannesburg has good land communications when you are familiar with the territory."

"And I can see that you are."

"Kind of."

They met one more time, a day before they were going to depart from Johannesburg. They shared a couple of drinks once again but Victor never revealed to Luis that he would be leaving town.

The next day Luis found an envelope under his door. Inside there was a poem that read—

> Tomorrow will be another day,
> Among the people another hope,
> Resting in peace, another soul.
> Tomorrow will be another day.
> Up in the sky, another star,
> Far away, another galaxy,
> France is in the Milky Way,
> Earth is our home.

At the bottom Victor had written: "This is the man you are looking for."

Luis Demetrius was only a couple of years older than Charles. His father and Doneli had been together in the war. Demetrius was a slim man, also the tallest one in his family, and he had a very large forehead, typical of intelligent people. His forehead was too big for his head and too long for his face; everybody could see it before they could even see Luis. He liked to be called Demetrius. Usually he smiled whenever it was possible and when his brown eyes held a frozen look, his mind worked very quickly, thinking and analyzing the subject matter. He told jokes for no reason and loved being single. Demetrius enjoyed his job and spent every moment of his life learning about investigating.

Demetrius arrived in New York City and went straight from the airport to Doneli's house. After sitting comfortably in front of a hot cup of coffee, he began to talk. First, Demetrius explained to Doneli how he had met Mr. Victor Corcega. Then he showed him the poem.

Demetrius waited until Doneli finished reading before he asked, with a funny expression on his face, "What do you think of it? Does this mean anything or is it just a joke to distract us?"

"It could be one or the other," said Doneli. "We have to see. These French agents enjoy being enigmatic. They love this kind of game. What did you say his name was?"

"Corcega. Victor Corcega."

"I'll try to find if it's true that he is an INTERPOL agent."

Later, that same day, Charles also learned about the poem. Doneli and Demetrius met with him in the office. Charles became extremely frustrated and visibly disappointed after reading it. His brother was dead, his life was in danger, and someone decided to write them poetry.

"I need to hear something more substantial than this," Charles said gruffly.

"I know, Mr. Merlenes," said Demetrius. "We will get there. But Johannesburg can't help us. We ought to find another place to start. And the mere fact of knowing that Johannesburg can't help us is already a great beginning."

"I'm not a detective. But as a lawyer...I hope you are right, Mr. Demetrius."

"I think Demetrius should spend some time in New York following the leads I provided for him," added Doneli. "Perhaps all that we need we already have here in front of our eyes. I believed that Senator Ashford sold his soul to the devil; and when we meet the devil, we will have the missing piece."

"Fine, Doneli. I'll leave these decisions to you, but please bring me some good news," Charles almost begged.

58

FOR MORE THAN A MONTH the newspapers wrote of Anthony's death. In an attempt at broadcasting something sensational, the journalists related lots of misleading stories and spread all kinds of unimaginable gossip. The newspapers shouted the subject as if they were competing for the headlines. The gist of them was: "Anthony Merlenes' death remains covered by hundreds of questions. Did Anthony really save the life of his brother? How did the dynamite get into the Ferrari in the first place? Is the Merlenes family hiding something?"

There was so much garbage written that Charles decided to grant a private interview to Rebecca Macklen. He needed her to try and stop the avalanche of gossip. Therefore, he invited her to the Merlenes residence so she could have the opportunity to personally meet Catarina, Elizabeth, and Victoria.

First, Rebecca spent a long time in the library with Charles. She listened to him attentively as he explained in detail the conversation he had with Anthony in his office the day Anthony arrived back from Africa. Then he related the morning conversation in the house that Saturday and why Anthony wanted to drive the Ferrari.

"He never had a chance to try the car before," said Charles. "He told me that every time he planned to do it, he had to leave on a trip."

With enormous patience Charles told her all that he knew wouldn't harm the course of Doneli's investigation and when he finished, he took her to talk with the rest of the family.

Rebecca met Catarina first upstairs in her reading room. The moment Rebecca set eyes on her, she knew she would very much like to interview her. Catarina's tenacious look shot down every wrong impression Rebecca had conceived about her. She observed how sad Catarina looked, yet calm at the same time. After screaming out her pain and rage when she first heard the news about Anthony's death, she had sunk into an unnaturally calm state. She spoke intelligently and freely.

"God is teaching us to be strong and we will learn that. We are a family, Miss Macklen. No one will destroy us. No one. It's my heart speaking for me..."

Following the meeting with Catarina, Charles guided Rebecca downstairs where she briefly spoke with Elizabeth and Victoria.

Elizabeth couldn't avoid crying when she uttered her words and constantly dried her tears. Rebecca sensed the anger in her voice.

"My husband served in the war only to come home and die on a mountain. Difficult to understand, but I have accepted it. Now, out of three sons, I have only one left. Can my heart bear it? No. I shall *not* lose Charles, and I hope that the gods of the world are aware of it!"

Victoria, whom the press had been hunting for in order to get an interview but had not succeeded, now sat in front of Rebecca playing her illusory role of the *sad widow* in order to protect her ten million dollar deal with Catarina. She wanted to finish quickly so she limited her time and words.

"I'm sorry, but there is nothing that will change what happened. I prefer not giving interviews. Nothing will bring my husband back."

She was indeed so tearful that Rebecca Macklen left convinced of her private suffering. But on that evening Rebecca had discovered that Victoria was a *pregnant* widow and added this information to her story. After all, it was fresh news.

Since Victoria's marriage to Anthony, her ambitions had grown as big as her ingenuity, an occurrence that led her to constantly fail in detecting the dangers on the paths she had selected to travel. Shortly after the incident in Bolevar, she received an unpleasant phone call from Peter Lacerda.

"Hello, princess!" he said when he recognized her voice. "How is my rich widow?"

"Oh, Peter, you are a miserable wretch! Why are you calling me here?"

"Because I have something very important to say and don't attempt to use such harsh words when you talk with me. They really don't suit you."

"What do you want now?" she snapped at him.

"To tell you not to believe in this terrorist story going around."

"What? You did that? Did you try to kill Charles?"

"I'm sorry, princess, I killed the wrong guy, didn't I?"

"Bastard!"

"Oh, Victoria! It is too late for those strong words. You owe me $3,000 dollars–the amount of money I gave the Puerto Rican who waxed the Ferrari. He kindly took me there."

"I don't owe you anything. I didn't ask you to kill people. You're crazy!"

"Be careful, princess. I—"

She cut him off by hanging up the phone.

Who was Peter Lacerda? He was little Alexander's father. Victoria had met him through Madame Perlaz to whom she had paid $10,000 dollars. She had placed her blind faith in this woman. Madame Perlaz was very popular in New York City for solving the problems of many rich women. She knew how to discreetly handle things with great attention to detail and made people feel comfortable in her presence. Her soft look, gentle smile, and genuine kindness rapidly turned her into someone worthy of that trust. No one ever had a problem doing business with her.

Peter Lacerda's profile, according to Madame Perlaz, met the requirements Victoria had stipulated. He was of Italian descent and had a very interesting background. Madame Perlaz even assured Victoria he was not in need of money; however, because he was a man with extravagant tastes, money was always welcome. So, in a steadfast manner, he became the healthy, intelligent, handsome man, with the discretion of which Victoria approved.

Of course any person with a shady background like Madame Perlaz would immediately see that Victoria was just as beautiful as she was stupid, and as stupid as she was naive. A beautiful angel trying to fly with new wings in a sky infested with vultures. Madame Perlaz would never turn her back on an angel.

Victoria had never heard the real story about Peter because Madame Perlaz had never told her he was her nephew, a poor impostor, a compulsive gambler, and that she, Madame Perlaz, was tired of paying off his debts. Therefore, Peter survived in this world because Madame Perlaz constantly arranged for him to meet rich women in need of something. Prompt to pay for special favors or sex—indirectly she supported his habit.

Victoria's sudden arrival and her needs turned out to be something out of the ordinary. Madame Perlaz decided Victoria would become an endless fountain of money that would forever fix Peter's life. She finally found the best opportunity to get her nephew off her back.

Wickedly, Madame Perlaz made her move. She confidently took care of all the small details so Victoria would find everything easy and charming. Then her good reputation and experience helped to convince Victoria that Peter was the most convenient person in New York City to father her child. Once they came to a full understanding, the other part just followed.

To persuade Victoria to go on with the crazy idea became as

easy as counting the fingers on her hands. Almost instantly, Victoria felt pleased with Peter and began to leave her luxurious nest to sleep with him in order to get pregnant. Peter handled their affair maturely and responsibly. She, who had not expected to gain any pleasure from it, indeed found some. He was an amazing man.

During her pregnancy Peter had humbly played the role of an ideal husband—patiently waiting to the end, and when Alexander was born, he felt very proud of himself. His son was born a healthy child with a silver spoon. He resembled a prince and his picture appeared in every major newspaper imaginable as Catarina's great-grandson, and of course, the creature that would put an end to his misery. Swiftly, Peter started his real game—everything now had a price.

Insolently, he initiated his business, which was blackmail. Victoria soon found herself dealing with the unpleasant surprise of Peter's sudden change in behavior. She grew excessively angry and trapped in a chamber full of demonic ideas. She didn't know what to do. In an attempt at avoiding any new turn of events, she agreed to pay whatever Peter asked. Deep inside, she knew the situation had to change, but at the moment she happened to be occupied with other things, and chose the easy way out.

She played his game and even thought about using him once more for another job. There were so many things to accomplish, that maybe he could fit somewhere else. Because of her inability in coming up with a quick solution to her problem, she shook hands with the devil for her own convenience, and kept Peter as part of her expenses for a while.

The day arrived in which she needed his expertise one more time. It was after her conversation with Catarina and the ten-million-dollar deal. She certainly was going to put her hands on the ten million dollars, but she desperately wanted Catarina to pay for it. Victoria couldn't bear the fact that she had to leave the Merlenes mansion after giving birth and her greed drove her insane. She decided to do something that would infuriate Catarina.

While struggling to survive in Peter's hands, she also became seduced by the idea of going on and using him one more time. Deliberately, she thought Peter could skillfully attempt an act against Charles' life, implicating Anthony. At the same time she would make it public that she was expecting Charles' child. When the Merlenes faced the scandal, she would put on her glass shoes, like Cinderella, and dance to the music of her revenge. Her idea rapidly shifted to something real and glamorous, and once again Peter entered the scene. Naively she revealed to him the story about the ten million dollars.

"Princess, I love your pregnancies. It is unbelievable how easily you make ten million dollars. I wish I could change my sex."

Victoria, instead of criticizing his remarks, just looked at him. None of his words would make any difference in her future. Anyway, soon he would be out of her life. She would find the right person to help her out with that matter.

But Victoria simply underestimated Peter—she moved fast but he controlled the game.

After she left him that afternoon, he realized that half of the money belonged to him because Alexander was *his* son. He turned excessively bitter with the news that Charles had entered the picture and was running side by side with him. Perceiving Victoria's happiness with this whole situation, Peter quickly saw Charles as a threat. Besides being very valuable, Victoria was also extremely beautiful. He decided he would not easily let her go and dreamed about having her forever—he loved her. Peter's mind sifted, looking for new horizons. Neurotically, he switched from being a normal man to a crazy one in love, impulsive and therefore doubly dangerous.

Pronouncing himself the master of the game, he never intended it to be Catarina, Charles or Victoria's way, but his. And according to him, Charles had to leave the picture. He hated both Charles and the white Ferrari. Suddenly, he thought of the word bomb and with that they would be gone.

Actually, Victoria just wanted an attempt to be made against

Charles' life so that her husband, Anthony, would be incriminated and provoke a scandal to break the family's peace.

However, while analyzing his fantastic idea and Victoria's wishes, Peter recognized that the moment favored him. It couldn't be more convenient. Instead of an attempt on Charles' life, it was better to really kill him. The terrorists had already started the ball rolling in Africa so he would just add more fuel to things in America. Easily this incident would be connected with the other and his best chance ever to leave without suspicion. Peter was indeed very clever in thinking this way. Unquestionably, destiny reversed all of these expectations for Victoria and Peter.

After the accident at Bolevar, when the news and the people were still talking about Anthony's death, Victoria, like the rest of the family, was shocked. She accepted what everyone said, that it was the terrorists. Not even vaguely did she imagine Peter could have been responsible for it. A bomb was never in the plans. Besides that, there wouldn't be enough time for Peter to come up with something. So until she had answered his call, she had just floated on the moment.

After she hung up on him, the truth started to bounce inside her mind, disrupting every stable thought she held. She ended up being very upset. Then, in the next conversation she had with Peter, he disdainfully told her that he had done it to scare her. He thought that the more she feared him the better.

Despite having missed Charles, Peter was able to scare her. In a way, his plan worked out quite well. With his action he had demonstrated to her how unpredictable he could be, and this new reality engaged her feelings in an energetic orbit of fears. She came to the conclusion that Peter must step aside. Now, besides being a threat to Charles, he was also a threat to her plans. He definitely had become too dangerous and out of control.

At times Victoria could be compared to an impulsive woman who forgets to take an umbrella, or fails to think of a newspaper or even a piece of plastic to cover her head, and rushes into the rain, to later spend time drying herself and taking hot baths to avoid a cold.

Stupidity rushed Victoria into the rain, and Peter Lacerda was the rainstorm. Now she needed a towel. Who on the face of the Earth was going to be her savior? Then she remembered the words which were spoken to her years earlier: *I am simply fascinated by your beauty. Ask me whatever you want, and I will give it to you.*

She heard those words for the first time in Greece at the beginning of her career. The man who uttered them had watched her on the runway and bought the entire Elizabeth Sfeel collection. They dined together, and he had asked her to marry him. Despite the fact he was sixteen years her senior, he was very attractive. She almost said yes.

In Paris, Victoria had told Charles that story. How the man proposed to her only a few hours after meeting her. Because of his prodigious, impulsive desire and mature behavior, Victoria had cautiously kept his words secreted in her mind. Now that her needs converged into almost a desperate, situation, she couldn't help but remember his attractive face and lovely words—*I am simply fascinated by your beauty. Ask me whatever you want, and I will give it to you—*

Looking in the mirror at her beautiful image she thought, *It is not about what I want, but what I do not want. I do not want Peter Lacerda around any longer.*

59

IN THE BEGINNING OF May, Charles attended the Industrial Association's annual dinner and helped pay tribute to his brother Anthony, whose life and work were to be honored that night.

He arrived around eight o'clock, and as soon as he entered the dining room, Mr. Henry Trasder, the president of the association, came to greet him. Afterwards, they stayed together talking about business and politics while enjoying a glass of champagne.

Many other industrialists approached to welcome Charles and to participate in the conversation as well. In spite of this being the first dinner of its kind in which he had participated, Charles knew most of the people present. And of course, they all knew him. Later he mingled with the guests, going from group to group in order to get acquainted with the new faces. During his meanderings, he saw someone he had not expected to see—Miss Macklen.

Purposely Charles walked over to greet her, "Good evening, Miss Macklen."

"Good evening, Mr. Merlenes!"

“I did not expect to see you here,” Charles added.

“I hadn’t planned to be here either. It was a last minute surprise. Yesterday, Mr. Trasder telephoned and invited me. He said he wanted me to cover the event. And in my job that’s enough to cancel any previous engagements.”

“I understand. And besides that, you are a workaholic. Right?”

“Quite true,” she admitted. “And talking about that, I need another interview with you. Mr. Trasder is counting on it as he has something prepared for Anthony. Did he tell you?”

“Yes, we spoke about it.”

Robert Delvalle, the cameraman who always worked with her, approached then cordially saluted Charles before leaning over and saying something confidential in her ear.

“Right, Robert. I will be with you shortly,” she said aloud to her partner. Then turning her attention back to Charles, she excused herself and left.

As Rebecca walked away, Charles silently followed her with his eyes. She wore a long black dress that emphasized the silhouette of her body with her raven tresses loose and skimming her shoulders. Charles found he was fascinated and that she was breathtakingly stunning.

During dinner Charles sat next to Mr. Trasder and as coincidence often has it, Rebecca sat directly in front of him. In the course of the evening their eyes met several times and silently they exchanged innocent smiles.

After dessert, Mr. Trasder took the floor and as had been planned, he paid a glowing tribute to Anthony. At the end Charles thanked him and the guests, and eventually everyone went back to their individual conversations.

Shortly afterwards, Charles granted Rebecca the interview she wanted. They sat in a quiet corner of the room where they talked for twenty minutes. When the interview was over, she closed her notepad, stood up, thanked him and said good night.

“Good night already?” asked Charles feeling somewhat disappointed.

"I need to work and get this prepared for tomorrow."

While she explained her urgency in leaving so early, another tray of champagne was brought to them. Charles immediately reached over and took two glasses, handing one to her.

"I do not believe you can sit down and work at this time of the night."

"Oh, I do it all the time, Mr. Merlenes."

"Charles... Please call me Charles. The interview is over. And if you don't mind, I'd like to call you Rebecca."

She smiled gracefully as she agreed. "It's okay with me. Actually I would like that better."

"I'm sorry, Rebecca. I do believe in what you said that you work late. Sometimes I do the same thing. After this glass of champagne, you are free to leave."

"Thank you...Charles. Cheers!"

"Cheers!"

Lately Rebecca had been thinking about Charles more than she really wanted. No other man had ever disturbed her as much as he. Behind the private walls of her apartment, she had surprised herself thinking of him in a dangerous and suggestive manner. She had even admitted to herself that his romantic green eyes were the most fascinating she had ever seen. If she persisted in her fantasies, she knew he would become the first man to really play with her desires.

Charles tasted the champagne and suddenly said, "I have something that belongs to you."

"You what?" she replied attentively. "Something that belongs to me?"

"Yes, a fortune cookie. Don't you remember? You forgot it on my table the day we met."

An interesting smile lit up her lips as she said, "Are you serious? Do you still have it?"

"Yes."

"Why?"

"I don't know. As a souvenir perhaps?"

Definitely this was the most appealing lie Charles had ever told. He had not, in fact, kept it but rather opened it. His curiosity had got the better of him and he just had to read it. But today he found himself in great need to come up with something that would keep her from leaving so soon.

"I have it in the car," he said, hinting at his intentions. "Aren't you curious to find out what it says?"

Silently she studied him then said, "Now that I know you kept it, yes, of course."

"Did you mean that if it wasn't me, you wouldn't be curious?"

"No...I mean...yes," she stammered and he could tell she was a little flustered.

"Is it no or yes?" Charles asked playfully.

"Oh, I think I lost track of what I was going to say, Charles. But I still want my fortune cookie. I think it would be charming to have it after seeing that your curiosity was kept so well under control."

"Excellent! You will have it then. It's in my car...how does it sound if I take you home?"

Suddenly she just looked intently at him. She took so long to answer that he excused himself and walked away for a moment. He crossed the room searching for a waiter. When he found one, he wrote a note to Lobo, his chauffeur on a piece of paper—

> Lobo, I need a fortune cookie. Please, have it in the car for me.
> Put it next to my bottle of whiskey. It's very important.
> When you have it, come pick me up.
> Thank you,
>
> Charles

He folded the note and handed it to the waiter. It was nicely tucked in a hundred dollar bill. He asked him, "Would you please go downstairs and deliver this to my chauffeur."

Looking at the hundred dollar bill, the waiter immediately said,

"Yes, Mr. Merlenes! I will do it right now."

For the rest of the night Charles and Rebecca remained together. She did not have the chance to leave with her cameraman on this occasion as it became almost impossible. After the fortune cookie conversation, Charles kept her to himself. Sometimes he even held her hand as he walked from one side of the room to another, letting everyone notice his sudden interest in her.

Rebecca, a successful young journalist both beautiful and intelligent, was an interesting and suitable woman for any rich candidate. With her extravagant sense of humor, outgoing personality, and air of independence, she could have chosen just about any man she wished. But Charles piqued her feminine appetite.

From a distance, Mr. Trasder had taken a moment to observe them. Then he had happily commented, "Those two make an attractive couple. They should take it seriously."

At midnight they said good-bye to everyone and left.

Lobo had accomplished the task at hand. The fortune cookie rested peacefully next to the bottle of whiskey. And while the limousine drove through the streets of New York, Charles and Rebecca speculated what could be written on the tiny piece of paper inside the cookie. Charles helped her come up with some ideas but intentionally listened more than talked.

When Lobo pulled in front of her building, he got out and opened the door for her. As she prepared to get out she said, "Good night, Charles. And thank you for taking care of my fortune cookie."

Suddenly he heard himself say, "No! I don't want to say good night yet. Why don't you invite me for a nightcap? We'll drink something, you'll open your cookie, and then I'll say goodnight. It's a promise."

"No. I don't think that's a good idea, Charles. Good night."

"All right. I'll walk you to the elevator."

"Thank you."

Much like the rest of the night, he held her hand as they walked into the building. They stopped to await the elevator.

"I can't believe that you are going to open this cookie alone," Charles commented with a very interesting expression, shadowing his appealing face.

"I will."

"I thought women changed their minds easily. I guess I was wrong."

She smiled, now looking at his amazing green eyes and thinking how much she wanted to take him upstairs with her for a nightcap.

When the elevator stopped and opened its door, she gave in. "Fine Charles, you won. You're right, now it wouldn't be fun to open this fortune cookie alone. Come in. Let's have our last glass together. But I warn you, after that—good-night."

Rebecca's apartment was a small one but with a spectacular view. She kept it clean and organized. Nothing was out of place. The extravagant modernism showed throughout the entire décor as it silently tossed in her fantastic good taste.

Upon entering, she left him alone to get acquainted with the surroundings while she walked to the kitchen. Looking around as he enjoyed the exotic decoration, Charles took off his tuxedo jacket and placed it half-folded over the sofa. Rebecca returned from the kitchen with two glasses and a bottle of champagne. Silently, he took the bottle from her hand, opened it, and filled the glasses.

Before sitting next to him to finally open the Chinese fortune cookie, Rebecca walked away and turned on some music. She chose Mozart. Walking back, she wore a soft, speculative smile upon her lips. Charles found her and everything around her so charming that he blocked her way, gently took her in his arms, and began dancing with her.

Mutely Rebecca let her body go, her mind completely occupied in following the steps for she wished to forever remember this moment—the day she had Charles Merlenes in her apartment, dancing with her.

They danced mesmerized with each other; her perfume intensifying the moment and her lips too close, too moist, too yearning. He no longer resisted the temptation and kissed her.

"Charles, now do you see why I told you that coming up wouldn't be a good idea? You just kissed me."

"What is wrong with that? I'm attracted to you."

"Are you?"

"Yes."

Satisfied with his response, she blissfully closed her eyes and let her body move according to his steps and the rhythm of the music.

Charles found it so wonderful having her in his arms that he followed his other instincts. Gently and slowly he unzipped her dress part way and began caressing her back.

"I want to make love to you," he whispered in her ear.

Her first thought was, *how can I say no to Charles Merlenes?* Aloud she said, "Oh, no, you won again."

The glasses of champagne, as well as the fortune cookie, were taken with them to the bedroom. As the night slowly gave away to early morning, their desires merged frantically into the path of many sensations they could find in their naked bodies. Touching each other, they exchanged gentle words, and disclosed the secrets of their souls.

Her firm body was soft velvet to his fingertips. "Let me give you all the joy you desire to have," he said. In response, Rebecca stretched herself next to him, allowing his hands to caress her breasts while his lips kissed them as well. Slowly she spread her legs, inviting his fingers to come in between and explore her innermost secrets. Gently and smoothly Charles touched her and deeply looked into her eyes to witness her joy.

She moaned and he closed his eyes to bring to his senses the warmth of her. His lips traveled furtively over her naked body like the soft wind combing the crest of the high green grass in a distant field. Rebecca uttered his name, dying with pleasure and ready to let her existence come to an end inside his arms. Soaked by the sensual greenness of his tender eyes, she caressed him and thirstily her lips wipe every drop of sweat that coursed his masculine body. Swirling with excitement, she opened herself and received him deeply inside of her. As he made love to her, Charles moaned with fiery passion, experiencing pleasure in every breath he took. Not just taking from her, but also giving back, until Rebecca felt his entire being within her.

At dawn, still naked in Charles' arms, she finally opened the fortune cookie.

"Love comes when we do not expect it."

60

THE RIGHT TIME TO TAKE ACTION was never very clear for Victoria. Though her thoughts were irrational, she believed they were practical. If she waited, instead of reacting, she would delay her glorious future. And only for that reason, she never held back making a decision. For her everything was either, "I want it or I do not want it." So she acted with the same speed as she thought.

After assuring herself that things must be the way she had planned them, she went looking for a card that she had always kept hidden in a safe place. After finding it she held it in her hand and thought as she remembered those words from long ago—*I am simply fascinated by your beauty. Ask me whatever you want, and I will give it to you.*

In fact, what had happened with Anthony had changed all of her plans, rushing her toward a new reality—her freedom. Almost frantically her thoughts flitted through her mind. *Now I can have Charles, and I will fight for him. Everything now favors me. Anthony's death has greatly affected Catarina, besides that, the woman is getting old and her mind—unstable. Then there is*

Elizabeth. She seems tired of so much suffering. She would be the easiest to manipulate.

For a moment, she stood in front of the mirror in her room, holding the card in her hand, proudly contemplating her beauty, and letting her mind continue to run heedlessly—*One day I will be in Catarina's place, and the people around the world will love me as they love her. Peter Lacerda is the only remaining loose end, but I'm going to surprise him. With this card I will have someone to protect me.*

The card she held was Hard Narquilet's very special "red" card. It listed twelve telephone numbers. Only a handful of people had one and she was among them. They were the telephone numbers of his many residences around the world.

When Hard had seen her for the first time, her beauty caused an extraordinary effect upon him, and even though she declined his wedding proposal, his experience whispered to him that his red card would one day bring her back. Hard seemed too good at inhaling the smell of his belongings when they mixed with the air. He knew so much and Victoria so little. Waiting became his journey toward her.

Glancing at the card, Victoria fingered the telephone numbers and chose to call the house in Greece. Confidently, she dialed. When the butler answered, he politely told her that Mr. Hard Narquilet was in his residence in New York City.

Hard Narquilet's servants had been instructed to disclose his whereabouts to whoever called one of his private numbers. For this reason the butler, without further question, had told her that Hard was in New York City.

Shortly after Victoria hung up, she called Hard's residence on Long Island. When the butler mentioned her name, Hard smiled in pleasant surprise. "Maome came to the mountain," he whispered.

He had just finished dressing for dinner, as he intended dining that night in the company of the extravagant luxuries he could buy.

"Hello, Mrs. Merlenes," he suavely said as he answered the phone.

Immediately she impulsively said, "Please, call me Victoria."

"I certainly prefer that," he replied. "Hello, Victoria! I'm deeply sorry about what happened to your husband."

"Thank you, it was terrible."

"I can imagine," he commented. "And to what do I owe the honor of this call?"

"If it is not asking too much, I'd rather answer that in person."

"It would be my pleasure," replied Hard. "Would you like it to be today? I can send a chauffeur for you. We are very close. Will you dine with me?"

Delighted, Victoria agreed. One hour later, Hard greeted her in his beautiful house.

She walked toward him with a pleasant smile on her lips. As soon as Hard saw her, he remembered how much he had wanted to have her. *Isn't she divine?* And since he never missed a single report by Rebecca Macklen, he was aware of her pregnancy.

"You look wonderful," he said admiring her.

"Thank you, Hard. You're very kind."

They sat together in his private living room and on the coffee table in front of them were delicious looking appetizers. Despite her pregnancy, she accepted a glass of white wine. Then intentionally Hard sat across from her in order to enjoy her delightful presence. He wanted to observe her responsive looks and beloved smiles, not missing one. That morning he couldn't have imagined that in the evening she would be in his home, drinking a glass of wine.

He told himself, *I love my red card, and I am glad I gave her one.*

To Hard, Victoria's presence was so incredible that he knew he could just sit and admire her for hours without uttering a single word. Just to contemplate her delicate, innocent and amazingly beautiful face pleased him. So on purpose, he allowed a moment of silence to pass. He also thought that a little time without words would make her feel more comfortable. Indeed it did. But the moment came when she sensed that he waited for her words.

Victoria found it very difficult to begin. Even though Hard would kiss the ground she walked on, she didn't know that. He had become so fascinated with her beauty that he could have worshiped her like religious people worship their gods. She was his obsession. Hard would pay any price or do anything just to please her. But she happened to be unaware of that. She possessed both the power as well as the ignorance. She felt insecure as if she lacked the net with which she could catch him. His presence emanated such power that it made her feel small and fragile; even her ambitions seemed to shrink when he looked at her.

They hardly knew each other but he urged her on by saying, "Feel free to talk to me, Victoria. I'm all yours." Noticing her hesitancy, Hard encouraged, "I know you're here for a reason; don't make it otherwise. You can ask me whatever you want."

Definitely those magic words rescued her confidence and restored her courage.

"Thank you, Hard. I needed to hear that and it is the second time you have told me that."

With a friendly smile and sly look, he added, "I never forget my words."

Smiling sweetly, Victoria finally dropped her hesitancy and plunged ahead. "I have gotten myself involved in a problem and now it is costing me too much money."

"If this is the case, you did right by coming to me. I would be glad to help."

After that she calmly mentioned Peter Lacerda's name and revealed that he was blackmailing her. To Victoria's surprise, Hard remained silent, looking at her, unconcerned as to why Peter was blackmailing her. In fact, his sudden discretion made her very happy and in order to keep it that way, she added, "Do you mind if I don't tell you the kind of arrangement I made with this man?"

"No. Not at all."

"Thank you. He—"

"One moment, Victoria," Hard interrupted, getting up as he politely stretched his hand out to hers. "Dinner is served."

They walked together arm in arm to the dining room.

During the rest of the evening they did not speak of Peter Lacerda again. Hard wanted to see her happy and avoided anything that would possibly destroy the moment. They both thought having the opportunity of spending the evening together was wonderful. From the beginning until the minute she had to leave, they not only enjoyed the dinner, but also each other's company. At the end of the evening, Hard said, "I will be flying to Italy tomorrow. But don't worry your problem is now in my hands."

The next day, before boarding his own private jet for Italy, Hard telephoned a man named Sandro Bonaveti. When Sandro answered, Hard said two words, "Peter Lacerda." That was all he had to say.

For many years Sandro Bonaveti had worked for Hard. He was skillful, secretive, and also extremely loyal to Hard. He had also become Madame Perlaz's business partner. Without him, she would not have succeeded or acquired the reputation she had. In other words, without Hard's money, she would never have started the business she now ran. So, through Sandro, Hard came to know all that pertained to Madame Perlaz.

Victoria had never mentioned the type of arrangement she had with Peter Lacerda, but Hard had not cared, as he had known about it from the moment it had begun. Peter Lacerda had been under Sandro's surveillance for a long time. Hard also knew that Alexander was not Anthony's son, and furthermore, that it was Peter Lacerda who had placed the bomb in the Ferrari.

* * * *

Peter lived in the same ten-story building as Sandro. It was located only a few blocks from Madame Perlaz's business. Two days after Hard left New York for Italy, Sandro planned an encounter with Peter. Around 9:30 p.m. Peter got out of a taxi, walked into the building and stepped into the elevator. Almost at the same time, Sandro ran in, gesturing for Peter to hold the door for him. Breathless, Sandro entered the elevator.

It appeared as if Sandro had just finished shopping because in his hand he held a bag filled with several items. While pretending to catch his breath, he said, "Peter, I have something hot upstairs. I have to deliver it now, and I need your help. We can divide the loot."

"What is it?" asked Peter.

"Cocaine."

"Where upstairs?"

"Hidden, on the roof."

"Half and half?" asked Peter.

"Yes."

"Deal."

Peter had no problem trusting Sandro because of the partnership between Sandro and his aunt. Besides that, they lived in the same building and this was not the first time they had split the profits from a job. Many times they had sat and drank together, and on more than one occasion Sandro had helped Peter get out of a jam as well as lend him money. In fact, they shared a decent friendship.

When they got out on the tenth floor, they looked around to make sure no one saw them. Then they walked to the end of the hallway where Sandro opened a small door that led to the roof. Once on the roof Sandro allowed Peter to walk ahead of him. He still had the plastic bag in his hand. Peter walked to the edge of the roof, and while looking down he asked, "Where is it?"

Quickly Sandro took out a gun from the bag and commanded, "Be quiet and don't move. Otherwise, I'll shoot you."

"What? Are you crazy?"

"Do as I say or it will be worse."

Studying Sandro's movements, Peter remained motionless and speechless. He obeyed, hoping that this was a stupid joke. But no, immediately after that Sandro took a bottle of tequila from the bag, opened it, and gave it to Peter saying, "Start to drink. And do it fast."

"You must be out of your mind!"

"I said drink it!" repeated Sandro.

Peter tasted the tequila as he watched Sandro with a quizzical look. He took three gulps and stopped. He thought maybe the joke was over. But Sandro cocked the gun as he commanded, "Drink more."

"What is this?" asked Peter now quite upset. "Are we friends or what?"

"I'm not here to answer your questions," responded Sandro. "Keep drinking."

Without any other choice and scared, Peter nervously began to drink once again. He was forced to drink until Sandro decided he could stop.

"Now get up on the ledge," Sandro ordered.

"What?"

"I told you already that I'm not here to answer your questions."

Next, Sandro placed the gun at Peter's back and forced him to the ledge.

"Please, stop joking!" said Peter. "If you want to scare me, you already have. Let me down."

"No," answered Sandro. "And don't forget that I am the one with the gun."

On the ledge, Peter opened his arms, balancing himself without looking down. He knew he was really fighting for his life. When he saw how well he controlled his balance, he began to laugh, an effect created by the tequila. His drunkenness made him see Sandro as a friend again. "Hey, Sandro, look at me. I'm doing pretty well!"

"Yes," said Sandro. "And because of it, I'm going to give you a present." Quickly, Sandro took out a toy from the bag. It was a jack-in-the-box. Sandro handed it to Peter who naively turned the handle and began to enjoy the music. Instantly the tequila made him regress into a giddy child with a new toy. He laughed and laughed until the music ended and the puppet sprang out. Startled by it, he instinctively jumped back and fell into the air. The grotesque smile on the puppet's face was the last thing Peter saw.

Early the next morning Hard received a phone call from Sandro Bonaveti. "The job is done, boss, but I have some bad news. News of the accident was covered by Miss Macklen."

Shit! exclaimed Hard to himself as he hit the table, causing his hot coffee to spill over his hand. *I really need to put an end to this.*

Aloud he said into the phone, "Damn that young lady!"

61

DONELI BEGAN WORKING SIDE by side with Luis Demetrius. He could not endure another minute knowing that the life of his son was in danger, and Charles was all Elizabeth had left.

Anthony's death dulled the brightness in Elizabeth's eyes, erasing the spontaneous smile her lips used to hold. Nowadays when she greeted Doneli, she held his hand tightly as if he were the only one capable of protecting Charles. Apart from dealing with the devastating wave of pain caused by Anthony's death, she also had to face what Victoria had done lately that had shamed her greatly. For a long time, Victoria had been someone very special to her but at the end she only brought disgrace to the family.

* * * *

While Doneli had immersed himself into the investigations regarding the *Serenata*'s destruction, Risley, and Anthony's death, the FBI had also started their own investigation. They had followed the paths of some terrorist groups already in existence. As a result, Doneli used the FBI's research files, as well as all the new information he had gathered, that could be considered relevant to the case. Merely as an act of precaution, he avoided sharing his information with the agency. He never mentioned the poem Luis Demetrius brought from Johannesburg to the FBI.

Because a French agent gave Luis the poem, Doneli decided to go to France to see if INTERPOL could help him decode the message hidden in those few intriguing words. As Doneli sat at his desk enthusiastically planning his trip and concentrating on all he wanted to do in Paris, he had an unexpected visitor. It was Mr. Abraham Bark, a detective he had contracted to follow Victoria. He came to see Doneli the day following Peter Lacerda's death.

Mr. Bark sat comfortably in Doneli's living room, and began informing him of his recent discoveries.

"I found out that Victoria knew the man who jumped from the building yesterday—Peter Lacerda. A few days before, she honored him with a visit and stayed in his apartment for approximately forty minutes."

"Hmm, interesting," commented Doneli. "Did you find anything else?"

"No. But there is something more to it—supposedly, the man committed suicide. You are going to love what comes next. She also visited someone in Long Island—Mr. Hard Narquilet."

"What?" exclaimed Doneli in disbelief.

"I knew that you would love it."

"What the hell was she doing with Hard?"

"I asked myself that same question," responded Mr. Bark.

"We need to find out," said Doneli. "Hard doesn't play to lose. He is definitely after something sweet."

"Maybe he is after her."

"She is pregnant," Doneli informed Mr. Bark

"So? That only takes nine months," added Mr. Bark.

"I don't think she is the 'something sweet' I'm talking about," explained Doneli.

"You may be a good detective, but when it comes to men and women's matters, you seem very naive. This woman is the most beautiful female I have ever seen. No one can resist the power of her beauty—he *is* after her."

"I don't know... You could be right, but we need to find out the truth."

After Mr. Bark left, Doneli returned to his desk where he found the poem that was amongst the scattered papers on his desk and once again read it looking for some clue. He read the poem out loud:

> "Tomorrow will be another day,
> Among the people another hope,
> Resting in peace another soul.
> Tomorrow will be another day,
> Up in the sky another star,
> Far away another galaxy,
> France is in the Milky Way,
> Earth is our home."

He had read it over and over but none of it made any sense to him. Frustrated, he put the poem aside and returned to his previous activity. As he shuffled the many papers he had on the desk, a few loose sheets covered part of the poem. Suddenly, he glanced at the verses from a different angle. It was then he saw that the first letters of the first word in each verse spelled something. He leaned over and looked more closely. Those letters—T A R T U F F E—spelled Hard's nickname, "Tartuffe," as he was known among the French agents.

"No...Hard is responsible for the explosion of the *Serenata*?" he said out loud incredulously.

Next, he remembered that Hard was the man behind Risley Ashford's political campaign.

To himself he exclaimed, "Of course! The 'devil' must be someone like him. Why didn't I think of it before?"

Doneli spent a moment enjoying his successful discovery, and carefully reviewed the accumulated facts so he could correctly put the pieces of the puzzle together.

"Definitely, this saved me a trip to France," he shared with the room at large.

An hour later, Doneli and Demetrius had a long conversation. Not only did Doneli inform him of his findings relating to the poem, but also explained to him how they would conduct the investigation from now on.

Confidently he said, "Demetrius, we finally know with whom we are dealing, so we have to be very careful. Hard Narquilet is our man; a dangerously important, affluent prey that is quick and furtive at the same time. For years he has had the knack of getting away swiftly. Besides that, he is capable of doing what we both can't even imagine. He cracks the almonds from the inside and before you and I have graduated from eating almonds, he knows that the shell breaks the teeth."

"In that case what do you think will be his next move?" asked Demetrius.

"I don't know. But let's look at it this way. If he attempted to eliminate Charles and failed, he will wait some time before trying it again. He is anything but stupid. His next actions will be tempered with, 'not jump so fast' and 'dig something new.' Now that he knows the police and the FBI are on the dance floor, hand in hand, Hard will play safely if he has to enter hell rejoicing. This will give us some time. Let's concentrate on following Risley Ashford's movements."

"Are you sure they are working together?"

"I'm positive. Only Hard has the power to have a man like Risley Ashford in his pocket. Hard can cleverly run the State of New York from behind the scenes if he desires. The senator's activities are already lapsing into electrons with movements around a nucleus—which energizes Hard's interest. Mr. Ashford has no way out."

"Interesting!"

"Demetrius, I guarantee that we have found the path to follow. We have Hard Narquilet, Risley Ashford, Victoria, and a dead man called Peter Lacerda. I don't know the name of the recipe yet, but we do have the ingredients. I think it is time to start making the dough. I need to know why Hard targeted the Merlenes family."

* * * *

As soon as he had finished his conversation with Demetrius, Doneli called Charles on the phone. "Charles, I need to see you. I have wonderful news. I decoded the poem. Can we dine together to discuss this?"

"Fine with me. But we should go out."

"No, I'll cook something."

"Again?"

"What's the problem?" asked Doneli "Don't you like my food?"

"Oh, I love it, but I think it's not fair to have you cooking for me."

"I enjoy it."

"Are you sure?"

"I really am."

"Since you insist, I'll be there shortly."

Charles spent the next few minutes making important phone calls. He also spoke with Joseph and informed him about his plans for dinner. Following that, he went down to meet with Lobo and then left for Doneli's.

At Doneli's house, Charles accepted a chilled glass of wine, and while he quietly savored it, Doneli brought him up-to-date on the latest incidents, including Victoria's visit to Peter Lacerda as well as Hard Narquilet.

"Charles, what do you know about Victoria that I do not?"

"Nothing. What makes you think that I would know something?"

"Well, you fucked her lately. That is why."

Genuinely surprised by Doneli's crude response, Charles indignantly said, "How dare you speak to me like that?"

"I'm sorry," uttered Doneli, realizing the harshness of his words. "I'm terribly sorry. I only had the intention of showing you the kind of woman she is. I think I chose the wrong way to do it."

"You sure did!" Charles responded with a hint of anger.

Doneli remained quiet for a few moments, thinking of what he could possibly say to ameliorate what had happened. He desperately wanted to find the precise words to start a new course of conversation between them. But he couldn't. Shortly, the temporary silence escalated the length and severity of the moment.

Charles spoke first.

"Now that your vile remarks have come to light, I'm wondering, what implicit secret lies beneath my existence and yours that you naively pushed yourself into the false assumption that you have the right to talk to me like that. Your whole attitude has surprised me."

"Please, forgive me. Your life is in danger, and I lost my mind."

"That's it," replied Charles. "Why do you worry so much? You once went to Italy to see me, and you told me that my grandmother asked you to do that."

"She did."

"Why? Why you, Doneli? She has the power to give orders to anyone she wishes. She could have sent my father or my mother. Why you?"

No words came out. Doneli sank into the most difficult situation of his life. He hated the turn their conversation had taken. And at that moment the aroma of his conscience—if conscience could have an aroma—was strongly disgusting.

"I have the feeling something is out of place and that you know what this is," said Charles.

"I really disrespected you, Charles. I chose the wrong words to express myself. And I think it turned out this way because I am very concerned about everything that has happened lately. You might not know this, but Victoria contacted the man that we think tried to destroy you. She is expecting your child! I don't know the plot yet, but my experience tells me that you have a great chance of losing."

"Please, do not change our conversation. Things between us have already become too tense to just remain the way they are. I feel that you have something to say. If you talk, I will listen, and if you don't, I will walk away without a clue as to what is disturbing my mind. You accidentally destroyed the pages of the book that my eyes are accustomed to reading, and now, my respect for you is in great danger, enough danger for me to never speak to you again. And this angers me very much. Did I make myself clear?"

"Yes, you did."

"Who are you?"

Doneli kept quiet. His mind rushed and reflected on the past before he could lose the present. Then taking a deep breath, he quietly stated, "I am your father." He couldn't help not telling the truth.

"You're what?" said Charles shocked.

"You heard me. I am your father."

Obviously, Charles ran out of everything that could minimize the collision this revelation caused in his mind. His green eyes widened as his stupefaction bestowed a series of strange expressions on his face—expressions unknown to him before. Crazy ideas unexpectedly collided inside his head, darkening his mind. Disorganized questions filled his mind, but none were asked. Charles couldn't rescue himself from his apparent comatose state.

He felt baffled as if his existence had suffered a 360-degree turn and had left him unsure of what the future might bring. Grabbing his coat, Charles prepared to leave, taking with him all the questions he didn't have the nerve to ask. At the door, he turned around and mumbled, "I need to be alone; my head is spinning. We'll talk some other time."

"Yes, we will," uttered Doneli. "Your mother is the only

woman I have ever loved. I hope that one day you'll allow me to explain it to you. I would like to talk about the war, because aside from it, Charles, there is nothing more to be known."

Silently, Charles left. Outside, he entered his limousine and asked Lobo to drive without a destination. He needed to organize his thoughts before returning home.

It was the middle of May and people dressed in light clothes were enjoying the warm nights, walking without rushing to return home. Dispassionately Charles watched them on the sidewalk and for the first time in his life, wanted to be just like them—a simple person, someone without a father, mother or diamonds. He yearned for a moment like King Lear had—totally deprived of his garments.

Lobo drove throughout the city until Charles gave him an address. He longed to see Rebecca. Definitely her arms were the shelter he needed that evening. In her arms, at least for a while, he might forget who he really was. Then suddenly he understood his role—he was his grandmother's peace of mind. Whatever wrong existed between the Casimiros and the Merlenes, his sole existence would fix it.

Charles quickly stepped out of the car at Rebecca's building, entered the elevator, and rode up to the ninth floor.

He knocked on the door and when Rebecca opened it, she gave him a welcoming smile. She had assumed it was Charles because no one else ever visited her. That evening, as Charles looked into her eyes, he felt like the happiest man in the world. Silently he stepped in, closed the door and took her in his arms and just held her for a long time as if she were the only thing that made any sense at that instant.

"Charles, are you okay?" she asked worriedly after a few moments.

"Yes, I am," he answered just to ease her fears. Then, as if attempting to escape from something that was suffocating him, he bluntly asked, "Do you love me?"

"Yes, I do," she replied unflinchingly.

"Will you marry me?"

"Charles!" she exclaimed now searching his face. "What happened? Why are you—"

"I am in love with you," he interrupted. "Will you marry me? Just say 'yes' or 'no'. "

"Of course I will. But..."

Gently, he placed his finger over her lips and said, "For now, that is all I need to know."

"Charles...I know that something is wrong. Let's have a drink and then we can talk. I have just arrived and I'm starving. Have you eaten?"

"No."

"Good! Then Charles Merlenes is going to eat what Rebecca ate yesterday—spaghetti with meatballs. Is that okay with you?"

"Yes."

Walking to the kitchen she wore a mocking smile on her lips, enjoying the idea that Charles Merlenes would eat leftovers for dinner. Meanwhile, Charles went to the bar and fixed their drinks.

Then he asked, "Would you mind marrying me tomorrow?"

"Tomorrow—" she shouted.

Just then a loud noise mixed with her voice. Charles turned his head and saw smoke coming from her stove. Worried, he dropped the glasses and ran to the kitchen where he found Rebecca lying unconscious on the floor. He quickly grabbed her in his arms and rushed toward the elevator.

Downstairs, Lobo came quickly when he saw Charles carrying Rebecca and helped them into the limousine. Lobo drove to the hospital at break-neck speed.

That night, Charles only went home after the doctors guaranteed that she would be okay.

From his home he telephoned Doneli and told him what had happened.

At the same time they were talking, someone phoned Risley Ashford and reported, “I made my first attempt, but I already know I did not succeed.”

“Damn it!” the senator cursed.

62

DONELI HAD BECOME OBSESSED with Hard Narquilet since he had discovered that he was the man who had begun the war against the Merlenes. Now, fearing what lay behind Hard's mind, Doneli worried even more for Charles. He knew Hard only spent time on matters that carried a great significance to fulfill his accomplishments. It seemed Hard always ended up with many options.

After the attempt on Rebecca Macklen's life, something else bothered Doneli's peace of mind. *Did Hard want to kill that young lady or was he using her to destroy Charles? If the second hypothesis is true, how did Hard know that Charles would be in her apartment that evening? As it happened, not even Charles had planned that.*

When Doneli carefully studied the situation from different angles, he concluded that the attempt was against her life, and then formulated a more complicated question. As he paced the room he spoke his thought out loud. "Why did Hard want to kill Miss Macklen? Does she know something that could put his operation in danger?"

Suddenly, Doneli knew the answer and continued with his

reasoning. "Maybe...after all, she arrived in Africa to cover the *Serenata*'s accident...went to Bolevar when the Ferrari exploded...and later appeared at the scene of Peter Lacerda's death with her news crew. She may not know it, but perhaps she knows more than she should. And now Charles seems to be attracted to her. Oh, who is she, anyway?"

Because Doneli didn't know the answer to that, she became another piece in his unfinished puzzle.

* * * *

The real truth of the matter never crossed Doneli's mind. He would never have imagined, not even vaguely, that Senator Ashford was the one responsible for the attempt on the life of the young journalist. Only Hard knew that.

Hard had felt threatened with Rebecca's intrusion in everything related to his activities. She got too involved with the Merlenes—talking with the family and especially, interviewing Charles. Little by little she was moving toward the heart of everything that was important to Hard. Because of that, one week before the incident in her apartment, Hard had phoned Risley Ashford and expressed his anger and frustration with the situation. That's when, innocently, Hard ignited the darker side of Senator Risley Ashford.

In his brief conversation with the senator he had said, "I want that young lady out of my business, Risley. Use your influence to make her disappear."

"Oh, Hard," replied Risley uneasily, "I can't do that. I have to take care of my reputation. She is only doing her job. How can she possibly be a problem for us?"

"She will be. Try to get her out of our way. Perhaps out of New York City."

"For heaven's sake, Hard—"

"Risley, I smell trouble," Hard interrupted.

Extremely disappointed, Risley said, "Okay. I'll see what I can do."

Risley had strongly resented Hard's request. After hanging up from the conversation, he stood up from his desk and began to pace the floor. *Damn! I don't know why Hard has become so concerned with this young journalist. And the worst thing about all of this is that he doesn't give me a choice!*

The senator's mind raced out of control...recklessly. His thoughts reached the wildest part of his imagination as he concluded, *I have to do what I have to do. This is how I'm going to take care of it.*

That same afternoon he contacted a man by the name of Matheus, and the following evening they met at the Alameda Country Club near Bolevar. Since Senator Risley believed that human beings do not make history by holding back their ambitions, Matheus became part of all that fit into this course of unusual events.

Matheus' expertise in handling secretive business for politicians, dated way back before Risley, and it was this kind of job that placed him in a comfortable apartment with an unbelievable view of one of the best parts of the city. He always worked alone because he didn't believe in partnerships, and pleasing his clients had always been his ultimate goal.

This evening he met with the senator, and they sat together in a safe corner of the bar to have their talk. Nearly whispering, Risley explained to Matheus the nature of the job and requested he make it appear like a sloppy terrorist job. "Let's confuse everybody," he concluded.

In making this request, Risley Ashford made two very costly mistakes. The first was in asking that the job be of inferior quality. His reason for making that specific request was because he knew of Matheus' fanaticism and crazy ideas. He could end up destroying buildings, and many innocent people would get hurt because one insignificant journalist must die.

Ashford's second and most colossal mistake was in thinking that Hard would be even happier with him by not having her just permanently out of New York City—but dead.

Somehow, when Hard made his request to the senator it activated Risley Ashford's hidden insanity, and his actions chipped away Hard's patience. After that, Hard's bad decisions took a rampant course.

By the time the news about Miss Macklen's accident had gone out and begun to cause speculations, Hard had already swept away all possibilities he could find to forgive Risley. Suddenly it seemed impossible to understand how quickly the days had stopped being ordinary and how far Risley Ashford dared to go. Hard could not afford to allow an outsider to gain enough power to start playing smart games—no, never. Supposedly, rules were to be followed—and according to the rules, Hard did the killing and the senator ran the state. So the attempt against Miss Macklen's life infuriated Hard to the point where his anger was almost uncontrollable.

Therefore it caused Hard to do some serious thinking about their relationship. *Your hostile ideas, Mr. Ashford, have begun to disturb my peace of mind. You have made me think that this will lead us nowhere.* He made new decisions.

After that, Sandro Bonaveti received one of the most important orders of his life. Hard called and said, "Go on with operation Telma Zurique."

From then on—there was Hard on one side of the path changing the course of his operations—and on the other, Doneli investigating Miss Macklen's life. Doneli had learned to trust his instincts and knew his investigation of her would eventually bring up something valuable. In this type of game, he who collects more pieces to the puzzle has a better chance on becoming the winner. Sooner or later something relevant will fall from above. Doneli had a detective on Victoria, and Demetrius was watching the senator's every step. Somehow, he was sure there would be a surprise that would come out of all this, and when that happened, he intended to be the man in the right spot at the right time. Doneli knew he was sitting in front of a refined banquet of fortuitous events.

When Sandro Bonaveti acknowledged to himself that

Operation Telma Zurique was activated, he spent a few seconds deep in thought. From now on he knew he would cease all of his regular activities. Going into his bathroom, he looked at his image reflected in the small mirror above the sink and said to himself, "The boss wants action. So this is it. Go on...nothing should be out of the ordinary. I was a good shepherd watching the lamb that became a wolf. Now..." he paused and took a deep breath, "I'm the hunter and I must fear nothing."

Then he solemnly washed his face as if he were leaving one existence to enter another. Drying himself, he returned to the living room to phone the woman he needed to contact for this operation. Her name was Angela Careli.

"Angela," he said when he heard her on the other end of the phone, "Operation Telma Zurique has been activated. You know what this means, don't you?"

With a dry taste in her mouth she hesitated before she replied, "Yes."

"When can it take effect?"

She made a quick reflection and then uttered, "Friday."

"No, I would prefer another day. Friday is a busy day. Lots of people travel for the weekend, and I have to be at the airport dressed like—you know."

"Friday is perfect because it is my birthday. I know for sure that our man will come to have dinner with me."

Sandro remained silent for a moment, thinking over the situation. Then he said, "All right, let's do it on Friday. Don't forget my things. I need a handbag, a ticket, and a taxi waiting downstairs. We should leave the apartment together. You stay in the lobby until I leave. Then, you can also exit the building in another taxi."

"Yes. I heard you. Be here at four o'clock."

Following their conversation Sandro left his apartment. He now had a number of important things to do before Friday.

* * * *

When Friday arrived, neither Sandro nor Angela stepped foot outside. They each stayed in their apartment, resting for the busy evening, studying the operation's plan, and eliminating any fear that could enter their minds. Above all, they must avoid the possibility of mistakes. In a few hours they would be leaving New York City forever as part of their lives had just collapsed.

Around two o'clock, after constantly checking his watch, Sandro immersed himself into the role he would play. He took a long bath and shaved his head and legs because when he left the country, he must be dressed as a woman. He would be Telma Zurique.

At exactly four o'clock, dressed like a man and using a hat to cover his shaved head, Sandro left his apartment to meet with Angela. In her apartment they sat together and clarified the details of their impending job. Then they ate some food that Angela had prepared, sat down, and waited. Angela had cooked a delicious dish for her birthday and sitting on the counter to accompany it was bread and a bottle of white wine.

When 5:30 p.m. arrived, she promptly got elegantly dressed and then led Sandro into the second room of the apartment where he could change and remain hidden.

Promptly at 6:00 p.m. Senator Risley Ashford arrived. Upon taking one look at Angela he felt dazed. Her beautiful long hair had been cut extremely short, much like a man's. The change was so unexpected and drastic, that he was speechless and for a moment or two didn't know what to say. He was so disappointed.

"What did you do to your hair?" he finally managed to ask.

"I just cut it. I am 32, Risley. Long hair makes me look old. I like to look young."

"Don't you think you should have asked me first?"

"If I had done so, you would have said, 'No!' "

"Right."

"That is why I didn't." Then she got closer and hugged him.

"Smart girl. Happy birthday, my dear!" he said as he embraced her with love and gave her his present.

Angela held the little box and excitedly opened it. It was a beautiful ring. She thanked him profusely, gave him another kiss and to express her gratitude even further, she gently leaned over and touched his prick just to see the pleasant change on his face.

"Dinner is ready, Risley. Shall I bring it to the table?"

"No, I have an idea. Why don't we make love first?"

"Why not?" she replied with a big smile. "Go on and get ready while I pour the wine."

Much like a good boy obeying his mother, Risley walked into the bedroom, took off his clothes, and lay down on the bed. He closed his eyes and in his mind sketched all he would do with her. While lost in the thrill of his sexual fantasy, Sandro Bonaveti entered the room, aimed his gun, and shot him three times. It happened so quickly that it seemed painless. Not a sound emitted from the room.

Sandro, thirty-three years old, with an interesting face, and a body that disclosed the sensuality that made him so severe, was dressed as an attractive woman. That evening he and Angela Careli, without rushing themselves, left the apartment to go to the airport.

Until then, everything had run perfectly.

If Hard Narquilet could have known that Doneli was trying to buy a ticket outside the theater in which his actors were performing, he would have probably announced that the show was sold out. But this did not happen. Hard had put Operation Telma Zurique into action at the worst possible moment—exactly when Doneli had decided to have Senator Risley Ashford followed.

Obviously, Sandro Bonaveti did not count on the presence of Luis Demetrius in the building the night he walked out, going to the airport as Telma Zurique. Also, he had no way of knowing that Demetrius just happened to be following the senator that evening and had arrived at the building and witnessed the senator entering Angela's apartment.

Demetrius waited, and shortly afterwards, he witnessed two

women leaving the apartment. Something intrigued Demetrius very much about their actions. They had come out of the same apartment but had then headed for different elevators. That quickly aroused Luis' curiosity and making a quick decision, he safely managed to appear in the hall and rushed toward one of the elevators—entering the one that Angela Careli had taken. Downstairs, he discreetly crossed the quiet lobby and ran to his car in order to prepare himself for any course of action. Only one woman took a taxi, so Demetrius decided to follow her. He raced after Telma Zurique

The taxi drove straight to the airport. Quickly, Luis got rid of his car and rushed inside. When he found her, he maintained a short distance—just observing. Shortly thereafter, she finished checking in and walked toward the terminal. Demetrius managed to move ahead, cut off a few passengers, and on purpose, though it seemed like an accident, bumped into her. The collision of his shoulder against hers caused the woman to drop her passport and plane ticket. While she picked up the plane ticket, Demetrius reached over for her passport. Quickly he opened it and glanced at the name inside before politely handing it back to her.

Sandro grabbed the passport and gave Demetrius a silent thanks with a nod of his head. He avoided uttering a word so his voice wouldn't give him away. Afterwards, he simply slipped away leaving Demetrius with his disquieting thoughts. *So long, Telma Zurique. There is something in the way you walk that intrigues me. I wish I knew what it was.*

Still puzzled by it, Demetrius headed outside of the airport with the firm intention of going home. He exited through the doors exactly at the moment that a taxi drove up and stopped almost in front of him. Automatically glancing inside, he saw the same woman with which he had shared the elevator. Her hair, cut extremely short, enabled him to immediately recognize her.

Am I lucky or what? Next, he imagined how interesting it would be to know her name too. So he stayed close waiting for her to step out of the taxi. Then to Demetrius' amazement something unexpected happened. She couldn't find her wallet and became extremely nervous and agitated about the situation. The taxi driver lost his patience, and they started a heated argument. Finding the moment very fortuitous, Demetrius swiftly arrived at the scene.

"Good evening!" he said looking at her. He expected her to recognize him from the elevator, and she did.

"Do you know this woman, sir?" asked the taxi driver.

"Yes," he lied. "We met this evening."

"Good. Then you can help her. She can't find her money."

"Of course I would be glad to help," Demetrius graciously added, already reaching for his wallet.

He paid the taxi driver, and it sped off leaving them alone.

"Thank you for being so kind. You helped me more than you can imagine. I really don't know what happened to my wallet."

"Oh, it was my pleasure. I am Luis Demetrius and you?"

"Denise," she lied.

"Nice to meet you, Denise. Are you leaving town?"

"Yes."

"Any place in the United States?"

"To London."

"Without money?" he queried.

"I live there, Mr. Demetrius, and I have someone waiting for me at the airport. So arriving without money will not be too complicated."

"Of course," replied Demetrius. "And you also will not lose your flight because of money. I guarantee that."

"I appreciate what you are doing. If I don't find my wallet, please give me your address. I do want to pay you back."

"Oh, you don't have to."

"But I insist."

She kept searching for her wallet nervously.

"Be calm," said Demetrius, now offering his hands to hold everything that she was pulling out of her purse. "You will find it."

When her passport came out and was put in the pile he was holding, Demetrius' eyes managed a quick peek inside of it and read only that her last name was Scoofio. *Denise Scoofio,* he repeated to himself.

Luckily she found her wallet and immediately repaid Demetrius.

"Here is your money, Mr. Demetrius, and thank you." Then, to be polite she added, "If you give me your address, I'll send you a postcard from London."

Smiling, Demetrius wrote it down for her. In order to cover his identity as a detective, he avoided giving her his card.

That evening, she almost missed her flight, and Demetrius drove home without knowing that he had spoken with Angela Careli.

63

DEMETRIUS DROVE BACK FROM the airport recapping the series of events that happened that evening. When he had rushed in, following that strange blond woman, he never thought about what might have happened with the senator. Only now did he surprise himself by remembering him. He found it very strange that those two women left the country.

Suddenly he exclaimed out loud, "Oh, no! Did I do something wrong? No...I did the right thing. They are probably part of the senator's sexual playthings. He looks like the type that needs two in order to get excited."

As Demetrius kept driving he kept thinking about the senator's sexual activities. To him it seemed to be the case. But then, in the back of his mind arose a question. *Why were the two women from another country? And why did they leave shortly after the senator's arrival at the apartment?*

Violently, Luis pressed his car breaks. "Damn! Something is wrong...really wrong. I can feel it!" he exclaimed worriedly. Quickly he turned the car around and returned to the apartment building.

* * * *

As they watched the 11:00 p.m. news, the citizens of New York found out that their senator was dead, and that it was a homicide.

For quite some time, Demetrius remained quiet, thoughtful and in disbelief. The apartment was in the name of Angela Careli and she had left her driver's license behind. The picture perfectly matched the woman he had helped in the airport—Denise Scoofio. Only the hair was different, as she had probably cut it on purpose.

"Doneli, I had those women in my hands."

"Yes, you did. But don't worry, Demetrius. They did not kill Risley Ashford. Hard Narquilet did."

"Do you think so?"

"Yes."

"Why are you so sure?"

"Because, I know how Hard operates. I knew the senator would have no way out."

"Yes...you did say that."

"I have discovered many illegal transactions that Risley had authorized. Things so well done that Washington could never begin to trace them—guns, bombs, and terrorist deals. He knew that Hard ordered the explosion of the *Serenata*."

"If Risley was so useful, why did Hard decide to kill him? It won't be easy for him to find another politician with a good face and ability to keep the game going."

"That is what we have to find out. Why did Hard dismiss him so soon? And please do not mention these women that you followed to the police or to the FBI. For the moment let them be connected only with Angela Careli and her apartment. The two women belong to us. They are part of *our* investigation."

"Doneli, if Denise Scoofio is a fake name, Telma Zurique is also a fake one."

"Right. But we know where they went. One is in Paris and the other in London. I think we are going to go on a trip, Demetrius. I have my connections in Europe. Let's find them before the FBI does."

"I like that idea."

"Of course you do. Aren't you a good detective?"

Smiling Demetrius replied, "You love this, don't you?"

"This has been my whole life, Demetrius. When I worked for the FBI, I got up every morning and I went to bed trying to solve cases. Investigating is quite an interesting career. I was never bored."

* * * *

Rebecca Macklen did not cover the death of Senator Ashford. Because of doctor's orders, she had to stay in bed. Charles had been at the hospital every single day, and when the doctor said she could go home, he had taken her with him.

He had found out that Rebecca's closest relatives lived in London, and her parents were both dead. Besides that, Charles felt responsible for what had happened. He strongly believed that somehow, the attempt against her life had occurred because she had become involved with him.

The day Charles took her home, he told the press that he was in love with her and was going to marry her. When asked, she just confirmed what Charles had said. She happily said that she was also in love with him.

* * * *

One day before his trip to Europe, Doneli went to speak with Charles and paid a visit to Miss Macklen. He needed to ask her some questions regarding the accident in her apartment. Doneli desperately wanted to discover from where she had come and other relevant details. Now because Charles was in love with her, he had to discover the true color of her thoughts.

When Doneli entered the house, he first looked for Catarina as he wished to talk with her regarding his latest decision—his trip to Paris.

They met and before Doneli could say anything she began,

"Doneli, someone killed the senator of New York, and he was our biggest shareholder. Do you have any idea what is going on?"

"Yes, Catarina, I do. Behind everything is the worst enemy that any person could have. And much like you, he is very rich."

"Then what could he possibly want from us?"

"This is exactly what intrigues me. I promise I am going to find out."

"Charles needs protection as well as that young lady. In fact, I think we can all use some."

"Yes, I took care of that already. Charles should not be involved in any social events until I return from Paris."

"Paris?"

"Yes. I am going after a mysterious woman. If I find her, Mr. Narquilet will have to see me."

"Who is that man?" Catarina asked. "Is he the one responsible for all these problems?"

"I think so."

Catarina remained quiet a few moments thinking about Hard Narquilet.

Then she asked, "Doneli, do you know that Charles wants to marry that girl, Miss Macklen?"

"I read it in the newspaper."

Then assuming what Catarina would ask, he volunteered, "I think she is fine. If I find something wrong with her, you will be the first person to know."

"Thank you, Doneli. You are quite a mind reader."

Doneli stood up to go see Charles' fiancée. Catarina hesitated a moment then asked another question. "What about Victoria? Do you still have someone watching her?"

"Day and night. She has been visiting Mr. Narquilet. Can you believe that?"

"Oh, I expect anything from her," replied Catarina. "Except for her to win this battle of hers. As I said before, if she insists, I will have her killed."

"I hope she gets what is coming to her."

"I hope so too, Doneli. I hope so, too."

On the way to see Rebecca, Doneli stepped into the music room to say hello to Elizabeth. He found her with her painting teacher. After Anthony's death, a psychologist had suggested that painting might help keep her mind busy with other thoughts. This was her twentieth lesson and she had a canvas full of sunflowers on the easel.

From the door, Doneli called her name announcing his presence. When she saw him, she quickly put down the brush and ran to him, kissed his cheek and pulled him into the room.

"Come and meet my teacher, Doneli. He is wonderful. Teofulo, this is Doneli."

"Nice to meet you, sir," said Teofulo. "I have heard only good things about you. Mrs. Merlenes admires you a lot. She said you are an extraordinary person and an excellent detective."

"Oh, Teofulo! Don't believe everything women say because they exaggerate when they desire," Doneli said with a laugh.

Teofulo joined in the amusement. In fact, what was said seemed quite right.

"What is happening now, Doneli? Do you have bad news?" Elizabeth asked.

"No, everything is all right. I came to say good-bye because I'm leaving for Paris tomorrow. I know who is responsible for the bombing of the *Serenata*."

"I'm afraid, Doneli. What will happen to Charles?"

"Nothing, Elizabeth. Everything will be fine."

"I'm tired, Doneli. I have been crying since I was young. I lost my mother at eleven. I don't think there is someone in this world that has cried more than me. God keeps taking away everything that shapes my happiness, and He is much stronger than me. I can't fight back."

"I hate to hear you thinking like that."

"God creates ugly things, Doneli. Don't tell me that this is not true. Look at those sunflowers. They are too big and too yellow. Why did God create those flowers? I hate yellow, and I hate sunflowers."

"I can't believe what you're saying, Elizabeth. You still have things that make sense. You have Charles. You have me. And I love you. Don't forget that. You have two grandsons and another on the way. Enjoy what you have, Elizabeth, before the next rain falls. Take the time to inhale the smell of wet soil until the new day dawns once again. Allow the water to wash away the pain and let some sunlight in to warm your heart. Otherwise, there will be no happiness. Without sunflowers, you would not enjoy the other beautiful flowers. Do not change, my dear. I like you the way you have always been."

Tears filled her eyes and they began to slide down her face. Lovingly Doneli hugged her as he always had—as an old friend.

Then before leaving, he glanced at the painting one last time and said, "If you hate sunflowers, Elizabeth, why paint them?"

"I was hoping to find out why they exist."

Leaning over to kiss her on the forehead, he added, "Do not ask so many questions. See them as they are." "Just flowers."

64

HARD NARQUILET AND SANDRO Bonaveti had met many years before in Italy. Their paths crossed because of Sandro Bonaveti's outstanding courage and audacity. He had been orphaned and at a very young age had learned about the realities of life on the streets of Rome. He had found out that living and surviving are instincts that sometimes are literally honed by the hour.

One day, as the gentle evening pushed away the afternoon, Sandro was roaming the streets searching for a way to support himself. Accidentally, he violated the Mafia's border territory and soon found himself inside a small room thick with cigarette smoke, loud music and a round table that seemed big enough for cards, glasses, bottles of alcohol, and six people.

Sandro immediately knew this was a place forbidden to him, but not for the heads of an infallible organized crime family. He had sneaked in with the intention of listening to what the six men were saying. Instinctively, Sandro sensed that something good might come from any information he might garner, so he hid in order to overhear the conversation. On that day, who knows what the devil had in store for him, and he overheard their plan to kill Hard Narquilet.

Knowing the Mafia's plans blossomed in him an enormous excitement. Sandro couldn't get it out of his mind. He had heard the name of the person who was going to kill Hard and he knew when, where and how it would happen. Plainly, Sandro saw the possibility of spoiling their plans by saving Hard's life. In his mind was information that could either kill him or sustain him. For the first time he felt enthusiastic about something.

Audaciously following his instincts, he went looking for Hard and eventually found him in a notorious spot in town. As always, very well dressed, wearing an expensive hat, Hard was never alone; he had three men following him around—his chauffeur and two bodyguards.

For some time Sandro remained outside waiting; planning his next move, which would come as soon as he could get near Hard to share the information he had. As he waited, he couldn't help but be excited about the whole thing. Every minute that passed made him feel more alive. He very much enjoyed the opportunity of having something important to do.

Hard's car was already parked out front when he walked outside with his two bodyguards. Sandro observed everything with keen attention to detail as if his plan was a Mafia plot and he, the head of it.

As Hard entered his car, Sandro ran past the bodyguards, into the car and sat next to him. This indeed was a crucial moment for Sandro. Immediately, he had two guns carefully pointed at his head. Hard's men just remained motionless waiting for the order to pull the triggers.

"They are going to kill you," said Sandro bravely. "I heard everything."

Hard studied Sandro for a second. He could tell Sandro was a very young and intense man.

"I swear to the saints that I'm telling the truth. You've got to listen to me," repeated Sandro.

"Let the boy talk," Hard said to the bodyguards. Then he snapped his fingers indicating for the chauffeur to drive on.

The bodyguards closed the doors and Hard's chauffeur drove slowly through the streets, maintaining the speed of the other vehicles. In the back were one of the bodyguards, Sandro, and Hard.

"Tell me what you heard. It better be good or else you will not see the sun tomorrow."

"They want to kill you."

Hard's lips creased into a quick smile as he said, "That is not news to me. Tell me something I don't already know."

"This time they have a plan."

"Who are you calling *they*?"

"Quivolati," said Sandro.

Antonio Quivolati happened to be Hard's worst enemy. Hard and Quivolati could never reach an agreement in regards to their business operations. They both wanted everything–the power, the money, and the respect. So this would not be the first time Quivolati had a plan to kill him. However, it would be the first time Hard would know it in advance.

Hard smiled disdainfully and ordered Sandro to further explain.

Sandro's information enabled Hard to make plans of his own. Antonio Quivolati was killed, along with ten of his men, as well as many of his family members. The massacre was appalling. The bodies lay everywhere, while their souls hurriedly left this world. Blood from their bodies flowed like dirty water staining the floor. While guns and bullets assumed the leading role in this gruesome act, men scrambled and jumped back quickly like graceful dancers in a great performance. It started with the snap of a finger and ended even faster as the horrendous noise abruptly stopped.

Antonio Quivolati's misfortune happened two days after Sandro braved a discussion with Hard. For Hard nothing went wrong, and during those two days he kept Sandro locked in an empty room.

After the massacre, Hard returned home, sat at his dining room table, which had fresh delicious food, and requested Sandro's presence.

"Sit down and eat," Hard ordered Sandro when he entered the dining room.

Sandro silently obeyed and ate voraciously. He had never been in front of so much food.

"What's your name?" asked Hard.

"Sandro Bonaveti."

"Where do you live?"

"Nowhere...anyplace on the streets."

"What about your parents?"

"I don't think I had any. I came from the gutter."

His response made Hard laugh long and hard.

"What do you want to do with your life? Do you have something specific in mind?"

"I want to be quick with a trigger."

"You're too young for that."

"This is not true. I have heard stories about you. You started at fifteen on the streets of New York City."

"I had a reason for that. At fifteen I had to take care of my mother but that is not your case. You never had one."

"No, but at eight I was already stealing in order to eat."

The conversation ceased. Hard pensively watched as Sandro devoured the food with a worried look on his face, as if the table would, at any moment, fly away. Something stirred in Hard and he felt sympathy for the young man.

"I'm going to think about it," said Hard. "About you being quick with the trigger. You can stay here if you want, but no guns yet. There is something about you that I like—your courage. If one day I change my mind and teach you how to use a gun, it will be because of that."

Soon after, Hard took Sandro with him whenever he traveled. Sandro visited all his houses, and met the people who worked for him as well. Hard discovered that Sandro had a lot of great qualities, and in turn began to enjoy his company. Sandro proved to be quick, intelligent, sincere and an excellent listener. In very little time, Sandro had captured Hard's trust and gained his highest appreciation and genuine friendship.

So, what Sandro wanted, happened. Hard welcomed him into his incredible world. Once inside, Sandro's honesty, which was the most remarkable quality he had to offer, separated him from the others. Sandro became Hard's most valuable and trusted man, and he was the only one who had the honor of knowing the deepest secrets of Hard's life.

Hard's employees used to say that Sandro occupied the place of a son in Hard's heart. That was, *if* Hard would have had a son, and furthermore, *if* he would have had a heart.

Sandro and Hard were always together except for the last four years. When Hard became involved with Risley Ashford, he had sent Sandro to New York City. Hard needed a trustworthy and clever man to foresee Operation Telma Zurique. Of course, Hard couldn't find anyone better than Sandro. Even though Sandro would have to move to New York, and their *father and son* relationship would end, Hard decided that Sandro would have to handle that operation. Indeed, Sandro accomplished the task, professionally.

* * * *

Three months passed before Doneli and Demetrius could make contact with Telma Zurique. In other words, it was the time it took for them to discover that Telma was actually Sandro Bonaveti. While they had spent some time flying from Paris to New York City, the FBI discovered that Angela Careli and Senator Ashford had been seeing each other quite frequently the past three years, and that she had left the country as Denise Scoofio.

Senator Ashford's murder and the news of his romantic involvement with Angela had caused such turmoil and shock that the political scandal came to a boiling point. It wilted the admiration the dead senator once enjoyed. The press made it their favorite pastime until October when Victoria Merlenes gave birth to a beautiful little girl. Catarina named her Giovana.

As agreed, one week after Giovana's birth, Victoria left the Merlenes' mansion with ten million dollars and of course, lost the love and respect of her Uncle Joseph. The Merlenes had been Joseph's life, and his loyalty to the family was unbreakable. Victoria's behavior broke his heart but didn't harm his soul.

As she entered the limousine that was to carry her away, she looked back toward the mansion and uttered, "I *will* come back, Catarina. For your diamonds and Charles! It will not be a dumb journalist who will keep them away from me. Hard Narquilet will take care of this Rebecca—exactly as I wish."

Two days later, the newspapers published a picture of her boarding an airplane headed for Greece. She left New York to marry the Syrian millionaire, Hard Narquilet. The news of their upcoming marriage caused fresh gossip, but more interesting than that was the story she left to be published later.

To hurt Charles' integrity, she revealed to the press the truth about Catarina's new granddaughter. She used her sweet, innocent face to play the victim and made discreet insinuations that gave the FBI concerns in regards to her husband Anthony's death. Of course, Giovana's existence fueled the fire. What was left hanging in the air teased the FBI's skepticism, and Charles ended up under investigation as well.

Quite content with the havoc she left behind, Victoria got on the plane to leave New York delighted with what she had done and with one main thought in her mind. *Dear Catarina, there is something your money can't buy—peace.*

65

TWO THINGS BECAME TWIN obsessions in Victoria's life—Charles and diamonds. No other emotion could touch her heart. She didn't miss her children and had never developed that special maternal bond between them. At times she vaguely remembered them, and would realize that they were part of her belongings and eventually expected they would come back to her. It was not necessary to worry or think about them. *The children will return to me along with the diamonds,* she often told herself.

Her marriage to Hard took place upon her arrival in Greece. Only three people were present at the wedding—the notary, the bride, and the groom. Hard was so happy with the fact that he had finally married her that it seemed as if he were walking on clouds. Victoria's beauty had the ability to stir the ecstasy of his adolescence. Just by looking at her he experienced the fruition of a fantastic excitement. Next to her naked body, he vacillated from one-seventh heaven to another. For her and her beauty, he would do anything drastic or impossible.

Despite his knowledge of Victoria's obsession for Charles, Hard had every intention of making her feel like a queen. Hard had no reason to worry about Charles because the Merlenes' destiny already lay in his hands. He would be nothing more than the winner. In reality, he was the major shareholder of Merlenes Industries because he had been the one that invested money in Senator Ashford's political campaign. He needed him as a front for that transaction. The shares the senator had acquired for himself had actually belonged to Hard from the very beginning. Legally, Hard owned them. For years he had spent planning and engineering a plan to take over the Merlenes Industries. And according to his facts, he was almost there.

* * * *

After Senator Ashford, the next important person on Hard's agenda was Sandro Bonaveti. He made Sandro his eyes and informer. From the outside Sandro surveyed all the paths between the Senator and the Merlenes, and then he related the events for Hard on a daily basis. Sandro knew about the Senator and the Merlenes as much as their chauffeurs and butlers, and he was only Madame Perlaz's partner.

Sandro was also responsible for introducing Angela Careli into the senator's life. She established the connection between Hard and the senator. For four years Sandro had been in charge of everything and kept the ball spinning beautifully. Things always ended exactly as planned except the senator's premature death. Even though Sandro knew the reason why Hard had killed him, it was still a big surprise.

* * * *

Now, all the news circulated around the Merlenes. After Victoria's insinuations, Charles made the front page of every newspaper for weeks, and the Merlenes' name was dragged through the mud because of the atrocious scandal. News spread so fast and out of control that it affected Rebecca and Charles' relationship. When Rebecca read what the newspaper insinuated, she became extremely disappointed and confused about her feelings toward Charles. It was then that she decided to return to her quiet nest—her apartment.

However, as she was getting ready to leave the Merlenes' house, Charles went to see her for one last conversation. He walked upstairs and stopped at the bedroom door, which was open.

"May I come in?"

"Yes, Charles."

He entered the room and saw her things already packed.

"So you are leaving?"

"I need to be alone, Charles. Please understand."

"I do. I am sorry. You have to know that I never wanted you to get hurt."

"I know. Things would have been different if I didn't love you. That is exactly what complicates everything. It's upsetting waking up one morning and finding out that you have fallen in love with a person you don't really know. I have never been in love before so I'm hurt."

"I had every intention of telling you the whole truth about Victoria and me. But I was waiting for the right time. Now, I see it was a bad decision."

"Yes, it was."

A brief silence filled the room. She didn't know what else to say.

"I love you, Rebecca," Charles said simply.

"I think you lost the right to say that, Charles. And please, don't make things more difficult for me. I want to leave, and I will."

"I have no intention of stopping you, Rebbecca. I understand how you feel. I came to see you because I want to do what I should have done before. This will not fix things between us, but you deserve to know how it all started."

"Please...Charles, don't."

"Rebecca, your most precious quality is being a good listener. Please don't lose it now that I need it."

Calmly, he took her hand and led her to the nearest chair. He also sat down, and began to speak—

"When I was nineteen, I fell in love with Victoria. At that time I called it love. I was young, and did not have another definition for it. She came to Paris and spent four days with me. She was my first. Then, I don't know what happened, but from one day to the next she chose to marry my brother. That is why I decided to stay in France and finish my education. I didn't want to be around. I had lost her, and wished to stay away. My grandmother allowed me to stay in Europe so everything worked perfectly.

"Later on, after I graduated I returned home thinking that things would be different. She was a married woman, also a mother, and I felt confident about my feelings toward her. I still felt attracted by her beauty, but she was also my brother's wife. Besides that, I had grown older and matured and knew how to control myself. What I expected was to find her playing her role in a respectable way. So I came home with some apprehension and avoided her presence. It worked well for a while. That is, of course, until she decided to change it. One weekend when Anthony was in Brazil, she came to Bolevar, knowing I was there. Late at night, when I was taking a shower, she suddenly appeared naked in my bathroom."

"Oh, please!"

"It's true," said Charles. "And do you want to know what happened?"

"We all know what happened, don't we?"

"Not really."

"What happened?" she then asked.

"I completely lost my mind. At that moment—like a fool—my eyes could only see her. After making love with her, I felt as miserable as when I had lost her.

"A few weeks later she came to my office telling me that she was pregnant and wanted to have an abortion. That day, I finally understood her game. She had done everything on purpose, to hurt me, and to have the power to somehow manipulate me. I didn't feel that she really wanted to have an abortion; she was just playing with my feelings. For the first time I saw her as she really was and I lost my tolerance. Immediately I took charge and stood up for my interests only. I treated her the way I thought she deserved and offered her five million dollars for my child.

"That same day I told my grandmother everything and she doubled my offer to Victoria if she would sign the divorce papers, and leave without her children. She walked out of this house with ten million dollars."

"What? Are you telling me that she sold her children?"

"Call it what you will, but it is the truth."

In dismay, Rebecca thought about Victoria. It seemed unimaginable that behind Victoria's angelic face lived that kind of woman.

"I'm sorry, Charles," she said at last.

"Thank you. And thanks for listening to me. I am going to call Lobo. He will drive you home."

"I would appreciate it."

Next, Charles walked her to the car, and nothing more was said.

* * * *

Days later, after much thinking and analyzing his words, Rebecca decided to write an article about Victoria. Rebecca thought that the world should see more than just a "close up" of the *lovely angel.* She felt comfortable disclosing Victoria's bitch side now that the Melenes had nothing more to fear or lose. The scandal clouding their name was already a fact, so her article would have two results—it would destroy Victoria's lovely image, and it would pique Victoria's annoyance. And just to accomplish the second one, Rebecca decided to go on with her idea.

Undoubtedly, Rebecca used the article to ease her misery as well. *What the hell?* She was in love, and considered herself intelligent and competent to fight a bitch battle. Her excitement escalated knowing she was doing this for love, and also realizing that Charles was too good to be given up just because of a *silly past.*

Skillfully she revealed everything she knew about Victoria, adding at the end how Victoria had sold her children for ten million dollars. Then, intelligently, she reversed Victoria's latest insinuations about Anthony's death—nicely engaging the FBI on a new journey. But what really surprised everyone, even Charles, was Rebecca's last statement. "DESPITE ALL THE ABOMINABLE TALES, I WILL MARRY CHARLES."

When her article reached the public, everyone's mind veered toward the new information and shifted their perspectives. Who would rise to victory—Victoria or Rebecca? The people were waiting.

* * * *

At the time, Doneli and Demetrius were on their fifth trip to Paris. Since Senator Ashford's death they hardly spent time in New York City. They also read the article.

"Do you see this, Demetrius? How interesting, a battle between two women. Not even with Hard at her side will Victoria win this one."

Demetrius laughed disdainfully and said, "Good! The FBI will be too busy with her endeavors, and we will have plenty of time to find Sandro Bonaveti. This is moving as swiftly as a racing horse."

* * * *

Their hard work finally paid off. Doneli and Demetrius discovered that Sandro Bonaveti and Telma Zurique was the same person. Doneli's contacts in Europe helped him discover Sandro's hideout in Paris. Twice a week Sandro shopped for groceries and never went more than one block from his apartment. Aside from that, he confined himself to his room.

Doneli wanted to contact him, but had no intention of handing him over to the police. He had something really 'special' planned for Sandro.

Finally, after taking care of everything they would need,

Doneli and Demetrius parked in front of Sandro's apartment and waited patiently. When Sandro stepped outside, they calmly got out of the car and walked toward him. Both approached Sandro, grabbed his arms, and quickly Demetrius shoved a gun into his back.

"I know you are Sandro Bonaveti," whispered Demetrius. "Do as I say without asking any questions. We don't plan to hurt you."

Sandro looked at Doneli and then at Demetrius before saying, "I hate Americans. They are all a pain-in-the-ass. They appear to be good in every way. If they want to find you, they will. If they want to buy you, you're as good as sold. They get whatever they want."

"I agree," replied Demetrius. "But Italians are a pain-in-the-ass as well. Always thinking they're smarter. They just don't understand Americans. For example, if I were Italian, you would be dead already, but because I am American, you have another chance. So get into the car."

Sandro entered the car quietly. Once inside, he looked at Doneli, who had not said a word so far. "I know you. FBI, huh?"

"Was," answered Doneli.

"And what difference does it make?"

"None. It is not supposed to make one. Is it?"

"What do you want from me?"

"You will know soon."

Demetrius drove to a discreet café in the city. Once inside, they sat away from the door and windows. They ordered some coffee and then Doneli spoke. "Sandro, I am not here for you. I want Hard Narquilet. We are working for Charles Merlenes. Also, we know for certain that Hard is responsible for the wreck of the *Serenata*. We also know that Risley Ashford made business deals with him, and we suspect that he fingered Anthony's and the senator's death, as well as the attempt against Miss Macklen's life. I know a lot, but I need more. I believe you can help me. Why did he start this war with the Merlenes?"

"I have always been faithful to Hard. You're wasting your time."

"Nothing lasts forever," replied Doneli.

"Nice phrase, isn't it? Why do detectives have the bad habit of thinking they know everything?"

"But we do!" said Doneli. "For example, we know that you left Angela Careli's apartment the day the senator was killed and on that evening, you headed to the airport and left the country using the name Telma Zurique. Soon after, Angela Careli also arrived at the airport bound for London as Denise Scoofio."

Sandro looked at Doneli with dismay. It blew his mind that Doneli knew everything. *How could it be? I planned everything so carefully.*

Quietly, Sandro turned his head, gazed at Demetrius' face and immediately recognized him. "You! You were the one who bumped into me at the airport."

"Yes. That was me, sweetie."

"How did you know what was going on?"

"I didn't. I followed the senator and entered the building behind him. I waited there until I saw you and your companion coming out of the apartment. It intrigued me that you both came out of the same apartment, and yet took separate elevators. At that point I became suspicious so my instincts forced me to follow you because you had a destination while your companion didn't. The rest you know."

"Excellent," commented Sandro. "How would I have known that the senator was being followed?"

"You had no way of knowing," replied Demetrius. "Besides that—that was my lucky day. As I walked out of the airport, Denise Scoofio was arriving. She had a slight problem that needed my gentlemanlike skills. She had a problem finding her wallet. I paid the taxi driver for her."

Sandro looked at him utterly amazed. He had no idea about any of this as he hadn't spoken with Denise since that day, and he would never do so for she was dead. A car had run her down on the streets of London. Denise Scoofio had been a part of Operation Telma Zurique and for that reason she could no longer live.

The three men talked until nightfall and, after a while, Sandro felt quite comfortable around them and neither one had pointed a gun at him. Even though Doneli had enough on him to turn him over to the FBI, this was not his intention. Understanding that, Sandro felt free to play by his own rules, trying to see how far he could go with the conversation.

Sandro showed interest in what Doneli had to offer in exchange for whatever more he needed on Hard. Doneli happened to be a very intelligent man, and Sandro knew it. Rapidly, Sandro grew curious about what Doneli had in mind.

"What do you have to offer, Doneli?" he asked.

"The most valuable thing for you at this moment."

"Are you implying that you know what that is?"

"Of course. I have been among criminals. You are a man who happens to have a good side. It is not your fault that this part of you is hidden. Our lives keep turning and suddenly we just stay alone in a big loop. I'm here to help you. I can offer you your freedom. I am the only one on the face of the earth who can offer you help. You have too much to lose, Sandro. The FBI will find you, or Hard will eventually kill you."

Doneli stopped in order to let Sandro mull it over. He calmly poured more coffee into his cup and waited patiently for Sandro's reply.

Sandro felt that Doneli definitely knew what he wanted. And how much he desired it—to disappear from a life of crime and start all over again in a quiet place. He was tired, and furthermore, unhappy with Hard. Sandro had been in Paris for months, waiting to return to Greece, and Hard had simply ignored him.

Hard had changed a great deal. Now, he was keeping himself busy with Victoria. Apparently, he had disconnected from his duties to engage in his new love life. Sandro could no longer remain in Paris without running the risk of being found. But Hard had just closed his eyes.

Denise's accident also bothered Sandro very much. He knew she had to die, it was part of the plan, but it needn't have been in such a cruel way. Sandro's disappointment in Hard kept growing. Victoria now was the center of Hard's happiness, and bad guys are not allowed to be happy. Bad guys can never fall in love. That was a law because love ends their lives. Hard had begun to dig his grave, and didn't even know it.

Considering all this, Sandro knew his destiny was uncertain. Doneli's words started to make a lot of sense. *The FBI will find you or Hard will eventually kill you.*

Confidently, Doneli continued the conversation, offering Sandro a peaceful place to live.

"I have arranged a passport for you," said Doneli. "New name—Virgilio Mozani, in case you accept my proposal—and you can leave France tomorrow morning."

"Oh, is that so!" exclaimed Sandro. "May I ask where to?"

"Brazil...Claros. There you will have a chance to start with a clean slate. You are a young man who can still live a decent life. You owe it to yourself to give it a chance. A world of crime can tire even the devil's partner."

Sandro embraced the idea of freedom. The possibility of sleeping at night and resting peacefully until the next day excited him. No crimes, no deals—just passing the time. It sounded so simple and decent. Indeed, Doneli's words made a soft rustle in his ears, and the sound of the words found their way into his soul like soft music comforting his senses. For an instant he waved away his dark past and without a word waited for a new beginning—the right to go on living and enjoying the calm aspects of life—even if for a short time.

"What makes you think that I'm going to trust you?" Sandro asked.

"You have nothing to lose and everything to gain," said Doneli. "You don't have to be brave to accept my proposal, but to continue to live on, in the situation you are currently in, you certainly need to watch your ass. And you don't know for how long."

Since Sandro's birth, this was the first time he had found it easy to visualize the good side of life. Quietly he savored a brief moment of happiness.

Maybe it is never too late to begin anew.

66

AS EXPECTED, SANDRO ACCEPTED Doneli's offer and that same evening left the cafe and went back to Doneli and Demetrius' hotel. They planned to fly to Portugal the next day where they would await the Merlenes' new ship, the *Blue Coast*, recently bought to replace the *Serenata*. The *Blue Coast* would take them to Rio de Janeiro. Once there, the Merlenes' lawyer would take Sandro to Claros. Doneli had planned everything ahead of time, assuming Sandro would flip the coin.

At the hotel, Sandro complied with Doneli's wishes, disclosed everything he knew about Hard Narquilet—indeed, more than Doneli had ever expected to hear. The secrets were no longer.

Doneli listened attentively to Sandro for over an hour. Sandro confidently brought to the surface everything Doneli wanted to hear, including telling him that Peter Lacerda was Alexander's real father. Then Doneli learned that it was Peter who had placed the bomb in the Ferrari and that Sandro had killed him at Hard's request. Also, Doneli found out the true story about the Merlenes' shares, and that Hard's ultimate goal was to take over the Merlenes Industries. Apparently, Hard planned to do to the

Merlenes what they had done to his father.

That evening, Doneli was made aware of Hard's life story. To Doneli's surprise, the Merlenes shared at least some blame for the choices Hard had made. As it was, Hard's father committed suicide in 1939 after being forced to sell most of his tailor shops at below market value in order to pay his debts. At the time, the Germans knew exactly what they wanted—WAR, and the world would soon begin to collapse. The only crop everyone planted was FEAR. Consequently, many businesses closed due to the uneasy situation in Europe and the threat of a total war. Peoples' dreams, as well as ambitions, were put on standby. The economy lost its peak, forcing multitudes of people out of work. Hard's father and the Merlenes were submerged in the same waters, so to speak. Unfortunately, one remained on the selling side while the other joined the buyers.

Catarina's husband went to the auction, waved his hand and closed the tailor shop's deal. Later on after the war, Elizabeth's name became well known in the fashion industry.

Hard was almost fifteen when his father lost everything and committed suicide. He and his mother lived from day to day without money or a place to live. They couldn't find help anywhere and, as a result, they quickly sunk into endless misery. Survival became the ultimate goal. They went on sharing their grief with strangers—all ordinary people who lived on the streets where the daily routine was stealing and killing. However, because of Hard's intelligence, he understood well the laws of the streets and skillfully tracked a convenient pathway out of their misfortune. If someone had to die in order for him and his mother to eat, so be it. Soon, his relentless spirit turned him into a tenacious leader and executor of well laid plans.

Except for his mother, no one ever gave him a complete explanation about what really happened to his father's business. She blamed the Merlenes and so did he. Hard remained behind the scenes without a clear picture of what really happened. In fact, the Merlenes had done nothing wrong; they had just bought what was for sale. But Hard never erased the name Merlenes from his mind. While he busied himself by controlling his clandestine deeds–the hatred and pain resided quietly but remained under the surface. Fearlessly, he took from life what life offered. His needs guided his decisions, and his astuteness assisted him in acquiring success. He floated with the turbulence of his activities without aim until the day he saw the first shop with the sign Merlenes & Sfeel above it.

Instantly, all the hatred and pain took hold of his heart with venomous force. From that moment, he swore revenge and this obsession became the purpose of his life. With each step bringing him closer to his goal, he mirrored Charles Merlenes–the young Charles who had left St. Denis in search of his own dreams. Except that Hard's dreams were those of enacting revenge.

That evening Sandro sang like a bird. Doneli and Demetrius listened eagerly and much of what Sandro related impressed them. Sometimes Doneli stopped Sandro to ask an important question for clarification. For instance he said, "Hold on a moment, Sandro... There is something I still don't understand, Senator Ashford's death. Why did Hard kill him if he still proved valuable?"

"That's easy enough to answer. The senator did something stupid," said Sandro, grinning some. "He tried to kill the young journalist, Miss Macklen. That was a big mistake."

"What?" exclaimed Doneli and Demetrius at the same time, looking at each other quite astonished. They would never have guessed it.

"It was the senator who tried to kill her?" asked Doneli.

"Yes," affirmed Sandro.

"But why?"

"Oh, that's another story—quite another story," said Sandro. "I can't tell you why the senator tried to do it, but I know that Hard was angry because of her involvement with the Merlenes."

"Then it was Hard who planned to get rid of her," concluded Demetrius.

"No," said Sandro. "I think Hard would never have wanted to kill her."

"He wouldn't?"

"No."

"Why?" replied Doneli.

"Because she's his daughter."

* * * *

Rebecca was born in New York City in 1943—the same year as Charles. Her mother was eighteen and Hard nineteen. Later, Rebecca moved to London where she spent her childhood in the company of her mother and Mr. Edward Macklen—a well-known lawyer, who married her mother and adopted her.

Edward Macklen possessed valuable documents and photographs that disclosed Hard's nine years of crime and illegal operations. Evidence that could, in the snap of a finger, send Hard to prison. But because Edward Macklen planned to marry Rebecca's mother and adopt Rebecca, he went forward and used it to corner Hard. Hard then had no choice but to give away his daughter in exchange for the evidence.

Mary, Rebecca's mother, was a fine English woman. At seventeen she had met Hard and immediately fell in love. She couldn't resist his charm, and he became fascinated with her exotic appeal. Her blue eyes and dark hair were not a usual combination. She was an exquisite brunette that swept the peace of his heart. Hard simply adored the idea of having her.

At that time Mary was living the worse moments of her life. She had lost her mother and father because of the war, and had to move to New York City to live with her uncle who, like her father, was a pilot away from home fighting the war. Mary felt utterly alone and scared.

Hard came into her life at that difficult moment. With him also arrived the opportunity of giving some direction to her life. Easily blinded by love and without her uncle's approval, she married him. In spite of being only nineteen, Hard seemed mature, and she really believed in their relationship.

For some time everything worked well. She loved him and worked hard to please him in every way. She even tried to accept his least appealing personal traits and he adored every gesture she made. They immersed themselves into a beautiful love affair, so meaningful that Hard for a while turned away from his illegal activities. However, later on when the reality of his criminal ties finally surfaced, Mary couldn't hide her frustration and disappointment and as fast as she had fallen in love, she lost interest in him.

Along with this terrible reality, Mary's life quickly sank into a fearful nightmare. She discovered that she was pregnant and realized that for this reason alone her husband wouldn't let her go. Her pregnancy spoiled her plan for leaving him. Hard not only refused to let her go but basically kept her as a prisoner for nine months. After she gave birth, he decided to let her go, but not with his daughter.

Mary once again felt utterly trapped. Toward the end of this first conflict with Hard she realized he would kill her if she tried something stupid. Also, she realized that in order to escape with her daughter, she would have to come up with a plan. Strategically she stopped being a fighter and Hard assumed she had given up on the idea of leaving. Then, safely, she secured all her interests behind his back. It took her two years to accomplish the task, with the help of her uncle and Edward Macklen. Afterwards, she married Edward and they moved to London. For almost three years Hard tried to regain custody of his daughter but nothing worked. Since then, losing his daughter had been his biggest defeat.

* * * *

Hard's plans to destroy the Merlenes family could smoothly move on for destiny was taking care of Charles' interests as well. Suddenly, Rebecca Macklen rushed in and landed exactly in the very same field. Ironically, she became Charles' fiancée.

Again the same old battle—love and hate like two demented cupids playing a twisted game with people's hearts. Or perhaps it was the furtive work of two wise hands that placed Rebecca in that soil where Hard had planted his seed of hatred. Whatever it was, it didn't matter. The great duel supplied the drama. Now, lay the expectation. Who would fire first?

Indeed, in every way Charles had begun to complicate Hard's plan. Even Victoria, who Hard had desired for a long time, planted her feelings in that same soil. And Hard wanted her so much that he vowed to grant her anything for which she asked.

She became like Salome in the Bible, except this time, she asked for Rebecca's head.

Facts and secrets scrambled together into an intriguing charade between Hard Narquilet and Charles Merlenes. Victoria did not know Rebecca was Hard's daughter, and neither did Charles. To Victoria, Rebecca was just an intruder who would meet her unlucky fate very soon. Professionally those two wise hands wove a trap for the great Hard Narquilet. Perhaps what Sandro said was true. "Bad guys can never fall in love."

* * * *

There is no doubt that everything became tangled like a spider's web. Sidney Maskuitiz, one of the Merlenes' vice-presidents who secured all of the share transactions for the senator, suddenly committed suicide. That incident aroused more speculation and suspicion. Since the death of the senator, the air had become contaminated with unplanned little incidents, and much of the nonsensical questions began to move up and down like a yo-yo. Hard did not want to see things run out of control or place himself into a situation that could jeopardize his safety. So in order to avoid any kind of mistakes, he ceased operations for a while.

Now that Victoria was his wife, and because of Rebecca's article, she became the FBI's interest as well, another reason why Hard prudently decided to play only the role of a husband. The journalists loved Victoria and everything she had to say, and one single misplaced word from her could be disastrous for him. Carefully, Hard eyed everything and concluded that in a situation like this, the best thing to do was to not do anything. He decided to extend his honeymoon by sailing the Mediterranean Sea.

* * * *

As planned, Doneli, Demetrius, and Sandro left Europe on the Merlenes' new ship, the *Blue Coast*. However, before leaving their hotel in Paris, Doneli called New York City and spoke with Mr. Vareda, Charles' lawyer. Quickly, Doneli informed him of everything he knew regarding Anthony's death. And at the end of their conversation without any discretion, Mr. Vareda asked Doneli his whereabouts.

"I am in Africa," Doneli lied, "still trying to discover who was responsible for the explosion of the *Serenata*."

After he hung up, Demetrius replied, "Africa?"

"Yes. It is none of his business, or the FBI's where the hell I am. Is it?"

"No. Of course not," uttered Demetrius shaking his head.

* * * *

By the end of November, Doneli, Demetrius and Sandro Bonaveti arrived in Rio de Janeiro. By now Sandro was traveling as Virgilio Mozani. He was introduced to the Merlenes' lawyer, who would take him on to Claros. Immediately after their arrival, Doneli called the lawyer for a private conversation. Doneli introduced himself as a close friend, and an international spokesman for the Merlenes family. Following that, Doneli explained that Mr. Mozani's stay in Brazil had an important purpose for the Merlenes' future affairs. He was to learn about the mining operations, for he would soon leave for Africa to oversee some of the operations there. Doneli thought this was enough of an explanation. Afterwards, Doneli turned his back and left, leaving Virgilio Mozani with his new and quiet life.

* * * *

From Rio de Janeiro, Doneli and Demetrius flew to Greece, where the ship *Maria Catarina* waited for them. Because Doneli knew that Hard was sailing the Mediterranean Sea, he decided to pay him a visit. The place turned out to be very interesting for a confidential talk.

Upon his arrival in Greece, Doneli called Charles. They hadn't spoken since he had left Paris, but Doneli felt an obligation to brief him on the latest details regarding the investigation.

"Doneli?"

"Yes, Charles."

"For heaven's sake, where are you?"

"In Greece," said Doneli. "On my way to visit Mr. Narquilet."

"I'm worried about you, Doneli. I don't know your plans, and I don't want you to risk your life for me. We still need to have that conversation about you, my mother and the war, do you remember?"

"Yes, Charles. I'm glad you decided to let me talk about that. We will do it as soon as I return to New York City. I promise."

"Why do you have to meet with that man?"

"Business, Charles...strictly business."

"I hope you know what you are doing."

"Oh, you can bet I do," affirmed Doneli.

"Okay, but be careful."

"I will."

After they hung up, Doneli said to himself, "Oh, you don't know what I know Charles...about your future wife. If Hard is a good father, this is going to be a family business."

67

SERENITY COVERED CATARINA'S countenance, showing that her confidence had been regained. She was ready to face the upcoming new era with tranquility in her heart and soul. A mystic look shown from her green eyes, so bright and tender, effortlessly, softening her sharp appearance. Having just turned eighty-one, she was still as lucid as when she was young. She knew everything that was happening around her and still remained calm and faithful. Not even what Victoria had done upset her. Quietly and almost painlessly she faced the scandal. It seemed as if new energy had developed deep inside her and kept her entire existence connected with some unnatural insight—something so strong and genuine, and indestructible. All of a sudden it seemed that she stopped worrying about the future of her family and felt nothing harmful would happen to Charles. She simply held on tightly to the idea that the Merlenes would overcome all these nightmares.

Her great-granddaughter, Catarina, turned five, and despite the fact she could not walk, she was a beautiful and delightful little girl. An elevator had been built in the family room in order to facilitate the child's access to the second floor. A live-in nanny, fluent in English and French, took care of the girl's education. Little Catarina's mother would be away for some time, and like her father, Jacqueline decided to become a doctor. And aside from blessing her decision, Catarina also gave her enormous support.

Alexander was now four. He was an intelligent child who adored little Catarina, his cousin. Once in a while he would ask the servants why his cousin could never abandon her wheelchair and play with him outside. His happiness and unpredictable questions captivated the attention and love of all those who lived with him.

Giovana, Charles' daughter, now into her second month, looked at her nannies, searching for that special being who she would later call mommy. Instinctively, she looked at the faces, not yet understanding the world around her. But one day she would. She would understand that the man who came by to see her every night was her father.

Full of pride, Catarina observed these children growing older. They were the heirs of her diamonds. She had paid for them with pain and money and would never forget the many tears she had cried, nor the happiness she had lost. What she had learned she would keep and pass it on to them. She thought that this was the reason for her having lived so long.

All she had endured helped her perceive that her family would be just fine. Her faith resembled an indestructible rock—perhaps as hard as a diamond. Her wisdom took her beyond the limits of where others were accustomed to going. Now she spent her days rocking in her chair enjoying the tranquility that life had finally given her with this clear wisdom.

* * * *

One morning Elizabeth joyfully entered the library with a newspaper in her hand. She announced, "Catarina, they found the guy who used to clean the Ferrari. He confessed everything. A man named Peter Lacerda placed the explosives in the car. Look,

...t page of the newspaper. Thank God that those ...urrounding Charles have finally ended."

...ndeed wonderful news," replied Catarina. "But I knew al... ...at these accusations were not enough to cause Charles any damage."

Just then Charles also entered the library with a newspaper in his hand. And before he could say anything, Elizabeth hugged him saying, "My dear, I am glad the nightmare is over."

Contemplating her happy face he added, "Do you know who made this possible?"

"I can imagine," she responded.

"Doneli did, didn't he?" said Catarina.

"Yes, he is doing an excellent job."

"Where is he now?" Catarina asked.

"Greece. Sailing the Mediterranean Sea. He is going to meet with that man, Hard Narquilet."

"Hard? Victoria's husband?" asked Elizabeth. "For what? I thought we were finished with Victoria once and for all."

"We did with her, mother, but not with Hard. He is responsible for the *Serenata*'s explosion. He is dangerous, and I'm very worried about Doneli. But Doneli assured me it was going to be a business conversation. I don't know what he meant by that."

"Charles," said Catarina. "If Doneli says he is all right, don't worry about him. Doneli was not born to die in the Mediterranean Sea. He will die at home."

Suddenly their conversation ended because Charles had to go answer a call from Mr. Varedas.

"Charles, did you read the newspaper?" asked the lawyer.

"I did. I'm glad the truth is finally out."

"This is one of Doneli's victories," added the lawyer. "I want to speak with him. When will he be back from Africa?"

"Africa?" asked Charles puzzled.

"Yes. The last time we spoke, he was in Africa, investigating the *Serenata*'s accident."

Immediately Charles realized that this might be Doneli's game plan.

"Oh, you're right. He was going to Africa."

"And he didn't?"

"I don't know, Mr. Varedas. Doneli is very unpredictable. At a moment's notice, he can call and say he is in China. He is like that."

"I don't understand how you can trust a person like him."

"Oh, you will never know why. But don't worry. He is excellent at what he does."

"All right, Charles. Keep him working for you, but be careful. I don't like people who don't offer clear explanations of what they are doing—especially if they are working for me."

"Thank you for opening my eyes. I will be careful."

Charles returned the receiver to its place and exhaled deep

"That man wants to know everything!"

"Charles, this is the first time I have heard you lie
Catarina.

"Oh, I have done it at least a couple of ti
grandmother. Don't be angry with me
really necessary."

He leaned over to kiss her goo
the same with his mother.

Flying to Gree
list that Victo
Hard Nar
as soon as
Hard was on
"Yes?" answe
"Hello, Mr. Na
"Who is this?"
"Giovani Doneli C
are very busy men, we

personally but I have heard very interesting stories about you. We need to talk face-to-face. I know everything about Operation Telma Zurique. I have come on Charles Merlenes' behalf, and I have a proposition to make."

Hard, who never expected to hear such a thing, immediately deduced that Sandro Bonaveti must have ended up in Doneli's hands. And if that was the case, he could be in big trouble because Sandro knew too much about him. So he found it prudent to go on and have this face-to-face talk with Doneli. Quite unhappily, Hard granted Doneli a meeting two days later on December 26th.

* * * *

Doneli and Demetrius spent their Christmas Eve in the company of the small crew of the *Maria Catarina* in the Mediterranean Sea, a few miles from Hard Narquilet. They dined in the captain's quarters, and afterwards, the captain and Demetrius talked until dawn. Spending Christmas Eve in the Mediterranean Sea turned out to be an incredible experience for emetrius.

* * * *

precisely 11:00 a.m., on December 26, Doneli and Hard sat face on the deck of Hard's yacht. Before Doneli was o sit, he had been carefully searched from head to toe. guards remained on each corner of the deck at all times, r one stayed below guarding Victoria. Hard had he was to be kept away until the meeting with Mr. ver.

ng, Mr. Cassarete," said Hard politely. He liked pite the type of business he handled, he had nners.

Ir. Narquilet. It's nice to see you."

fully Hard said, "Let's talk business. What is Sandro Bonaveti?"

ndoned in Paris and I found him."

"Where is he? Did you torture him?"

"No...I negotiated with him. He gave me the information I wanted, and I offered him a good deal in exchange. Sandro Bonaveti is dead. I gave him a new identity, and you will never find him. Leave him alone, Hard. He was faithful to you for a long time. He deserves some peace."

"Usually people don't tell me what to do."

"I'm sorry," replied Doneli.

"Sandro is a valuable man, and I want him back," explained Hard. "I don't know what type of deal you plan to make with me, but let me warn you, I will not do anything until I have Sandro back."

"Forget it then. You will not be able to see him again. From now on, he will have my protection. Let's get straight to th matter, Hard. If you have to kill Sandro for what he knows will have to kill me, too. Things are already too comp know that you are responsible for the explosion of and that Operation Telma Zurique was mean Ashford. I also know about the shares."

"Don't try to be smart with me territory," said Hard firmly.

"Hard, vengeance destroys Doneli. "Why go on with Macklen is your daughter?"

Unexpectedly, Do Syrian. Abruptly to the railing out onto t of him. His spread across observed him, returned to the tab

"That son-of-a-bit without my consent. will pay for this. If you w to be mine. Do you understand? The son-of-a-bitch just ruined my plans."

"No, he didn't," added Doneli, playing the master position. "No one spoiled anything. No one lost here. Your daughter is marrying Charles and after that, on whom will your vengeance fall? The wedding has already been planned for the 31st of this month. She is the sole heir to your shares so it will all remain in the family. They will become the Merlenes and Narquilet's property as well. You are a clever man, Hard. Can't you see that the game is over?"

"Bullshit!"

"No...it's a perfect ending."

Once again, Hard's anger took over, and once again he walked away from Doneli.

To lessen his fury his eyes gazed into the immense sea while his mind penetrated the massive horizon. The ocean's erratic plight and the smell of salt intruded upon his senses. The waves of the ea rocked his spirit gently, and the soft breeze blew away his adness.

When he returned to the table and sat down and lit a cigarette, tually felt that he was in a friendly mood.

mly he asked, "What kind of proposition do you have in

t you to stop this war with the Merlenes. In exchange all y will remain here, between the sky and the ocean. No ow that we had this meeting. When the FBI discovers Bonaveti murdered Risley Ashford and that he ce, all they will find in the INTERPOL files will So you will be safe. Without Sandro, they have est you."

don't know me, Mr. Cassarete," commented of many resources. I do not fear the FBI or w that. Your mere words cannot convince

, it's not about me, you, or Charles; it's

about your daughter."

"Mr. Cassarete, leave my daughter out of it."

"No, because she is already a part of it."

Angrily, Hard smashed his cigarette in the ashtray and looked thoughtfully at Doneli. He felt trapped in his own cave, and he hated to make decisions when he lost the top position.

"I'll tell you what, from now let's leave things as they are. We'll meet again in January. Then I'll tell you what I am going to do."

Doneli felt a little disappointed with Hard's decision, but preferred not to show it. He could afford the wait and diplomacy counted with individuals such as Hard.

Politely Doneli said, "Nothing would be as perfect as that Mr. Narquilet. Let's bury the old year first. We will talk again."

The next day, Doneli and Demetrius returned to New York City. Somehow, Doneli hoped that at least once in his life, Hard would use his *heart* to make a decision. He expected to see Charles and Rebecca's wedding taking place without any complications.

Following Doneli's visit, Hard isolated himself and spent hours thinking about how to fight his battle. He still could do something on behalf of his cause, but needed to keep his heart completely out of it. He had the upper hand. Victoria wanted Rebecca dead, and he wanted the Merlenes' assets. Quite simple and quite difficult, but still it was a game.

Hard loked deep inside himself, assessing his life, enjoying what he had built, and smiled at infinity. While his gaze danced in front of the gigantic horizon, his mind reached its verdict. As always, his decision would please himself. Silently, he turned his back to the ocean and ordered to return home.

* * * *

Of all his houses, the one in Greece was his favorite one.

Upon Hard's arrival, he called an old friend who was also a great jeweler. He asked him to buy a Merlene's diamond of no less than three carats. A few hours later the man returned with a beautiful stone, which cost $13,000. Hard held it close to eye its beauty, then asked to have it grounded down completely.

At that moment, the request only held meaning to him.

68

IT WAS DECEMBER 31ST. THE DAY of Charles and Rebecca's wedding. In New York City Rebecca was busy with the last minute details of the ceremony.

In Greece, Hard Narquilet was busy preparing a small feast to celebrate the New Year. He had bought Victoria a beautiful red dress for the occasion. After all, red was her favorite color. For him, he had decided to wear black and white.

At 8:00 p.m. they went into their room to prepare themselves for the evening. After bathing, Hard fixed drinks for them and made love to her and then promised her the world.

"In the most distant blue that my eyes can reach, there is your smile fading away," he said passing her a glass of champagne. "I can look at you for hours because you are the most beautiful thing my eyes have ever seen. I am going to buy you an island."

"Oh dear, first, I want Rebecca dead. Afterwards, all of the Merlenes' diamonds. Then the island."

Hard smiled and kissed her passionately, "You are going to have everything you wish. I never forget a promise."

As the evening went on, Victoria's contentment radiated all

over her angelic face, and no one else besides Hard knew the reason for such joy. She was on the verge of fulfilling one more of her whims. Hard had said that this was the day their happiness would be of great glory. Since morning, she had pictured Rebecca Macklen dying on her wedding day and could hardly wait for the New Year to hear the wonderful news.

Because of her excitement, she gladly accepted the second and third glasses of champagne Hard offered her. Then she reached out for the forth and the fifth, and when the guests arrived, she was the perfect hostess—cheerful, beautiful, and sexy. The sensual movements of her tender body inside the red dress seduced even the men least interested in women.

"You look wonderful my darling," Hard whispered at every opportunity. All night long he remained by her side worshiping her existence. From time to time, he discreetly glanced at the clock on the wall. He would soon receive a phone call from New York City.

Their guests enjoyed the evening mingling, drinking and eating, and some of them exchanged their excitement and hopes even further because of the upcoming New Year. At exactly 11:50 p.m., the call from New York came in. Hard excused himself and went to his office to answer it.

"I'll be back shortly," he said. "I have a phone call from New York City."

He walked away and Victoria watched him smiling. *Could this be the news I am waiting for?*

When he entered his office, Hard carefully closed the door, and answered the phone.

"Everything ended as you wanted," said the person from New York City.

"Did you stay at the ceremony until the very end?" asked Hard.

"Yes, exactly as you wished."

"Was she happy?"

"As happy as any bride could be on her wedding day."

"Thank you, Mr. Varedas. Thank you for the favor."

Afterwards, Hard returned to his guests.

As the clock struck midnight, he ordered the waiters to serve more caviar and champagne, and also asked the band to play livelier music. While the guests entertained themselves wishing one another a "Happy New Year," Hard took Victoria by the hand and furtively exited the party.

They entered his office where he had a cold bottle of champagne awaiting them. He held it and said, "My darling, let's celebrate the end of our struggles."

He popped the cork and filled the glasses. Hard took out of his pocket a folded piece of paper that contained the ground up diamond.

"We shall toast with champagne and diamonds to extend this moment towards eternity." Contemplating her beauty, Hard poured the sparkling grains into their glasses.

"To your beauty and all the diamonds in the world."

In the darkness of his office, Hard and Victoria drank their champagne with the ground diamond in it. She did not realize it was a real diamond as she had been drinking for hours and did not question Hard's actions. She was overwhelmed by what might have happened in New York.

They emptied their glasses and returned to the party holding hands. Like a couple very much in love, cheerfully they danced. Their bodies turned lightly following the music and moving all across the room. Hard looked and smiled at everyone. It was his farewell to his friends, for he knew that he and Victoria had little time left to celebrate.

Mixing grounded diamonds into a drink as a way to kill someone was an old Persian custom—a subtle and cruel way to exterminate an enemy. The pain was excruciating. The clear grains cut the stomach into little holes, causing fatal internal bleeding, and the victims painfully contorted their bodies until the end. Hard had become a great admirer of Darius, the Persian son of Cyrus, and he spent an enormous amount of time reading about the Persians. So his sudden inspiration came from these old times when men died bravely.

He chose to end his and Victoria's life expensively. Victoria had never read about the Persians, but she died like one of their enemies—

* * * *

Rebecca became what the Merlenes' family loved most, the new Mrs. Merlenes, Charles' wife. They were married in the ballroom of the Merlenes' mansion and only the family's closest friends attended the ceremony. Despite being the oldest person at the wedding, Catarina's presence energized the occasion. Her happiness was genuine and contagious.

She spent most of the time at Doneli's side and after the toast, she said, "I have the feeling that you know something I don't. Am I right, or is this the effect of the small amount of champagne I drank to toast the bride and groom?"

"Oh, Catarina! Who could ever hide anything from you? Yes, I know something you don't."

Leaning toward him and with a keen look in her eyes, she whispered, "What is it?"

"It is good news."

"Then say it."

"Our dear Rebecca is Hard Narquilet's daughter."

"No! How did you discover that?"

"Nothing unusual and perhaps everything that a father could do for a son."

"Detectives...that must be the answer. Do you know something, Doneli? The good will of people are like diamonds, hard to be destroyed. My diamonds brought pain as well as happiness to this family, and also straightened our hearts."

She paused, as her eyes looked up to contemplate her adorable Charles.

"Thank you, Doneli, for always handling things so remarkably. You are a great man and Elizabeth is a very fine woman. Because I have Charles, you both will never know the intensity of my gratitude. My mother brought such pain to my life that my diamonds became God's gift to minimize the consequences of her deeds. Now in my old age, I have accepted the idea that in this family nothing is confused...nothing is irrelevant...and everything makes sense. The many events around these diamonds were just shadows of a legacy. Indeed, the Merlenes' unique and lovely legacy."

* * * *

Like many lovers, Charles and Rebecca went to Hawaii for their honeymoon. They planned to stay there for two weeks. However, on January 2nd, they read about Hard and Victoria's deaths and immediately returned to New York City.

Because of Alexander and Giovana, Catarina wanted Victoria to be buried in the Merlenes' mausoleum. When her body arrived in New York City, the police and the press escorted her coffin from the airport to the cemetery. At the cemetery, the press found Catarina and Rebecca side by side, dressed in black attire.

The day before the funeral, Catarina had called Rebecca to her and said, "Rebecca, it is not easy being a Merlenes. It doesn't mean you will be happy. I want you at my side at the cemetery, dressed in black the same as I. I wish for every journalist to see us together. You will not do this for me or for the Merlenes, but for the man you love, and for his daughter."

Surprised by Catarina's request, Rebecca asked, "Will you forgive me if I refuse to do what you ask?"

"I don't know Rebecca. My heart sometimes endures feelings that surprise even my own soul. But let me tell you something. Charles needs you and love is exactly that."

Thoughtfully, Rebecca looked at her. She had just awakened to a new reality. Now, her life belonged to the legacy of the Merlenes' diamonds. Whereas before she covered the news, she now became the news. Exactly the way Catarina was long ago.

"My love for Charles is more than all the salt water found in the four oceans; however, it is not enough to wash away the difficulties I will face representing this family. But I made up my mind and I have a genuine heart. I would rather die than fail my duties as Charles' wife. I'll be there next to you."

"How do you feel, Mrs. Merlenes, having to cut short your honeymoon to attend the funeral?" was the first question she heard from the press.

"I am fulfilling my first duty as a wife," she said. "I am attending the funeral of the mother of my husband's daughter."

* * * *

A month later, Rebecca inherited the greater part of Hard's fortune which had been estimated at sixty million dollars. Doneli told her everything he knew, and for the first time she heard the name of her real father.

* * * *

Leisurely, the month of July arrived, bringing the typical warm and humid air of summer. The bright days came and went, dancing under the sunrays, diminishing at every hour, until moonlight appeared in the sky and carried them away.

The ship *Maria Catarina* entered the port of New York with a great surprise for the Merlenes. The new geologist in charge of the mines in Brazil, Mr. Parcel, had brought with him the first and only emerald found after one year of excavation. The stone was the size of a small lime.

Mr. Parcel met with Charles at the Merlenes' mansion on the same afternoon the ship arrived at the dock. He gave Charles the emerald and briefly explained the strange way in which it had been found.

He told him that Virgilio Mozani, the man who had recently arrived in Claros, woke up one morning talking about a dream he had. In his dream he saw a little girl on a swing. She suddenly left the swing, came to him, grabbed his hand, and took him to where they were excavating for the emerald. With a thin branch, she drew a circle on the ground, and then disappeared. In the morning, to satisfy his curiosity, Virgilio went to the place he had seen in his dreams. He found the circle with the branch embedded in the middle of it. They started digging inside that circle, and two days later found the stone.

The story left Charles mesmerized. He solemnly contemplated the emerald as his eyes admired its beauty.

"Do you believe this, Mr. Merlenes?" asked the geologist. "A spirit communicating with us through our dreams? I always thought that this was people's fantasies."

"I don't know what to say, Mr. Parcel," replied Charles. "The only thing I can assure you is that this stone is not a fantasy."

Next, Charles asked Joseph to serve Mr. Parcel something to drink, and he walked upstairs to show the stone to his grandmother. Catarina was sitting alone on the balcony.

Silently, Charles approached her with the emerald and placed it in her hand. Surprised, Catarina held the stone with both hands, and gazed into the transparent green depths of it. Her look kept growing with intensity for inside she saw her little girl Ana on the swing. Ana was laughing. The swing kept moving back and forth. And perhaps because emeralds symbolize immortality and faith, Catarina understood that she hadn't lost Ana. Her little Ana had never died. She had just passed from one life to another.

"Charles," she said handing back the emerald. "Please, don't cut this stone. I want this to be my present to my granddaughter Giovana on her fifteenth birthday. And I want that in my will."

"It will be as you wish."

After Charles left, Catarina stood up and walked toward the balcony and placed her hands over the railing. Her eyes looked up and she contemplated the portion of the sky that covered her mansion. Quietly, she thanked God for her life, her children, and the entire universe. She admired her beautiful garden and happily breathed in the sweet fragrance of the flowers.

"My dreams...and my faith," she said with a genuine smile of contentment.